A TEMPLAR'S JOURNEY: UNDER THE CROSS AND CRESCENT

by
WR Chagnon

with
Judith Anne Chagnon, Contributing Editor

First published by Dog Ear Publishing
4010 W. 86th Street, Ste H
Indianapolis, IN 46268
www.dogearpublishing.net

ISBN: 978-1-4575-3449-2

This book is printed on acid-free paper.
This book is a work of fiction. Places, events, and situations in this book are purely fictional and any resemblance to actual persons, living or dead, is coincidental.

Printed in the United States of America

A Templar's Journey Trilogy
WR Chagnon & Judith Ann Chagnon, Contributing Editor

The Squire from Champagne Dog Ear Publishing, 2010

Under the Cross and Crescent Dog Ear Publishing, 2014

Coming Soon

The Final Glory

To our loving parents,
whose roots in history
shaped our way of life.

Auntie,
You Too were part of
my "roots". Love
"Enjoy the journey"
Billy
April 28, 2015

Introduction

The years 1185 and 1186 proved to be a turning point for Lord Roland of the House of Champagne in the first book of our trilogy, *A Templar's Journey: The Squire from Champagne.*

It has been more than one year since the young Roland, under duress from his family, took the road toward righteousness. The year-long journey of the squire from Champagne was sometimes painful, occasionally humorous, and many times dangerous, but for the most part, it was outright adventurous.

So how did this adventure begin, you ask? And why? The young squire's many comely features unlocked a goodly number of France's most noble ladies' and village maidens' hearts. For the boy from Champagne, often, the same key that led to a fair maiden's heart also unlocked a dark door that led to a pathway of disaster.

His many casual love encounters with the fairer sex had perhaps been instrumental in causing the death of Lady Joan of Metz, a young noble lady who was having Roland's child before marriage.

If life on earth was to be miserable for Roland, the Catholic Church assured the boy eternal damnation in hell with excommunication if he did not mend his ways.

Roland indeed had tumbled from grace and had fallen afar from his lofty position of wealth and respect. What could go wrong in Roland's life had gone wrong; however, when one door closed, another door seemed to open for the wayward lad.

Directed by the pope and by the grand master of the Knights Templar, Roland was assigned to two renowned Templars: Brother Walter of Mesnil and his secretive Templar sergeant, Brother Martin of Brittany. They became Roland's reluctant mentors and tutors.

Walter of Mesnil is renowned in France, Spain, and the Holy Land (or, as the Franks call it, the *Outremer,* overseas) as the best knight to have ever entered the Templar Order. Sergeant Martin, the Celtic soldier from Brittany, is known for his combat prowess, and equally known for his unruly and unholy ways within the Order.

The former squire from Champagne now finds himself living life as a penniless, yet prayerful, lowly Templar squire serving these other fabled Templars. Each day, the poorly fed and simply dressed young man from Champagne leaves more of his past behind as he grows in mind and spirit.

Still, his old life follows him along the new pathway. Roland's inner light still glows and guides him away from the darker Templar policies and spiritual beliefs. Because he has not accepted Templar ordination, he still has some free will, unlike his mentors, who have sworn their blind obedience to the Templar Order.

It would at first appear that Roland must face his soul-searching trek alone, yet in some of his darkest hours, a bright light comes into Roland's life: his fellow Templar squire Aaron. In their first chance encounter, Aaron knew that Roland was very different; he knew Roland had many secrets, and he knew just how to uncover those secrets.

Aaron has a certain rustic charm with the ladies also. At times, the young redhead can be a merciless and brutal warrior. Aaron has used his many skills to keep himself alive during a brutal time on the streets of Paris.

The redhead knows many ways to kill a man and to pick his pockets before his victim's body hits the ground. During the course of the year, Aaron's street skills have played heavily in saving Roland and their Templar mentors from death many a time.

Along Roland's path is Doctor Jacob, a renowned Jewish physician. Jacob has taught the boys much about science, religion, language, and the arts.

Jacob has also exposed the boys to the workings of his true practices within the Knights Templar: master spy and counterspy. These skills may prove most important in the lads' knowledge inventory, because the Holy Land abounds in intrigue.

But all is not warfare and brutal training. When Squire Roland first cast his eyes upon the beautiful Lady Marie of Baux, he knew she was different from the other young women in his life. He also knew that he must *earn* this lady's love and affection, as he now has nothing else to offer.

What started as a fleeting chance meeting between two young people has matured into genuine love. When Marie is in trouble, Roland always seemed to somehow, and often with unorthodox techniques, save her life.

The roads from Roland's courtly and ancestral home in Troyes, Champagne, to the coast of the Outremer have been laced with much training, hardship, intrigue, and blood. It is in this backdrop that Roland, Aaron, and Templar Knights Walter of Mesnil and Sergeant Martin of Brittany, and their band of Templar brothers, along with Doctor Jacob and Marie of Baux, continue their journey to the shores of the Holy Land.

Roland may be seeking the way of redemption of the Christian cross but may find his destiny under the shadows of Islam's crescent. Who knows? A templar's journey continues...

Prologue

"To open the blind eyes, bring out the prisoners from the prison, and them that sit in darkness out of the prison house."

Isaiah 42:7

E dward gazed down at his aged father, thinking about what exactly could be done. In a muted tone, he spoke to his two brothers, seeking their counsel. "Do we rouse him or inform the grand master and bishop that Father is in no condition to continue his ordination ceremony?"

The eldest brother, Edward, looked again upon his resting father, and then slowly—ever so slowly—he turned to his two brothers. "Well brothers, what do *we* do?"

Gilbert, the youngest son, and most like his father, was quick to answer, "Father may be old and frail, but he is still Roland. If anyone tries to stop this ceremony, Father would still take that sword at his side, or that dagger he still keeps in his boot, and wage war with his last breath. No, Edward, no one will stop this ceremony now, save Father himself."

Robert, the middle son and always the diplomat, wore an expression as to calm his brother. Quietly, he redirected the question. "What would Father want, Edward?"

Armand of Périgord, the grand master of the Knights Templar, had sent word that the ordination ceremony would take place in a few minutes. Here was Edward's aged father, the infamous Roland, in a trancelike reverie, looking east, directly at the hot sun. The aged knight was looking more and more as if he were blind or perhaps, worse, near death.

Roland had been in this same position for several minutes now. Initially, his sons had believed he was dozing. They had thought this brief nap would serve the old man well, and perhaps energize him for the rigors of his ordination as a Templar monk.

Edward now felt remorseful for allowing his father to drift into this nearly comatose state.

Robert announced in a loud tone that he thought perhaps would rouse his father, "He must be revived now. The grand master and bishop are doing this ceremony out of respect for Father's standing in France, in the Order, and in the Outremer."

He continued, "This entire ceremony itself is highly unusual, since normal Templar investments in the Outremer occur at Templar headquarters in Acre. It was Father who requested the ceremony be conducted in the same fashion as it was before the city fell to Saladin so many years ago. Father insisted that it must be done here in Jerusalem, in the original Templar headquarters above Solomon's Temple, and not in the new headquarters in Acre."

Robert reflected inwardly as he approached his father. *Here we are, nearly surrounded by Muslim warriors just miles away. We use the old Templar chapel, near the Dome of the Holy Mount for the ceremony. This whole drama will eclipse Templar tradition in many ways. Father is seventy-two years of age, and we all know that his life is coming to an end. This is foolish that an old man wants to take the vows of obedience, poverty, and chastity at this time so late in his life's journey.*

Yet here was Roland, perhaps the greatest knight in Christendom, ready to answer the call of Templar ordination. Roland was dressed in the white raiment of a Templar knight, with the bloodred cross emblazoned upon his body. In just minutes, the nearly crippled old man was to take the required vows in the presence of the grand master of the Temple, and Robert of Nantes, the bishop of Jerusalem.

Edward joined in his brother's appraisal. "The very Papal Order that authorized this break with tradition came from the leader of the Knights Templar, Pope Gregory. I received this papal bull from His Holiness's own hand. I orchestrated the progression of events as dictated in the parchment. I am now regretting my actions."

Edward would later discover the papal order was one of the last documents signed by Pope Gregory before his death. Edward continued, "We have had nothing but evildoings from the time I received the pope's order. This papal bull is cursed and perhaps foretells the outcome of today's ceremony?"

Edward approached Roland's relaxed body rather timidly. "Father, in God's name, please move."

Roland's eyes remained continually open with no change as he gazed at the blazing sun to the east.

Edward eyed his father carefully, and the reality came to him as Roland's body appeared still and perhaps beyond this world? Edward thought, *God has taken him; what shall I now do?*

Gilbert sensed his brother's concern and approached his father. He knew the words to stir his father to action. In a loud tone, he bellowed, "Lord Roland, the enemy is at the gate."

With that alarm, Roland's eyes rolled and his right hand slipped to the sword that hung by his side and his left hand assuredly approached the dagger hidden in his boot.

An odd smile, perhaps drawn from his youth, crept upon the aged man's face. "Ah, Gilbert, you remembered how you would awaken me to go hunting when you were young. It was a trick that the great Islamic leader Mustafa used on me once. Now, *he* was a soldier."

With the deportment of nobility and the élan of youth, Roland then arose. "I was in deep thought. It was an art taught to me by one of Hassassin's warlords to ward off the pain of torture."

The old man arranged his clothing, adjusted his sword, and finally spoke to his sons. "Edward, I am not dead," he said, savoring the reflection on the next word from his lips: "*yet.*"

The old knight continued, "I was in deep thought...recalling what brought me here to the Outremer the first time, ah those so many years ago."

The old man looked toward the sun and smiled. "I believe I arrived here in the morning. There, just off the coast. I was amazed at the sun's brilliance. It nearly blinds you and draws the very color from your eyes—perhaps that is why all the inhabitants have black or brown eyes?"

Then he looked, up at a small window in which lepers could see the services when this hall was used as a chapel. "Yes, all here have dark eyes, unless they have a Frankish father and a Greek slave mother's eyes."

His smile turned deadly. He was remembering the many, many blue-eyed Islamic Mamlukes; all those whose light-colored eyes he had looked into before he had hacked them to death in combat.

Roland continued, "The land seemed to be aflame, as if it were a caldron ablaze. It was warning me, but alas, Edward, I did not heed the sign."

Then, the old man floated off mentally and lost his balance momentarily. He briefly lost his sight and had difficulty refocusing. He spoke of the shortcoming. "Age does that to you, Edward, when you try hard to concentrate. It is a sure sign that my journey here is coming to an end. Then again, I also had the same question more than fifty-five years ago as I do today. What will the journey bring forth? Perhaps at this stage in my life, I should ask the question, when will the journey end?"

He now directed his discussion to Gilbert. "Had I only known that the pathway of my road would be so harsh, I would have taken the advice of an old friend, Father Williams, back in Sicily and traveled back to Champagne."

The old man continued after a pause, "Alas, Gilbert, had I taken the good priest's advice, you would not be here, since it was the Outremer that brought your mother and me together as one."

The old soldier calmly lowered his right hand into his boot and took out a rather long dagger. He pointed the steel toward the northwest. "Gilbert, out there to the north is the ancient city of Tyre. After today, you need to visit the place."

Roland looked out at the walls of Jerusalem and remembered. "In the walled city of Tyre, we held out for two months against Saladin's massive army. It is where I was knighted in the Cathedral of the Holy Cross on Christmas Day. Just days later, your mother and I were married on January 1, in the Year of Our Lord 1188."

Roland continued, "Many brides and grooms fail to remember their wedding day. Your mother and I surely remembered our day. We were married in the midst of the battle for the Christian soul of the Outremer.

"After we wed, we went to the walls and battled Saladin's host for twelve hours. She was excellent with a bow. What a woman she was." With that, Roland looked upward to the heavens and commented, "I will see her shortly."

Edward was growing pensive by the minute and wanted this event to happen soon. He looked to the entrance door and noted several priests at the hall entrance, making a motion for Roland and the sons to come forth for the ceremony. With one bob of his head, Edward acknowledged the nervous priest and told his father solemnly, "The grand master and the bishop await you, my lord."

Roland acknowledged his son with a small hand gesture. He then turned ever so slightly and looked to a distant corner of the hall. The old man's eyes could barely make out the rather battered script's table and chair tossed in the corner. A broad smile, as if he had just seen an old friend arrive, came upon his face. "Edward, tell them to wait."

Robert, wanting as always to be the peacemaker, spoke. "Father, with all due respect, sir, you can't keep the grand master and the bishop waiting."

Roland's response, while not one of anger, was reproachful. "Robert, ah...but I *can* make them wait. They or their ilk have pressed me for over fifty-five years for this day. A few more minutes will not bear harm to the grand master or the bishop." With a trembling hand, Roland pointed to the corner. "Gilbert, please bring me that chair and table."

Several attending squires overheard Roland's command and ran to the tattered furnishings to bring them to Roland. One small young squire pushed an older, larger, boy clear out of the way to obtain the chair and place it at Roland's feet. All wanted to see the famous Roland, some more than others.

Roland smiled. "Thank you, Squire, for delivering my old friend to me." The boy looked puzzled. Why this chair? To this lad Roland could do no wrong. Roland was the truest hero of the boy's life.

The old knight understood the boy's puzzlement. "I was not much older than you, Squire, when I first sat in this very chair many years ago. Turn the chair over and see my name upon the seat's bottom. I did the writing out of boredom one day. I remember mumbling as I did it, 'Well, at least my dagger got a workout.'"

The boy turned the chair over, and his eyes lit up as he noted the name carved there: *Roland from Champagne, 1186.*

The boy beamed. "I sit in the same chair, my lord Roland, when I keep the numbers in the journal for the commander of the Temple." The boy continued, making a brief but impassioned plea, "I pray each day I could be in the field with the knights and you, sir, rather than sitting here doing numbers, my lord."

Roland, looking deeply into the young squire's eyes, announced earnestly, "Keeping the numbers is an important task, boy. I did that same job and discovered much adventure in doing so. Do the task well; you will soon be with the knights."

The old knight now touched the chair and table in turn. "Yes, my sons, I was not much older than this boy. Perhaps no more than seventeen years old, when I sat in this chair and worked upon this table. This hall was filled with much activity."

Roland's aged eyes looked to the window again, toward the sun. Then he looked first at the young squire, and then at his sons. "My first few days in the Outremer were almost my last.

"If not for the skills of Brother Walter, Sergeant Martin, and my friend Aaron, I would have been buried a long time ago on the Joppa Road. In those days, I could not see the many dangers that surrounded us. My old taskmaster Mesnil would often say that I was blind, but made to see with the good grace of Jesus."

Roland crossed the room very slowly, as if carrying a great burden. He looked west out the window, toward the many roads, including Joppa Road, which had brought him here. He turned, then searched the room for his youngest son, Gilbert, who was visiting Jerusalem for the first time.

"Gilbert, see the only road from the east that ends by the Golden Gate near the Kidron Valley? The Turks sealed it over 400 years ago to keep the Messiah out of Jerusalem. We Christians reopened it, knowing the Messiah did ride through it as announced in the Old Testament. Jesus rode through it over a bed of palms to that hill of death for our very souls. We always dismounted before the gate and walked through it with heads bowed."

The old man's failing eyes shifted left to the Joppa Road, then followed the road west for a few yards, until all went dim. He rubbed his eyes. "I cannot see well this day, Gilbert."

His eyes were very bad, but within his mind, he could see the road's end at Joppa, the beginning of his Outremer journey. He could also feel a strange tightness in his chest and a pressure in his head. The old man knew that the Lord was sending him a message; it would be soon.

"Squire, please bring me my old chair. Perhaps there is still magic in it to get me through the day." Once the chair had been brought, Roland sat, and as if by magic or the Holy Spirit's touch, his memory of Joppa's harbor was suddenly crystal clear as he closed his eyes.

Gilbert knew that their father was not here in their world, but rather back somewhere in the deep recesses of his mind. "Let him be, Edward," he told his brother. "I will inform the grand master and bishop of Jerusalem that the Holy Spirit is within Father and we must delay the ceremony for a few more minutes."

Robert, always sarcastic, added, "They should wait. Father's rather large donation to the Order and Church demands at least a few minutes of toleration. Yes, I agree with Father; they **can** wait a few more minutes."

Roland had closed his burning eyes as his sons approached, yet he could hear his surroundings well. He turned his head to capture the voices and many languages abounding in the streets of Jerusalem.

He could understand the Greek man calling out in his language, "Yes, this is the *true* thumbnail of Saint James." He heard the Arab fish monger calling out, "Fresh Saint Peter's fish here." He could understand them all today, but it had not been so on his first day in the bustling port of Joppa.

His sons could see their father smile and then heard him mumble as if speaking in tongues. First he spoke a few words of Greek, then recited a short prayer in Latin, mumbled some Arabic, followed by some Italian phrases, and closed with a prayer in Hebrew.

These were all languages the old man knew well and heard on the streets and alleys of Jerusalem. His smile deepened as his mind went searching for answers into the very recess of his head...into his past adventures.

He was no longer in Jerusalem now but on the high hills overlooking Joppa. He could see the blue sea and those ships tied up to the quay in the harbor. The ancient knight breathed deeply and could smell the refreshing brine. He felt the cooling breeze blowing on him once again.

In the distance, a fast ship approached Joppa. He strained to see the Templar-bannered vessel. Roland could still see Aaron, the friend of his youth, high up in the ship's mast.

He could also see a handsome, blond-haired young man dressed in the attire of a humble Templar squire. The squire stood with the ship's steering tiller in hand, guiding the vessel into port. The tall young man on the ship's quarterdeck seemed strong, and very sure of himself.

This figure of a young man was looking at him now, directly eye to eye. He knew that young man very well, for the young man was himself, so many years ago.

Chapter One

"Yet man is born unto trouble, as the sparks fly upward."
Job 5:7

Roland was looking into the eye of the storm off toward the east. "Master Henry, it seems like a cauldron with fire and smoke below, and steam bellowing above into the sky."

Henry, the ship's master, pointed with his well-worn hand toward the east and what appeared to be the land and sea ablaze in flame. "When the weather is just so, both the sky and land near the sea seem to be on fire as you approach the Outremer. It is out there, Roland. Joppa is out there." The old shipmaster Henry knew the phenomenon well. "The Outremer plays tricks with your eyes and head, Roland. This is but the first trick; many others will follow."

The young, redheaded Aaron had the eyes of a hawk, and it was his sharp eyes that first noted the Outremer in the fiery morning haze. It was he who alerted all from his station high in the raven's nest. "Master Henry, land, due east. I can see land and a port." He had used Doctor Jacob's seemingly magic green glass to penetrate the sun's haze and mist to see the land very clearly from his raven's nest high in the main mast.

A cheer went up from all the Templars, pilgrims and crew alike. Henry cautioned, "Not so fast, friends. Perhaps Aaron has eyed a port, but we may be many miles from Joppa. We could be many miles north. Perhaps it is Caesarea to the north, or many miles south near Ascalon. Aaron, can you see black rocks, forming a barrier, perhaps two hundred feet north of the quay?"

Aaron strained his eyes and moved his green glass closer to his eyes. "Yes, it appears that a large patch of black rocks are anchoring the barrier to the north."

The old Jewish doctor, Jacob of York, announced in Greek to Roland, " χ ναι, ότι η outcropping ήταν το μαύρο βράχια της Ανδρομέδας. Δηλαδή όπου Ανδρομέδα αλυσοδέθηκε αναμένει το Kraken και σίγουρο θάνατο. Που έσωσε Ανδρομέδα από το Kraken, Roland" meaning "Ah, yes, that outcropping would be the Black Rocks of Andromeda. That is where Andromeda was chained, awaiting the Kraken and sure death. Who saved Andromeda from the Kraken, Roland?"

During this adventurous year with the Templars, both squires had grown into more than just battle-hardened warriors. Doctor Jacob had also educated the lads in science, history, languages, religion, mathematics, and much more. Roland had read the entire mythological story of the Olympian gods and the Greek Titans as part of Jacob's plan to educate him on the long cruise. "Yes, Jacob, Perseus saved Andromeda with the help of his winged sandals, and he killed the Kraken with the head of Medusa. Those are the rocks that Greek mythology tells us that Princess Andromeda was said to have been chained on in the harbor because her mother had boasted of Andromeda's beauty. Perseus supposedly rescued and married her."

Jacob smiled proudly, thinking, *Just perhaps we may make the boy a scholar as well as a soldier.* Jacob knew that the Order of the Templar Knights had more requirements for Roland and Aaron than sword and shield, and he was educating them to deal with their new environment.

The old shipmaster Henry had taken the Templars from Barcelona to the Outremer in safety, but his job was not completed yet. "Well done, Aaron! If those are the Black Rocks of Joppa, we have arrived. Keep a keen eye for pirate ships from the south, as it is possible for them to come this far north and attack when you least expect it."

Henry continued, "Roland, keep the sails full. I need to go to the forecastle to make signals with the tower at the port entrance and to look for the Templar secret code displayed from a banner in the port. It would not be the first time a Christian ship sailed into a port that was in Arab hands or an Arab ship sailed into a Christian port. Very embarrassing for the shipmaster," said Henry with a smile.

Henry was one of the best star navigators in the Templar fleet, and he believed he had gotten them very close to the city of Joppa during the night, but he wanted to leave nothing to chance after such a journey. Another smile came over the old sailor's face as he announced, "Yes, this is the port that the Bible tells us that Job used to try to escape God's direction and wrath. Praise the Lord, it is Joppa."

Aaron came down from his high perch and landed in front of Roland, saying, "That being true, Doctor, we must be over the sea monster, the Kraken." He quickly grabbed Roland's head. "This head is much uglier than Medusa's head. No snakes, but lots of small bugs to scare the Kraken to death."

Roland, the lad from Troyes, Champagne, had found an enduring friendship and a bond of unbreakable brotherhood in Templar squire Aaron, formerly from the gutters of Paris. In the past year, Roland had come to understand what it meant to have a true brother and friend in Aaron. This brotherhood, with its trust and caring, was forged in battle and tempered in the many common hardships they shared.

The ever-stoic Templar Walter of Mesnil, always observing the operation, said, "Stop this talk of pagan gods, all of you, to include you, Doctor Jacob. All here are *supposed* to be men of God. Take no joy in such pagan talk. Jesus's beloved Peter, the rock of our church, worked his first miracle here at the tanner's house, yet you talk of winged sandals.

"Now, all of you take to your knees as we thank our Lord for delivering us, and be prayerful that He has directed Henry so well. No other shipmaster could take us within ten miles of port after ninety days of sailing. That was exceptional sailing, truly exceptional, Master Henry. Praise the Lord for your skill!"

Henry smiled broadly, as Mesnil was critical about most things and had few compliments to offer under the best of circumstances. "Thank you, Brother Walter. Yes, it is Joppa; I can tell by the towers to the left of the harbor and the heathen rocks that Doctor Jacob pointed out.

"We should arrive in port within two hours. The date is February 10, in the Year of Our Lord 1186—a rather good crossing with most of the pilgrim and animals in good condition. Keep those sails full. I want to be first into port."

Roland was always happiest when he was on deck and at the tiller with the breeze upon on his back. This was when he came alive. "Yes, Master Henry, I will keep her full speed."

The distant land became clear, and Roland now could make out the mystic port of Joppa in some detail. Roland kept a steady hand on the tiller as he positioned his thumb on the port and counted in his mind the ten thumbs in distance from the port to the ship, an old sailor's trick that Henry had taught him to measure distance.

The lad smiled. *Old Henry put us ten miles north of the port after sailing for over ninety days! I wonder if I will ever be that good.*

The other ships in the Templar convoy that had been in the lead yesterday, were now trailing badly. Each of those ships' captains pondered how Henry had made it past them during the night unobserved and undetected.

The port of Joppa was the very essence and the center of the Latin Kingdom's transportation hub, so goods were constantly imported and exported here. It was a busy port. Roland could now see that four Templar ships, and perhaps ten Venetian vessels, were being off-loaded with military impedimenta or uploaded with spices, fine pottery, and silks. Other ships were going north, making their way to other ports such as Acre.

Henry directed, "Roland, take her to the quay with the other Templar ships."

About 200 feet away from the quay, Roland commanded, "Take in the sails, and make ready to port." Ever so gently, Roland brought the vessel alongside the quay as if he were an experienced sailor with many years under his belt rather than just a few months of training under shipmasters Henry and Lamont.

The ropes were tossed out and secured as the ship halted. Walter gathered all the men and said, "Let us pray and thank our Lord again for safe our journey."

Roland was the first to kneel and inwardly thanked the Lord for this day. *Lord, I believe you have something for me to perform here that is your will? You have kept me standing when all around me have fallen, and I thank you for that. I will try in your name to do your will, and I ask for a continuing journey. Please keep my friends and the Lady Marie in your grace. Amen.*

Not many months ago, it would have required Walter's or Martin's not-so-gentle pushing on Roland's shoulder and commanding "kneel, boy, and pray" to make the unrepentant boy from Champagne take a bended knee. Today, he did it willingly and without pressure.

This small and seemingly insignificant event was noticed with much interest by Martin and Walter. Both men looked at the boy and smiled with a father's pride.

Even the former Paris gutter thief, Aaron, was thanking the Lord for the safe journey's end. Of course, Aaron would always thank the Lord in his own words. For certain, the prayer of the scamp from Paris was not to be found in the Bible. *Lord, so far from Paris, and I now understand why you sent me here. After seeing some of the desert women around the port, this is my penance for my past sins of the flesh. I will try to do better, as I can't do worse here. Amen.*

After the prayer, the crew began quickly off-loading barrels and sacks of goods that they had brought with them for the outlying Templar fortresses. Most of the horses and mules had made the journey alive, but a few were ill from the sea journey. Now they were being off-loaded with a sling over the side of the vessel and onto the dock.

Roland's mount, Sirocco, was the first over the side. Even with the many stops in port for the animals, many had not eaten in days. Roland went to Sirocco and unfastened the shipping harness while addressing his Arabian steed. "You will be fine, boy! Let me walk you to the paddock and find you something to drink and eat."

As both man and beast tried to regain their land legs, they made a comical sight walking down the quay. They were wobbling as if drunk and it appeared that Roland had just come fresh from the pub. It looked like that to those on the ship as well, and all the Templars and pilgrims laughed.

Only the old salts understood what was happening to man and beast. Soon, the pilgrims also joined the parade of wobbling puppet-like characters disembarking down the quay.

The other Templar ships from their convoy finally began making port. They quickly began off-loading pallets of weapons, clothing, grain, and other foodstuffs, but one ship had someone aboard of much more value to Roland than these implements of war and trade, and that was Lady Marie of Baux. Roland and Sirocco stopped along the wharf. Roland began searching for Lady Baux. "Where is she, Sirocco?"

Another horse was being off-loaded directly overhead. It was ever so close to Roland, and yet so intent was he on his search for Lady Baux that he didn't even notice the horse until its rear hooves unexpectedly struck him on the head, sending him flying into the bay.

Immediately, Aaron began to laugh and yelled out a warning, "Roland, your swimming lessons will come in handy now. You best pay attention to work and to what other ships are off-loading." Aaron knew precisely what Roland's attention had been centered on.

Brother Mesnil was not amused with the unholy comedy. He thought of poor Job, who had departed from this very port on his belly-of-the-whale journey to redemption. He mumbled to himself, "Wherever that lad goes, trouble appears and sparks to the heaven flow."

Mesnil then commanded, "Sergeant Martin, this is hardly in keeping with Templar rules. Go get *your* charge before he drowns—*again.*"

"Yes, Brother Walter, we shall save the boy from himself." The always faithful Martin ran quickly because he knew all too well that although Roland's skills were many, swimming was not one of them.

Roland had never done well swimming, and in fact, drowning was his only fear in this world. His attempts to move his own tall and muscular 200-pound rock-hard body with a dog paddle brought roars of laughter from the entire port.

Roland approached the dock as two small sailors attempted to pull him onto the dock. Roland's wet mass was too much for the sailors to handle, however, and in due time, they too were pulled into the glimmering bay. Even Mesnil laughed now, wondering what else he could do.

This water circus also got the attention of one beautiful young woman on a nearby ship that had just docked. It was none other than Lady Marie of Baux, the cause of Roland's lack of focus.

Yvette, Marie's cousin, was the first to laugh on her ship, and point to the spectacle. "Marie, it appears that your poetic warrior, '*Song of Roland,*' is instead the court minstrel Roland when it comes to the water."

Trying to compose herself, Marie thought, *Think of something else, woman, and perhaps you can remain composed.* She instantly remembered the first time she had seen the boy from Champagne at her home. He somehow had hit the stacked silver on the side table, tumbling them. They had crashed to the floor with a noise that had been heard in the entire castle. Far from helping her to not laugh, however, this memory caused her face to break its stern composure.

Then she smiled as she recalled the time she had first seen Roland's nakedness as he and Aaron had crossed a log after bathing on a Greek island. Poor Roland had been so embarrassed that he had dived into the cold river and unceremoniously dog-paddled downstream with his backside high in the air. Dog-paddling as he was today.

Marie's final humorous memory was of when Roland had saved her in Sicily as they had escaped from twenty drunken knights by setting a castle on fire.

By now, her ladyship was rolling with laughter as she watched four more sailors try with difficulty to pull the wet squire from the bay. Bringing the humor under control, she commanded, "Enough, people; the boy may be hurt from the horse hitting him."

She saw that Roland was on the dock now, waving welcome to her. She started laughing again and touched her heart with her right hand, signaling Roland of her concern.

Chapter Two

"And Allah did not make it but as good news for you, and that your hearts might be at ease thereby, and victory is only from Allah, the Mighty, the Wise."

The Quran 3:126

"Alms for a poor Christian soldier nearly blinded and crippled for Christ." This plea for pity immediately turned the heads of unsuspecting pilgrims making their way into the small tanner's house where Saint Peter had worked his first miracle of raising Tabitha from the dead.

Leaning against a tree was a ragged beggar man with a patch over one eye and a worn crutch next to him. More often than not, when a passing pilgrim was visiting this holy site, the pilgrim would drop a coin into the beggar's plate. Who could refuse such a pitiful sight? Was this what they were seeking on their way to Jerusalem? Were they to be as generous as Jesus was? Nearly all reached for a coin within their purses for this poor man. And he a wounded Christian soldier at that!

When a coin hit the plate, the beggar would respond, "Bless you, friend, and for another coin, I will kill a heathen Saracen in your memory when Jesus cures my leg and I can once again defend Christendom." Most passersby dropped a second coin in the plate and mumbled their names, praying that the old soldier would say it as he plunged a dagger into the heart of a Muslim soldier in the next war.

This was perhaps the best spot in Joppa to beg alms. For a small price, the old priest in the tanner's house allowed Guy the right to sit by the door, under the shade of a palm tree. Besides the steady stream of pilgrims visiting the tanner's house, a cooling ocean breeze kept the heat bearable, and the well water was always cool. The site also offered a pleasant view of the entire port. All this made it the premier location in town.

So, each day, Guy made his way high above the port of Joppa to the shadows of Simon the tanner's house. Here, he sat on a small stool near the door and observed all the ships arriving and departing the port. No one other than Guy of Sicily, the former soldier who was now a blinded and crippled beggar, occupied this spot.

All of the locals knew Guy was a soldier–at–arms, a brave soldier who had fought and been maimed in the last crusade with King Louis of France. He was a noble and kind man. At least this was the story they all repeated, so it must be true.

When pilgrims were not directly in sight, Guy would scan the port for activities. Today, he observed several Templar banners marking arriving ships, which took his immediate attention. He slowly took his plate and stool to the door of the tanner's house and informed the old priest that his wounds were so bothersome today that he must make his way to his dwelling.

As always, he gave the old priest several of the larger-valued coins. "Bless you, Guy, for your charity," the priest told him.

The beggar looked up and smiled. "I was raised that one should give charity each day, Father." With that said, the beggar made his way down the hill to the port.

Nearing the port, he made his way to the Templar quay to observe the off-loading. He focused on one ship, carefully scanning her crew and passengers.

Satisfied with his newfound knowledge, he traced his way back to the market and disappeared into the crowd, periodically turning slightly over his shoulder to see if he was being followed. He then turned into a dark alley not far from the Joppa port.

A short distance later, he made his way through the peddler's marketplace and farther onto a narrow alleyway into the warehouse district. The locals, who noticed that he was looking over his shoulder, would comment that Guy was only concerned that thieves would steal his hard-earned money.

In the shadows of the buildings overlooking the port, along the rear of a warehouse, a door was suddenly unlatched and opened quickly as Guy approached. As if by magic, the beggar disappeared behind the door. His operative closed and latched the door quickly.

The beggar quickly removed the patch over his eye so this eye could adjust to the light as he climbed the ladder to the second-floor loft. Had a miracle just occurred? Miraculously, Guy could fully see as well as walk as nimbly as a young man in spring.

No longer the beggar who was called Guy of Sicily, he was now Rashid-al-Damascus, a principal spy in Saladin's wide net of international operatives. Tomorrow, he would return to being Guy of Sicily and beg for alms on the hill, but now he had to report his daily activity to his master, the great Saladin.

Rashid, walking along the narrow loft, reviewed his accomplishments. "A busy day, Hussein; we have much to report to our lord Salah-al-din-Yusuf. Our old friends Mesnil and Brittany are back. The younger member must be Champagne, the one we have heard much about.

"Oddly, he does not have the look of a dreaded warrior, as we have heard, but more of a clumsy buffoon. Our colleague also arrives from France. We must ready for his arrival and orders."

Hussein had followed Rashid to the loft and nodded his head in agreement, for that was all he could do. The Templars had cut his tongue out some years ago when they believed him to be a spy.

Rashid, the beggar-turned-spy, had of course observed the arrival of the Templar convoy closely. His job was to count the newly arriving Templars and other warriors, and to make note of the ships' cargo as well as any other activity that may warrant the attention of Saladin.

In noting all activity, Rashid also had seen some other familiar faces among the new arrivals. He wrote the intelligence in code and placed the script carefully in a hollowed-out loaf of bread then he plugged the hole. He placed the unremarkable loaf in a basket along with several other unremarkable loaves.

He motioned to his assistant, Hussein. "Take this basket to the drop point and pick up the empty basket. Then stay by the door and watch for our friend from France."

Once Hussein had left, Rashid searched an empty basket that Hussein had just returned that morning. In it, he found a hiding place beneath a false bottom, where a coded message that looked much like a bread recipe lay.

Rashid grabbed his decoding script from a hollowed timber in the loft. He wrote out the message, promptly read it, and then burned the paper immediately. He smiled and repeated, "God is great," several times as he quickly washed his head, face, feet, and hands to prepare for prayer.

Rashid found his small prayer rug hidden between the walls. Turning east toward Mecca, he rolled out the small rug, raised his hands in supplication to the heavens, and dropped to his knees, bowed in prayer. "There is no God but God, and Muhammad is his messenger. God the merciful, all praise is yours. Merciful God, with you by our side, our forces near Constantinople have won a great victory in your name. Soon, God willing, we'll be in your holy city, Jerusalem."

Rashid, the familiar beggar, as Guy, at the tanner's house, seen each day on the hills above Joppa, and known to buy wine for the men who worked the harbor as porters and carters, knew that his days of suffering would soon be over. In his daily prayers, Rashid hoped that the great Saladin would not forget his four years of living dangerously as a spy.

He also understood from the secret message that the victorious Seljuk Turks would soon be released from the lands near Constantinople. They would move south and join Saladin's forces. Rashid knew these experienced soldiers existed in such great numbers that the Christian army couldn't begin to match them.

His heart was overjoyed that nearly eighty-six years of Christian rule would soon be over. The tide in favor of Islam was approaching. Saladin had united Sunni and Shiite Muslims as brothers throughout the land. A mighty Jihad was about to be unleashed upon the Christian lands, and he was a part of it.

After prayers, Rashid went back to a high warehouse window, where he continued counting the newly arrived men and material from the Templar fleet. He watched as wounded and sick soldiers were also brought on for their return trip to Europe. Rashid smiled. Soon, the master spy would be here with new orders concerning preparation for the invasion.

He closed his thoughts with words from the Quran, *And victory is only from Allah, the Mighty, and the Wise.* Rashid closed his eyes and bowed, saying aloud, "God wills it."

Chapter Three

"The more lowly your service to others, the greater you are. To be the greatest be a servant."

Matthew 23:11–12

I t took only minutes for Brother Walter to stop the laughter and to bring organization back to Templar reality. Just in time, too. Aaron announced ten mounted Templars approaching the port from the distance. He could see one of the knights pointing to their ship. He ran to Brother Walter and exclaimed. "Templars riding in, and they look rather important, Brother Walter."

Aaron's keen eyes then narrowed with menace as the cowardly Preceptor Daniel of Lans walked down his newly-arrived ship's gangway. Preceptor Daniel was rushing to meet the riders' leader. *Surely he will report and advise that Roland should be arrested for insulting the preceptor for his actions in Sicily, not to mention me tossing the guard off the wall and surely killing him,* Aaron thought.

The beauséant, or Templar war banner, of the marshal of the Temple was being carried by the riders, indicating that a Templar senior knight was among the riders.

The principal rider dismounted and approached Daniel of Lans as soon as he disembarked the ship. "Welcome to the Outremer, Brother Daniel! Praise God for your safe journey and quick passage. I am Brother James of Mailly, Marshal of the Temple and Commander of Troops. Brother Ridefort, Grand Master of the Temple, sends his regards and bids you welcome! How many brothers did you bring with you?"

Lans was in no mood for providing logistical data. "Before we discuss that, Brother, I want you to arrest Mesnil and his slapdash gang of highwaymen. I am *Preceptor* Daniel of Lans, and I—"

James lowered his voice menacingly. "I *know* who you are, and mark well that *I ask the questions here*. You, Preceptor, *will answer them*. That's your sole purpose in life right now. I don't care about your needs, Brother Daniel. *Now answer my questions.*"

Daniel looked left to one of his men for the answer. That man quickly nodded. "Brother Marshal, we have brought you twenty-two knights, thirty-eight sergeants, and eighteen squires. Brother Daniel's entourage consists of the preceptor, six knights, and three squires," barked the preceptor's second-in-command.

Daniel added, "I will travel to Jerusalem with my men to pay our respects to the grand master of the Temple. I intend to bring this matter of Mesnil and his pirates directly to the grand master, and then depart for France within the month."

James smiled. "Brother Gerald has ordered that all brothers be committed for duty immediately once they are here. That order includes you and your entourage. I have the written order here in my hand. You and your men will be based at Chastel-Blanc, about a six-day ride north. I want you to escort several wagons of supplies up to your new home. Two of my men will guide you to the fortress."

Lans, completely distraught, said shrilly, "I protest this move. I demand to see Ridefort now!"

James grabbed the arm of the preceptor and moved him to a more isolated position, out of hearing distance of the other Templars. "You, Brother Daniel, *were* the preceptor in Paris. Here, you are just another Templar who will obey orders. You *had* the right to command in France and across the ocean; however, once that ship tied up at *my* dock, you and these men belong to **me**.

"The grand master did not request your presence, and I command all Templars here in the Outremer. Let me remind our Rule of Order to you, Brother: 'Let only those brothers whom the master knows will give wise and beneficial advice be called to the council; for this we command, and by no means everyone should be chosen.'

"You, Brother Daniel of Lans, have not been chosen as one of the grand master's counselors. I am his chief counselor on placement of the troops in the kingdom. Do your duty, Brother, as *I* have ordered."

James continued in a louder tone for all the newly arrived Templars to hear, "We have lost a great number of men due to fighting and disease. We need all of you to do your duty for Christ."

Turning back to Lans, James continued, "Due to your poor recruiting effort, the numbers here have not increased. We have thirty sick or dying brothers who will make the journey back to France as soon as these ships can be off-loaded. The men you brought in will just barely replace them, much less the dead from recent engagements and illness."

James Mailly, who was a hardened warrior many times over, sized up the soft Parisian Lans and found him wanting. *A Parisian crème puff in body and spirit, in soldier's clothing,* he thought. He told Lans, "I suggest you pen an impassioned letter to your replacement in Paris and beg him for 200 more men. Brother Gerald assures you that when the 200 men arrive, you, Brother Daniel, can go back to France. Now, gather your belongings and follow Brother Boniface."

Daniel was shocked at the rude treatment, simply shocked. In Paris, he had lived a style of rather high living. He had never believed he would actually fight. He would bide his time for now, he thought as he moved along the dock, toward the awaiting horses.

James continued down the row of ships, passing orders and requesting that all pilgrims assemble in the distant courtyard in preparation for the near sixty-mile journey by foot to Jerusalem.

When he got to Henry's vessel, he noted Mesnil supervising the off-loading. He stopped. "If I live another day, my dear Lord, my eyes will not see a more sorry sight! No soldier doing the Lord's work was ever uglier than Sir Walter of Mesnil! I believed that the pope had a special place for you in his dungeon, dear Brother."

Walter roared back, "That pope died, Brother James, and our late grand master Arnold broke me out of prison, along with Martin. You still may get your wish, as I am fairly sure our new grand master will return me to prison."

James just laughed. "Well, at least I have two good men out of this entire bunch. Not to worry, Walter; our dear Brother Gerald has a special place in his heart for you and your lance. A wretched place called Castel La Feve. Yes, my dear friend, the famous Fortress Bean, near Nazareth, just for you."

The near-by Martin added, "Wretched is La Feve's very watchword. Still, the Bean is worse than most and better than a few. Please tell me, Marshal that Lans will not be in command there?"

Brother James smiled. "Lans will be our honored guest at Castel Blanc as quartermaster. Brother Walter will command the fortress at La Feve."

The three Templars chatted for a few minutes, and then James left the ship to ensure that Lans was readying for his journey north.

Walter recalled to Martin and James the last time he had been in Joppa. "It was near eleven years ago that I was at the end of a short rope, on my way to Rome to stand trial for my attack on the Hassassin's envoys to the king. In some quarters, I was a hero, but not to the king. Today, coming back here, I am still on a short rope that only the grand master holds."

Walter cleared his mind. He continued watching the pilgrims assembling for the trek to Jerusalem or Galilee. Then he said, "Martin, look at them! Even the knights on pilgrimage are acting like sheep. All of them are trying to emulate our Lord; not a sword among them, only the walking sticks of a pilgrim and songs of praise to ward off the enemy. The knights should at least be armed to assist us in an attack."

The ever-faithful sergeant Martin was also concerned. "Brother James said he has less than 600 knights, sergeants, and auxiliaries fit for duty in the entire Outremer. The Hospitallers are no better off than we are, with barely enough warriors to man their castles and hospitals. All the people believe that Saladin will be good at his word and maintain the truce, until the odds and numbers favor him, that is. James is more afraid of the likes of Prince Reynald, or our own Grand Master of the Temple Ridefort, being the first to break the truce."

Walter confirmed Martin's assessment. "The truce between Saladin and Raymond of Tripoli, acting as regent to the young King Baldwin, has brought pilgrims to the Holy Lands in large numbers. Unfortunately, the truce also brought indifference on the behalf of the various Christian kingdoms as fewer knights have volunteered for the military orders. Even paid mercenaries are becoming harder to find in the Outremer."

Martin could see that the few Templars they had brought with them would not make much difference in the balance of power, as hundreds more were needed. While enroute to Greece, the Templars had observed several ships that had mercenaries from France, Italy, Germany, the Lowlands, England, and other lands who were going to Constantinople to serve the Byzantine Empire for much more gold and silver than the Kingdom of Jerusalem offered.

In his earlier days, Martin had been such a mercenary. Now, looking at Walter, he noted, "Sir, most of the secular knights will fight for the riches offered in services for the Byzantine Empire. Constantinople can afford the mercenaries' pay. The empire is wealthy, and they can pay much more money and offer a better lifestyle than could the Order, or even the king of Jerusalem."

Walter of Mesnil added, "The Byzantines have been fighting against Islam for hundreds of years and have taken most of the Islamic pressure, but soon, that pressure will shift to us, Martin, and we are not prepared. This truce also allowed the Islamic warriors to concentrate their power against the Byzantine Empire. Martin, we will see our enemy again soon, truce or no truce. Gather up the men, as we will be on the march within the hour."

Chapter Four

"Then the angel of God, who had been traveling in front
of Israel's army, withdrew and went behind them."
Exodus 14:16

Once on the quay, Brother James Mailly took Walter aside.
"You and your men will return with me to Jerusalem and
then escort these pilgrims on to La Feve." James' eyes were wandering the deck as if he were searching for someone. "We understand
that you have the King's nephew, young Champagne, with you?"

Walter answered, "Yes, this is true. The boy is the brother of
Count Henry of Champagne, as well as the son of Maria of France; he
is the third son, named Roland."

James pressed, "We don't need to be caring for the boy—it is too
dangerous for the Order. He is to go back on this ship with the
wounded tonight."

Walter was quick in rebuttal. "He is good, James—very good
indeed; in his own right, he could be a knight today and a great
leader of France tomorrow. Imagine a Frank with a bloodline to the
crown of France who was trained by us and truly understands what
we face here on a daily basis. That is why Grand Master Arnold
and Pope Urban wanted the boy to be mentored by the Order. They
had hopes that one day he would be a leader at the king's side—
whether that uncle be either Philip of France or Richard of England. With his connections, it is possible for him to be king of
Jerusalem one day. Better still, a grand master of the Temple. James,
old friend, I believe he is the one who will carry on when we are
gone."

Walter continued his impassioned request. "It was his great
uncle who formed this Order and came to the Temple in the early
days. The boy has the bloodline and, God knows, much courage. I
believe that it will be fitting at the right time for Roland to carry the
Order's secrets."

James was still searching for young Champagne when Mesnil directed him, "To your left. He is in the squire tunic, and I keep him anonymous for security reasons. He is that massive lad on the quarterdeck."

Mailly looked at the boy. "He has reddish-blond hair like his uncle Richard the Lionheart and is fair-skinned like his mother. Must we place him within Jerusalem in order to protect him?"

Walter whispered, "Marshal, that boy fights like no other knight I have ever seen, other that his uncle Richard. See the bony lad next to him? That is Aaron, a street thief from Paris. Teamed up, they can kill the enemy in great numbers. Unlike us, they don't take kindly to blind obedience. They are more like Martin—cunning and crafty."

The old warrior-monk continued, "I watched Roland with his longbow kill some of the finest crossbowmen in Iberia, then continue the mêlée to dispatch another five of the emir's best knights in close combat. He wanted to take Zuntain to task, and I believe Roland would have killed the traitor had I not stopped him. The other lad killed three or four in the same combat. None can touch them, Brother. No, we don't protect Roland and Aaron—they protect us!"

Walter continued, "Any others who took the chances those two have taken without God's special protection would be dead by now. They have a warrior angel by their side and a halo around them that protects them like any of the warriors in the Old Testament! I have to take this as a message from the Holy Spirit."

James was rethinking his decision. *Perhaps I should let Ridefort make the decision concerning the king's nephew?* Still in self-examination, he said aloud, "Walter, I agree with you. He will come with us to Jerusalem, and I will let the grand master make this decision.

"We travel to Jerusalem this very day. We have about eighty pilgrims we must escort, so it will easily take us five days. The journey, even with the pilgrims, should be peaceful, since we have few Islamic attacks now. Our concern these days is more the occasional rogue marauder outside of Saladin's influences. These highwaymen look for easy prey and fat pilgrim purses. When they see Templars, they normally don't attack. No harm should come to the boy between here and Jerusalem. Once we get him to Ridefort, I will wash my hands of the matter. We leave within the hour. Make your men ready. Oh, and

Walter, although I am looking hard at the boy, I have to tell you…I see neither angel nor halo."

Walter looked at his old friend, and a rare smile crept upon his leathery face. "You will, Marshal! You will see both the angel and the halo before this journey to the Holy City is complete."

Chapter Five

"Do not fear the people of the land, for they are no more
than bread for us; their protection is removed from them,
and the Lord is with us; do not fear them."

Numbers 14:9

An old man with a sack of grain joined the line of porters carrying items off the Templar ship and placing them in wagons
on the quay. He then joined two carters pushing a wagon and slowly
left the port. This barely visible man found a lonely corner of the old
city and off-loaded the few sacks into a small shed. In between bags,
he quietly held a discussion with his fellow porters, who also happened to be the last two members of the Jewish community in Joppa.

Within the hour, the quiet figure rejoined the empty wagon for
its return trip to the Templar ship. He joined the line of waiting
porters on the quay and came aboard, presumably to unload additional sacks; however, this silent porter quickly melted into the crew.
He went below deck, toward a quiet, ignored corner, where he
approached Walter.

Walter, reviewing ledgers, was not pleased that the porter was
interrupting him. "Yes, man, what is it you want?"

The dirty porter removed his headpiece and shawl, only to reveal
the aged face of the familiar Doctor Jacob. Walter had had no idea
that this dirty porter was his friend of more than thirty years!

The old man smiled as he whispered into Mesnil's ear, "We must
be quiet. You were correct, Walter. Events are shaping for the final
battle. My people inform me that Saladin has ended the discourse
between the Sunni and Shiite tribesmen in both Cairo and Damascus.
Now they act as one people. He has complete control of the cities of
Cairo and Damascus.

"Walter, did you not notice the rather pleasant green trees blowing in the breeze as we landed? I noticed the blooming gardens as we
rode past the city walls. Yes, finally a rainy season, with full wells and

running streams. Now the land can sustain an army, perhaps 20,000 men, on the move for the first time in many years. Saladin only awaits the arrival of the Turks to launch his attack. Perhaps that will be in some months, certainly not more than a year. Saladin will move cautiously after his defeat by Baldwin. He will perform much work to know the land before he travels upon it."

Walter's face grew dour, and briefly, he closed his eyes and said, "God's will be done."

Jacob's head bowed in agreement as he continued, "Also, your concerns about a Frankish spy were not unfounded. While we don't know the name, we know that he *was* a part of this very convoy."

Walter was mystified. "The spy is one of our own! I was hoping and praying that my beliefs would be disproven."

The old man continued, "Yes, he was under our nose and we did not know it. He is very good at his business."

Walter, searching the area with his one good eye to ensure that they were alone, said, "Jacob, you did well! I see your network is still good. Your information and reports will be of increased value in the days ahead. The time must be near for Saladin to attack, or he would not risk such an asset so freely. I knew that a spy was close after we were attacked at sea. We must be ever vigilant. You must stay behind and uncover Saladin's spy network here. Start with this port, and then go east to the Jordan. We *must* make Saladin blind. Godspeed, Jacob. Shalom, my old friend. Watch the boy—he *is* the key."

The doctor and sometime-Templar spy gathered his clothing, medical supplies, and books. He once again joined the porter line in off-loading items, making his way to the wagon once more.

Aaron and Roland completed packing their few belongings. Aaron, the consummate pickpocket, had honed his considerable skills of observation, and he noted Jacob's rather bizarre goings and comings. "Yes, Roland, it is Jacob under those rags. He is under the assumption that he must do this, as the enemy spy may even be on this ship."

Both remembered some of the discussions they had had with the doctor at sea during their journey to the Outremer.

Aaron said, "Roland, remember Jacob informing us of the practical matters of spying? His very words were, 'I can't be seen in the presence of the Templars, as my identity would soon be known to our enemies. I work from the dark corners, alleys, and back rooms. I am never seen and always unknown.' It would appear the doctor is working the spy trade today."

His friend responded, "Yes, Aaron, Sergeant Martin also had some experience in the matter and offered his advice during the voyage, 'Remember, lads, there are two types of spies: the ones who are out of sight and nearly out of their mind for doing such a deed, and the dead ones.'"

Roland continued, "Jacob believed that we were being followed, and, on the three occasions when we were ambushed—at sea, in Gerona, and in Greece—that those attacks were arranged by the same person."

The squire from Champagne surmised that Jacob had been directed by Walter to stay with his people and investigate along the ports. "Aaron, if anyone can find the spy it will be Doctor Jacob. It takes a spy to know a spy. Still, we must watch all around us. We shall focus our attention on the pilgrims within our charge, since most of them traveled with us in the convoy."

The slim redhead looked at Roland with a grimace and noted, "Brother, I believe this spy is after *you*. It is *you* who are the center of these attacks. This enemy spy knows who you are. You are of royal blood, and these Templars can't hide that forever." Aaron then patted his two long daggers hidden beneath his tunic, saying, "The twins and I will be watching your back."

Roland smiled as he departed to get Sirocco from the paddock.

Marie and her cousin were standing on the dock and were talking to Marshal Mailly. Marie presented Mailly with a document with the papal seal upon it, which the Marshal read. Within a few minutes, he produced two local Templars who would escort the two young women. The men brought along a cart to transport the ladies and their belongings to a waiting ship.

The ladies thanked the Marshal, who quickly disappeared to attend to the details of orchestrating his detachment to escort the pilgrims to Jerusalem.

Roland mounted Sirocco and soon came abreast of the cart as it approached a coastal vessel about to depart for the northern city of Acre. He quickly dismounted and approached the two maidens. "Good day, ladies. I see you are leaving!"

Marie spoke first, and as always when she spoke to Roland, she did so in a light and airy tone. "Good day, Roland! Yes, we are leaving on a Venetian ship for Acre, and then we'll caravan to Tiberius on the Sea of Galilee. Our cousin, Eschiva of Bures, is the countess of Tripoli. We will visit her and attempt to visit my birthplace. Of course we shall visit the sites of Jesus' ministry. We then will journey to Jerusalem and return here in some months."

Yvette finalized, "And on to Provence—and home."

Roland's face turned white with remorse and disappointment. He had wanted to believe that Marie would go to Jerusalem, like most of the other pilgrims. He had thought if they spent some time together, he could convince her to marry him. He knew that if she would marry him, his whole life would be more focused and complete.

Now he would have to continue his trek toward the unknown. He explained to Yvette and Marie, "I am to join a Templar lance and escort a group of pilgrims to Jerusalem." He turned to look directly into Marie's eyes. "Perhaps in the future, it will be my good fortune to see you again?"

Marie blushed and smiled. Then she did something totally unexpected to both of them. She pushed Roland away from her cousin, out of Yvette's earshot. She finally asked the question she had wanted to ask when she had first met the handsome young man. "Roland from Champagne, who are you truly? Please don't lie, since I know that you are not some squire from a small village in Champagne."

Roland was taken aback by her action and the blunt comment. He quickly recovered and whispered into her ear in a low tone, with all the skill of a courtesan, "My lady Baux! Such a blunt and pointed question! I can't tell you any more than I have, yet does it truly matter to you who I really am? Who am I? I am one who loves you most in this world, the man who will someday be your husband and the father to our children—but not yet, my dearest one."

Marie was so startled that she had no words to offer back, but her smile and continued flushed face communicated her innermost desires.

Roland's bluntness had hit home, so he continued, "Our time is not yet here, Marie, but it will be soon in coming. I ask that you keep yourself for me. My claim to your uncle Raymond for your hand will be just, honorable, and soon."

Marie's retort was simple. "I believe you have just proposed betrothal and marriage, Roland? If so I accept, my darling."

Now it was Roland who was speechless, but his eyes and face told all! The young squire's well-tanned face was swept away in an instant and replaced by a blush of deep scarlet. His inner being overcame his soldierly demeanor, and love replaced Templar conduct. He gently embraced the beautiful maiden, mumbling, "Templar rules be damned." He gave her a passionate kiss. As he kissed her, he pressed forward, wanting to hold her forever.

In lusty return, Maria's tender frame melted into Roland so that both lovers formed a perfect silhouette of one.

Roland gently broke the kiss momentarily to whisper into Maria's ear, "Yes, I did ask for your hand in marriage—a thousand times over."

Marie had never received such an embrace and passionate kiss in her life! Her back strained to push her body forward into Roland's sculpted frame. She wanted him to cradle her body. She wanted to escape that very minute to some place they could call their own. Her one desire was to give herself to this incredible young man.

Roland had never felt like this in his life. Not with any girl, not with any woman. All the rest of it had been playacting, leading to this moment of pureness.

He was flabbergasted at the emotions; he backed away from his beloved Marie, knowing that for now, duty and honor must rule over love and desire.

His face went from a blush to ashen gray as he heard his name from Aaron and the attendant warning, "Either run away with her, Roland, or get your arse on that horse before Mailly or the other Templars see you." Aaron's harsh alternatives rang true.

Reality swept Roland back into the real world. "Marie, you are the most important person in my life, but we both have a service and duty to perform."

The gentle Lady Marie, her eyes tearing, touched Roland's rough hands. "Yes, Roland, we must do what we must—for now. The time will be short that we are parted. I pray that it will go by quickly. Stay safe, my love, and come back to me soon."

Roland's heart was heavy as he gently placed her comforting hands by her side. "I can hardly believe the sweetness that is you.

Marie, please send word to me if you need me. If you call, I will come. Always. And forever. May our Lord bless you and keep you, my Marie of Baux."

Roland backed away, bowed, mounted his horse, and turned to the ladies, saying, "By your leave, ladies, for I must depart!"

He rode down the dock to meet the Templars preparing for the journey east. Outwardly, he looked calm, but his heart was hammering in his chest. He had faced the most daunting and dangerous people and forms of death, but never before had he felt his heart pounding as it did now.

Yvette scurried across the dock to join her cousin as Roland was riding off. "Did you ask him the question? Who is he, cousin? Who is he? I heard he is the nephew of the king of France. The Castilian sailors say he is the nephew of the queen of Aragon. Others say he is Count Richard the Lionheart's bastard son."

Yvette continued to twitter like the youngest handmaiden, "So, who is he, Marie? I saw him kiss you. I've heard he is quite a scamp!"

Marie made a hand motion to her cousin, telling her silently, "Be calm, be relaxed, and remain in control. All is fine." The Lady of Baux smiled confidently and announced to her cousin, "He will be the father of my children, Yvette. He will be the father of my children. Now that we have sorted that out, let us go, cousin; the ship is ready!"

Casually, Marie looked at the stunned Yvette and, with a snap inserted into her words, stated, "Let us depart for Acre. *We have a duty to perform!*"

Yvette was aghast. "He will be the father of your children? For God's sake, Marie! Make some sense, girl, please! This heat has gone to your head, poor girl—it really has!"

Marie added, "Of course we shall marry before we have children, dear cousin. Now, let us board and get about the business at hand and see our cousin, Lady Eschiva."

At the corner of a warehouse near the dock, a set of familiar eyes had watched the couple's tender moments very closely, with much guarded interest. The same set of eyes had watched at the Commanderie at Orleans, on the high seas, at the court of Emir Mutamin, and in the alleys of Greece. The same set of eyes that had sworn to kill this boy and his mentors, Mesnil and Brittany! He would not fail this time.

The spy had received a starling message as he was walking in the shadows in port of the Greek island of Zenta just weeks prior, when a burly man had stopped him, saying, "A message from your master, Saladin."

A gray pebble had been pressed into his hand; this was the final warning symbol, and it meant that *any* further failure would result in his own death. The spy could not fail. The next sign, a black pebble or black ball, meant death was imminent.

Forced to painfully recall his past mistakes, he watched the boy take flight down the Joppa dock. *I've miscalculated your luck or capabilities, Champagne. It will make no difference in the end, for we will kill you, Roland. We shall kill you just as we did your forebear uncle Theobald, who started the accursed Order. Yes, we also set upon your father with poison for his foolish meddling in our affairs. If your brother, Count Henry, becomes imprudent and involves himself in the Latin Kingdom, he too will die! Yes, boy, we shall get to you very soon.*

The agent knew Roland would never understand why he was to die, because as it is with all cult inner workings, it was a secret!

The master spy walked within the bazaar, making his way toward a yet unseen warehouse, and thought, *The fool of a child does not know why he is so valuable to them. By now, he has passed any test that Mesnil could ever envision. You, boy, will not be the bearer of the secret, nor will Mesnil or the other four trustees be able to give you their segments of the Templar secret. Our man is in position within the very Templar walls, to soon obtain the other trustees' names. Death will find them as well.*

The man continued on to his appointed place, the back alley of a Joppa warehouse. Suddenly, a door was unlatched and quickly opened as he approached. He entered and greeted the awaiting Hussein and Rashid.

Rashid briefed the dark man of Frankish heritage, focusing on only the man's eyes, as the master spy kept his face masked with a shawl to make it impossible for Rashid and Hussein to identify him. The man's eyes were expressionless during the entire conversation. He was well experienced, and so he gave nothing away as to his background, comings and goings, or anything that could link the three men.

The master spy spoke. "Rashid, the time is close for our master, Saladin, to attack. The four Templars who landed can cause problems to the sultan's plans if they live. They must be eliminated. They will not expect a full attack on the road to Jerusalem. We can kill the entire lot and bag Mailly as a bonus. Our master will be greatly pleased. Get me Halmid now, as we have no time to waste."

Chapter Six

"And as for him who asketh of thee, chide him not away;
and for the favors of thy Lord tell them abroad."
The Quran 93:10

The Damascus court of Sultan Salah-al-din-Yusuf-ibn-Ayyub, known to the Christians as Saladin, was very busy today, as usual. Military leaders were clamoring for more men; judges were seeking legal guidance; countless minions pressed personal concerns and sought favors.

Saladin spoke in a rather soft tone to those assembled this day. "Gather, my friends and see who favors us today with his presence and plea."

One such inner-circle councilor was Ali ibn al-Athir. Ali approached the throne; he could not believe today that the most hated Frank in the Islamic world, Brins Arnat, known in the Christian kingdom as Prince Reynald of Antioch, was standing in front of his master.

Ali smiled and spoke to his friend Baha al-Din, who was the boyhood friend of the sultan. "Praise Allah, they have captured Brins Arnat and this time will kill him for sure. I don't normally do such things with a knife, but I will ask the sultan to allow me the honor of cutting that piece of camel dung's throat."

Baha replied, "No, my old friend. Brins comes to the throne room *pleading* for Saladin to return some land that our soldiers captured in a recent attack."

Ali believed his friend was making a joke. Baha could see the puzzled expression on Ali's face. Moving his head, Baha responded, "On my son's eyes, I would not joke about such things. Our sultan gave the old fool safe passage to come to Damascus to assert his concerns about his southern holdings near the Red Sea."

Ali al-Athir turned to his dear friend and colleague Baha al-Din and offered a critical comment. "Any one of us would kill that old fool Brins and be honored in paradise for it, yet our lord sultan allows him here? How the old fool Brins lasted so many years in prison is a testimony that the mind is stronger than the body."

Baha corrected his old friend, "Brins has no mind; our prison took it away. For nearly fifteen years, we had him imprisoned. His own family would not pay the ransom for the fool. They knew something that we did not know: The man is not worth the air he takes in."

Ali walked, as requested by the Sultan, towards the gathered council and continued speaking in a low tone to Baha, "That my old friend is a good sign for both of us. Look at him, Baha. The man who makes the Franks tremble and the Arab world stand up and notice is not more than half the size of that old Frank, yet that small man who has conquered Arab, Turkish, Kurdish, and Christian lands is entertaining the most hated man in Islam."

Ali smiled as he continued, "As he talks to Brins, he has completely encircled the Christians from the north, east, and south. Yusuf just waits to attack them when the Turks arrive, and the treasury will fill to pay the soldiers and purchase a fleet to seal the fate of the Christians."

Baha agreed, "He has the Arab world from Cairo to Damascus under his control. We gain more strength each day as the quarrelsome Christian state of the Kingdom of Jerusalem is slipping away fast, yet the man who set this in motion has nothing in the treasury, you say? Still, today, Yusuf-ibn-Ayyub is willing to return enemy land as a gift to that deranged idiot Brins?"

Ali looked to the throne room and saw the great sultan agreeing to Brins's plea. "Baha, his generosity is truly as famous as his courage. While we can sometimes constrain him with our war counsel, we can't seem to slow him from his outpouring of kindness. He cares more for the foreigners than for our own people sometimes."

Baha al-Din and Ali ibn al-Athir were perhaps Saladin's most trusted agents. The two understood Saladin better than his own family. They had seen the courage and kindness of this frail man for more than thirty years.

Baha continued, "I won't understand Yusuf-ibn-Ayyub until the final chapter is written. The sultan is Kurdish, yet he was unfeeling when we attacked Mosul and killed his own countrymen in great numbers. He will do what he must to unite our people against the Franks. He tolerated the Cairo followers of Fatimid until they revolted. Remember, old friend, when the Shiites tried to bring back Fatimid's cult, and he dealt with them in a most cruel fashion?"

Ali was the sultan's personal scribe and recorded all such events so others could repair their ways. He answered, "This is true, Baha. I can still hear the screams of the hundreds of Shiites crucified along the roads into Cairo. Some took two days to die—so cruel. I have watched him slaughter an entire Christian garrison, yet allow a Christian woman to walk away with her baby under safe passage. This is the same man who will allow this fool, Brins, safe passage here today yet tomorrow will order twenty men who stole bread to their deaths."

Baha shook his head and whispered into his friend's ear, "Later, he is to see Raymond of Tripoli's man, Ali al-Mosul. I go to the prison after this council to release all of Raymond's knights as a gift from the sultan to Raymond to celebrate the event. He could have received 10,000 dinars as a ransom, but he lets them go free as a gift."

Ali watched as Brins left the throne room and another favor seeker made his way into the room. Ali could see Ali al-Mosul lying prostrate upon the floor. Saladin took the letter from Ali and motioned to Baha. "Come, Baha, read this Frankish writing to me, please."

Baha noted the great seal of Tripoli and the signature of Raymond. "Yes, Lord Sultan. It is from Lord al-Sanjli in our language for Count Raymond. It is in his own writing; Lord al-Sanjli sends his regards and wishes you a long life." Baha's eyes focused on the second paragraph. "Here, he requests that his lands be spared, and in return, he will allow safe passage to our caravans and military to pass through his territory to assure you that he has not prepared for war. This reconnaissance must be accomplished in one day only. That would limit use to perhaps twenty miles within his lands, my lord."

The sultan's eyes flowed across the room as he spoke. "I, as a token of my gratitude, will release all of Count Raymond's knights from my prison. Ali, come to my side and record a message to Raymond that I accept his offer of friendship and welcome him to my court."

The sultan then directed, "Ali, come with me, and let our friends drink refreshments." Saladin, with Ali in tow and six Mamluke guardsmen trailing, walked to an ornate water fountain. Its large waterfalls spilled water several feet. It was the perfect place to hold private conversions, with the water's rush masking voices.

Saladin informed his old childhood friend, "Ali, old friend, I recently discovered that several within our court have actually employed people to observe me and read my lips. Will it never end? In any case, old friend, watch the waterfowl and fish within the fountain as I speak to you."

Saladin was looking at a black cygnet and a white cygnet gently swimming across the pond in perfect pace with each other and continued, "I have a task for you, old friend. I want you to go to Jerusalem and tell me what is truly happening within its walls. We are now in the third year of the five-year truce, and I need to know if the Occidentals are preparing to resume hostilities. I hear many conflicting reports concerning their war preparations, and I can't tell what is true or false. I also hear that their leadership is falling apart. Please confirm or deny these rumors, old friend. Take the imam Khatib Yusuf Batit with you, as he has many contacts in Jerusalem that can help you. Be careful, old friend."

Ali bowed. "Yes, my lord, and I thank you for this mission of trust. Lord Sultan, may I ask you a question, as an old friend, not my sultan?"

Saladin quietly bowed his head. "Of course, dear friend, you may ask your question."

Ali continued, "With due respect, Yusuf, why did you let Brins live, much less let him have his land back? We know that he designed the attack on Mecca. The man is an outrage, not only to Islam, but a curse to the Jews and to his own Christian people."

Saladin smiled. "Ah, old friend, it was much easier when we were young. Things were very black and white, like that pair of swans. When you and I were younger, we would see an injustice and we would act without much deliberation to quickly correct the injustice. Perhaps we were creating even greater injustices by not taking counsel and being patient?"

The sultan continued, "Today, Ali, I must look down the road through the distant haze of time to see the future. This is not easy, my friend. I must see past the laments of life to glimpse the greater good. I see us soon at the gates of Jerusalem in my dreams, but I also see thousands of Christian warriors manning the walls. I see their pope and kings sending thousands of warriors to *our* land to defend the city and to defeat us. More important, they will come to wash away Islam."

The sultan continued, "Ali, I need the Christians to come out of their cities and fortresses, and to follow us out to the desert, as did the Great Prophet's enemies. Once they are out of their dens of filth, a single mistake on the part of a Frankish commander could lose the entire Christian army."

Smiling now, Saladin went on, "Once their army falls, so will the fortresses and cities, and with them, the whole kingdom. I need that old fool Brins to counsel their king to attack us at a place of *my* choosing. Brins will remember this day, when he *believed* he humbled the sultan of Damascus and Cairo. He will tell his king that I am weak and afraid of the Christians. I gave him back miles of desert and two small towns—nothing. In return, he will deliver the Christian army to my door and give us back Jerusalem."

Cautioning Ali, Saladin pointed toward the desert. "We must draw them away from their fortresses and into the desert. It is in the desert that our people and our ways of attack serve us best. We, dear friend, will get it all, yes *all*—the kingdom and our holy city—back. Now go, and be my eyes and ears."

As soon as Ali rather nervously walked back into the small anteroom, Baha cornered him. "What did the sultan ask of you, Ali?"

His old friend Ali looked grim when he answered, "Now I am to be a spy on the Franks. I need to prepare for my death, Baha, for while I am a fair councilor and good scribe; I am, alas, a poor spy. I fear that surely I will be caught. But when the Christian sword touches my neck, Allah and paradise will be my last vision in this world. I leave tomorrow for Jerusalem. Pray for my soul, old friend."

Chapter Seven

"Then he said, "Jesus, remember me when you come into
your kingdom.' Jesus answered him, 'I tell you the truth,
today you will be with me in paradise.'"
Luke 23:42—43

Walter had dispatched his lance of twenty-five Templars to
Fortress La Feve in northern Galilee to reinforce the small gar-
rison. That task accomplished, he joined Mailly's entourage of seven
Templars, along with Sergeant Martin and Squires Roland and Aaron.

James hailed Walter, "Brother Walter, take your men and be the
rear guard. Have your sergeant come forward, as I know he has
knowledge of this road. He and one of my men will go forward as the
advance guard. If we get five miles today from this soft bunch, we will
be lucky."

Mesnil acknowledged the command and took his men to the
rear. Martin ordered the boys, "Roland and Aaron, drop back and get
those pilgrims who have fallen back gathered up."

Roland noted, "Yes, Brother Walter. At least we won't have to
listen to the pilgrims singing."

Walter remarked, "That will stop as soon as the temperature rises."

In fact, just two miles west of Joppa when the summer's heat
climbed, the pilgrims stopped singing and began begging the Lord for
rain.

Aaron, aboard his trusty mule, Paris, informed Roland, "Brother
Walter said it would be so hot that the birds can't fly except in the
morning and evening. I thought he was pulling my leg even though
Brother Walter doesn't really joke. It is even hotter than it is in Iberia
or Greece. I am sure that the pilgrims can't take the heat and we'll
soon be busy as hell."

Aaron was correct, and the progress was very slow. Within a few
miles, several of the pilgrims from the Low Countries and England
had heat exhaustion and required medical care.

The eleven Templars guarding the eighty pilgrims were hard pressed keeping the weary band together. Already, several pilgrims were falling behind, making themselves prey for bandits, or for Muslims not observing the truce.

Sergeant Martin and another Templar were in the vanguard, scouting the road and looking for ambush sites and signs of enemy activity. Roland and Aaron were with the baggage train with eight pilgrims who were too exhausted to move and had been placed in carts.

The group managed to travel just five miles and spent the first night in one of the Templars' fortress-like way stations at Casal des Plains.

As the pilgrims ate supper and rested, the two squires had to accomplish the routine camp tasks, such as hauling water from the deep well, finding wood for the fire, and assisting the sergeants with caring for the animals. After prayers, the pilgrims fell fast asleep as the Templars were assigned night watch. Walter's lance was assigned the first and third watch, meaning they might sleep about six hours.

Commander Mailly was also busy as he inspected the small fort's garrison of eight Templars and then ensured that all was ready for tomorrow's journey. He was pleased at how quickly Walter's men adapted to their duties.

He also noted that this band of pilgrims was in poor physical condition after the long voyage. He told Walter, "We shall depart at dawn's light and walk until noon, then seek shelter until late afternoon, and move for another hour or so until dusk."

He expressed concerned with the slow pace. "At this rate, we won't be in Jerusalem for seven days. Every day out here offers bandits more opportunity and makes us weaker."

Though they were hardened to the Templar life and the high heat of Iberia, even Aaron and Roland were having problems adjusting to the difficult road and extreme heat after the inactivity of a long sea voyage.

Both squires had the third hour guard with Martin and another sergeant. Aaron was peering over the rampart into the hot desert night and said, "Roland, did I see something out there move?"

Roland strained his eyes and noted a small desert hare jumping across the ground. "It was only a rabbit."

Aaron insisted, "It couldn't be a rabbit. It was an Arab crawling on the ground. Perhaps I need to call out to the guard?"

Young Champagne peered over the rampart again and pointed toward the animal. "Now you are seeing small Arabs hopping across the desert. What next, Aaron? Either we need an engagement to keep us focused on not seeing small hopping Arabs, or these pilgrims need to walk fifteen miles per day to get to Jerusalem quickly. This environment and climate make you see things that are not there. The water we carry from here will only last seven days, and we can't count on any wells since the drought has dried up so many of them."

Aaron agreed, "Twice today, Brother Walter chastised pilgrims for drinking too much water. I am already exhausted from the heat, and we've only gone a few miles. Today we lay within a Templar castle that no one would dare attack, but tomorrow and until we reach Jerusalem, we will be out on the open road—alone."

The second day was even worse than the first day. The going was very difficult because the terrain and road went higher into the hills toward Jerusalem. The many months at sea had caused muscles to soften, not only on people, but also on animals, so the stone road soon took its toll on the horses and mules. Sirocco and Paris were not in proper condition yet, and both were nearly lifeless and unresponsive to commands.

Walter approached Martin. "Sergeant, your mount is coming up lame. I will stay with the scouting party. See if you can replace your horse, and then come forward." Walter went ahead with the two squires and one sergeant. Each squire took a position on the left and right flanks. Sometimes they would drop behind the party, to ensure that they were not being followed.

After several hours of this patrolling routine, the canyon broadened out, and Aaron and Roland were within talking distance. Roland saw that Aaron's face had turned nearly the color of his carrot top.

"Roland, I am near used up, and it is just noon," Aaron said. "Both of our animals are suffering as well; one more mile, and I know Paris will just sit on the ground. This outriding assignment has caused us to do perhaps fifteen hard miles of weaving and doubling back on our trail. Still, the pilgrims have only walked five miles after all that."

Roland was beat up, too. He could not seem to maneuver his large body around some of the trees and undergrowth. He had hit several trees or prickly vines, making him and Sirocco jump in pain; then, when he had tried to rest his mount by walking off the trail, that had hurt his tender feet. "Aaron, my feet are killing me. I know we have been walking eight to ten miles to keep the horses fresh in case of attack, but if I hit one more damnable tree limb, I will scream to the heavens." Roland was rubbing his ribs from his latest encounter with the small, wiry trees.

Then he rubbed his slightly bleeding leg. "Better still, I'll head to the harbor and board the first ship west. I discovered Sirocco hates snakes. He's so nervous about the snakes that one second he's looking all over the ground, and then he's looking over to the trees."

The tall blond continued as he wiped his forehead. "If I get tossed off Sirocco just one more time...ugh...this is crazy. Hell, Aaron, my body feels as sore as it did when we quintain-trained in Barcelona."

Aaron came back with his usual encouragement. "Hell is just around the corner, lad! So, buck up, soldier of Christ, and back into the saddle. Remember, there is a pretty girl serving ice-cold water behind every well."

Roland looked puzzled and said, "Aaron, there *are* no wells!"

Climbing back into his saddle, Aaron retorted, "There are no pretty girls in this forsaken country either, except for your Marie and her cousin Yvette."

Roland knew his friend was trying to encourage him, and he knew that Aaron was nearly played out as well.

Aaron smiled. "Truth is that I can't take much more of this either, Roland. The beads of sweat never stop streaming from my skin. I sometimes pray that Sergeant Martin would have just left me swinging in the gallows—rather that than taking me on as a Templar squire."

Roland was rather surprised. "Just keep moving, Aaron; we stop in just an hour. What do you mean by 'swinging in the gallows'?"

Aaron explained without his normal humor, "I never told you how I got to be a Templar? I first met Sergeant Martin in the jail in Paris. I was standing on a small barrel with my hands tied behind my back and a hangman's rope around my neck, about to have my neck stretched. I still can see the damn fat, drunken hangman and hear him say to me, 'Let us see how you can dance at the end of this rope, thief.'"

Always a clown, Aaron tied his rein around his neck. "There were about six of us, all in a row, ready for execution. The crowd gathered near the Seine River's edge to watch the daily hanging. I was third in line. I saw this Templar talking to the hangman and noted that some silver passed from the Templar to the hangman."

Aaron nervously raised his hand near to his neck, then rubbed his neck and continued, "The man to my right says, 'Boy that is how them Templars gets recruits for the squires. This is the last time in this world you can save your arse. If that Templar asks you to serve, say yes. I am too old, so he will pass by me.'"

Squinting into the sun, Aaron continued, "The old man was right. The Templar passed by the first man, who only had one arm. The hangman kicked the barrel, and the man kicked, pissed himself, and danced for about ten seconds. Martin then looked at the second man, and that guy said to the Templar and the hangman, 'To hell with you, bastard Templar. I would never join you. I'd rather go to hell.'"

Aaron smiled. "This Templar looked at the second man and said, 'You are right about the hell part.' The Templar *himself* kicked the barrel, and the man swung in the breeze, doing the dance, wetting and shitting himself, as the crowd all laughed. Soon, they would be laughing at me soil my clothing."

Roland looked at his friend in amazement. "Good God, Aaron. Are you making this story up?"

Aaron traced the small Templar cross emblazoned on his tunic and said, "Hope to die."

The boy from Paris continued. "Oh Lord, no, Roland, and trust me, it gets better. When this Templar started to look me over, the hangman informed him, 'This one, Brother Sergeant, is the worst of this lot, a professional thief who has *no* respect for the law or the Lord. I have been waiting two years to bag this one. Half the crowd here today are people that this redhead pickpocketed from or stole from. I could not take your money for him, even if you wanted him."

Aaron looked pale just remembering it all. "Roland, I truly thought it was all over. Martin started to walk by, and the bastard hangman was going to knock the barrel away."

Roland stopped his horse and looked his friend in the eye. "My God, Aaron, you *are* telling the truth."

Aaron went on. "I screamed to the Templar, 'Our Lord loved the repenting thief on his cross, and just like that thief, I will be in heaven today, with Jesus.'"

"Lightning-quick, the Templar placed his boot in front of the barrel, just as the hangman struck, blocking the blow. Still, the barrel almost went over—and I pissed myself," laughed Aaron nervously.

Aaron continued, "I owe my life to Martin. He stopped the hangman. He looked me over closely and asked me, 'What're you here for, boy?' I said, 'I was a thief, and a good one at that.'

"Martin laughed a little and said, 'The Templars do not need thieves, boy. We need brave young men willing to defend the Holy Land. You do know something of Jesus. He did perform a miracle with that thief, and at least you know one part of the scriptures.'"

Aaron started to adjust his sword and spoke again. "I told Martin, 'You, too, Brother Templar, have worked a miracle and converted me. I will be the best squire the Templars will ever have.' I still remember the odd look Martin gave me when he asked, 'What miracle would that be, thief?'"

Aaron chuckled and continued, "While all this talking was going on, I had untied my hands. The crowd stood there in amazement. I suddenly brought the rope to the front, slipped the noose from my neck, and jumped off the barrel in one seamless move. The gathered mob began to laugh, and I did one of my backflips, and they all began to applaud me."

Roland broke into laughter as Aaron continued. "That is the same thing that Martin did, laugh. I passed the rope that bound my hands to Martin. The sergeant said, 'I guess you *are* a good thief, lad. Know any more tricks?'"

Aaron then did one of his coin-behind-the-ear tricks for Roland as he continued his story. "I said, 'Yes, my lordship, I know many more.'"

"Martin looked at me. 'But alas, for you to show them to me, you must be a Templar man. Come, boy, and remember this day well. You will need today's vision of desperation to get you by the desert's hot days.'"

Aaron smiled. "So here I am, in one of those hot days, so I am having that vision he talked about. The funny part of that whole thing is that hangman then complained that Martin did not give him the normal two pieces of silver for the released prisoner. Martin reminded the hangman that he had said just minutes before that he would not take Martin's money for me, and we walked out. He used the silver coins in a bawdy house next to the jail so that we could have some time with a woman and drink a little before we went to Beaune."

Roland laughed as he adjusted himself lower in the saddle. As they passed still another low tree branch, he exclaimed, "God bless you, Aaron, and I believed my story on how I arrived here was rather complicated. It pales compared to your tale of woe."

He smiled and continued, "Jesus is not in my story at all. The Templar grand master, a few kings, several queens, and some counts, perhaps. Oh yes, a marshal of France, several young women, and even a pope or two, but somehow, Martin is also in my story, along with a rather large oak tree, and swimming lessons as I was drowning. My story is mild compared to your story. But one day, I will tell you how I got here."

Aaron smiled in return, and the boys continued their scouting duties.

All in the caravan were exhausted when Brother James called a halt, and the party stopped during the major heat of the day. But unlike the pilgrims, who fell fast asleep next to the wagons, the Templars stood watch and, of course, prayed. No rest, little water, and hard work were their only rewards.

For the Templars, the third and fourth days were about the same as the others—long days and short nights with mediocre food, little sleep, and excruciating heat. By now, all the Templars and pilgrims were exhausted, and the pace had slowed even further.

To add to their anxiety and dread, the water was running out. As predicted, two more wells along the way were dry. Several pilgrim parties going west from Jerusalem to Joppa and other ports reported that the Holy City was peaceful and had plenty of water, but they had little to share now, knowing that the next two wells were dry.

The only good news was that Jerusalem was now less than ten miles away. But ten miles in the Outremer can be deadly dangerous.

The squires were positioned in the rear, with most of the baggage, and were not assigned to scouting on this last day of the march.

Brother Mailly rode to the sergeant who was escorting the baggage train with Roland and Aaron. "Keep them going, Sergeant! No one rides in the carts! Squire, why are you letting that pilgrim ride your horse while you walk? You must be ready to defend them, and you can't do it exhausted."

Roland continued walking as he replied. "I understand, sir, but the gentleman is ill and can't walk. I am fine, sir, and I can move quickly if we are attacked."

Brother Mailly, wanting to prove the squire wrong, quickly pulled his sword and was about to hit Roland with the flat side of the blade to get his attention. Roland, who was equally as fast, parried the sword by pulling his dagger from his boot and yanking James off his horse and onto the desert floor in one easy move, almost simultaneously placing the dagger to the marshal's throat.

Mailly moved the dagger from his throat and slowly stood up. He was shocked by the way he had been manhandled by the squire! In one swift movement, he, the marshal of the Temple, had been tossed to the ground by a boy. He was the third best fighting knight in the Order, after Walter and Martin, that is.

"Sorry, Brother Marshal, it was a reaction. May God and you forgive me? I pray I didn't hurt you, sir."

James, without one word and in total embarrassment, remounted and rejoined the main party. After the initial shock of being dismounted by a lowly squire wore off, he began smiling as he rode away. As he galloped forward, he said to himself, "No halo, but just perhaps he may be the one. The boy is quick, for certain."

Walter had observed this spectacle and prayed that James was still the good soldier who had some humor. Hopefully, he had not been infected with the grand master's arrogance or irrational bad temper.

As the marshal approached, Walter could not resist a barb. "Ah, Brother, I see your horse tossed you. I hope you are okay and suffer no broken bones?"

Mailly looked at Mesnil. "You know I was not tossed by my horse, Mesnil. I was manhandled by a boy. He is quick and very strong, Brother Walter, but can he fight?"

Chapter Eight

"O sing unto the Lord a new song; for he hath done marvelous things; his right hand, and his holy arm hath gotten him victory."

Psalm 98:1

Martin came from his vanguard at a gallop. The second sergeant trailed, slightly wounded from an arrow in his arm. "Brother James, it looks like twenty to twenty-five raiders are nearly upon us—a mixed lot of Muslims and mercenaries. The sergeant pointed to the right of the road. "We uncovered them waiting in a draw, ready to ambush as we pass. They have us in this flat land with the only hills about 400 yards there," he said, pointing south.

James looked south to see the dust about 200 yards away. "Let us try to make for the hills; it may be a running fight, but that is better than us being penned here. Martin, take Brother Harold and get those people to the hills."

Martin and Brother Harold gathered the pilgrims and pointed to the hills. "Bandits are coming, friends; stay together and run to those hills. We will be defending you the best we can. Now, move." Martin and Harold formed a picket line twenty feet behind the pilgrims to stall the attack.

James directed the remaining six Templars to turn toward the road to make it appear as though they were leaving a battlefield. "Let's us pray they take the bait and go for the pilgrims. We will move forward fifty feet or so, and when they come abreast, we shall turn and charge. Keep together, men! I will be in the center, Walter on the left, and Thomas on the right. We hit them hard and then make a right turn. Then re-form and hit them in the right flank."

Walter thought the marshal of the Temple had picked the best tactics for a bad situation. Had the same event happened to secular knights, they would have abandoned the pilgrims to escape harm's way in the face of such overwhelming numbers.

Walter knew that, being well-led and trained, the Templars had an even chance of surviving the day and keeping their pilgrim charges alive. More importantly, each knight knew that if he was killed in combat, he died for Christ and, as such, would surely gain entry to heaven.

It appeared to the raider leader that the knights were leaving the pilgrims to be slaughtered. The leader, Halmid, turned to his men. "Cowards! See them flee! Run down those two in the field, and we shall have them! After we kill the sheep, we look for the boy. Allah is great!"

James Mailly was correct. More than twenty warriors went behind the knights, speeding toward the pilgrims. He glanced over his shoulder to see that the raiders were in a nearly-perfect line in pursuit of the pilgrims. It was then that he gave the command, "Now, men, about-turn. March."

As if on parade, and having had hours of practice, the horsemen executed the 180-degree about-turn perfectly. James stopped the men in line and placed himself in the center of the formation. He raised his shield and announced in his booming voice, "Brothers, may our Lord Jesus keep us or welcome us today in heaven. Charge!" Then he closed with the Templar battle cry, "Be glorious."

Aaron noted that a second band of undetected raiders was making its way to the left of the road toward them. "Sergeant, look to the left, behind that small hill—dust! They want the baggage train and to cut off any retreat."

The sergeant in charge of the baggage train was an old warrior and knew the best way for the Templars to fight the enemy. "The carts and pilgrims will make for the hills. We'll stay behind them and try to break up the attack the best we can. Going by the dust, it looks to be about eight to ten of the sons of thieving whores. You boys ever use a sword before?"

Roland was stringing his bow, and Aaron was putting on his crossbow belt and quiver. Roland, looking to his flank, could see the raiders emerging from the brush and nearing the road. "Yes, sergeant, we know how to use a sword as well."

In a few seconds, Roland analyzed the battlefield. He understood what Mailly was attempting to do and knew that he must assist the vastly outnumbered Templars quickly. First, they must break up the second attack fast, and keep this new enemy from joining the main attack and overwhelming Mailly.

"Aaron, we must draw them off Walter and the others. We must offer ourselves as the sheep. We must empty a few bowmen's saddles first. But to make this work, you will mount up and flee in the open towards the pilgrims very obviously so we can draw the leader's attention to you. I believe they will go after you and the pilgrims. I will cover you! Once we kill four or five of them, they will run and we can help out Walter."

Aaron had his first bolt in place and was pulling the draw-string into the crossbow's locking device. He looked up as he said, "Great plan, Roland! Why am I always the one who is the bait? More importantly, why do I even agree to this foolishness?"

Roland looked at his bow. "Two good reasons, Aaron: because I can shoot off eight to ten arrows in one minute to your one shot, and I can hit most of the targets at this range. They have bowmen trained to shoot from horses, and we don't want to be caught in the open taking any chances."

Roland turned to the old sergeant, "Brother, we need to take down the bowman first. We can do the most damage from those small bushes and few trees yonder. Trust us, please? Take these people and carts, and get them to the hills."

The old English sergeant had heard Martin say the boys were good in combat, and that was sufficient for him to make a quick decision, as well as offer a comment with a discerning glare. "A countryside Frenchy with an English longbow, and a Parisian with an ivory Genoan crossbow; never heard of such things in my long years as a Templar. Do your worst, lads! Do your worst!"

The Templar turned and moved toward the hills and the main party with the carts and pilgrims.

Aaron just shook his head. "We need to share your wonderful plan with these bastards coming down the road trying to kill us to make sure it works. Maybe once I can cover you! Let's go, Paris, towards those trees!"

Young Champagne prayed aloud, "Bless us, oh Lord, and welcome us to heaven this day." Marie's smiling face crept across his mind's eye. He smiled and commanded, "On, Sirocco." The animal's response changed from exhaustion to renewal. Sirocco knew it was his time to rise in battle, and the lean Arabian ran like the wind into the trees.

Halmid believed the main attack was going well for his men because the Templars were fleeing like old women. Now as Mailly turned his small band of Templars and was in position to attack Halmid's troops, the Muslim's smile turned to fear. In just a few brief seconds the hunter was now the hunted.

The raider leader was good at his trade. He could see that if he and his men continued to attack the fleeing pilgrims the way they were, that the Templars could then attack in the flanks or, worse, to their rear.

This was a trap, and Halmid knew it. The problem was that he had stopped, while the other twenty-four of his warriors had not. The leader did his best to halt the charge, but that made matters worse because the troops were spread out and were trying to regroup.

Halmid also noted that his second troop had come up on the road and were closing in on the fleeing wagons and pilgrims. He tried signaling to recall his second troop to assist him in killing the Templars, but he saw two of his bowmen in the second troop fall from their horses, and soon, a third bowman tumbled to his death. Halmid's exceptional plan was rapidly coming apart. *What is happening?* he screamed to himself.

Halmid turned to hear the thunder created from the Templars' massive Percheron warhorses on his right flank. The Templars' feared bannered lances had already pierced two of his warriors' backs, and now they were approaching him.

Halmid sensed that he would die during this battle. The second troop was on their own, as he had bigger problems. He looked over the battlefield and thought; *These Templars are insane, attacking so many with so few."*

Just 200 yards away, Halmid could see what the Christians called a David-and-Goliath battle occurring between the small Templar rear guard and his second troop of men.

He needed to kill the "sheep," spread out in front of the attacking raiders. It should have been easy, so easy, and they were so close. Some of the younger raiders were smiling, while the older, more experienced raiders looked stern.

Halmid had fought so many battles that he was well aware that this may be his last. Even in these last moments, two very young Templars, squires, he believed they were called, had caught his eye. *It is the one they call Roland and the redhead, the one they call Aaron.*

Halmid could see Roland's stern face in the distance, yet the one they call Aaron was laughing as he loaded his weapon. The raider leader was well aware that each man goes into combat with a certain combat face, an élan or style. Some face death very quietly, almost serenely—others, not so much.

Aaron was the "not so much" type who would talk to himself out loud, or cheer himself to give self-encouragement in combat. "Not bad shooting, Aaron; you hit him on your second shot. Clean shot in the upper chest, I believe. I wonder what prizes he has in his pockets?" mused the lad from Paris. Aaron always searched his victims for booty. If Brother Walter saw him doing the evil deed, Aaron would yell, "For the poor, Brother Walter, for the poor only," and then muse quietly, "That would be me! After all, who is poorer than a Templar squire?"

Now the Parisian squire was readying his third shot as Roland killed the third and last bowman.

As he neared his friend, Aaron said with mock concern, "Roland, did I notice that it took you three arrows to kill the first bowman?"

Roland was packing his quiver in his belt as he replied, "Yes, I am out of range here, and I need more practice hitting mounted men. It took me two arrows to bring down the second bowman. Let's hope these warriors also need more practice! Mount up and head toward the carts; I will cover you. Now, Aaron, the tide of battle favors us, as we have the only bows on this battlefield."

Aaron mounted Paris. He checked his sword, shield, and bolts for the final time. "Well, Paris, it is rather sad to know that while we draw off these bastards, the squire from Champagne who will cover us is *in need of practice!*" He patted his trusty mule, asking, "Paris, I wonder if mules go to heaven." The young animal's ears twitched, and Aaron knew he understood. Aaron spurred on Paris and yelled, "Be glorious!"

Halmid's second troop leader stopped the attack on the fleeing carts. Realizing that they were ambushed, he led his three surviving men toward a small grove of olive trees to root out the attackers.

He noticed a Templar on a mule exiting from the back of the stand of trees, now going toward the carts. He would butcher this

Templar slowly for killing three of his men. "See? He runs—the coward. After him!" he told his men.

The enemy band was in pursuit of Aaron when they came within twenty feet of Roland's cover, giving the squire the best angle of attack. After his earlier missed shots, Roland critiqued himself; he could almost hear Big Red, his archery mentor, warning him, "You must estimate how far you are to your prey. At thirty feet on a fast-paced horse, lead your shot ever so slightly between the horse's mane and the warrior's chest." Roland judged the distance to be about thirty feet. "Here we go," he mumbled as he sighted the bow between the horse's mane and warrior's chest. Roland encouraged himself and spoke aloud, "Now stand and deliver. Steady the bow, draw it, and gently release it in one movement."

With that, the squire calmly rose from hiding. He stood steady as a rock, drew a deep breath, and, with harmony of mind and muscle, released a perfect shot. The arrow made its way toward the lead rider, finding his left rib cage. The rider grabbed his chest as if to clutch his heart and fell upon the hot desert floor.

The second rider was soon in Roland's sights, and the deadly arrow soon on its way took its toll with a second perfect kill. The third man realized what was happening and turned quickly toward Roland while the last rider continued on his mission to kill Aaron.

The man in pursuit of Roland was an excellent horseman mounted on a well-trained horse. The warrior would not provide an easy shot to Roland. He first weaved left, then right, and then was very close to Roland, perhaps only forty feet away. Finally, the rider was so close that Roland could see the beads of sweat on the warrior's forehead. Roland also could see the hate in the man's eyes—and a determined smile creeping across the man's face as the raider lowered his lance and charged ever closer. Just feet from Roland, the man's entire body rose confidently in the saddle, with the lance pointed toward Roland's heart.

The lad from Champagne held his ground. He calmly stood and discharged an iron-shafted armor-piercing arrow in perfect form just twenty feet from the enemy. Roland could see it all in his mind's eye even as it occurred; it was as though he were separated from his body and watching the scene. It came down to this one moment. It came down to Roland's few years of training, albeit with the best archer and warriors in the world, matched against another man's many years of training and experience. It was just that simple in the end, but it meant certain death for one of them.

The warrior's horse continued to close the distance. For some reason, home, Troye, flashed in Roland's mind. Roland would fight his older brothers in the training ring, and whenever the battle was going badly for him, his sister Scholastica would scream, "Roland, run away and fight another day." He could hear her once again call out, "Run and fight another day." Who would turn first today and run?

The unknown warrior chose to come and did not run this day.

It was Roland who dropped his bow and rolled to his left, barely escaping the lance and charging horse. Roland's mind was screaming at him, *How did you miss at such a close range?* He scampered toward his weapons under the tree some feet away. Would he make it before the warrior turned his horse and pierced Roland with his lance?

The young Templar could hear the horse stop as he grabbed his sword and shield to make a stand. He readied himself for the charge and what he knew would be certain death. He got a side view of the rider amidst the dusty whirlwind looking toward the sky. He then saw the forlorn hope of eternity revealed as the man closed his eyes for a final time on this earth. The young archer had had not missed his quarry after all.

The well-experienced warrior had misjudged the young man's talent for killing. The power of the bow had been so strong at such close range that the arrow had gone through Roland's adversary's armored mail and exited through the cavalryman's back. The man tumbled from the saddle onto the arid ground.

The battle was not over for Roland, however. He searched the battlefield to find his best friend also near death. Aaron was being pursued by a lanced warrior with revenge on his mind.

"Aaron!" screamed young Champagne as he saw the enemy warrior's lance approach the Parisian's back. Roland's own bow lay many feet away, and he was powerless to help his friend in time.

As he ran to his bow, Roland spoke softly, as if in prayer, "It is in the Lord's hands now."

The fleeing redhead could hear the horseman approaching at a full gallop. Without turning, the boy mused to his noble mule, "Perhaps he is about fifty feet away from you, Paris."

Aaron knew the sounds that animals made when they walked, trotted, or galloped. He had learned that technique in Paris as a thief when he was being pursued. He could tell how far behind him the city guard was by the hoofbeats. The mule, Paris, had a unique gallop, which could not be confused with a horse's gallop.

"Well, Paris, old friend, it is about that time to stop running."

Aaron sensed that the rider was closing rapidly. The boy pulled up hard on the mule's reins, and the animal stopped as if by magic. Aaron called on the animal to give him the best opportunity to kill his tormentor. "Paris, steady girl, steady."

He then pivoted in the saddle with one of his acrobatic moves. Doctor Jacob had described the tactic best: "The Parthians let the Roman cavalry near them and would turn in their saddles with a short but very powerful bow, to fire upon the enemy with great destruction. They gave the Romans a parting shot, if you will."

In one smooth motion, Aaron raised his weapon and let go a bolt that squarely hit the last enemy rider who was not more than fifteen feet away—when he was a mere second from killing Aaron. The power from the bolt sent the man backward in a rear trajectory, sucking the air from his lungs and instantly killing him.

The old English Templar sergeant observed this slaughter and remarked to himself, "Praise the Lord, we shall live another day. They killed those seven men in less than five minutes. I have never seen such things."

Aaron and Roland quickly regrouped and made their way in a hurried but unremarkable fashion over toward the main mêlée. "Pretty good shot, Aaron! You never even turned your head before the shot. How did you know when to make it?" asked Roland.

A smile spread across Aaron's face. "Paris told me when to shoot."

Sergeant Martin could see that his charges and the wagons had successfully escaped to the hills. "Brother Harold, please stay with the pilgrims in case one of those bandits breaks through. I will try to help out the main force."

He would work his way back into the fracas and hope he was not too late, because he could see only four Templars remaining to fight the fearsome enemy.

Martin looked at Roland and Aaron who just completed their dance with death. Where seven of the enemy had been just minutes before, now, only horses stood by corpses in the dry fields. A flash of concern crossed his face then quickly disappeared when he spotted two riders approaching the main fight, one riding on a mule and a second on a beautiful Andalusia of Arabian descent. Martin smiled.

The boys neared the skirmish. They stopped at point-blank range to discharge their weapons, and two more of the enemy fell from their saddles. The two squires again rode forward in tandem toward the enemy.

Martin could see his boys re-arm and let go a second flight of death toward the enemy. Again, two enemies fell to their deaths. Now, both squires attacked with lance, battle-axe, and shield as the fighting was at close quarters, with still many bandits and too few remaining Templars.

Martin had often believed himself close to heaven's door in the midst of a fight. He sometimes could see an image inviting him in to heaven. He wanted to go to heaven, but not for the same reason that most people had in mind. He wanted to see a man who was in heaven for sure, a man whom he had murdered many years before. He mumbled to himself, "Not today, Becket, but one day soon."

Martin was a Templar monk, but oddly not a particularly religious one. The sergeant did have a few favorite Bible scriptures, mostly dealing with fighting and whoring. Now, upon seeing his boys in action, his favorite fighting scripture came to him: "His right hand and his holy hand hath gotten him the victory." He closed his visor and charged into the slaughter pen.

Halmid could see that he was being hit in all directions. *This is not what I expected. The spy said that my band of thirty-three warriors would overwhelm the few Templars.*

The seasoned warrior was down to ten men, and most were wounded, as was he. The Arab knight saw no help from his left because they were all dead. He made the decision to leave the battlefield.

As quickly as the battle had started, it was over. Halmid was in shame, as well as despair and pain, as he galloped away from this accursed place. *Victory was in the winds but for the two who slaughtered my men,* he thought. *It was the one called Roland and his friend. Alas, victory was not Allah's will. Why does he favor them?*

Halmid looked at his men as they rode into the hills. He saw that arms were missing and that holes gaped in their bodies. Halmid knew that most of them would soon die because of these horrific wounds. He too had an arrow in his leg from some unseen enemy with a long-bow and he was bleeding out rapidly.

In much pain and looking down at his leg, Halmid had a last thought: *A parting gift from the one called Roland, surely.* A short distance away from the battlefield, Halmid tumbled from his saddle to join the parade of dead.

James and Walter were surveying the battlefield as the remaining Templars and pilgrims bound up the wounded. Other pilgrims began to bury the four dead Templars. The vultures and wild animals would feast on the many enemy dead.

James looked to Brother Walter. "You were right, Mesnil; the two squires turned the battle in our favor. The boy from Paris is agile, daring, and deadly with a crossbow. A very brave young man indeed."

The Templar commander then looked toward the distant figure nearly aligned with the afternoon sun. It was Roland, standing alone. "Roland is cunning, and he laid the perfect trap. Henry's son is calm in battle, and when confronted, he thinks before he acts. He is his mother's learned son, and his uncle, Richard the Lionheart's, perfect warrior."

Mailly looked at the carnage of the battlefield. "Between the two squires, they killed seven or eight in that glen, six more here, and fatally wounded two or three more. You were correct to make him as the future grand master of the Temple."

Walter responded as he looked over the carnage that he had observed many times before. "We have had several wise, good and kindly grand masters of the Temple, but none had the traits so early that Roland has, which you have just heralded."

The old warrior paused to collect his thoughts. *If this boy continues to grow stronger and wiser, perhaps he could carry the secrets, or in fact be the grand master one day. But many things must fall into place, and much is on the table of who rules Rome and our house in Jerusalem. Will Ridefort give me more time with the lad or take him away from me?*

Walter looked at his old friend James and continued, "As of now, the pope has other tasks for the boy to accomplish once we are certain of his character. He has been successful to date with his trials by fire. His military prowess and resourcefulness are equal to those of his warrior uncle Richard. Frankly, the boy may be better."

Mailly had other doubts. "Can he read the scriptures?"

Walter smiled. "As you said, Brother, he has his learned mother's insight. His ability as a scholar has been tested by Jacob. As expected of a Champagne, he speaks and writes in five languages. He also has a good grasp of many arts and sciences."

Martin approached the gathering and heard Walter inform Mailly, "I have seen Roland's loyalty, yet it has limits and it is not blind. The boy is truthful to a fault. He could have used his family connections many times to relieve his plight, yet he still wears the tunic of a poor Templar squire. Still, he has three more tests to pass before I take him to the pope."

Marshal of the Temple James looked amazed. "What could the boy do better, Walter? What challenges other than the battlefield?"

Walter cautioned James, "Look no further than our present grand master's fast rise for your answer. Roland is interested in Gerald's rise, and the system that made that possible." Mesnil pondered, "The boy soon will be confronted with corrupted power of the secular world *and* the military monastic orders. His faith and loyalty will be challenged. The lad will soon see clearly that most present in power today are not in awe of our Lord but favor riches and fame."

Walter of Mesnil touched his heart and continued, "The second test sailed away to Acre, in the form of Lady Baux. How he copes with the depths of that love will also test his inner sprit. That test will come in some months. It has been so long since I have seen love that I may not understand its effects upon the lad."

James smiled as Walter continued, "But love is a powerful force, and when understood, it can be a force in the world, either for good or bad."

Mailly agreed, then asked, "I am curious, what is the third and last test?"

Mesnil looked at the leader. "My friend, it is easier for an army or soldier to be victorious. Victory has many fathers. Defeat is but a bastard child. The true character of a soldier comes to bear witness in defeat. Both you and I have seen the character of men severely tested in defeat."

Martin finally spoke up, agreeing. "All here have been captured, imprisoned, beaten, and tortured. I have gone thirsty and hungry for days on end, only in my anguish to lick a sweating wall in prison or eat a roach."

Walter quickly remembered the fact that he had not seen sunlight for three years in prison. "This torment can last months and years. We have been forlorn, in despair, in prison. We have watched our own Templar knights renounce Christ and embrace Islam to save their lives. I have seen brother renounce brother for a scrap of bread."

James agreed, "True to all you have said, Walter. I too have seen men steal food and water from the sick. But the ones who survive this most severe test with dignity will surface as better men for it. What comes from this crucible of suffering are strong men of great character—men who can handle adversity."

The one eye of Mesnil searched the battlefield. "To date, Roland has witnessed victorious days and feted nights. Out in that desert, he will find the wind and heat that will forge his very soul. That test will be for our enemies to administer."

James agreed with Walter's appraisal and smiled. "Mesnil, you are wise. I am glad that the Pope let you go. You have done well with these boys." The commander scanned the battlefield and in the distance noted that Roland was assisting a wounded Templar. He could barely see the squire against the bright sun, which was directly behind the boy. "Walter, perhaps you are correct. I do see the boy's halo, and perhaps that haze is an angel above his shoulder!"

All three of the Templars laughed for perhaps the first time that day.

Once the battlefield was cleared of the wounded and dead Christians, the group gathered and moved west. The pilgrims no longer needed coaxing to move swiftly and to stay together. The pilgrims and Templars now traveled to Jerusalem unabated and in near-record time.

As they approached the city in the distance, they could see the sacred walled city of Abraham, David, Christ, and Muhammad upon the seven hills of Jerusalem.

The hills surrounding the Holy City were aglow in the setting sun. It seemed that the stone walls surrounding the city glowed as if they themselves were made of gold. As the city came into each pilgrim's sight, they in turn went to their knees in prayer, with both men and women weeping. The Templars stood still, completely motionless and silent, as if in a trance.

This was the Jerusalem that the travelers had heard about from their youth: from returning crusaders, from their priests and bishops, and from surviving pilgrims. This was where the final days of Jesus of Nazareth's life on earth had occurred, his painful betrayal, his crucifixion and resurrection.

The pilgrims also knew that this was the holiest place for the Jews and the Old Testament's heroes. This was where Father Abraham, King David, the wise Solomon, and, of course, the holy Temple, stood.

Jacob often told Roland and Aaron that Jerusalem was also sacred to their enemy, the Muslims. "Remember, boys, this was the focus of the messenger Muhammad's night journey."

Jacob, pointing to a map of the city, had shown them the Rock of the Dome. "In the journey, Muhammad travels on the steed Buraq to 'the farthest mosque,' where he leads other prophets in prayer. He then ascends to heaven, where he speaks to God, who gives Muhammad instructions to take back to the faithful the details of how and when to pray."

The old mentor had continued, "Understand this, and you will see that the Muslims will keep warring with the Christians, Rumi, Jews, or whoever controls Jerusalem. Then, they will fight to the death to see if their own Sunni or Shiite sect will control it. No peace will ever come to this city."

The astute young scholars thirsted for every ancient chronicle as they saw the city for the first time. Even they looked upon the city and wept, for this was the holiest place on earth, and now they, too, were here.

Roland dismounted first before any of the others and knelt. "We are here, Aaron! We made it! I can now understand why we fight for it as we have. You can see the sun shine upon it! Look to the right—the Rock of the Dome. And there, just left, is the home of the Templars."

Aaron looked at Roland. "I am more scared going into the city than at any other time during this journey. I don't know why, but I have a strange chill—a funny feeling all over. Look, my hands are shaking."

Roland pointed to the center of the walled city. "See beyond that knoll? That is the Church of the Holy Sepulcher. The area is Golgotha. That is where Jesus and the good thief were crucified, my friend."

Roland continued, "Aaron, I too have grave concern here. When I was trying to help an enemy warrior after the battle on the Jerusalem Road, he told me something important. He told me that he was a Christian in the service of an Arab called Halmid. He was moved that I was trying to save him, and he confessed that he was being paid to kill *me*. He pressed these silver coins in my hand and said that I was kind and undeserving of an assassin's death. He rolled his eyes, and spoke his dying words, 'Watch for the man named Pilot; he is your Judas.'"

As the squire from Champagne rose into his saddle, he looked at his best friend. "Why me, Aaron? Why am I the marked man? Who is this man called Pilot? Maybe he wanted to say Pilate, the Roman who gave Jesus the death sentence? Is this another Templar test or secret?"

Chapter Nine

"A talebearer revealeth secrets: but he that is of faithful sprit concealeth the matter."
Proverbs 11:13

Ridefort was pacing in the Great Hall like a new postulate monk on his first day as a Templar. "Albert, where are they now?"

Albert Fontainebleau was the Order's newly appointed seneschal, who was now in charge of all administrative and logistic functions for the Knights Templar in the Outremer. The grand master expected Brother Albert of Fontainebleau, as the chief logistician for the Order, to know where all patrols were at all times. "They have arrived, grand master, and they are stabling their horses. The boy is with them. He is alive and well! They were attacked along the way and lost four men."

Gerald Ridefort himself was just getting comfortable with his new position as grand master, but he still had many detractors within the Order—including those close friends of the late Grand Master Arnold, such as Mesnil. "Albert, please tell me that our dear Brother Walter of Mesnil and his man Martin were among the fallen warriors."

Albert looked down at the casualty list. "Not this time, Grand Master, but we are working on it. We have need for Mesnil's lance to replace men at La Feve. What better place for our two wayward monks to be afforded an opportunity to enter the kingdom of heaven?"

Ridefort smiled. "Ah yes, La Feve! That assignment should kill him off, along with Sergeant Martin of Brittany, in just a few weeks. I believe it is the water. In any case, we must keep Mesnil away from the boy. I will assign our young squire to you. I understand that he is a rather intelligent young man. Who knows; if you fail me, I can make him the seneschal."

Albert did not find any humor in that comment. "I will find work for the boy. Ah, here they are now, with Mailly in the lead."

James Mailly gave Ridefort a brief report concerning the journey from Joppa. Ridefort wanted his marshal to know that he was well advised. "I know of these things already, since your advance rider has informed me of the attack. Now tell me something I don't know, Commander."

Commander Mailly closed by saying, "It appears that it was a mixed lot of brigands. We would have been wiped out had it not been for the Champagne boy and the other squire, named Aaron."

Ridefort knew of the matter and spoke. "Yes, Mailly, the entire city is talking about the young Templar named Roland. Excellent public relations, is it not?"

Without answering the grand master, Mailly continued, "Mesnil informed me that he rescued several pilgrims in Sicily as well. The men from the Order of the Knights of Our Lady of Montjoie, who recently arrived from Iberia, also informed us of his fighting skill, as well as his favor with the king and queen of Castile. Still, I am greatly concerned. I recommend that he goes back to France immediately."

Ridefort took charge. "Yes, we have a large risk placed before us. The boy's luck will run out at some point. And his mother, the king, and his uncles Richard and Louis, who care greatly for the lad, will make *me* bear the pain if something does happen to him. No, we must watch this boy carefully and let no harm come to him. I have sent word to his mother that when all is safe, I will send him home," Ridefort said.

Gerald Ridefort had not risen from the dirt to command the Knights Templar from a position of impertinence. He knew all too well that Roland was very important. He also knew that Mesnil was under direct orders from the late grand master, as well as Pope Urban, to care for the boy.

The grand master spoke again. "Mailly, I understand how important the boy is to his family. Certainly, he is too important to be entrusted to Mesnil and the crazy Sergeant Martin of Brittany. So, what do we do with young Lord Roland of Champagne? If the boy wants to join the Order, I can mold him into an asset for our purposes."

Ridefort smiled and planned out another alternative. "Commander, if the boy does not want to join the Order perhaps we can find him a fitting wife and make him a count. Better still, perhaps he will be the king of Jerusalem one day. Tripoli's crown may soon be available, since Raymond has no sons, and like his father, he may die suddenly, particularly if the soulless traitor and coward continues to maintain his friendship with that heathen, Saladin."

Pacing the floor, the grand master continued, "Yes, just perhaps with some help from our friend Reynald, we could get our dear Raymond to the doors of hell rather quickly. Then think how easy it would be to lift our charming Roland to his throne. Yes, that would be an excellent plan. Think of it, Brothers; this boy knows every royal house worth knowing in Europe. They love the boy. They would love him more if we made him king. If we were attacked, they all would come to his rescue, tripping over each other to get here first."

Ridefort turned to Albert, "Yes, I am sure that his mother would be very appreciative. That relationship would bind us well with many in France, Iberia, and England. I believe the pope may like either of those two possibilities. Albert, send our future king in now."

Albert brought the entourage into the Hall of the Knights, where James of Mailly began the introductions. "Grand Master, this is Brother Mes—"

Ridefort interrupted him. "No need to introduce me to two such legends, Commander! All of Christendom knows of these two monks and the squires who accompany them. Brother Walter of Mesnil and Sergeant Martin of Brittany—of course I remember them well. Welcome home, Brothers! Your reputations have preceded you, gentlemen! These four warriors have been very busy of late, have they not, Brother Albert?"

Albert had several parchments in his hands. "Yes, Grand Master, we have three letters here. One, from Lord Tancred of Sicily, addresses certain actions that took place within the Kingdom of Naples at Sicily. In the letter, it discusses our intrepid heroes as maliciously wounding several beloved Christian knights. It goes on to describe the willful destruction of property, to wit, the burning of his castle. It also appears that a guard was either killed or somehow walked off the ramparts to his death during the visit of our dear brothers!"

Albert was taking much joy in undermining Mesnil's reputation as he opened the second parchment. "The second letter is from the Venetian ambassador, discussing incidents of mayhem involving

Templars at the Greek port of Zakymthos. It appears that the bodies of five men were found on a road that our dear Brothers Walter and Martin were traveling upon; so much for the parable of the Good Samaritan?"

Moving on to the third letter, Fontainebleau openly chuckled. "Excuse me, Grand Master. This allegation is just too rich. The third letter is from two noble knights from Castile who claim money is owed to them by Sergeant Brittany. It appears that some money may have changed hands in regards to a jostling match in Barcelona involving our squires Roland and Aaron. Further information must be forthcoming in this matter. I am sure that other concerns will also surface, Grand Master."

Ridefort turned to Mesnil. "We have received reports that everywhere you have recently traveled, Brother Walter, carnage, burning ships, burning buildings, wounding, and death were left behind. Our dear Brother Albert feels that these were felonious acts. I tend to believe you can accomplish the same level of destruction upon the enemy."

The Grand Master looked now at both Walter and Martin. "Mesnil, work in your new assignment as the commander of La Feve as you did on the road from Joppa. Then again, we are at peace with the Muslims, but given your lance's reputation, I estimate that within a few months, the truce will soon be broken, thanks to you and your Sergeant Martin. I would be grateful for that, dear Brother. Equally important is to bring the traitor Raymond to the high court for treason."

Now Ridefort's eyes went to Roland. "Who do we have here, Brother Walter?" He turned to Mesnil for a response. Walter then turned and introduced Roland and Aaron.

"Yes, so legends do live up to expectations occasionally, now don't they? While we do not often recall the history of members of the Order—it is against rules, you know—your exploits, young Roland of Champagne and Aaron from Paris, are the talk of all Jerusalem. Squire Aaron will also go to La Feve."

The grand master eyed Roland from his feet up to his head. "The reports are correct in describing you, Squire Roland; you do favor your mother, Princess Maria of France. Then again, your father, Count Henry, may the Lord keep him close, was rather a large man.

I remember him well from the recent Crusade with the sainted King Louis. Your father was a good warrior, generous to this Order, true to the Church and loyal to his kinsman. Unlike most we have today in this kingdom, like our heretic Raymond of Tripoli, who strides around in Muslim clothing, reading the infidels' own Quran and entertaining his Arab friend Saladin. Oh yes, we too have spies working for the Order."

The Grand Master continued, "Let's address more pleasant things for now. Yes, Roland of Champagne, we know who you are. You are every bit the warrior that all inform me you are! But we simply cannot have you fall into the hands of the Muslims. No, that would not be good for the Order. So you will stay here in Jerusalem, until we can seek counsel from the pope, as well as from your brother the count and from your mother on your final disposition."

Roland's face went from indifference to outrage as Ridefort pronounced his decision. All in the room could see that Gerald's decision had far-reaching impact.

Before Roland could erupt, Mesnil said quickly, "Sir, may I address you on this issue?"

Ridefort raised his hand to stop Mesnil, and he reinforced the sign and his decision with his words. "I have spoken, Brother Mesnil, and my word is final. I will not be questioned further.

Suddenly, the grand master spewed venomously, "Why, in God's dear name, Arnold ever gave this responsibility over to you is not only questionable; it's simply unpardonable. Had this boy been killed or captured in the care of the Templars, we would be ruined. It would be one thing if the boy were a knight and had already taken holy orders, but to steal him away as a common squire and expose him to such harm and mayhem was lacking in common sense, Mesnil."

Ridefort sidled up to Walter so Mesnil was within earshot as he said, "To place him into *your* hands is one issue, dear Brother, but for you to place Richard's favorite in the hands of Sergeant Martin—and yes, I know who the man *really* is—while you were in your sickbed in Castile is beyond the pale of reason. The man is crazy, perhaps more so than Reynald of Chatillion. No, this is an order, and you do obey orders from your grand master, do you not, Brother?"

Walter looked at Roland and then answered, "Yes, I will obey orders from the grand master."

In a soft, calm voice, Roland asked, "May I speak, Grand Master?"

Ridefort nodded his head.

Roland told himself to be logical, to speak with no emotion, to be the voice of reason now. He looked at Martin and then, with a slight bow, continued. "Thank you, Grand Master. I accept your kind offer to work here in Jerusalem until you receive the information and guidance needed. However, I must clarify that on no occasion did Brother Walter or Martin have anything to do with my decisions to act in the field. The fact is that they, on many occasions, shall we say, tempered my actions. It is my fervent wish to serve the Order where you dictate, and I will do so with devotion."

Ridefort's distaste had turned to confusion. "As you know, Champagne, you have been sent to us for the specific purpose of a life as a Templar. Is that your wish?"

Roland strode over to the Grand Master and responded, "With all due respect, Grand Master, I was not sent to the Order for life. I have received word from my brother and mother that I am welcomed back home. Frankly, I was thinking about being knighted and serving my uncle Richard, or perhaps accepting the offer of my aunt, Queen Eleanor, and dear uncle, King Alfonso, of Castile—to serve them. My aunt and uncle pressed hard for a marriage to the count of Barcelona's daughter."

He then looked toward Albert and continued, "Then again, perhaps Uncle Philip Augusta, King of France, would want a kinsman to serve him. So many offers to consider, Grand Master, and here I stand before you, a humble squire. My mother, the regent of Champagne, and my brother, the upcoming count of Champagne, have called me back to France, yet I stay on as a squire, as I do want to serve the Order and our Lord."

Roland felt like he was at his best as he commanded the room. His years at court showed his élan to full advantage, and he spoke effectively, playing with his words. "I do this service because of Brother Walter's and Sergeant Martin's training, counsel, and wise guidance. They have come to make me understand what is valuable in life. Frankly, sir, they are equal to my uncle Richard in battlefield knowledge and display of arms, and to my uncle Philip in diplomacy. It is an honor to serve under them!"

With imposing yet authoritative charisma, Roland turned to his dear friend Aaron and continued, "It is my friendship with Squire Aaron that makes me stand proudly and deliver in combat due to his demonstrated *real* brotherhood. His friendship is something that has caused me for the first time in my life to place another before myself. He is a knight much like the ones my mother's poet, Chrétien, writes so ardently about. He is much like Perceval in search of the Holy Grail."

The lad looked directly at Ridefort and continued earnestly, "Sir, I have issues of the heart, and yes, I could follow another path. All in all, I am not ready for holy orders, nor am I ready to return to my beloved Champagne."

Roland finished as he gazed at Walter, "I understand the concerns at hand. I understand that while I want to stand with Brother Walter and go to La Feve, I can't. It appears that nearly everyone in the Outremer knows who I am, and that was not my intent; that will bring every danger possible to the people I care for most in this world. It is best that I stay here until my brother Henry sends word to you."

Walter felt proud to know this young man. He knew at that exact moment that his young charge had turned from boyhood to manhood. "Grand Master, may I talk to Squire Roland privately before we leave for La Feve?" Walter asked.

Ridefort was pleased with himself. He felt a sense of tranquility in the room because it was Roland who had made the ultimate choice of staying in Jerusalem. It was the grand master who would now benefit the most from the boy's decision. "Yes, Mesnil, you may say your quick good-bye. Then report to Brother Albert for your orders."

Walter took the young man aside and walked to the far end of the hall. "I have come to understand, Roland, that you have a *faithful spirit* that makes you unique. I have watched as your talents and character traits have developed into manhood in recent months. The Holy Spirit has called upon you to accept a challenge. I could be burned at the stake as a heretic if you just inform Ridefort of what I am about to tell you."

Roland took Walter's hand. "You have been a father to me, as Martin has been like my older brother. Nothing you can say or do would cause me to turn or renounce you, so help me God."

Walter felt tears form in his one good eye, his first tears in many years. "I believe you, Roland, and I thank you for your kindness, as well as the many brave and righteous deeds you have performed."

During this, Mesnil was ever watchful of the busybody Albert and the prying grand master. "I don't have much time, but it was not by accident that this day has arrived. You have been chosen by many for a sacred task: to guard a secret that is so critical that, if compromised, our Order would literally cease to exist. Many would be happy for that day—all the enemies of our Lord Jesus. Some you know first-hand, like the Moors and the Arab hordes. Others are much closer, like Tancred. And many others, you will grow to know here in the Outremer."

With that, the old knight looked once again across the room to Ridefort, who was discussing events with other Templar officers. "Yes, Roland, some are very close; there are Christians who claim they act in the name of our Lord, but they really act in their own interest. Roland, should I stop now, or shall I continue on your path of commitment?"

Roland looked deep into Walter's face, staring into the older man's very soul, and then he said, "Continue, Brother Walter."

Walter turned to see a knight walking by, and he stopped talking until the knight passed by. "It is the duty of the person entrusted with the secret to train another to take his place when he feels that he can no longer carry the secret. I hold the secret now, and I wish to pass it on to you. Saladin grows in power every day while the child-king Baldwin grows sicker. Once Baldwin dies, the effort to obtain his throne will cause civil war among the Christians in the kingdom. I will be in the forefront of those mishaps. Saladin hates the military orders and will grant us no quarter if we go to war. I, along with Martin, Aaron, and the others in the northern border castles, will be the first to die."

Roland was shaking his head. "No, that must not happen without me. Brother Walter, don't say such things."

Walter hugged the boy like a father would. "Roland, we work for our Lord, and when he foretells such events, dear son, we can't stop the sands of time. He has set the banquet table and has many rooms in his dwelling place. It will be a glorious day when he calls me home. I hurt, and I am always tired. Something happened to me that day we fought Zuntain, and my body has not mended well."

Roland looked at Martin and Aaron, who were in a far corner. It was as if they knew what Walter was saying, as they nodded toward Roland, Aaron giving his tight smile.

Walter knew that young Champagne, who just minutes before had stood his ground to the grand master, was now in despair. "I know you are ready; you are young, but you have demonstrated courage and wisdom beyond your age. Our enemies would think that another, more senior, man would carry the secret; they would never expect you—a man with, shall we say, a troublesome reputation—to carry such a secret."

Roland smiled as Mesnil continued. "Martin and I have tested you many times over the past year. We've given you trials, and we know you are the one to carry such a burden. We had the trust of the past grand master and the pope in this matter. Your mother knows of this matter as well, Roland."

The squire was confused. "My mother knows of such things?"

The old knight nodded. "Your mother is the most learned lady in Christendom, and she has many contacts. Your family carried the financial secrets of the Order and, to an extent, profited from it—and that is not sinful. I am certain that Arnold was in Rome to discuss these issues with the pope when he was taken ill or made ill." Mesnil again looked over at Ridefort.

Roland asked, "You trust me in such things, Brother?"

Mesnil answered, "With my life, Roland, and the lives of Martin and Aaron. I believe that your oath is that of a Templar, save one advantage that you have. You are not yet a Templar monk and have not taken the vows of blind obedience; therefore, you are not bound to the blind obedience that Martin and I must adhere to. You are a freethinker, Roland. You see a problem, and you do well sorting out the best path. Thus, for now, being a Templar monk would be a disadvantage due to our present leadership. I believe that one day you will be a Templar knight, as was your uncle Hugh, but not now. Do you accept the honor as a trustee of the secret, and the attendant pain on your soul that if you pass this secret on willingly, you will renounce Jesus' name in so doing? Do you understand that our way of life will change if this secret is broken?"

Roland knew that he had come to Jerusalem for a mission of faith, but to accept this level of commitment and challenge seemed to be going one step too far. "I know we have only seconds, Brother Walter, but this seems of extreme importance, and frankly, I have failed at so many things that I question myself in carrying such a burden."

Mesnil smiled and pointed toward the Church of the Holy Sepulcher. "We can't find the perfect person, Roland, because he was nailed to a cross over 1,150 years ago on that hill."

Walter went on, "This is not a first for your family. Most of our Order's founding members were from Champagne and supported by your great-uncle Hugh. As you know, Hugh gave up his entire kingdom to your family line and then joined the Order. He was one of the first trustees to guard one of the four secrets of the Order, the secret of Solomon's Temple."

Walter closed his one good eye as if searching deeply in his mind. He summed up the challenge for Roland. "It is the qualities of courage, self-denial, wisdom, and many others that must be given and observed. Assessing involves risk and requires observation. Trials are required to validate commitment under the most trying conditions."

The old knight looked in the direction of the Dome before continuing. "I was evaluated by Grand Master Arnold and found acceptable to carry the secret. Frankly, I asked him the same question you are asking me; why they would ever elect me, but I see now that he was correct. The secret must be protected, and material objects must be moved from time to time in order to do so. My secret is protected by Templar Brothers who believe they serve another function—they know not what they truly protect. When you move the secret, you will understand the reasons for secrecy much better. You will then fully know the secret and quickly understand why we can't expose what you will find. Do you know what discipline that will take?"

When Mesnil saw Roland nod his affirmation, he continued, "Remember the six chests, and how we carried them? That was part of the trial. You never asked to look within, yet you were within inches of riches beyond belief. I believe you can do this better than any man I know. We must keep the chest and the contents within until such time when the keepers of the Church and Islam are not so ignorant. To allow the secret to be exposed would cause a panic that we can't fix, and it could do more damage than the Islamic hordes at our gates. These secrets we hold will tear Christendom asunder if exposed. The war we are in now with the Muslim people will pale in comparison to what will happen if this secret is exposed."

Roland asked the next logical question. "Why don't we destroy it or toss it into the sea?"

Mesnil responded, "This would be the easy path. The secret is sacred to many, and we can't do that. We must protect it with our very lives. One day when man is wiser, our followers will correct the gravest of foul deeds—taking what was not theirs to take. But not now, because mankind does not have the skills to repair what has been done without disturbing world order. Will you bear the secret's burden?"

The young man's breathing was shallow, and in a rare instance, some panic crept over him, yet he whispered, "Yes, Brother, in God's name, I will bear this terrible secret."

Walter nodded. "Remember what we told you in our travels about marking a certain place?"

Roland nodded, remembering the hilltop fortress in Greece.

Mesnil told him, "Take this seal and present it to the brothers who guard the vault."

Roland could see that it was the Templar coin with an inscription over the picture of two knights riding one horse on one side, and the reverse side was the Dome of the Rock with an inscription. "It is important to tell them that the picture inscription says in Latin that it is Solomon's Temple."

Roland looked at the seal and noted, "It is not the Temple; it is the Dome of the Rock." Walter agreed.

Walter added, "Look in your Bible, in Mark 16:3 for the answer to how you will find the entry way. Once you find the entry way, look to your left and find the seal of your house. Press the two fleur-de-lis and find your burden within. It must be moved upon my death to a location that only you will choose. *You* must remove it, guard it, and discover a safe place for it."

The wise warrior continued, "Then begin the process of picking another to take your place. While the grand master has knowledge of the other three secrets that deal with the welfare of the Order, you have the key to world order. The other trustees are appointed by the grand master. Grand Master Arnold once said that after much prayer, he was moved by God to appoint me the guardian of the fourth secret. Thus, Roland, God has moved me as well, to appoint you to be the secret-bearer."

Mesnil could see that Ridefort was getting interested in the intense conversation. "I must close our discussion. I leave you with this warning. The same intelligence that drives you well in so many ways can be dangerous in the act of secret keeping. Mostly, it is a thing of the mind; a kept secret weighs upon the owner and may overcome his mind. Still, I know I have chosen well. I now can leave in peace and accept my reward in heaven."

Mesnil started walking toward the door and said, "I also agree with Martin that we are close to death's door. Martin's vision is closer now, and he sees his friend beckoning from the dark door. We must go now."

The parting was very sad, as these men were closer to Roland than his family was. Their bonds of friendship were built on trust and abiding fellowship. The small band of brothers was gathered by the chapel ready to go north to La Feve.

Roland went to Martin and said, "Sergeant, I could not have completed this part of my life's journey without your help. The beginning of the road was indeed difficult, but today I understand why you made that road so difficult. I think of you as my older brother, surely unlike my brothers in France."

The Celtic monk, who knew that this may be the last time he would see Roland in this world, smiled gently. "Thank you, Roland. I see a young man who each day grows wiser and stronger in so many ways. Roland, you have gifts that God gives to so few. You now will travel a different path from Brother Walter and I. You always had the tools inside of you; they only needed to be sharpened. Jerusalem will be challenged in the days ahead, more than any other time in its history, and you will be in the eye of that storm. Remember what our Lord said to Peter in the storm: 'Take courage! It is I. Don't be afraid.' Keep us in your heart and prayers."

Roland looked into his mentor's eyes as he said, "I shall remember always, Martin; I will never forget. Sergeant Martin, I am not sure about your vision, but ever since we started this quest, you have said your vision is getting stronger. I believe that only God, and not this vision, can call you out. When he does, you will gain entry and your offense will be forgiven. Thank you for all you have made me be, Brother. I shall remember."

Martin turned away, weeping into his cloak as the band walked slowly to the stables. They were all starting a new journey that none wanted to take without each other along.

Aaron was mounting old Paris while holding the reins of several other horses. He was trying to be his lighthearted self, and as always, when he was most serious, he looked toward Roland but not at him. "I understand that the fortress is near Galilee and that it is cool and the water is fine. Then again, others tell me it is hot and not to drink the water from the fortress's wells but rather from the river. Once again, squire from wherever, you have the easy life while I must listen to Martin's jokes and Walter's sour comments while I get kicked by Paris."

Aaron patted his two long daggers, which were always tucked under his belt, "Remember, my Brother, that for the first time in over a year, the twins won't be watching your back. That is where they will try to strike you, as no one man can take you from the front. We will be together again, my friend! Keep me in your prayers, and keep the food coming our way!"

With that, Aaron tried to mount Paris and was manhandled from behind by Roland. Aaron found himself flying into the air and then landed on the ground. This was the same trick that Martin had done to Roland in the woods that first day when they had met. Aaron got up off the ground, and Roland gave Aaron a big bear hug, nearly crushing him. "You are my Brother and dearest friend. Yes, I will see you again, and yes, I will keep the food coming."

Roland walked with the convoy though the alleys of Jerusalem, moving north toward the Damascus Gate, sadly looking at his friends for what may be the last time. As Roland stopped and watched the riders clear the gate, Walter turned and raised his cross shield, saying, "In God's name, be glorious, and continue your journey."

Chapter Ten

"Be ye not unequally yoked together with unbelievers."
2 Corinthians 6:14

The routine at the Templar headquarters was much different from that of Roland's past year. He would rise early from his cell-like room below headquarters, but not as early as he had with Mesnil. He would then go to the stables and feed and care for Sirocco, and check his equipment.

As with all things Templar, there was a routine for prayer times and work calls. Where the routine was very different and unlike that of the past year was the absence of hard training, as well as few challenges and no adventure. Now, Roland was mostly glued to a clerk's table, keeping books and ledgers for the seneschal.

He was so bored one day that he carved his name and the date under his chair: *Roland from Champagne, 1186.* "Well, at least my dagger got a workout," he mumbled. Roland would sometimes escape from his table to the training fields and find four or five good Templars to train with; these were seasoned Templars who had survived many engagements.

All the knights came to respect the boy's skill with sword, battle-axe, and shield. Rumor had it that Roland had been trained by Martin of Brittany and that Martin had schooled Roland and Aaron to be relentless. The sergeant from Brittany removed the word "chivalry" from their vocabulary when it came to combat with a sworn foe.

Champagne would continually work his challenger hard in the training ring, in the same manner that he did in actual combat, never holding back anything. Sometimes his training partners grew angry and had to beg for quarter several times before Roland stopped his hammer blows.

Roland was trained to do what it would take to kill his adversary fast and without mercy. He worked on his shortcomings, such as using the dagger. He had formerly believed daggers to be the tools of cowards and assassins alone. In general, the nobility believed daggers, crossbows, and longbows to be the instruments of soldiers-at-arms, certainly not of knights, but watching Aaron save his own life on many occasions using the daggers that Aaron called his best friends or the twins, had only proved the point, so to speak, that these were killing tools. Now Roland kept a sharp icepick dagger in each boot and was getting nearly as good with them as Aaron was with the twins.

Many times when his training adversary believed that he had disarmed Roland, the knight would find a dagger at his throat and would quickly call, "Yield," "Mercy," or perhaps "Quarter," sometimes all three.

Even when it appeared to others that Roland was not perfect, he really was perfect. One such training session was observed by the grand master on the field. On this particular day, the lad from Champagne was fighting two of the best Templar knights in Jerusalem at the same time in the combat ring. Roland took out one knight but fell to the ground while the second knight still stood over him. "I have you, squire, and no dagger at my throat today. What say, do you call quarter?"

With a smile, Roland remarked, "Well, sir, besides your throat, what other part of your body can't you do without? Look down, sir, and call for mercy."

Within a second, the knight had looked down to his manhood to see a bright dagger within a half inch of his most prized possession. The combatant dropped his sword and screamed, "I yield, Roland." He repeated his plea in earnest when he noted that the dagger was edging closer. "Mercy, squire! For God's sake, quarter."

Ridefort had watched as his best warriors had been bested in perhaps two minutes by this boy. The grand master smiled then turned a stern face toward Albert, snidely saying, "It is good that he is on our side. I almost feel bad for Saladin's soldiers who face this squire in combat. If his mother and the Church allow him to stay, and if we do go into combat, Roland is to be by my side, Brother Albert."

Sometimes Roland would saddle Sirocco and join a few others to venture to the hill country surrounding Jerusalem. They would practice with lances and would poke at olive tree limbs or pods much as they did with the jostling rings.

Roland would often longbow target practice for a few hours to maintain his capability with his best offensive tool. He even perfected hitting mounted armored Templars with blunted arrows, remembering how poorly he had done in hitting moving targets in his recent clash on the road from Joppa.

Roland also sharpened his political skills as he watched and listened to visitors discuss what was happening outside the headquarters, in Jerusalem and the other baronies. He soon found out that political events in Jerusalem were at a fever pitch.

The grand master often had Roland provide refreshment to dignitaries. During these times, the learned squire would listen to the rumors, debates, and lengthy discussions and would gather insight as to what was happening. Champagne deduced from all the conversation that once the sickly King Baldwin died, all hell would break loose in the Outremer. Either civil war or Islamic invasion was on the horizon. Roland's only question was *What will happen first, civil war or Saladin's invasion?*

With all these pressures, long days of paperwork, and trying to maintain his combat prowess, Roland had gaps of attention and focus occasionally, and he let his mind float some rather bold thoughts about how life with Marie might be in France one day soon.

On one particular spring day, he thought that it was a close match to that fateful spring day in 1186 when Walter first "got his attention" in his palace home in Troyes and sent him on his Templar faith journey.

"Squire Roland, stop daydreaming and bring me the Pilgrim Travel ledgers. Don't dally, boy; I want them now," yelled Albert.

Roland gathered his books, retorting respectfully, "Coming, Brother Seneschal, I am coming," but he thought *I would like to get that little man in the field for a few days alone.*

The weasel-like Albert examined the ledgers, then said, "Very good, Roland; your sums are indeed correct. Perhaps we will make a good clerk of you yet."

Roland grimaced. *Perhaps you weasel-I will make a dead man out of you yet.*

Albert was looking at bits of parchment and continued, "Sadly, these three pilgrims were murdered. You must write a letter to the next of kin explaining and add the usual bit about how they loved Jesus, or they were wonderful pilgrims for the Lord, that sort of thing. Make them more fanciful with the more funding they have in their account."

Albert passed Roland the pieces of parchment and instructed, "Next to the name of the dead pilgrim is the amount of money they owe the Order. Deduct that amount they owe and inform the Paris bank to pay the next of kin the balance."

The tall squire looked puzzled. "Brother, perhaps you have the receipts the pilgrims signed so I can post the sum owed to the families?"

The seneschal's whole body went rigid. Not a muscle moved. Then his eyes narrowed as his head stretched back slightly and he gazed down the length of his long, thin nose at Roland. "Did you just challenge me, boy? Are you that ill-mannered or perhaps just stupid? How dare you challenge my authority? I said to mark the book with the numbers I gave you. You, squire, will mark what I tell you to mark. Now get back to your table—*now*," he added menacingly.

The grim-faced Champagne picked up the ledger and acknowledged Albert. "Yes, sir. I will make the postings."

Roland noted that the other five clerks just smiled and attended to their own books. *So that is how he is making money. He is doing the same evil thing with the other accounts. Yes, let me watch you much closer, you weasel. This information may come in handy one day.*

Roland took after his parents, who were proficient with money, accounting, and business in general. His mother was exceptional at rooting out dishonest tax collectors, and it appeared that her son had paid close attention to her. *Just today, our dear Albert seized about ten gold bezants from my ledgers, and perhaps he did the same with the other lads. He could be stealing fifty gold bezants or more each day. So how is he getting the coins from the safe room to where they are stored for his use? Perhaps he has a contact in the city? Could the grand master be in on this evildoing as well? I must be cautious and show patience.*

Roland began watching the comings and goings of Albert more intently. He needed to follow the seneschal and see whom he interacted with.

Roland's opportunity came quickly. Just days after the incident in the counting room, Roland was working in the stables, brushing Sirocco after combat training. He was in the shadows of the stall, when he noticed the seneschal passing the stables with a cloak in his hand, carrying a small bag.

Roland thought, *The weasel did not notice me. Why is his usual Templar knight attendant not with him?* It appeared to Roland that the seneschal was making his way, rather clandestinely, into the streets of Jerusalem using a seldom-used rear door.

Roland thought about following him. *Jacob would be really proud of me; one minute a squire and the next a spy. Let's find out where Brother Albert is going.*

The lad grabbed some worn toweling he was using on Sirocco and draped the rags over his own head and shoulders to conceal his Templar tunic and his blond hair. He then tucked one of his daggers into his belt to access it easily. Roland was pleased with his new Bedouin look. He then found an empty basket to make it appear that he was shopping in the bazaar, and into the streets he dashed after Albert, muttering what Walter would tell him, "Time to get out of the boat and walk upon the waters, Roland. Trust in the Lord and no other."

Roland watched Brother Albert cover his white Templar tunic with a plain cloak and hood that he had been carrying. As both men walked among the crowded alleys of the Holy City, Roland thought, *Why would the esteemed seneschal be without his usual bodyguard and traveling incognito? The little man is working evil.*

Fontainebleau occasionally turned his head, checking to see if he was being followed, as he weaved through the dark streets of the Armenian Quarter. Roland feared that perhaps Albert would notice the slouching grubby farmer with a basket on his shoulder, so he was careful not to get too close. *Where is he going?*

Albert moved into the marketplace then paused before the old Syrian monastery. He went right toward the citadel, then veered left to the Mt. Zion Gate. Finally, he walked toward the Church of St. James and disappeared into a side door.

The squire looked up to see a magnificent cross on the church roof. *"So the thief works his sin under the cross of Jesus."* Roland saw a wandering band of pilgrims approach the church. He needed cover if he was to enter the church without Albert noticing him. He called to a crowd of pilgrims, "In here, dear friends, you will receive over 500 days of indulgence from Saint James for your visit."

Roland opened the door, and the band of pilgrims entered the church. In their midst he stooped to match the crowd's height.

Roland moved from the center of the pilgrim circle just in time to see Albert enter a confessional box. The boy moved from the crowd. He stood in the shadows of a church pillar, under an icon of Saint James the Greater. Less than a minute later, the seneschal exited the confessional. He departed immediately through a side door and went into the crowded street.

Roland smiled. *Ah, Brother Albert, you're just so pure that you had no sins to confess, no prayer to say in penance? So, who is this priest that hears your confession and is so kind not to reward you with a few prayers for your thieving ways? Wait, what happened to the bag you were carrying?*

Roland looked to the picture of Saint James, who he was now eye-to-eye with in the dim light and prayed, *Dear Apostle James, as you did say, 'A double-minded man is unstable in all ways.' I believe one such man just walked out your door but still another remains in your church. Expose him to me.*

The squire was rewarded for his prayer to Saint James when a man exited the booth, hastening to place a small bag in his boot. The man quickly made his way into the streets. Roland noted the man's swarthy features for a brief time. Roland also noticed something else. *You wear no cross upon your breast. Certainly you are no priest. You are too dark-skinned to be a Frank; perchance you are an Arab or a Turk.*

Roland began his chase anew, shadowing this new player. *This man is not as crafty as Albert and displays no concern that he may be followed. That is strange if he is a messenger or money courier. He appears to be walking toward David's Gate.*

Two guards who held shields bearing the coat of arms of the Kingdom of Jerusalem appeared from a concealed alleyway, also making their way toward the man. As they closed in behind the swarthy man with a rush, they suddenly pushed him up against the wall. "Make one move for a weapon and I will run this blade through your liver, you bastard of an Arab," screamed the city guard hatefully.

The other guard followed up his comrade, speaking with a Castilian dialect. "Why do you move so fast, Arab? Perhaps you were stealing something from the church? What is the likes of you doing in a Latin church, and not an Orthodox one or a mosque? Speak, or I will run this blade into your infidel heart."

The swarthy man clearly did not understand what the soldiers were saying. He replied in broken Frankish, "I Christian. Syria," then pointed to himself. "Me. No Arab. Christian."

The second guard remarked, "Syrian Christian, yes. All you desert thieves say that when we are about to cut your throat. Tomas, see what he stole from the church."

The guard then pressed his sword to the man's throat. "Move, Arab, and you join Allah."

Tomas started to search the man for booty as Roland removed his hasty disguise and moved toward the crowd that was gathering to watch as the guards nearly stripped the man. *Surely they will find the bag of gold coins and take the proof I need that Albert was stealing from the Order and the pilgrims. I need to talk to that man.*

But the guards failed to search the man's boots, though they did find a small map of Jerusalem under the man's cloak. Roland watched intently as the guards shifted their discussion from stealing a few coins to something more sinister. The Castilian guard waved the map in his hand, saying, "You are a spy. I will kill you where you stand, Arab."

Roland was instantly taken aback. *A spy? My God, Albert is a spy working for Saladin and also a thief. This is too much to believe. Quick, Roland, don't let them kill this man without getting him to someone of higher authority to confirm that Albert is his contact. Think quickly.*

Roland approached the guards and spoke in Castilian. "Good day, sirs. Perhaps we need to bring him to the lord sheriff for questioning?" He could smell the wine and see that these two fools were nearly drunk.

"Move on, Templar. This is not a matter for your concern. Besides, if we brought every Arab to the Lord Sheriff, he would make us spend our entire day torturing them. That is too much like work. No, we shall kill him and collect the silver piece as a reward."

Roland thought quickly and smiled as he searched his own boot. He removed a gold coin and displayed it to the guards. "I have something here much better than a silver piece. This new gold bezant is worth ten silver coins. I will give you this gold coin if you let me kill the swine. I then can write to my family to say that I killed my first Muslim. They would like that."

The guard looked astonished. "You will pay us a gold coin to gut this pig? Here, boy, is my dagger. Now start low, near his bowels, and rip towards his heart. That way, his stomach will fall out into his hands. Step to the left side so you will get less blood, and less guts, on your nice pretty Templar garb. Got it? Oh yeah, first the gold coin, if you please?"

Roland slipped the coin into the guard's hand.

With a sword to his throat and a tall young man holding a dagger to his front near his gut, the captured man knew that death was close at hand. In a low tone that only Roland could hear, the man whispered in near perfect Frankish, "God praise your name. Please be merciful and cut my heart first."

Roland gripped the dagger and ordered, "I will grasp his throat and gut him; lower your sword."

The guard lowered his sword and warned his compatriot, "Stand back, Tomas. When he guts him, the blood will flow like a newly tapped keg of ale. The sergeant of the guard will be pissed if we show up with blood and guts all over us."

The squire held onto the man tightly then suddenly lunged at him with the dagger. Roland clearly and purposefully missed and pushed the captive to the right, thereby sending the spy running for his life down the darkened alley.

The guards were amazed. Tomas screamed, "You damn ass Templar, you missed the bastard."

"Sorry about that. Perhaps a few more coins will help to ease your pain." Roland quickly dropped a handful of coins on the ground, and the crowd rapidly mobbed the area around the guards' feet, blocking them from any further immediate pursuit.

The young Templar ran down the alley, calling back to the guards, "Don't worry, I will soon have him back."

The escaping man first raced toward the grain market. Then he made a quick left down a small alley. He occasionally turned his head toward Roland, only to see the boy getting closer.

Roland was much quicker than the dark man and could see that the man in front was failing fast. The lad's long legs and athletic ability soon had him within ten feet of running down his man. The boy thought, *Very soon now, my friend, you will tell me what I want to know, or I really will gut you.*

Then the man disappeared into an alley that had laundry hanging in the evening breeze to dry. Roland gripped the dagger tightly. He slowly moved the linen aside to search for his prey... and found only a city wall.

Roland was about to turn around when he caught the slight side-line vision of a man armed with a crossbow aimed directly at him.

"Stop, Christian, where you stand. You have seen enough of my friend Yusuf to know he has a crossbow aimed at you. You have saved my life and I owe you much. Why you did that noble service I know not. However, we have no time to discuss this now. Your friends may be nearing us, and I must take your leave. Please do not follow us. While I owe you my life, Yusuf does not owe you his."

Roland heard the city guard getting closer in pursuit. The man called Yusuf whispered in Arabic, "We must go. Now."

The unknown spy continued, "Templar, if you are outside of these walls and need a friend ask for Ibn al-Athir. I strongly caution you not to mention my name to any other Christians, as you will face the rack for not killing me when you had the chance. You and I are both yoked together by your act of kindness, and I return your charity by not killing you now. Thank you for your service and mercy. Now we both go in Allah's name, and peace be upon you."

Roland heard a door opening, then footsteps. He slowly turned around, only to see linen being removed by an old woman—that was all. He cautiously opened the door the woman had come out from, only to see a short hallway leading to a door. He walked to the door to open it, but it was locked.

He retraced his footsteps to the alley and saw the two guardsmen searching for him and the Arab. He hid within the doorway until the guards passed.

He took a cloth from the laundry line and wrapped it about his head and shoulders in the Arab fashion then he slipped into the market place undetected.

The lad from Champagne made his way back to the Templar headquarters. He was just in time for Vesper prayers, which were being led by none other than Brother Albert.

Roland smiled as he took his place in the long line of Templars making their way into the chapel. *So now, Brother Albert, where do we go from here? I know two of your secrets—you are a thief and a traitor—but I still don't know where the money is going or who this Ibn al-Athir is. I uncovered one Templar secret, only to discover two new secrets.*

Chapter Eleven

"Now when Jesus heard that John had been arrested, he
withdrew into Galilee; and leaving Nazareth he went
and dwelt in Capernaum by the sea, in the territory of
Zebulon and Naphtali, that what was spoken by the
prophet Isaiah might be fulfilled."

Matthew 4:15—16

Many miles to the northeast of Jerusalem, Count Raymond
of Tripoli was looking to his future that spring day. At this
moment, his life was in turmoil and in a constant state of flux. He
looked out from his castle at Tiberius over the Sea of Galilee.

He could not help but think that he and his wife were the pro-
tectors of many of the locations in the life of Jesus. He looked to the
still water of Galilee and noted the fishing boats. These boats were
akin to the very one that Jesus had spoke from to the multitudes on
the shores of Galilee. The crafts taking their nets with loaded fish
today had not changed much in design and function since Peter, along
with his brother Andrew and the brothers John and James, had cast
their nets into this same sea.

The view from his walled fortress also rested just miles north of
the head waters of the River Jordan. He walked along the rampart,
now looking north, toward Capernaum, where Jesus had spoken to
the multitudes and fed 5,000 followers bread and fish.

Not far from Raymond's perch above the Sea of Galilee, Jesus
had also cured the sick and spoken of a new way to gain the rewards
of heaven. "Will I gain those rewards for my work here on earth?"
wondered Raymond.

Within Raymond's domain of Galilee were Nazareth, Cana, Capernaum, Mount Tabor, Tabgha, Magdala, and many other holy places. His
inner voice reminded him, *It will take one of Jesus' miracles for us to
retain this place.* Raymond's eyes looked toward the Golan just eight
miles away from his castle. *Damascus is just a three-day march from the*

Jordan. Any time Saladin wants us, he can come get us as he did at Jacob's Crossing.

Raymond clearly understood that the election of Ridefort shifted the center of influence from his side of the political landscape to that of his increasing enemies. Raymond recalled just months before, Grand Master Roger Moulin, of the Hospitallers, making it clear: "Tripoli, if you continue this truce agreement with Saladin, I care not one penny for your life."

Raymond's thoughts continued as he looked west toward Nazareth. *We can live in peace with Islam. But someone must act boldly to show that peaceful coexistence with the Muslim world is possible. This warring can't continue.*

Raymond's family was descended from the old Toulouse Saint Giles clan. His grandfather had been one of the principal leaders of the First Crusade and had founded this land for the Christians. His Toulouse family, although powerful, were not true Franks; they were more inclined to be vassals of the king of Aragon rather than to the king of France. They were always more liberal than the Franks.

Raymond was a learned man. He read books and studied several languages, including Greek and Arabic, yet he was a warrior as well. He and his family had been fighting the Muslims in the Outremer for over eighty-five years. Raymond of Tripoli knew that it could not continue this way.

Life was not easy for Raymond. He still recalled the day when his father had ridden into Jerusalem to be crowned king of Jerusalem, only to be stabbed to death when a fanatic follower of Hassan ibn Sabbah, the leader of the Hassassin sect of Islam, had leapt from the walls and upon his father, killing him.

As with all atrocities, especially personal ones, rethinking the assassination was horrendous all these years later. *I was only twelve years old when I took over the lands of Tripoli in my father's stead. I know how to lead our people, unlike fools like Guy Lusignan, who come here for one year and believe they know the land and its people.*

Raymond, a warrior, had many scars to prove it. He too had had bad days. Truth was, he had had many years of evil times. From the deep recesses of his mind, he brought out the horror of August 12, 1164. *It was so hot that I burned my hand when I touched my shield with my bare hand. We believed the warring task ahead to be easy, yet all hell was around us when Ad-din-Zengi ambushed us at Harim.*

Raymond's emotional pain continued as he recalled, *The Christian army was defeated, and ten Arab warriors closed in on me and offered me quarter or death. I should have chosen death, yet I chose imprisonment in Aleppo, waiting for my family to gather 80,000 gold bezants for my ransom.* Raymond could recall nearly every day of the nine years he had spent in anticipation of his release.

I chose enlightenment over ignorance. I chose talking to an Arab scholar and learning his language rather than silent isolation. I chose reading the Quran over wandering ignorantly in my cell. Yes, I did learn Arabic in order to read the books of art, science, and poetry, and the Quran. And I am a better man for it.

The count turned to the window once again, watching the fishing boats upon the Sea of Galilee with fascination. *When others around me were dying after a few months in prison, I, Raymond, survived; the essence of me survived. Each day, I found some way to keep my sanity, along with my physical health. Each day of the nine years, I exercised both my body and mind. While other men went out of their minds in prison, I learned to use my mind and better understand our adversary.* Yes, Raymond knew how to survive in such political climates and under severe hardship!

He smiled as he recalled that just yesterday, he had been walking by the port of Tiberius. *Few noticed me except that three guards were trailing me with swords drawn."* He loved that he was one of the people!

Raymond looked Arab because he dressed in Arab garb and because the skin of his forebears from southern France, the region of Languedoc, was darker. But it was his Arabic ways that concerned his Christian brethren. Raymond was content with peaceful coexistence rather than with fighting the Arabs, unlike Guy and the others. He was by far the most visionary of all the Christians who lived in the region. He understood that the sheer Arabic, Turk, and Egyptian population numbers were against the Christians.

After talking in their own tongues to many of his subjects in port on the previous day, Raymond had ridden back to the castle near the port.

Raymond now retired to his inner sanctum. He smiled. Immediately upon entering his chapel, he felt a rush of warmth and an inner peace. This was where he was the most happy. His chapel was bright and airy, without the usual icons or symbols of Christianity. It was totally unlike his wife's chapel, the expected dimly lit Christian place of worship. Raymond's chapel looked more like an Islamic mosque than a Catholic house of worship.

Even his wife, Princess Eschiva, chided him for maintaining such a place. "Husband, you have no icons, as in the orthodox style, nor do you have marble statues or pictures of our Lord and the saints as in the Latin style. Raymond, you have just a simple cross on an altar and a small wooden box to house the Host. You call this place a chapel? No, my husband, this is a monk's cave in the wilderness. What will the royalty say? Think about what the priest and bishops say after they come here to celebrate the mass. They see a few chairs and you sitting on a perch of cushions like a Bedouin." She was referring to the way that he sat upon his beloved cushions, Arabic style, during his daily spiritual meditation.

He sat now on his cushions. For some reason, fleeting thoughts of Baldwin kept nudging his mind. Just a few months ago, Raymond had given personal guardianship of Baldwin over to the boy's grandfather, Joscelin. He had hoped to ward off any questions or deflect doubt that the barons may have that Raymond was somehow involved in the boy's sickness or death. The child-king and his guardian were in Acre, fifty-five miles west of Raymond's fortress.

He repeated the facts of the situation to himself: *The boy king grows weaker each day and perhaps will not live out the year. As regent, you must take over the leadership of the kingdom soon and seek out a co-king while the boy lives, as did his uncle when he knew he was dying.*

Raymond recalled the particular day just years before when King Baldwin IV himself, and all the barons and princes of the kingdom had agreed that, should the boy die during his minority the regency would pass to "the most rightful heirs." Of course, who knew that those adjudicating the rightful heirs would require the approval of the king of England, the king of France, the Holy Roman Emperor Frederick I, and the pope?

Raymond shook his head in disbelief. "*None at the table that day ever believed that Princesses Sibylla and Isabella would be contenders for the throne, yet today, it is probable, since many of the "most rightful heirs" are either dead or not living in this country to pick up the crown.*

Even Raymond's normal inner calm splintered with turmoil and uncertainty. *I should be king. Had the assassin killed my father after the coronation, rather than a few minutes before, the line of succession would have fallen to me. Who better understands the many peoples of the kingdom? Who but me can lead the Franks to peace? Yes, I understand Islam, Judaism, and the Latin and Orthodox Christian ways of the life better than all others here in the Outremer, yet they will not follow me.*

The count again tried to clear his mind. He had pressing business today. He was being briefed by a Kurdish spy who served as his secret diplomat to the court of Saladin at Damascus. This cover of a Kurdish spy was important, because if Jerusalem discovered that Raymond was communicating with Saladin officially, they would think him a traitor, but the court at Jerusalem always enjoyed another spy's input.

The count left the chapel and retired to his throne room to await Ali.

On time as always, Ali made his way into the throne room though a rear door. In a measured, almost melodious voice, he spoke in a formal style. "My Lord al-Sanjli, greetings. I bring news and salutations from Sultan Saladin. Lord Saladin is seeking continued peace with you. He sees you as the only hope the Franks have in maintaining peace and order here. He supports you; however, he wants to be assured that the Christians are not building an army in Galilee as a means of attacking Damascus. Thus, he seeks your permission to continue reconnaissance operations within the region. While no harm will ever come to your people, the sultan does insist on an exception to that: the blood of Reynald of Transjordan. Lord Saladin will strike him when he can."

Raymond nodded acquiescence. He knew that Reynald was a dangerous man. Ali continued, "The fool continues to raid Arab caravans, even when they had safe conduct through the lands of the Franks. His raiding is one thing, but Reynald insisted on murder and a complete disrespect of anything Arab or Muslim."

As he addressed the spy, Raymond knew that Saladin had a special place for Reynald. "Reynald is crazy from the fifteen years he spent in Saladin's prison. His own family never came up with the ransom. That's a pretty strong indication of how Reynald is respected among his own! Reynald practices revenge each day for the fifteen years your countrymen kept him captive. They drove him crazy yet failed to kill him. Why Saladin's son released the fool from prison is beyond reason. Now our Reynald, or Brins Arnat, as your people have named him, is a madman, and he plagues both Christians and Muslims alike, yet the priests here think him a messenger of Jesus."

Raymond drank some wine and then continued, "That fool Reynald has even raided pilgrims on the Red Sea going to Mecca. The most horrible was his attempted raid on Medina, and his plans to violate the tomb of the Prophet Muhammad in the Mosque of the Prophet to steal the Messenger's bones. Were it not for a barking dog, he and his Templar friends would have accomplished the deed. He is crazy with hate, Ali. He has made this into a blood lust that Saladin can't ignore much longer."

Raymond continued, "The entire Islamic world is calling for Jihad against us due to that fool Reynald's attempt to steal the Messenger's remains. Never mind his continued raids under a truce. When the sounds are loudest from the street, Saladin will hear them, rise up, and strike. Ali, go to Saladin and tell him I want peace between us. Yes, his troops may perform inspections of the borderlands between our two countries. But Ali, tell Saladin that his soldiers must not encamp in my domain and they must be in and out of Galilee in one day."

The count lowered his voice even though he was in his own home as he continued, "The tide is rising against me, and I fear my own people more than Saladin. Now go to Damascus and ensure that we have peace between us."

Raymond had concerns for his family and the stepchildren from Eschiva's previous marriage. "Ali, please thank Lord Saladin for the safe conduct and escort for my wife's cousins, Lady Marie of Baux and Lady Yvette of Baux. They visit Antioch and the home of Lady Marie's parents." Lady Marie and Lady Yvette had departed just two weeks prior for a visit to Marie's homestead.

Ali had just barely cleared the room when a messenger from Acre made his way into the throne room.

The messenger bowed deeply and spoke to Raymond. "Your Excellency, I bear sad news from Acre, from lord William of Montferrat and Lord Joscelin, grand uncle to the king. I regret to inform you that King Baldwin is on his deathbed. Lord William and Lord Joscelin beg you to come to Acre to attend to matters of state."

Raymond had played out this scenario many times in his head before, but here was the day. He offered, "Yes, refresh yourself, and I will provide you with fresh mounts. We shall attend to the king's business."

The count of Tripoli looked out the window at the Sea of Galilee and could see storm clouds gathering. He said aloud, "Now it begins."

Chapter Twelve

"Professing themselves to be wise, they became fools, and incorruptible God into an image made like a corruptible man."

Romans 1:22—23

The count of Joppa and Ascalon, Guy of Lusignan, was seemingly mesmerized by the Mediterranean Sea, off the Palestinian coast, this very hot day.

In a reflective mood, Guy thought, *In many ways, I am much like the waves in the ocean, with many peaks and an equal number of extreme valleys in my life. Today, the afternoon tide brings in fresh Templars and many other knights. We may soon have ample men to strike out at Saladin and defeat him, but Jerusalem needs a strong king to achieve victory. My stepson, the king, is sickly and near death. This is a good omen that I soon will be king!*

His eight-year-old stepson was now the king of Jerusalem, after his uncle, King Baldwin, had died the year before. Guy believed his death had been a stroke of luck.

Guy looked to the ocean once again. *Baldwin, saint that you were, your rotting manhood left the throne childless. Montferrat, most likely in hell, your corrupt loins did not do much better, producing such a sick child. Now it is my turn.*

King Baldwin V, as the young child was crowned, was the son of his wife's late husband, William of Montferrat. Guy recalled that William, who had died in 1177, was the eldest son of one of the greatest magnates in northern Italy. *God knows the family had many royal and imperial connections.*

Guy was envious because William was also known for his military prowess and his exceptional good looks. Guy's archenemy, Raymond of Tripoli, had once said aloud to a gathering, right in Guy's presence, "We arranged the marriage of our country princess to William the Younger, of Montferrat, who was handsome, brave, wealthy, and the most unpretentious man who ever walked into this kingdom. Now she lofts with a man from a family of cattle thieves."

"Yes, Raymond, perhaps we were cattle thieves, but we did have the sense to view the rosebud up close before we picked it." Lusignan knew that the life that William had led, bedding most noblewomen in Italy, and his drinking, had most likely resulted in him having the pox. The count mused, "That is why he did not marry until he was well into his thirties. That is why the child has been ill his entire life. You had the curse upon your loins, William."

William had been among the most eligible bachelors in Europe. When the young Lord William had failed to find a wife, his father had tried, but even then, several misfires had happened along the way to the wedding chamber. His father had tried to arrange marriage for him to one of King Henry II of England's daughters, but that had failed because of consanguinity; the boy's mother, Judith, was related to Henry's wife, Eleanor of Aquitaine. In some frustration, the elder Montferrat had set his eyes on a smaller kingdom, Jerusalem.

Guy laughed aloud and with warped pleasure thought, *Yes, here I am bedding William's wife, living in his house, and now the owner of his titles: the count of Joppa and Ascalon. I must remember to thank to you, Raymond, the next time for such hard work in arranging the marriage. I also owe you, leper king, a thank-you for allowing your sister to marry William.*

This chain of events had placed Guy and his wife, Sibylla, in an excellent position within the kingdom. The count continued pondering, *The barons did not trust me or the boy's mother to be the king's guardian. They appointed that Arab-loving bastard Raymond as the regent and the boy's great-uncle Joscelin as the boy's guardian. How rich. While I fought this arrangement, now the results are pleasing to me. Now I will not be blamed when the child dies, and die he will.*

Guy paced the room. *The moon is aligning with my fortune.* He thought about his friend and ally, Gerald. *Gerald de Ridefort has been elected as the grand master of the Temple. This plays well too, since Ridefort is the leader of the most powerful army in the Outremer, the Templars.*

The count smiled. *"Yes, perhaps now I can spring up from this self-imposed low-key life—one of many valleys—and finally rise up to my highest peak!*

Lusignan ran various plans through his mind. *This will work out in the end. I will be the king of Jerusalem. The boy is sickly and will die in a short time. Perhaps I finally have the means to gain additional power at the expense of the Muslim-loving Raymond of Tripoli.*

Guy recalled, *Just a few years ago, my marriage to Sibylla prevented the great Count Raymond of Tripoli from taking over the kingdom. Now it is I who will have this kingdom. How rich the reward.*

He still smiled every time he thought about that fast path to the altar. He had been called to the Outremer by his older brother, who at the time had been bedding the princess's mother, Agnes. Just a few months after meeting Sibylla, he had married to her. The Eastertide wedding had foiled Raymond's plans to force Sibylla to marry his vassal Baldwin of Ibelin.

As these memories passed through Guy's mind, he thought, "*Yes, Raymond! That expression upon your face when you entered the hall to see us married was memorable! It will live in my mind forever! It was so rich to see your expression—knowing your route to the throne was destroyed. Perhaps your good friend Saladin could help you as he has done in the past. That truce you have signed with your dear friend the murderous Saladin may just be your own death warrant. Yes, Gerald Ridefort was correct to let you have all the rope needed to hang yourself. You, Raymond of Tripoli, are so close to the end of the rope—so very close.*

Guy's marriage to Sibylla five years ago had paid him major dividends, which he considered as he walked toward the courtyard. *I am not a bright man, but at least I made one good decision in allowing my brother to arrange my marriage to Sibylla.*

The count was rather pleased with himself on this beautiful day. He looked out to Jerusalem Road to see a band of Templars escorting many pilgrims eastward to the Holy City. As he continued his walk into the courtyard, he thought, *How life can quickly change for the good and the bad. Bad is when the gallows are just a few feet away, as they were seventeen years ago. I was so foolish! To think how close I came to be hung by Richard the Lionheart.*

Guy recalled how Richard had been the acting duke of Aquitaine and Guy's overlord. The Lusignan clan had made a tragic mistake and had mistaken a returning pilgrim with a fat purse from the Holy Lands for easy prey.

Guy had acted unwisely and broken church rules by attacking a pilgrim. He had also violated Henry's royal orders that anyone who did attack a pilgrim be hanged.

The count remembered the day well. *The fool earl of Salisbury was dressed as a pilgrim and traveled without an escort or retainers. Salisbury was not easy prey, and he put up a good fight with just a pilgrim's staff. He nearly took my brother's head off with his staff. I remember well plunging my sword into the man's back.*

Guy shook his head. *How were the brothers Lusignan to know that this Englishman was not just any Englishman? No, we murdered none other than the earl of Salisbury, the friend of Henry II, King of England and Richard's father. It was lucky for us that our family was held in some regard by Richard and he was fighting his father at the time of our death decree.* Chills ran from Guy's neck down his spine at just thinking of how close he had been to "dancing the rope."

Guy recalled his luck. *Richard tried our entire lot, and rather than hang us, he banished us.*

Lusignan could still remembered being hired out as a common mercenary wandering in France. *Cold, hungry, and poor most of the time. Amalric, bless you, brother, for calling me to Jerusalem as a marriage candidate for the recently widowed Princess Sibylla.*

Guy smiled. *To think that I owe this chain of events to my whoring brother with his pillow-talk suggestion to the Queen Mother is beyond belief.*

This rather strange event had been staged by Amalric, who had made his way to the very door of the bedchamber of Queen Agnes, mother of the leper King Baldwin IV.

Guy was actually smiling to once again think how the Lord looked upon him. *Yes, Lord, you have picked wisely in your next king in Jerusalem. You will see what a healthy king can do with these infidel Muslims. With this marriage, I became count of Joppa and Ascalon, and bailie of Jerusalem. Now that I have planted two daughters within Sibylla, it is rather difficult for her to have the marriage annulled, as her brother wanted. I need to get working on a boy. One worthy of following in my footsteps in leading this kingdom.*

Although life was good for Guy, he knew that much more work was needed to foil Raymond of Tripoli to make life even better. He looked out from the garden and noticed how busy the road to Jerusalem was with parties of Templar knights.

He smiled. *Just months ago, Templars came into the port, thinking that they would elect Templar Commander Erail.* He smiled to think just how far they had come for nothing. *Too late, gentlemen; you arrived too late. Our dear Gerald had stolen the election from Erail. Yes, Gerald and I get stronger each day, and Raymond's days are numbered in months, maybe weeks.*

A servant came along with some fruit juices, as was the daily ritual for the count about this time each day. Guy stopped and examined both drinks. "Ah, let's see, what shall I have today?"

The servant announced, "The orange juice is particularly sweet, my lord."

Lusignan looked at the cups more closely, "Yes, it does have a nice color."

When the blond Count of Joppa reached for the orange juice, the servant quickly pointed to the second cup. "The lemon juice with a touch of honey is also very refreshing, Your Excellency. It is said that lemons and honey increase one's desire in bed."

Now Guy reached for the lemon drink and looked to the servant, who said, "Yes, my lord, that is a wise choice." Guy smiled and took the glass.

The servant walked to the kitchen, thinking how he had once again talked the count into taking the fruit juice that he wanted the count to take. *He is so dimwitted, he falls for the same ruse every time. Whatever is the last thing said, the count will then do.* The servant drank the cool, sweet orange juice and smiled.

Guy did not really like lemon drink, so he drank only a small amount. *Too bitter. How can anyone drink that potion, even if it does increase your bedding desires?* He continued to walk in the gardens and was still walking when Princess Sibylla approached with his two daughters. The youngest was just months old and in the arms of a lady-in-waiting. Sibylla instructed the young maiden, "Lady Suzanne, please take the children. I need to talk to the count."

The lady-in-waiting bowed and took the children to the outer gardens. Sibylla said to her husband, "Guy, what wonderful news we have! Ridefort has informed me that he has a new addition to his headquarters staff, none other than one of the count of Champagne's sons, Roland. We understand that he is Richard's favorite and is well liked by his uncle King Philip. This surely will tie us better to the homeland. With Ridefort and Roger Moulin of the Hospitallers, we now have two friends in power. Things in this kingdom will change, and Raymond is surely doomed."

As usual, Guy agreed with a simple yes, nodding his head in agreement. Sibylla continued, "The monks were outraged by Raymond's appointment as regent, and many believe he has secretly converted to Islam. They really hate Raymond's relationship with the Muslims and his damnable truce with Saladin."

Guy heard only the part concerning the truce. "Yes, the truce was Raymond's sign of weakness. We must not be weak."

The fact was that Raymond and Saladin had only agreed to the truce because a three-year drought had made the entire Outremer nearly devoid of water and food. The entire area had not been able to support military elements of more than 2000 men, much less an army in the tens of thousands, until now.

Like the servant, the princess also knew that Guy often focused on only the last words spoken. "Yes, husband, it is a damnable truce with the sworn enemy of our Lord Jesus. Just last week, Reynald of Chatillion was crying out for Raymond's head under the axe."

Guy looked at her. "Yes, Raymond is a traitor, and his head should roll."

Princess Sibylla reminded her husband, "My dear brother would never have allowed Raymond to fraternize with Saladin. Why in God's name my brother Baldwin ever appointed Raymond as regent, rather than you, is beyond reason. If you were regent, you would order Raymond's death, would you not, dear husband?"

Guy looked toward the sea and answered, "I don't fear Raymond. I would have his head on a pike!"

The count fully knew the truth. Raymond was no coward. Guy remembered that he had failed in battle not too many years prior. Guy had been given the duty of bailie, only to lose it for failure on the battlefield. His brother-in-law, King Baldwin, had been so annoyed that Lusignan had failed to assist Raymond in fending off Saladin when the Muslims had attacked an outpost that belonged to Raymond that the king had tried to have Guy's marriage to Sibylla annulled.

Guy remembered that valley in his life. How, in a few months, had so many events in Jerusalem changed? The tide was changing not only off the coast but also in the very halls of the Kingdom of Jerusalem.

The count and Sibylla walked up the stairs to the rampart. "We must rid ourselves of Raymond, but how?" From this high perch within his castle, Guy could see the busy port of Joppa, where ships were off-loading pilgrims, grain, animals, and all the other resources the kingdom required each day to survive. He and his wife also noticed two riders approaching the castle at high speed.

Sibylla could see that the two men wore the livery of her uncle Joscelin. "They are messengers from my uncle. I will greet them."

The count observed the scene as his wife walked to meet the visitors. *It smells like a fish market here,* Guy thought, hiding his nose in a cinnamon-scented cloth as the unpleasant smells of drying fish wafted across the castle. *Soon, I will be moving to more opulent quarters, and the smell of fish and animals will be a thing of the past.*

Guy could see the dismounted riders approach Sibylla. One of her maidens rushed to her side. The count began walking down the stairs and toward the courtyard, mumbling as he walked. "Now what pain has come upon us? What is this news that they bring to Sibylla."

As Guy approached the gathering, Sibylla turned and cried out loudly as she fell to her knees. "Baldwin is dead. My son the king is dead."

Chapter Thirteen

"And I looked, and behold a pale horse: and his name
was Death, and Hell followed with him."
Revelation 6:8

The sun was high in the midday sky, and the slight wind only added to the misery and heat. The bare ground and rocks seemed to reflect the intense heat and helped in baking Aaron's fair skin.

This was a normal day, and each day seemed like the last at Castel La Feve in the Jazreel Valley, in the district of Galilee. Today, Aaron was with the small patrol of turcopoles, the Syrian Christian auxiliary cavalry in the pay of the Templars, led by Sergeant Martin. The patrol was searching for Saladin's crafty raiders, who had recently been reported in the area.

Aaron, walking on a sandy knoll, was going north from the fortress in the direction of Nazareth. "Well Paris, here we are again, in the middle of nowhere. Once again, we are the bait, along with the two horses we are towing. I pray that our Muslim raider friends attack quickly and just kill me so this penance can be over. Then again, Paris, if not here in the desert, I would be standing guard atop the walls of Castle the Bean and be baking there.

Aaron found humor in talking to his trusty mule. Sometimes he believed the mule to be the only intelligent being in this forsaken land. The boy was not alone as he walked the lonely path north.

Looking out over the stark desert, Aaron patted Paris. "It is no small wonder Brother Martin hears voices and sees visions of dead people. Another month of this foolishness, and I too will be talking to myself and not to you."

"I heard that Aaron," voiced Sergeant Martin of Brittany. The sergeant and five turcopole archers were below the crest of the hill, near the bottom. This position placed the patrol out of sight from any enemy coming from the northern or western approaches, and within only seconds of helping Aaron if were attacked.

"Aaron, mules are neither male nor female. Why do you call that mule Paris?"

Aaron was quick in return. "I get along much better with females than I do males."

Martin smiled and added, "Any raider will see your mouth going and know we are about."

"Right you are, Sergeant, like they would never think that the sun, lack of decent water, or the desert has made me crazy. Talking to oneself is okay, Sergeant. It is when you answer yourself that you have gone mad. I am talking to Paris, who is the only intelligent being here."

The boy rode a few more feet as he said, "I will just talk low to Paris; she expects me to talk to her. Last question, Sergeant—why am I always the bait? Perhaps you or our turcopole friends would like to come up here and get an unseen arrow in the back in my place?"

Martin too had a Celtic sense of humor and added, "The Turks like redheaded young boys much better than worn-out sergeants or desert-beaten turcopoles."

Martin added quickly before Aaron could voice disapproval, "They want the horses and will not fire arrows, taking a chance of killing an animal or such a prize as you. Now shut up and keep your eyes open."

The redhead said rather sarcastically, "Thank you, Sergeant, for making my day. The Turks will not kill me, only sodomize me and sell me into slavery. Any more ways you can brighten my day?"

The now-smiling warrior answered, "Yes, we must circle around a dry stream bed of large rocks. This will take us out several hundred feet from the knoll. We will rejoin you about a half mile north. For that period of time, we can't help you if you are attacked."

Aaron just shook his head. "Paris, this is even worse than when Roland uses me for bait. At least he covers me most of the time. Let's move along quickly, old friend. I wonder if Martin was just joking about the Turks liking young redheads."

As he rode across the knoll, Aaron could see that Martin was about 600 feet away from him. He was thinking that his present situation was bad but certainly not the worst of days at La Feve.

The three months at La Feve had been difficult for him and the other Templars. The fortress was always hot, undermanned, poorly equipped, and ill-supplied.

The indispensable turcopole auxiliaries had not been paid in three months and were now positioned to leave the place any day.

To make a bad situation worse, every day, there were reports of enemy activity abounding in Galilee. It seemed to Aaron that Templar headquarters was indifferent to their situation.

Even Aaron, a lowly squire, could see that the fortress was a key Templar stronghold. He knew that it was at the intersection of the western coastal road from the port city of Acre to Saladin's capital, Damascus, in the east and the intersecting northern Acre road to the southeastern Jerusalem road.

In addition, it was just south of Nazareth, Jesus' boyhood home and a special place for pilgrims to visit.

The politics and bad blood between Count Raymond of Tripoli and the Templars did not help the many problems. Count Raymond at times forbid any of the local farmers to sell items to the Templars, so the Templars sometimes took what they needed to survive, creating more ill will between the fort and the locals.

In spite of all this, somehow, Walter of Mesnil managed to keep the fortress actively engaged, knowing that he guarded the invasion route that Saladin most likely would use. He mounted two patrols daily to keep the enemy off-balance and managed to keep the forces of Saladin at bay. It was one such patrol that Aaron was on today.

The squire from Paris scanned left and noted seven or eight riders on a parallel course about 100 yards north.

He saw them pointing at him, a single Templar with a fine-looking mule and two healthy horses. The lad shook his head in disgust and spoke to Paris. "Of course, Paris, they would see me now with Martin and the others on the far side of that rock bed."

His quick look to see Martin making his way around the dry riverbed told him that help was at least a long four or five minutes away from his position. "They can't help us now, girl. Let's move, Paris, and quick."

The young Templar looked forward to a slight rise about 200 feet away that had large rocks facing the northern approach. "Come on, Paris, move. If we can make that rock bed, we can channel them to only one path. Just maybe we can hold out until Martin gets here."

The enemy leader, Hashem, on a pale, nearly white, Arabian, was in fact on a reconnaissance patrol deep within Christian territory for his lord, Salah-al-din-Yusuf.

This act was clearly a violation of the truce between Baldwin and Saladin but was allowed by the count of Tripoli to show that no Christian army was making preparations.

Hashem's orders were that he must act silently and move unnoticed in the lands of the count of Tripoli while gathering intelligence.

Saladin had cautioned him not be captured and that it would be better to die in combat that suffer Saladin's embarrassment with the Christian king.

Hashem well remembered. *I still can smell the rotting bodies hung on the crosses along the road to the south after the Battle of Montgisard just ten years ago. Many were my friends and family who had fought bravely, yet they too were hung to die upon the cross. Even the wounded were crucified by Emir Saladin.*

Saladin made liberal use of the cross for failure. Now sultan, Saladin had had hundreds of his own men crucified after the defeat of his 26,000-man army by a Christian army of fewer than 2,000 men because of his own bad generalship.

Unfortunately, two of Hashem's horsemen's mounts had gone lame and could not make the more-than-ninety-mile trek to Damascus. He needed those horses that the boy was traveling with to make it back home.

Hashem knew that failure was not an option, as that would result in Hashem being hung from a cross at the gates of Damascus. On the better side of the ledger, he knew that the boy may fetch a good price in the slave market.

Hashem cautioned his men, "No bows. We don't want to risk wounding the horses we need, or the boy. If the boy puts up a fight, kill him. Now, let's make this quick. All praise to Allah." He and his men charged across the open desert toward Aaron.

Aaron made the rock bed and had just enough time to remove his implements of combat from his pack. Now he could face his stalkers in this rocky slaughter pen. *Okay, Aaron,* he told himself, *place the horses and Paris behind you. They will not use bows for fear of shooting the animals, so says Martin. Now, mental checklist time. One fine Genoan crossbow, one small crossbow, bolts from my backpack. Now ready my lance, shield, and the twins. Last drink of water, and here we go.*

Aaron's favorite tools of his trade were his matching eighteen-inch daggers with pearl palm grips. The twins were a finely crafted matching set of long steel icepick daggers.

In the hands of a good soldier—and Aaron knew he was one—these daggers could find their way home into the best of armored chain mail of a knight and could easily penetrate the average soldier-at-arms's leather tunic.

The redhead cranked the small crossbow back and set the perfectly balanced bolt in place—none too quickly, either, as the lead rider moved up the path only feet from the crop of rocks. Without panicking Aaron queried himself, *Does the first man have leather or bronze chest plate armor?* Based on the answer, he had to pick from his two crossbows.

The first enemy had reached the rocky summit and grasped for the reins of one of Aaron's horses when he noticed the boy with a toy-like crossbow that was aimed at his chest.

The man smiled for a brief second, thinking, *Once I kill this thin boy, that toy crossbow would make a fine gift for my son in Damascus.* This was the warrior's last thought. The small but well placed shot buried itself deep within the unarmored Arab soldier's chest.

To Aaron, the warrior had a pained look of surprise and wonderment on his face. The dying man could not get out the words, but his face said it all: "Has this toy put a pointed shot but an inch above my heart and killed me?"

The warrior clasped his chest, looked to the heavens, and fell. The brave warrior was dead before he hit the ground. He had sadly misjudged the power of what appeared to be a toy crossbow but was in reality a killing weapon. The Islamic knight would not bear any more gifts to his young son in Damascus.

The second enemy cavalryman swept away his fallen comrade's horse in an attempt to get at the young Templar. The experienced rider needed only to close about five feet more on the boy to prick him with his sharp lance and end this foolishness.

He had almost completed his task when Aaron suddenly shouldered his mighty Genoan crossbow. The man prayed to Allah that his double chain mail would hold back the power of the massive crossbow.

The squire from Paris winced as he felt the mighty recoil and painful backward pressure in his shoulder as the bolt launched.

Aaron had once checked the ability of the massive Genoan cross-bow to penetrate oak. At thirty feet, the bolt had quickly disappeared within a mighty oak tree and then split the eight-inch-wide tree in half.

The experienced cavalryman felt the power of the bolt hit him squarely in his chest. The air was sucked from both his lungs. Immediately, his eyes went blank as he was lifted from his saddle in a backward motion.

The third horseman, directly to the rear of the downed second enemy warrior, grimaced as he saw his friend lifted from his saddle and flown backward toward him. Through his mind flashed the prayer, *May Allah look after his soul.* The warrior looked quickly to see if he too had been hit, as he was covered with blood and the entrails of his lifelong friend. "All praise to Allah for sparing me. Grant me the strength to kill this infidel."

With this prayer of revenge said, the Muslim warrior realized that although he was not hit, his mount was badly injured. The heavy bolt had lodged itself into the horse's right shoulder.

The squire from La Feve had dropped the crossbow and now gripped his lance. The wiry lad ran among the enemy to create panic among the horses in the confined space of the rock channel.

The wounded horse panicked and collapsed upon the rocks, sending the rider tumbling backward to heavily strike a large rock. The warrior, dazed from the fall onto the rocks, looked up into the blue sky to see a figure standing above him. The knight was thankful that his friend Hashem had killed the boy. "You are welcomed here, my old friend. Help me up so I can finish off that infidel?"

But it was not Hashem who had found the warrior lying prostrate with a raised hand among the rocks. Rather, it was the infidel.

Aaron had no idea why the man's hand reached for the heavens beyond. He could not understand what the soldier said in Arabic. Perhaps he was begging for mercy? The lad did not weigh these gestures or appeals.

The tiring redhead quickly plunged his lance into the warrior's bare throat. He knew that he would receive no quarter should he fall in combat this day, and thus, he granted none. The boy now moved on to the fourth rider in line.

All Aaron's actions today were practiced. His education from his mentors, Brothers Walter and Martin, had taught him how to plan this defense upon the rocks. His inventive mind had created the miniature but powerful crossbow that had killed the first warrior. His untiring crossbow training had schooled him in killing the second knight. His relentless lance and sword training with Roland had taught him how to efficiently kill the third enemy warrior. Now he would call upon lessons learned in the gutters of Paris to hopefully displace the next enemy.

This enemy would not be easy. By now the enemy warrior certainly knew that Aaron was no mere boy but rather a skilled adversary. Both the Islamic rider and his mount were a matched set of combatant perfection. The man was outfitted in the best Arabic armor of the day. He was also armed with the finest Damascus steel scimitar. Aaron judged him to be a well-trained and exceedingly experienced knight.

The man was aboard the finest Arabian that Aaron had seen in a long time. The stallion was a first-class warhorse with strong lines. Sergeant Martin often talked about Arabic warhorses. "They are trained to rear up and strike the enemy with their sharpened hooves in combat. Never get directly in front of such an animal," he had warned. "If you do, you will be trampled to death or you will be shredded to pieces. Don't go behind an Arabic warhorse either, since it has been trained to rear up and kick you to death."

The young squire remembered this and had picked this rocky outcrop to take away such advantages of his enemy. Today, this warhorse needed to keep all his hooves on the ground in this rocky and loose gravel hell.

The redhead managed a brief smile. *I may die, but not due to being trampled to death.* Aaron had not simply trapped the men in these threatening rocks. The loose rocks and channel also rendered the animal's combat weapons near useless.

Martin had said that Aaron's thin body and flaming red hair would make him valuable in the slave markets of Damascus. Today, the young Templar decided to die hard, rather than surrender to be hauled away to the slave market. Running toward his enemy, he yelled, "Taking me prisoner won't happen today. Not today or any other day."

He stopped just feet away from the Muslim patrol leader, making a taunting motion with his hands. "Come, Muslim, a little closer, just a little closer. I have something special for you."

This only angered his adversary further. Hashem, as he urged his horse closer, in Aaron's own Frankish language, screamed, "You dare to beckon me, infidel? You are beckoning death. It will be you who gains the gates of hell today. I will cleave you in two pieces this day and piss on your body lying in these rocks."

Okay, Aaron me boy, you got him real pissed. Now what are you going to do?

The boy was ever so quickly blinded by the sun's reflection on the boulders. Perhaps God was sending him a message? Seeing this surreal vision unfold in front of him, Aaron's mind went to the Bible passage "Behold a pale horse and his name was death."

To Aaron, this was a hellish place of rocks that were afire and oozing blood. The dead bodies lay either face up, gazing into the sky and heaven, or face down on the rocks, looking into hell. The surviving riderless horses were wincing in pain brought about from wounds or falls. All taken, this scene was a pictorial inferno. *Living hell, Aaron; this is what hell will look like. So move, boy, or join the dead.*

Aaron instinctively ran up on a rock and set himself nearly even with the pale horse and its rider in bright ornate armor. Both man and beast were impressive, the man massive and strong, mounted on the perfect animal.

Now the young warrior must focus on his next prey. To the thin redhead, both the horse and man seemed larger than life. Aaron had never seen an Arab this large.

He was within inches of the Arab and could smell the man's breath and see the perspiration dripping from his forehead.

The enemy knight, much larger than any of the local Arab men, added to Aaron's fear factor. Aaron now knew what other men faced when they looked up to Roland's large frame extended by a large horse.

Suddenly, the expert warrior raised his sword arm, readying to cut the boy down in perfect form. Aaron would have had a quick death if not for his agility and training. He knew that this warrior was the leader and that he had won that position because he was nearly perfect. Aaron had one chance to convince this warrior that he was unarmed and to induce him to ask Aaron to surrender, or to feel certain that he could quickly kill the boy.

After watching three of his friends killed by this boy, the warrior opted for quick revenge and screamed to the heavens, "Allah, forgive me for striking an unarmed man." He began his downward slash.

As if by magic, Aaron made two larger-than-life daggers appear in his hands. Aaron's twins were extended in a defensive move, forming an X in front of him. The warrior's sword was committed to the downward swing, only to be cradled in the set of daggers, nearly locked.

This was but a momentary setback for the knight. He began to use all his power against Aaron's daggers, trying to break the block.

Hashem could not gather the strength needed to break the block, however. In a lightning-quick move that came from years of training and experience, Hashem quickly disengaged his sword. He raised the sword high in an overhead swing. He smiled, because he knew that in a second or two, he would cleave this young redhead in half.

In that brief time between life and eternity, the man's eyes locked on to Aaron's. He searched Aaron's blue eyes to see what fear may be lying in wait for this boy's journey to hell. He saw none.

The boy's face was emotionless as the scimitar neared the boy's throat. The boy's face revealed firmness of will and a fearless inner strength. It was then that Hashem glanced right to discover that his sword arm had dropped for no reason.

He looked toward the boy and noticed that the second dagger had disappeared from the X and the boy had parried his scimitar harmlessly out of his way with his remaining dagger.

Hashem's heart pounded in his chest, and he felt a slight pain under his right armpit. He asked the Christian aloud in Frankish, "Where is the dagger?"

Aaron replied with a smile. "I made it disappear by magic."

The man had a puzzled look upon his face. This was Hashem's last memory on earth as he fell to the right of his horse among his dead comrades, praying aloud as he tumbled from his saddle, "Allah, be merciful."

The squire used a killing technique taught to him when he was ten years old on the streets of Paris. He still remembered his older brother, Tom, telling him, "Timing, lad; it is about timing. When they raise their sword arm, they expose the armpit—no armor under the armpit, as it binds the soldier and he can't move his arm well. You gots to use a long dagger. Stick um fast, hard, and good. The dagger goes into both of the lungs. They die real quick, they do."

Aaron thought, *My brother would be proud of me. But that was my last trick.* He looked to his rear and saw two warriors making their way toward him, a remaining soldier closing from his front.

The boy from Paris was exhausted, surrounded, and out of moves. He removed his dagger from his last victim's underarm and got set to make his last stand.

It was then that the closest large warrior, no more than five feet from Aaron, went down. "Thank you, dear Jesus, for that. No redhead for you, you arse," Aaron screamed, pointing to the dead man.

Aaron saw that the warrior had been struck by several turcopole arrows and not by the direct hand of the Lord. He spun around to face the last two warriors, only to see Martin cleaving the last cavalryman in half and a lance protruding from the second warrior's back as he lay upon the rocks, also dead. They had never seen or heard Martin's approach; they had been too busy tracking Aaron.

"Bless you, Sergeant Martin, for delivering me from those bast... I mean Muslim knights. God sent me a message on that bit of advantage. That was too close, way too close, for comfort." Then the lad mumbled another "way too close" for added closure.

Aaron looked closely at the dead raiders. "Sergeant Martin, these men don't appear to be the average warrior. They appear more like Franks or Germans in size, and this one has blue eyes, yet they have a desert appearance and dress in desert clothing."

One of the turcopoles looked closely at the dead leader, crossed himself in the Byzantine Christian fashion, and said but one word, "Mamlukes."

Aaron was mystified. "What is a Mamluke, Brother Martin?"

Martin looked closer at the dead leader. "Praise the Lord, it is so, and they all are Mamlukes. This is not good, Aaron, not good indeed. You are lucky to be alive." Martin went on, "Mamlukes are Egyptian warriors of the best class. Sometimes they are bred as warriors with Turkish warrior fathers and young white slave women to increase the size and mass. Others are white children or slaves who converted under the sword or were raised since birth to Islam and then trained as warriors."

Martin closely examined the others. "These raiders appear to be all about the same age and perhaps have trained for years together. See that they are all much larger than most Arab warriors. We must report this to Brother Walter."

The warriors were stripped of anything of value. The food and few coins discovered on them were given to the turcopoles as a form of some payment. The horses, armor, and weapons were valued at La Feve, but the information they carried and the knowledge of who they were was invaluable to Walter of Mesnil and the Templars.

The entire engagement had lasted perhaps five minutes. No quarter was asked, and no quarter was given. And so was life and death at La Feve in the land of Galilee, not far from Jesus' ministry on earth.

The patrol arrived back at La Feve late in the day. They were greeted by Walter as they cleared the fortress gates. "You are just in time for Vespers, Martin, and for our squire, a bowl of stew. I see you found the enemy. Any prisoners?"

"Good day Brother Commander," Martin replied. "Yes, we found the enemy, and no prisoners, as the seven fought to the end. It took us some time to get back, as two of the enemies' horses were lame and a third injured."

Martin added, "They were heading to Damascus and wanted the squire's bait horses to replace the two animals. They had these maps and some interesting information with them." Martin displayed the paper to Walter. "One of the turcopoles noted that this form of parchment is used by spies. He placed the juice of a lemon over the blank parchment, and behold! It reveals its secrets to us. It is a map of all the water holes, streams, and wells at Cresson, Sephoria, and the village of Hattin, and all of the other watering holes between La Feve, Nazareth, Tiberius, and in much of Galilee's central lands to the Mediterranean coast. This mark next to the well point indicates when the well or stream is dry during the year."

Martin continued speaking as he placed a special type of dagger on the table. "They were not the average Arab warrior. I have six other daggers just like it."

Walter of Mesnil looked down at the ornate dagger and in a worried voice announced, "Mamlukes this far north. Impossible. Saladin only uses them when he has need for the most important of tasks. He puts them up front as shock troops. If he has drawn them from Egypt, then the time must be getting close for invasion."

Walter nodded his head. "Well done, Martin, and you too, Aaron. I have a mission for you, Martin. Take this map and the other documents we collected in the last two weeks and get them to Jerusalem. Take Aaron and three turcopoles with you."

The old warrior continued, "Martin, you must plead our case. I have penned a note to the grand master telling him how desperate we are, and how lacking in most implements of war. He must understand that we need reinforcements, food, and equipment to build up the garrison for the expected invasion."

Mesnil waved Martin's map in his hand. "This and the Mamlukes are proof of Saladin's intentions to invade soon. Go as quickly as you can to Jerusalem, old friend."

Just then, a rather large convoy of seven wagons under the Templar flag appeared beyond the fortress walls, with twenty-five to thirty Templar knights and sergeants as escorts. "Finally, food, equipment, and replacements!" cried Mesnil.

Aaron smiled and announced, "It appears the note I sent to Roland worked."

Martin looked at the mounted men and exclaimed, "They are but a small down payment for what we will need soon. Still, it is good that Roland somehow got Albert to send us these provisions and men. But how did Roland convince Ridefort or Fontainebleau?"

Chapter Fourteen

"Two are better than one, because they have a good return for their work: If one falls down, his friend can help him up. But pity the man who falls and has no one to help him up!"

Ecclesiastes 4:9–10

Fontainebleau slammed the door to the Knight's Hall as he ran toward the grand master's suite, waving a parchment in his hand. "That damnable boy; I will have him whipped for this."

The seneschal continued ranting as he ran down the hallways. "Using my name to advance his friend Walter both men and supplies at La Feve while I was in Joppa is too far a breach. I will have his back stripped raw."

Making the turn to the inner office, Fontainebleau screamed, "In my name, that damnable boy ordered men and supplies be sent to La Feve!" He paused to get his breath at the grand master's private secretary's table. "Brother Edward, I **must** see the grand master now. Now, I said, *now!*"

Edward looked up from his table and spoke commandingly. "Brother Seneschal, compose yourself. The grand master cannot be disturbed. He is in conference with Sergeant Martin of Brittany from La Feve, and Squire Roland."

The seneschal's nose flared, and his face went red. "*What?!* Martin and Roland are meeting the grand master, and you deny me entry? We shall see about that." Albert sped to the door and quickly opened it with Brother Edward on his heels.

"Brother Grand Master, I must render apology for my entrance. However, I wish to report—"

Grand Master Ridefort looked up. "Albert, I see that you are back from Joppa. No interruptions, not now." Ridefort waved a map in one hand and a dagger in his second hand. He looked at Martin and Roland and announced, "Brother Martin has just provided me with the information I needed to convince the barons that the regent, our dear friend Raymond of Tripoli, is in treat with Saladin. Martin has proof that Raymond is allowing Saladin to reconnoiter Galilee to prove that we are not preparing an army to attack Saladin. This map and dagger of the Mamlukes' leader, and Brother Martin's words, should send Raymond to the axe."

The grand master looked toward Roland. "Roland informs me that La Feve could not have accomplished this intelligence coup without the reinforcements and supplies sent north by you. Wonderful insight, Albert. Now that you are here, why did you nearly break down my door and run over Brother Edward? You wish to report something of great value?"

Fontainebleau's face went blank in response.

Roland saw an opportunity and spoke in Albert's defense. "Grand Master, I am sure that Brother Seneschal is taken aback by your praise. He always is looking out for the best interest of the knights in the field. This is just normal duty within our bureau. He has trained us all within his bureau to act in his stead, as if he was present, and look out for the troops."

The young Templar continued, "Matter of fact, I know that he is trying to organize a second convoy to La Feve, with additional men and supplies. He knows that the enemy will strike first in Galilee through to the coastal plain. I am sure that is what he wanted to report." He thought, *You owe me your ass, Albert. You live today, you no good bastard of a traitor and street thief, because my friends need that food, equipment, and men. Once that convoy moves north, you are on borrowed time.*

While Albert noted something odd about Roland's look, he came alive. "Squire Roland is correct, Grand Master. I wanted you to know this so you could inform Brother Martin to assure Mesnil to count on further help."

The grand master nodded in agreement. "Albert, you *do* have the makings of a good soldier. Excellent work, Albert, excellent. Now let us get on with business and—"

Brother Edward broke into the conversion with a stern face. "Grand Master, please excuse me, but a herald from the court of the king of Jerusalem has just informed me that King Baldwin has passed into heaven. His remains are coming south to Jerusalem as we speak."

Gerald turned immediately toward the Rock of the Dome and began to speak as if into a void, not paying attention to anyone present. "We all knew this would happen. Edward, inform all our fortress commanders and the brotherhood to expect Saladin to raid or attack during this time of confusion. Second, send a detachment to Joppa to escort the remains of the king and the royal princess Sibylla to Jerusalem. Also, continue to reinforce and supply our fortresses in the north."

Gerald shifted to the window overlooking the headquarters of the Knights of Saint John. "I must see the Hospitallers' Grand Master Roger quickly. So it begins, Brothers. What will our friend Raymond do? He knows the crown should go to Sibylla. He will not let her coronation stand. If he can't get the crown, he will ensure that Princess Isabella will, as he can control her. What will he do?"

Chapter Fifteen

"For they have sown the wind, and they shall reap the whirlwind: it hath no stalk; the bud shall yield no meal; if so be it yield, the stranger shall swallow it up."

Hosea 8:7

Raymond arrived at Acre as the child king Baldwin was being placed in his coffin for the journey to Jerusalem and the Church of the Holy Sepulcher. The barely eight-year-old was now at peace after years of suffering. "Lord Joscelin, on behalf of our people, please accept our deepest sorrow."

Joscelin's family had once been a powerful entity within the kingdom when the County of Edessa, now lost to the Muslims, was once a major principality. Now, Joscelin had to survive on his wit and a few scraps of poor land near Acre. The aged man spoke softly to Count Raymond as the coffin lid was placed over his great-nephew's body. "Raymond, I and the boy's grandfather will take the king to Jerusalem. You must gather the barons and lead the discussion on who will be crowned. As you know, King Baldwin knew that the child was sickly and planned in his will for the possibilities of an early death of the child. It was his wish, and the wishes of the kings of France, England, the Holy Roman Empire, and the pope, to be involved in the election of our next sovereign. We should have a monarch with connections to Europe, don't you agree?"

Raymond interrupted, "Lord Joscelin, we both know that vetting process sounds good, but that could take many months to realize. Our kingdom needs leadership *now* to keep her enemies at bay. My duties are clear. I am appointed as the kingdom's regent and bailie, and as such, I will rule the kingdom until a sovereign is elected, *as also directed in Baldwin's will.*"

Joscelin was excellent at chess and always outplayed his adversaries by at least four moves. The old chess player knew what words would come from Raymond's mouth next, and cunningly, he made his move to force the words forward. "Raymond, then as regent and bailie, you need to the gather all the kingdom's princes and barons at Tiberius. I also strongly recommend that both the grand masters of the Templars and Hospitallers be included in the discussions. It is imperative that you keep that meddling patriarch Heraclius out of the process. I will attend to the king's funeral at Jerusalem. You attend to the matters of state. When you are ready, we shall gather in Jerusalem for the decision."

Raymond believed that with Joscelin's help, he had just completed a coup that might lead to his choice, the malleable Princess Isabella, being elected as queen. He looked at Joscelin and said, "I agree."

With that, Raymond and his bodyguard rode toward Nablus, southeast of Acre, not toward the west and Tiberius. Nablus was the center of Baron Balian of Ibelin's stronghold. Equally important to his position was that Balian was stepfather to Princess Isabella, who had good claim on the crown.

Joscelin looked to the small coffin of his great-nephew. "Yes, Baldwin, my dear child, I will fulfill the promise I made to you. Your mother will be queen. Neither Count Raymond, nor your aunt Isabella, will dare approach the throne when I am done with them.

Joscelin watched Raymond's entourage's dust in the distance going southeast. *Just as I believed Raymond would do, he rides to Nablus. Once the count arrives, he will weave the next part of his plan to gain the support of Balian and the baron's stepdaughter, the Princess Isabella, and her husband, Humphrey of Toron.*

The old man called out to the captain of the royal bodyguard, "We sail to Joppa within the hour. Did you deliver the message to Princess Sibylla?"

The captain of guard replied, "Yes, my lord, the princess understands what must be done. She read the patriarch Heraclius's letter concerning the annulment of her marriage to Guy, Count of Joppa. She understands it may be necessary in order for her to be crowned queen in her own right and, thus, making her free to marry a European noble to strengthen our ties and in due course have him crowned as king."

Joscelin smiled. "Well done, Captain. By her ridding herself of that weak man, Lusignan, she would make herself a candidate for an improved marriage. However, she will not wait months until a recommended contender from Europe shows himself here—if ever. I soon will become her senior advisor, and our family will once again rise to a position of power within the kingdom. I have outplayed Raymond."

Within two weeks after his death, the child-king Baldwin V was taken to Jerusalem and placed in a tomb next to his uncle, Baldwin IV, within the Church of the Holy Sepulcher. After the service, the family and their supporters went to the Templar headquarters for discussions. Fontainebleau was cautioned by Ridefort to ensure that the headquarters was fully prepared for such an event.

"Albert, I want only a few in attendance today. The information that will pass here today is to be maintained in secret. I don't want some buffoon passing wine and spilling it on the next queen of the kingdom. Wait, I believe that Squire Roland should be here. Yes, he has seen firsthand Raymond's treason, and it will not hurt that he is a Champagne and favored by Richard and Philip. Being a Frank aligns him well with Fredrick of the Holy Roman Empire, who eyes the Champagne region from his perch across the Rhine. Yes, clean up the boy and have him assigned to me."

Albert, still concerned that Roland would soon be in the grand master's favor, retorted, "Grand Master, he is but a boy. Are you sure he needs to be in attendance? There are too many in attendance as it is."

Ridefort thought deeply before responding. "Yes, Albert, perhaps we have too many in the room. Only I, Marshal Mailly, and Champagne need attend. Dismissed."

"Yes, Grand Master." The disappointed Fontainebleau was going to protest but thought better of it. *Because of complaining, I now will not be in attendance. Why is all this of my concern? I can listen to the proceedings from the side door and gather information for Saladin without being suspected. Still, that damn boy keeps climbing higher in Ridefort's esteem. I will have him yet.*

At the appointed time, Gerald Ridefort escorted the bereaved extended family from the royal quarters to the Temple grounds and into his refectory office. He gazed over the gathering gloom and spoke to Sibylla. "Your Royal Princess, I recall you once informing me that as a young woman you had visited France and particularly enjoyed

Troyes and the hospitality shown by Count Henry and Countess Maria?"

Sibylla thought of better times and smiled. "Yes, Champagne is truly beautiful, and the count and princess were most kind. My dear husband often recalls his days of travel in Champagne as well and, in fact, once soldiered for Count Henry. Your order, Grand Master, has a special place in its heart for Troyes, does it not?"

Ridefort replied, "Indeed it does, madame. Troyes is where the Poor-Fellow Soldiers of Christ and the Temple of Solomon were supported and chartered as a holy order. Perhaps in your travels you may remember the count's family? To my right is Roland of Champagne, third son of Count Henry and Princess Maria."

Roland bowed deeply. "Your Royal Princess, you have the deepest sympathy from me and our family." Now Roland's charm took over. "I was but a child of six, but certainly, I remember your visit. I was so struck by your very stately presence. If I remember correctly, I asked for your hand in marriage and demanded that my mother keep you in Troyes until I was older."

All in the room laughed, perhaps for the first time since this trial of sorrow started. Sibylla smiled. "Of course, I remember. I was but fifteen or sixteen at the time. Many times, I wished that I could have accepted your offer. What are you doing here in Jerusalem, Roland?"

The squire responded, "It is a long story, madame. We shall say that once again, a Champagne is serving the Templars. However, in the interest of all gathered, I know the Grand Master, you, and this gathering have important issues to discuss for the kingdom's sake." Roland bowed and took a position near Gerald.

Ridefort was rather pleased with himself. Roland had set the stage for important discussions. "Princess, the Templars stand with you and believe you are the rightful heir to the throne."

The princess asked the group, "Where are the Hospitallers on this issue?"

Ridefort was quick to answer, "You noted, Princess, that after the burial ceremony, Grand Master Roger excused himself and returned to his headquarters. The Hospitallers want to be neutral on the issue. Roger does acknowledge that your claim and Isabella's claim to the throne are complicated by marriage. Technically, if you were crowned and married, your husband would become king."

Ridefort was cunning and always looking out for himself. He was also a survivor and knowledgeable about how best to play his hand. "Master Roger also is concerned about the oath we took to your brother to wait for the kings of France, England, and the Holy Roman Empire, and the pope to jointly decide upon your suitor."

Gerald now looked to Guy. "I am sorry to bring these points up, Count Guy, but I must."

Guy, looking at his wife, said, "We both understand what must be done. The kingdom is more important than our personal love. The church will annul the marriage on whatever grounds needed. I will not stand in the way. I will waive my rights to a Church court. I have to wonder what our friend Lord Humphrey will do when Raymond asks him the same question concerning annulment of his marriage."

Sitting in the back of the room was the prince of Transjordan, Reynald of Chatillion. He stood and addressed the gathering. "The princess Isabella's mother may be of your blood, Sibylla, but Humphrey is my wife's son and my stepson. The boy will ally with us, not with that Arab-loving Raymond."

The hum of conversation was busy across the room as the barons and royalty momentarily chatted among themselves. In time, all in the room agreed with Reynald's assessment.

The old warlord Chatillion continued, "Humphrey is but a boy and is only interested in Princess Isabella's beauty and body." All laughed as Reynald continued, "Humphrey will not be concerned with matters of court. He will not submit to a divorce and thus will make Isabella ineligible for the crown."

In between long drinks of wine, the old man Reynald spoke. "Listen, friends, I am more concerned with Raymond's latest poison rumors than with the princess Sibylla's illegitimacy. He can turn his lies into votes against us from the High Court and grow distrust among the kings of Europe and the pope."

Gerald grimaced. "Yes, it is truly sad that it has come to this, Your Royal Princess. I too have heard the count of Tripoli has this vial of poison to spread. All in this room acknowledge you as the rightful heir to the throne. Raymond tells all who will listen that you are illegitimate and a pretender to the throne. What say you, Patriarch, to these vile lies?"

Heraclius rose but stumbled over his words. "Yes, I have heard this allegation, too. However, I am not sure how to combat this rumor."

The room turned silent, until Roland whispered into Gerald's ear. Ridefort smiled and thought that it was well worth having Roland present. "Princess, young Champagne has researched this matter."

The squire, now turned canon court lawyer, spoke, "Madame, it is sad that you must be present for this discourse. However, with your kind permission, I may be able to enlighten all about this matter."

Sibylla was completely enamored with this handsome young man. Not only was he handsome and the son of France's leading family, but the lad seemed to be a scholar as well. "Please continue, Lord Champagne," she told him.

Roland bowed and continued, "Sadly, madame, these cowards call upon the reputation of your mother, who is no longer with us on this earthly kingdom to defend herself; thus, while others attack her reputation I will defend her honor."

Ridefort smiled and thought, *This boy is good. He has his grandmother's, Queen Eleanor of Aquitaine, wit.*

Roland continued, "It appears that your now deceased mother's reputation was challenged when she was required to have her marriage annulled so your father could be crowned king, much like what you face today. The official grounds were the appearance of the lack of a male child and further inability for your mother to bear children—and *not infidelity.*"

The tall blond walked to the table, where he picked up some loose papers. "I have read into the official record of the church on your parents' annulment. In 1163, the church ruled that you were the king's lawful daughter and thus his rightful heir under the traditions of the Kingdom of Jerusalem. The church has not changed that position."

The squire looked at each person present, commanding the stage. "I happen to have those documents and present them to the patriarch for his review." He then passed the papers to the patriarch.

Young Champagne then turned to see Sibylla's delight expressed on her face. Also noted was a short exclamation from Guy's brother Amalric, who had bedded the same woman Roland was defending,

Queen Mother Agnes. Roland had heard the story of how Amalric had bedded Agnes to gain favor for his brother. The young man would file this memory for future use.

Roland turned again to Patriarch Heraclius. Heraclius was also startled, as he, too, had had an affair with the queen mother, in order to get his present position. Roland's smile indicated that he had done his research and most likely knew about these later affairs after the death of her husband, the king.

Amalric of Lusignan, the constable of Jerusalem and the man responsible for the security of the city, returned them to business. "These are all wonderful words. They will help our cause in France, England, and the Vatican. Still, Raymond will not stand for these proceedings. He has access to many more men-at-arms then we do. Knowing that traitor, he may make another treaty with Saladin. He will surely come to press with his army to force us to accept Isabella."

Again, the young warrior whispered into Ridefort's ear. "Another excellent recommendation, Roland," the grand master exclaimed.

The Grand Master turned to the gathering. "We must not act independently, or Raymond will defeat us all in turn. He will come here and amass his force as Lord Amalric suggests. As Roland points out, the key is Humphrey's decision to either support his wife's claim or his parent's wishes. Also, the timing of the decision is critical to the outcome. Reynald, we must get to Humphrey soon and know his mind."

A broad smile came across Reynald's face. Here he was amidst the entire court, advising the princess on her claim to the throne, yet he saw an opportunity to advance himself. The old fox flashed on an opportunity to seize the crown for himself. *I can convince my weak stepson to divorce his sixteen-year-old princess. She then could be crowned and later remarry Humphrey, and make him her regent. I can pull the puppet's strings of kingship. Better still, I can convince the lovebirds to abdicate and turn the kingship over to me.*

To Prince Reynald of Transjordan, this was but one more wager at the table of the game of life. This time, the wager would be his head, because that's what the stakes were in the game of high treason.

Reynald, with much bravado in his voice, boomed, "Assuredly, Raymond or his friend Baron Ibelin will not allow me or mine in his keep to talk to Humphrey."

All the room broke out in a hearty roar because everyone knew that Raymond hated Reynald and would deliver him to Saladin in person if the opportunity presented itself.

Amidst the laughter, Roland offered, "Perhaps a clandestine note outlining your desires could be brought to Lord Toron on your behalf, Prince Reynald?"

The old man Reynald looked to Roland. "Sound advice, Champagne. I must get a note to my stepson telling him to support Sibylla's claim to the throne. But we need someone trustworthy and cunning to deliver it."

Little did the gathering know that Reynald's note would try to convince the twenty-year-old Lord of Toron to claim the throne in right of his underage sixteen-year-old wife, Isabella. Reynald would ally himself with Isabella's mother, Dowager Queen Maria Comnena, and the Ibelin faction. Oddly, the baron Ibelin had a kill-on-sight warrant for Reynald for his many crimes.

Roland saw a window of opportunity for his case to ask for Marie's hand in marriage. "Sir, perhaps I can deliver the note? I have business also with Count Raymond's niece at Tiberius. Along the way, I can clandestinely deliver the note to Lord Humphrey."

Ridefort announced, "Brilliant, Roland! I pray you better luck than I had with Raymond when I pressed him for Lady Botrun's hand."

Again, all in the room laughed, since the whole kingdom knew how Raymond had cheated a much younger Knight Ridefort out of Lady Botrun's hand in marriage. Ridefort smiled and announced to the nobles, "Not to worry, for I am sure that soon, the count will be repaid for his treachery, with much interest." The others again laughed and agreed with the plan.

The old fox Reynald needed to know what chess pieces could be played in this game. He stood up and stated, "While I believe that you, my princess Sibylla, have the most evident claim and are the rightful heir of the kingdom, how does one get by the marriage to Count Guy? The princess cannot be crowned with a husband. What says the Church in this matter?"

The patriarch asked Sibylla, "Will you allow me to annul your marriage?"

Sibylla rose and looked at all the attending officials and kingdom leaders, but it was Roland that she focused upon as she spoke. "I understand that the annulment will clear the way for a possible strong connection in marriage with a close member to the throne of our chief Christian kingdoms, England and France. You must promise me that you will allow me to pick my consort and *swear* none here will oppose my choice."

Many in the room followed the princess's gaze toward Roland. Again, muffled conversion between all took place. Yes, of course the House of Champagne, related to both kings, was wealthy and available. Ridefort surely noted the connection.

Most of the men in the room looked toward the patriarch and agreed. The elderly patriarch approached the Bible on Ridefort's table and said, "Remember that we did swear on Baldwin's deathbed that we would uphold his will. That is, to seek the consent of the pope and the kings of Europe to our choice. How do we reconcile this?"

Roland spoke up. "Grand Master, may I offer an observation?"

Ridefort smiled and whispered to Roland, "To this point, counselor, your observations have been most worthy. Speak."

Roland looked at Sibylla, then toward the patriarch. "Your Eminence, did you, in the company of Grand Master Arnold and Grand Master Roger, go to visit each of the kings, Henry of England, Philip of France, and Frederick of the Holy Roman Empire, seeking their support and *interest* in the Kingdom of Jerusalem just months ago?"

The patriarch nodded and mumbled "Yes," having no idea where the young man from Champagne was going with this.

Roland walked closer to the old priest, ignoring the others, and continued, "Sir, did you not inform the royal kings about our young king's health?"

Again the patriarch spoke. "Yes, I informed them, as did the grand masters of the Templars and Saint John."

Roland looked toward the grand master, then again toward the patriarch of Jerusalem. "Did you not make it clear the great forces that Saladin could array against the kingdom, and the grave threat to the land?"

Again the patriarch mumbled, "Yes, of course we did."

Young Champagne retorted, "I understand that they were *all* sympathetic. So where are their soldiers? Perhaps my brethren sent one of my princely uncles to act in the king's stead to answer such questions as to who shall be queen? I don't see such a prince seated here today to offer you guidance. All that are here from those courts is your humble servant—me."

All in the gathering, enjoying Roland's wit and courtly manner, sang in near unison, "Hear, hear!"

Roland continued as he walked toward the princess. "My observation, madame, is that, sadly, you are on your own. My uncles will be here outside the gates when Saladin is feted at this table, and not before. They are far too busy trying to keep their own heads, and their crowns upon them. I can't speak for the pope, but does this kingdom not have a patriarch, appointed by the pope, rather than a king-appointed bishop? Does not the patriarch speak for the pope in such matters?"

The boy commanded the room. Not a voice spoke, nor a chair was set ajar; all was deadly quiet. The squire closed by focusing on the princess. "I am just a squire, a scribe, and yet even I can see the issues at hand. This kingdom must come together soon and act as one in the face of Saladin. I beg your indulgence if you believe me wrong or unworthy, but we must have a crowned sovereign soon or this land will be torn asunder from within. What will be left will be easy taking for Saladin."

A total hush came over the room. Princess Sibylla rose and spoke. "We owe you a great debt, Grand Master, for having such a wise young man address us. For that you have my total gratitude!"

She grew very stern. "I will lead the kingdom against Saladin and protect our Savior's land from the infidel. My family is from this land, and I will die fighting to protect it."

With those words said, all rose and bowed toward the soon-to-be queen and announced, "Long live the queen."

The smiling Ridefort closed with Roland's last recommendation. "We must crown the queen quickly. Then it will be Raymond who will be on the defensive. Get me Humphrey's intentions, Squire.

"Marshal Mailly," he continued, "you and Champagne go north with the second convoy to La Feve. Roland will travel with you until the turn from the Jordan to Nablus. Champagne, you and a few men will go to Nablus, deliver the note, and return here quickly."

Ridefort announced, "We shall meet here in three weeks for the ceremony. We must all be vigilant. We must secure the seaports and cities under our control. Don't let the count of Tripoli enter Jerusalem with his army. The next move is up to Raymond and his supporters."

Chapter Sixteen

"Shall trouble or hardship or persecution or famine or nakedness or danger or sword? As it is written: "For your sake we face death all day long; we are considered as sheep to be slaughtered."

Romans 8:35–36

The thirty Templars and turcopoles, with Marshal Mailly in command and Roland in the rear guard, left Jerusalem two days after the royal concave that had agreed to crown Sibylla forthwith.

The troop, or lance, was escorting ten mule-drawn wagons loaded with provisions and military material for Brother Martin and Fortress La Feve. Many of the escorting Templars would be assigned to the fortress to reinforce the small garrison.

As the convoy headed out of the Damascus Gate and took the Jericho Road northeast, Roland looked over his shoulder to see the Holy City of Jerusalem, perhaps for the last time. It would be a long and dangerous ninety-mile journey to La Feve.

The road was rough, and the hot weather made the first day nearly unbearable for Roland. As he often did, he whispered into his steed's ear, "Sirocco, both of us are out of shape. Without Brother Walter's and Sergeant Martin's constant nagging, we have fallen victim to the headquarters' easy life."

The lad turned his head toward the teams of mules, which were surefooted but slow. "Sirocco, I have not seen my friends and my beautiful Marie in many months, yet, boy, we travel at this snail's pace. Is the entire world, including mules, against me?"

Sirocco was in no mood to care about his master's problems. He too was hot, and tired. He cared not one bit for low limbs of scrub oak hitting him and goring his legs. His sore hooves beat upon the rocky soil of this God-forsaken country for hours on end. The horse wanted a barn with proper food and water. He wanted France!

On a hot day in the Outremer, you quickly find yourself in a trance of sorts. Roland pondered many unanswered question as he listened to his horse's steady beat on the stone-weathered road that many traveled that day.

Roland welcomed this state of mind, as he could think better in this trance. His mind would slowly drift from subject to subject. Sometimes, he would chuckle to himself thinking of Aaron. *I wonder how that redhead is doing at La Feve? I bet he is having the soft life.*

Other times, he would see Marie in his mind. His recall of her was so real he could feel her tender flesh. He could see her making her way to him across a spring meadow. The vision was so clear. He had imagined both of them gently kneeling in a field of flowers in France above the Rhone. So real, he just needed to reach out and touch her!

Then reality fell on him, and he yelled. He came awake to the unpleasantness of Brother Mailly's lance tip ever so slightly jabbing him in his backside.

The old warrior was in Roland's face. "Wake up, boy, and stop drifting off. You had the look on your face that you were perhaps just entertaining impure thoughts? You will report to the chaplain and make an act of contrition as soon as we stop. If a Muslim arrow settles in your heart, you will be cast down to hell for that look upon your face."

The weathered warrior continued, "Roland, you are on the same road that Jesus, the Apostles, Paul, and many of the heroes of the Old Testament walked to the Holy City, Jericho, and the River Jordan. That should keep you awake with a busy and righteous mind as you do your duty."

The young squire straightened in his saddle. "Yes, Commander, I was drifting off. I will do better, sir."

As the commander made his way to the front of the formation, Roland made an irreverent comment as he rubbed his sore backside. "Sirocco, think about it, boy; King David's and King Solomon's horses walked these very steps we walk today!"

Sirocco's ears failed to twitch. The horse, like Roland, frankly, did not care who walked this road. While Roland wished for a gentle touch from his beloved, Sirocco wished for an oatmeal treat that Roland carried under his cloak as a reward.

Each hour, Mailly made the men dismount and walk for fifteen minutes on the stoned byway, still another Templar rule. This walk upon the stone road quickly ended Roland's trancelike state as the stones seem to come up through his thin leather boot soles. His feet had also grown soft with garrison duty.

For the fifteen minutes, it seemed like he was walking barefooted along the road to Jericho. He said aloud when the command to remount was given, "Thank God."

Back on Sirocco, Roland again let his mind slip into a nearly hypnotic trance. Perhaps it was the heat, but he slipped into one of his sex-filled trances, believing he was walking naked upon a beach in France with a perfectly formed Marie. *"Marie, let's go into the water, then find a perfect spot under the palm trees and then—"*

The boy jumped two feet into the air as he felt the rather untender prick of Mailly's lance upon the unprotected nape of his neck. Roland screamed. "I've been hit." He had failed to note that Mailly had slipped behind him from the flank of the column.

The commander screamed at the boy, "You only wish you were hit by an arrow. That, Squire, was a gentle touch of my lance that got your attention. Had it been an enemy lance or an arrow, your pretty blond hair and blue eyes would be on the roadway. Do you have a death wish, boy? Pay attention, boy!"

The weather-beaten soldier lowered his voice as his eyes penetrated Roland's inner being. "You are not the highly trained soldier that I saw in battle some six months ago."

The marshal grabbed Roland. "No, you are a soft garrison soldier who will last perhaps one minute in combat. Your carelessness will get the rest of us killed. Get your head out of your arse, Squire, or I will boot it out."

Now the other men in the convoy had picked up on Roland's failure to perform his duty as rear guard. One Templar sergeant in particular showed his disapproval with Roland as Mailly rode by him. "Begging the commander's pardon, may I speak to you?"

Mailly had known this old Templar for many years. "Yes, Brother Hugh, speak."

Hugh glanced back at Roland, "Sir, he will never amount to much; too soft and untrained. His kind has not known the hard life like you and I know it to be. Perhaps his duty and responsibly should be left to other, better-trained soldiers?"

Mailly understood what Hugh was getting at. "I've seen that boy in combat, Brother Hugh, and he kills like a machine does. Pray for him tonight that his mind comes back to us. Not much danger on this road until we near the Jazreel Valley. He will be either dead, or with us in mind and body." Then the commander rode to his position in front of the convoy.

The convoy's first night was to be spent near a small abandoned inn along the byway about twelve miles from Jerusalem. As they passed the worn inn, Roland observed two men wrapped in white standing in front of the old structure. They wanted to ensure the Templars saw the small green cross emblazed on their chests.

As the Templar convoy passed, one of the men began to ring a small hand bell. Mailly quickly viewed the men and gave the command, "At a gallop." The convoy moved gingerly past the inn.

The squire had been in the Outremer long enough to know what isolated people wrapped in white and ringing a small bell meant. This was a sign that lepers were present. Roland had never been this close to a leper, since lepers were allowed in Jerusalem only at night.

The lad from Champagne saw the men and contemplated. *Is it true that this disease is a curse for transgressions from their past? If Jacob ever heard me say that, he would beat my ears in with his cane, like the cane that leper has.*

He looked toward the abandoned, weather-beaten inn, *Perhaps this was the very inn that the Good Samaritan brought the wounded man to, to recover from his attack after he was beaten by the thieves? What is wrong with you, Roland? You should stop and see if you can give these poor brother knights and Christian's assistance as Jesus did.*

Then something within told to him, *If you get this disease from helping them, you too will die on the side of the road, alone. All the Samaritans, good or otherwise, are long gone. Just do your duty and get out of here alive and clean.*

Roland had not been in the Outremer when the leprous King Baldwin had been alive. Baldwin had died of the disease in 1185, at twenty-four years of age. When the young king was alive, he had done much to relieve the plight of the lepers in the kingdom. Once he was gone, people had quickly forgotten to be charitable toward lepers.

Sometimes the young squire would hear the lepers' bells and required leper warning, "Unclean, make way for the unclean," from his perch on the Temple walls. He would see residents scamper out of the way, cover their mouths, or sometimes run away from these poor outcasts.

At night, he would hear the bells and see the many lanterns as he observed long lines of lepers making their way along the alleys to the holy sites. Many times, they would be escorted by the Knights of Lazarus, named in honor of the leper in the Bible whom Jesus had cured.

During the leper king's time, the Knights of Saint Lazarus had found special favor. These same knights not only escorted and protected the leper pilgrims; many of them had the dreaded disease, too. They were also outfitted in white mantles similar to those of the Templars, with the exception of an emblazoned green cross. They were *always* cloaked in their hoods, however. The diseased knights often wore gloves and linen masks.

About 200 feet past the ruins of the small inn, the Templars formed the wagons in a circle, or lager, and placed most of the animals in the center. The mules, because of their noisy and mean dispositions, were placed in an old shed near the lager.

The squires, Roland included, checked the wagons and greased the wheels. Champagne's specialty was oiling the tack, as well as grooming, feeding, and watering the animals.

With those tasks complete, it was time for Roland and the entire lance, save three guards, to attend Vespers given by Commander Mailly. After the brief reading of the Bible and a brief chant, the squires were dismissed to help Brother Cook prepare and serve the meal of dried meat, fruit, and wine to the brother knights.

In keeping with Templar rules, the three squires and the ten sergeants ate soup with some rice, and whatever fruit the knights did not eat. The turcopoles made a dinner of a goat they had roasted.

After supper, the squires cleaned up the pots and bowls, a task Roland hated. To his relief, Roland did not have to clean the pots and bowls. Rather, the young warrior was assigned the task of patrolling the area around the lager and checking for possible enemy activity with two turcopoles.

Brother William, Commander Mailly's second-in-command, made Roland the patrol leader. "I was at the ambush on Joppa Road and saw your many skills, Squire. Display these same skills once more. Go no more than 300 yards around our perimeter. Take your bow, and if you find our enemies, kill them."

Near the old inn, the patrol noticed the two lepers were still there. Immediately, the turcopoles ran back thirty feet from the lepers.

Roland did not. One of the lepers in a soft voice said, "Stand where you are, Templar. Do you not know who we are?"

Roland countered, "Yes, friends, I know who you are. I brought you some fresh water, some bread, and soup." He placed the items on the ground and stood back a few feet as the men went for the food and water.

The taller leper remarked, "Thank you, friend. This is very welcomed. May our Lord bless you for your charity."

Roland replied, "I and the others are searching out for ambush and looking for bandits or Muslim warriors."

The older man with the cane said, "Brother Templar, thank you for your kindness. It may interest you to know that perhaps seven or eight riders came down the road, faces hidden, perhaps an hour before you arrived. I did not note arms, but they did have two pack animals with bundles. Perhaps weapons?"

Although his face was covered, the second leper spoke in a familiar tone. "This is the inn that Jesus talked about in his parable as He walked this road." The leper slowly raised his hand and pointed, "See those ruins there. They are the ruins of an ancient church to commemorate Jesus' famous parable of the Good Samaritan. Not many good Samaritans are willing to shelter lepers. We have no place to lay our heads, so this seemed as good as we can get."

Roland seemed to recall the voice, but from where? He then offered, "If you are here tomorrow, I will fetch some bread and honey for you to eat." He was about to walk away when again the familiar voice beckoned from the shorter leper.

He spoke in Greek, " εν καλά λόγια για έναν παλιό φίλο?" which Roland understood as, "No kind words for an old friend?" The man continued in Greek, "If you have them, speak them in Greek so none other may hear."

Roland turned and smiled. He then returned in Greek, "Είναι π σας Ραβίνος υπό το μανδύα του λευκού," asking if it was the rabbi, Jacob, under the white cloak. The boy continued in Greek, "Jacob, what are you doing here?"

The old man smiled and replied, again in Greek, "Just doing my job. Don't come closer as to reveal our relationship. Send your soldiers to scout the road and behind the ruins."

The young patrol leader dispatched the turcopoles on their way and then asked in the language of the Franks, "Jacob, who is your friend?"

"This is a Lazarus knight, Roger of Beaune," Jacob said.

The unseen man cloaked in white slightly bowed. "At your service, Roland of Champagne."

Jacob continued, "Before Roger contracted the disease of leprosy, he was a Templar knight and close friend of Walter."

"Any friend of my master Walter is a friend of mine, sir," stated a concerned Roland. The thought raced through his mind. *Had the doctor contacted leprosy?*

Jacob was an expert in reading facial expressions, both as a doctor and as a master spy. "Aha yes, you are thinking that I too have the disease? Let me explain. Only a few can get the disease. I appear to be immune and have been in contact with many lepers over the years. For a spy, it offers us nearly perfect traveling conditions. No one nears us, do they, Roger?"

The boy smiled. "Only you, Jacob, would be so crafty. What have you been doing?"

The doctor first requested that Roger secure the rear of the inn and remove himself from the conversation.

The old man then continued. "It has been a long six months, Roland, since we parted. It took me that time to find who the spy named Rashid in Joppa was and to destroy his network. I had to visit the house of the tanner in Joppa many times to discover Rashid's clever observation methods and disguises. I ate much bread to find his many messages to Saladin, before I took Rashid and his colleague down."

Jacob continued, "Yes, Rashid told me much prior to his untimely heart attack. Sadly, sometimes the medicine reacts differently on each of us. I must do more research when I have time."

The old man from York continued, "Rashid informed me that a Frankish spy ordered your death, Roland, on the road to Jerusalem."

Roland agreed, "Yes, one of the enemy was a Christian mercenary and told me that I was the object of their raid. Why is this so, Jacob?"

The old man replied, "For certain, he knows that you are close to the thrones of England and France. But it is much more. I know you have been chosen, Roland, to carry the Templars' prized secret. You must get out of here soon. You must fight this man on your chosen ground, not on his terms and time. I believe the enemy is close at hand."

Jacob cautioned, "Be watchful on the road near the Jordan. This is where they will ambush you. They will hit and run across the Jordan to Saladin's land. Now we have talked too long. Go. I will next see you at my namesake's well, south of Nablus, after you complete your mission."

Roland was puzzled. "Doctor, I did not say I was going to Nablus."

The old man chuckled. "That is why *I* am the spy and you are the squire. I have sources within the palace. This was not a chance meeting, lad. I have been waiting for you since this morning."

Jacob could see that the Turcopoles were returning and added, "Oh yes, thank you for reconsidering coming back to help us. I could see you grimace when you rode by—very normal when dealing with lepers. But you came back. Well done. Now leave."

The turcopoles arrived at the edge of the inn, not risking closer contact with the lepers. Roland waved to the lepers and walked away in deep thought of what was just said.

The men continued their wide search and reported back to Brother William that no raiders were present. The squire informed Brother William, "The lepers along the road said that seven or eight men came along the road just one hour prior to our arrival."

William nodded. "Good work. Now get some food and perform your duties. You're on first watch."

The lad continued his long, eighteen-hour day by standing first watch. After watch, he barely got to his bedroll and placed his head on his saddle before he was asleep. He slept soundly, only to rise early and face another day in the Outremer.

As on all days, he first joined in prayer, checked equipment, and tended to Sirocco. At the first opportunity, he went to the inn with water, bread, and honey, but alas, Jacob and Roger were gone.

The second day on the road was uneventful, considering what had happened on Roland's first day out of Jerusalem. The convoy arrived at Jericho late in the day.

Roland had wanted to see the city, but he saw that years of war had laid the place in ruins. Roland observed that the famous walls that "came tumbling down" were mostly gone.

The convoy route took them into the town of about 200 people living in an area about one mile from the ruins. Thinking of the story of Jericho, Roland recalled, *Most likely, they remembered Joshua's cursing any man who rebuilt the city of Jericho. Joshua threatened in the name of God that the price of building would be the loss of their firstborn sons.*

The squire had been haunted by the story Jacob had told him while he was aboard the Templar vessel enroute to the Outremer. "Many believe that Jericho is the oldest city in the world, even older than Baghdad or Cairo. The peopling of Jericho started perhaps 6,000 years ago. They were among the people that emigrated from Arabia to Syria, and Jericho was one of their most important cities in the region."

Pointing to a map laid out on the deck of the ship, Jacob had continued, "Jericho is the first city the Israelites attacked after their forty years in the desert. Our great Hebrew leader Joshua made the army march around the city walls seven times. With horns blasting, the wall came down."

Jacob had pointed out, "Our faith believes it was the power of God that made the walls come down. The city was completely destroyed, and every man, woman, child, and animal in it was killed by Joshua's army as an offering to God."

The doctor from York had continued, "Only Rahab, the prostitute, and her family were spared, because she had hidden the two spies sent by Joshua."

Roland noted a few women in the town dressed in scarlet just within the doors of some seedy hovels, looking out his way into the alley. *It appears that some of the descendants of Rahab are still working their trade.*

Doctor Jacob had informed Roland that the name Jericho-to the original occupants-meant "the moon." Roland smiled. *Jacob was right, it does look like the moon. Nothing but limestone rubble and pockmarked lands.*

The town had a small garrison of ten of the king's men, whose leader pointed out a courtyard where the convoy could stay.

The Templars pulled into the small courtyard and immediately knelt in prayer, as it was about time for the afternoon prayers, known as Nones. Then it was time to care for the animals, followed by more prayer, at Vespers.

After a meal of watery soup and bread, Roland collapsed onto a pallet in the stable only to be awakened a few hours later to stand guard.

After watching Commander Mailly's small Chartres hourglass for two trips, or about two hours, he awoke his relief and slept soundly for just two hours. Then the day's routine began at four AM with morning prayers, known as Matins. Matins were followed by checking equipment, and feeding and grooming the horses, with more prayers at five o'clock in the morning, known as Prime. This routine was then followed by a quick breakfast of porridge and fruit.

After breakfast, the thirty person convoy departed northeast, toward the Jordan River a few miles away. The convoy continued a slow pace north along the cooling river. They would, however, now be closer to enemy territory and on the axis where raiders entered the Christian lands from the east side of the Jordan River. That was the land of Saladin.

Roland was assigned to the rear guard, along with another squire and a Templar knight. Their duty was to ensure that the enemy did not perform a surprise attack on the convoy.

The young soldier and Sirocco drifted back about 200 yards from the last wagon. Roland looked over his shoulder to see two men leaving the rooms of the ladies of the night, and he pondered, *I wonder if those harlots know Sergeant Martin?*

Mailly was everywhere, it seemed. Now, riding along the convoy, he encouraged all to keep a sharp lookout for raiders from Syria. "If I see you men making idle talk and not paying attention, I will stop this convoy and have you whipped!" screamed the old Marshal.

He knew more than any living Templar, save Mesnil and Brittany that brigands would dart from Syria into the kingdom looking for easy pilgrim prey. Sometimes the brigands, in haste, would mistakenly attack Templars going north to Nazareth, Galilee, or Tiberius, or returning south.

The mule-drawn wagons were much too slow for Roland's liking. *This slow process is torture, and still another way the Templars are keeping Marie from me for their self-serving reasons.*

During the five times a day the Templars would stop to pray, the lad from Champagne found himself praying for the mules to travel faster. He caught himself mumbling in prayer, "Lord, is it possible to help these animals move faster? The best of days, this convoy travels twelve miles. Perhaps you can help Brother Mailly's eyesight. The man sees things that are not there. Lord, if we keep stopping to look behind every tree, I shall never see Marie."

At other times, Roland would pray, "Lord, these are not roads. I see why you walked to Jerusalem along the Jordan; it is more like a trail than a road in many places. Please give these animals wings to fly upon. Amen."

Brother James Mailly was a brave yet cautious leader. His many years in the Outremer had taught him to trust no one, including himself. He knew that Roland was anxious to see his Marie, but to Mailly, the consummate professional, one day was like any other day. The Brother James today was only one more day of many to serve Jesus. He gathered the men after a rest halt and mid-morning prayers, called Tierce. "We will only work the animals eight hours today. Yesterday, Squire Champagne picked our campsite two miles beyond our travel limits. Today, Brother Edward will pick the campsite near the road to Nablus if God wills it."

The savvy warrior looked down the line of monks bound to be replacements for La Feve. "I will check every water barrel and water skin to ensure they are full." He went on. "One of our number yesterday failed to refill his water skin and thus drank water designated for the mules and horses, so today this man will walk with no water for the remainder of the day."

The tough commander barked, "Come forth, Squire Champagne, and surrender your mount to Brother Arnold and enjoy the walk. Yes, take your armor, sword, and axe with you. You may just need them. If you fall behind, perhaps an Arab will have you as a slave or your head on his lance."

Roland knew better than to say anything other than, "Yes, Brother Mailly." He surrendered Sirocco to Brother Arnold and walked toward the rear of the column, cursing under his breath.

Just as the men were preparing to mount and travel on, the marshal spoke again. "Oh yes, I want you all to see the three thieves we captured that were behind that shepherd's hut, in the grove of trees, trying to steal the wagon mules last night. We found them due to the vigilance of the two brother knights of Saint Lazarus."

The men walked around the hut to see three bodies hanging from a short tree. The marshal pointed to the tree. "Today, we hung three thieves. Tomorrow, the enemy could turn the tables and it could be you swinging from the branch. Pay attention to the surrounding area; look behind every tree. Saladin pays one gold coin for a Templar's head. Saladin does not take Templar prisoners."

The old warrior swung his horse around to face the dejected squire. "Remember that, Squire Roland, as you are walking and begin to fall behind. Chaplain Baldwin, if you please, see to the squire's act of confession, as his soul needs to be purified due to some rather unkindly words just spoken and, I believe, impure thoughts. Now, all of you stay focused, or you will join the squire."

Roland's daydreaming had again cost him. *Another Templar that can read minds. Curse that life in Jerusalem.* Within one hour of marching on rocky roads and trying to avoid the many animal droppings, he had many aching muscles and bones, and much-fouled boots. Each step was sheer misery. *Lord, please send an Arab to kill me early in the day.*

Just as the lad was nearly played out, stumbling every few feet, he heard Mailly call a halt to the day's journey. The boy fell to his knees and thanked God for delivering him this day. *Merciful Jesus, I only survived the day because I knew you too walked this miserable path going to your death. Thanks for keeping me alive another day. Thanks to Brother James for calling the halt. Amen.*

The exhausted squire was glad that the troops had done about ten miles that day. Still, he had had to run many times to maintain contact with the convoy.

Several times in the long hot day, he believed he had seen a brief shadow of a horseman following him in the tree line. At other times, in a near delirium due to the lack of water and the heavy load, he had daydreamed of his times with Jacob, studying Greek mythology. *Where are Perseus's flying shoes when I need them?* He had found himself thinking, *Keep moving, Roland, or you will be vulture bait.*

As they were setting camp for the day, the old warrior commander approached the praying Roland and asked, "Did we learn anything today, Squire?"

Roland's dry mouth could not answer the question. The commander began a diatribe as he passed a water skin to the boy. "One day you're a hero, Champagne; a counselor to the grand master and cherished by the queen. The next day, you're a mindless buffoon endangering our mission, your comrades, and our animals. Oh yes, and reeking of animal dung. This is why Templar rules forbid discussing past victories or failures."

Mailly looked toward the Jordan, "In that God helped you to clear your mind and see about you more clearly; perhaps you noted that we were being followed? I saw that you ran a few times about the same time my old eyes picked out riders in the olive groves."

Roland nodded in agreement as he spoke. "Yes, Commander, it was a day of reflection and close danger, to be certain."

Mailly looked at the squire. "I promised an old friend to keep you from yourself. It is fine to rise up for promise and opportunity. I would not be the commander of the Temple and marshal of the troops in the kingdom if I just sat around being unproven, mindless, and thoughtless."

The marshal pointed to the distant clouds. "But Roland, keep your feet firmly grounded when your head is nearing the clouds. Tomorrow you shall do better. You will take care of the animals, your comrades, and yourself. In turn, you shall see your friends and Marie. Now, go wash, and scrape that dung off your boots, soldier of Christ."

The seasoned warrior James was more alert and watchful after his nearly fatal trip some months ago when he had been ambushed along the Joppa-to-Jerusalem road. Mailly explained the ambush to the lance as part of their training. After several days of travel along the Jordan, Mailly knew that they were nearing the Jazreel Valley. This too was a favored place for the enemy to appear.

The next morning, the marshal ordered, "Sergeant Hugh, take Squire Roland and scout north a few miles. We should be near the road to Nablus."

Mailly then looked into the distant hills and saw in the haze a fortress outline many miles away. He had a soldier's flashback as he remembered the many battles and sieges near that fortress, Belvoir, in his younger days.

The Belvoir fortress in the high mountains was virtually impregnable—a castle built in concentric design and strategically located on a number of primary trade and access routes. It had never fallen in a siege and was key to pinning Saladin in his lands east of the Jordan.

James ordered Hugh, "Take the battle standard and raise it before you approach any riders. Be careful; we are closing in on Hospitallers' grounds near the Fortress of Belvoir. A Hospitaller's arrow will kill you just as quick as an Arab arrow. Lastly, stay together."

The middle aged monk, Sergeant Hugh of Burgundy, was no Martin or Walter, but he was a skilled warrior with several years of experience. His leathery face told the story of many years in the desert. He acknowledged his chief with a simple "Yes, sir."

The monk then looked at the squire and commanded, "You heard the marshal, boy. Fetch a standard, and be quick about it. We ride fast. You do know how to ride fast, Squire?"

Now Roland really missed his friends as he addressed the Sergeant formally. "Yes, Sergeant, I can ride rather well." He thought, *If not for Marie and my friends at La Feve, I would give Hugh a piece of my mind. As my mother often said, "Roland, nothing good comes from Burgundy, even the wine."*

The marshal turned to the lance and announced, "We will soon be leaving this land of milk and honey to march up onto the high ground, northwest toward Belvoir and on to La Feve. Be as watchful here as you were on the road to Jerusalem."

Roland thought as he rode after Hugh, *I am not the same young squire that arrived in the Outremer some months ago.* He now had a beard, mostly blond stubble, but still it was a beard. That was not the real sign of change, however. The real changes were from the things he had seen and heard.

He turned Sirocco loose along the path next to the beautiful Jordan and let the breeze flow though his heavy chain mail. He, as he had so many times, whispered into his horse's ear, "Yes, Sirocco, I have seen the politics of the court and, alas, participated in making recommendations that may change the course of events in the Holy Land, yet yesterday, I nearly died because I was a fool. Keep me alive, Sirocco; keep me alive."

The lad continued the dialogue to his mount as if expecting a response. "Remember that day I was brushing you and we saw Fontainebleau taking his ill-gotten gains from dead pilgrims to his outside contact?"

Sirocco's ears twitched, as if he truly understood Roland. "See, boy, you understand me. Yet I am at a loss on how to turn Fontainebleau in to the grand master." He patted his horse's twitching ears. "Maybe I should do nothing, as soon, my old friend, we shall be returning to France, if I can gain the hand of Marie in marriage."

After a few miles, Hugh slowed the pace to a walk to rest the animals. As Roland came abreast of the old soldier, Hugh remarked, "I asked the Marshal not to enlist you on this journey to Nablus."

Before Champagne could say a word, Hugh said, "I know your friends Mesnil and Brittany. Mesnil is living on his reputation, as do you. Brittany is renowned for his crazy behavior. You, Champagne, are neither seasoned nor a warrior. Well, boy, that will not stop a Muslim arrow in your heart or sword down upon your neck."

Roland was going to protest, but suddenly, Sirocco's senses came alive, and he whinnied. Roland knew that something was wrong. "Sergeant, we are being watched."

Sirocco again whinnied. The pair slowed to a trot as they approached a bend in the road. Hugh had no patience for this boy. "Squire, is this more of your inexperience, or is it a display of cowardice?"

The young warrior ignored the sergeant, searching left and then right. He then noted people, perhaps pilgrims, praying in the grove. "Sergeant, look right, in that grove. It appears that some pilgrims are praying. But one is on guard about one hundred feet to the right."

The old warrior now consented to Roland's appraisal of the situation. "Boy, we best see if those are Christians in that field by the Jordan. They may be lost or unescorted and, if so, in danger." Hugh went on, "Then again, they could be bandits or Arab warriors waiting for prey. Stay directly behind me and watch that beggar in the woods." Then the sergeant turned his horse toward the band of men in the woods.

Roland trailed directly behind the sergeant, slowly removing his bow and quiver from the case that was strapped on Sirocco.

As they closed on the group, Roland could see six men dressed in Christian pilgrim garb. The squire armed his bow and made ready as he saw the guard beginning to run back toward the main group.

The squire noted, "Brother Hugh, the guard is running back to the group. I see only staffs, no weapons at all. They wear Christian pilgrim garb, as well. Two of the men appear to be praying. Do you believe them to be enemy warriors or pilgrims?"

Hugh drew his sword as they closed to about 200 feet from the band of seemingly harmless pilgrims. The sarcastic Hugh looked back toward Roland, taking his eyes off the pilgrims. "I understand, boy, that you are now the grand master's counselor and now have *all* the answers."

The sergeant shifted in his saddle to better observe the pilgrims. "Well, Champagne, yes, those Christians are praying, perhaps noon prayers, Sext? I will raise the banner to identify us. That will ensure we have no confusion."

Roland spoke up. "Brother Hugh, I would not do that. Those people could be observing Islamic noon prayer, called Dhunhr. They are clearly facing east, across the River Jordan, toward Mecca. Even the most misdirected pilgrim would know Jerusalem is southwest, towards the road they were traveling on."

Hugh turned to the pilgrims and raised the banner. When they saw the Templar banner, three of the six men picked up bows and prepared a welcome volley for the two Templar men. The guard to the right also had a bow under his cloak and was making it ready.

Roland screamed a warning to Hugh. "Down, Sergeant, get down!" Roland dove off Sirocco to his right, as an arrow missed his body by only a few inches.

The boy, who had been sleepy, achy, and rather indifferent the whole march, now came alive. He was once again Roland of Champagne, and soon to gain the respect of this band of raiders. He was now in full warrior mode.

The old sergeant lacked Roland's split-second agility and took an arrow to his body. The shaft passed though Hugh's chain mail and settled deep in his right shoulder. Though he was badly wounded, his warrior's training made him tumble to the left off his mount.

Hugh prayed to the heavens as the sharp pain almost caused him to pass out. *God Almighty, my fighting arm is useless. I am done.*

In great pain, the old warrior crawled to an olive tree to await his assured death. Hugh thought with a certainty that the boy would last but a minute. Those seven warriors would soon outmatch this crazed and inexperienced young squire. *Both of us will be lying dead in minutes,* he thought.

Hugh yelled, "Boy, save yourself. Get to the convoy, save yourself." He looked toward the young squire but saw only the boy's horse, not knowing that the squire had leapt from his mount. Hugh knew the boy from Champagne was dead. Now the old man could only watch his own martyrdom play out.

In what could be his last minutes on earth, in his near delirium, the old Templar could think of only one prayer suitable for his impending death—one that many a Templar said with his last words on this earth. "Dear Lord, for your sake we face death all day long; we are considered as sheep to be slaughtered. Amen."

Champagne was not conceding life, not just yet. "Sirocco, down!" screamed the young warrior as he rolled along the ground. The well-trained warhorse took to a kneeling position and then quickly rolled onto his side with his back toward the enemy.

Sirocco had positioned himself to form a shield for Roland to fight behind, and if required, the noble horse would take the enemies' arrows and deliver Roland from death.

The young warrior's reactions were nearly automatic. Nothing that the squire was doing in this grove on this day was random. He was a superbly trained soldier and would make the enemy pay with their lives for these trespasses.

He was calm and thought, *Don't panic. Just see the battlefield, nothing else.* As if by magic, Roland's mind deleted trees, ground cover, and even the Jordan River from his awareness. All that was present were seven men.

The boy's mind and logic continued, *Good, now where is the leader? Find him and kill him.*

He had seen this same drama many times before. His training under Mesnil and Brittany would serve him well. His close combat skills with the best warriors, perhaps the best in the world, would come forth this day.

The tall Frank cautiously looked above his saddle. The boy could see the men shedding their pilgrim attire with the small red crosses emblazoned to reveal standard Arab warrior knight garments.

Champagne patted his horse as he removed his sword from his scabbard. He set his shield on Sirocco's back to create an armored wall to protect the stallion as best he could. He took an armor-piercing arrow from the quiver and set it in the bow string. "Good boy, Sirocco. *Stay down.*"

Roland examined the landscape to his front, picking potential firing positions. He called out to Brother Hugh, who was about twenty feet away to his left, "I must take out the man on the right and the leader next. Be calm."

Hugh was in deep prayer, but the warning to be calm made him bittersweet. *This idiotic boy is telling me to be calm as we face eternal rest. He has no mind or talent for this venture.* Hugh again commanded, "Save yourself, boy. I am ordering you, save yourself. It is in God's hands now."

Without panic, the young squire quickly rose, knowing he had but a second or two before four arrows would seek him out.

He targeted the man approaching on his right as he thought, *Hugh is right; it is in God's hands.* He loosed his arrow at the moving target without watching to see if it struck home.

He quickly rolled to his left as three arrows struck hard where he had been kneeling just a few seconds before. *I counted three arrows. Either I hit him or he is a bad shot.*

Champagne seated a second arrow and whispered, "Thank you, Lord, for your favor." With that prayer of thanksgiving said, he knelt and sent another missile of death on its way toward a second archer.

He then dropped down and crawled a few yards right as two enemy arrows sped overhead and landed where he had been kneeling. "Two down, but where is the leader?" he muttered.

The multiple screams from the two wounded archers caused immediate panic among the surviving Arab warriors. Instantly, the entire band of men developed a sudden respect for the lone Christian archer with the rather large longbow. The screams soon stopped, as both archers lay dead along the banks of the River Jordan.

The lad from Champagne noted that the rearmost archer was trying to coax his comrades to stand and attack. "Aha, so there you are," he said quietly. "Not much of a leader, directing from the rear. No matter; I will kill you."

As one swordsman began to stand, Roland launched an arrow that hit the man's shield with a power and force that drove the enemy back a few feet.

The swordsman rethought his options and dived to the ground, placing his shield over his head, knowing that other arrows were coming his way. One soon crashed into his shield, cracking the metal and exposing the warrior's hand. The fear soon generated a prayer in the swordsman. "Allah, be merciful this day." He knew the next arrow would surely kill him.

Roland had learned from his previous encounters one principal maxim: Kill the leader and the others will surrender or run.

He ignored the other three swordsmen, who were hugging the olive grove floor even more closely after seeing the killing of their friends and another being beaten to the ground. Now it was the third archer's and the band's leader's turn to face death.

The boy screamed a command, *"Up, Sirocco!"* The agile Andalusian warhorse quickly knelt and then stood facing the enemy. The well-trained horse then reared up, as if to charge the enemy.

The enemy's attention was drawn toward Sirocco's display of élan. The tall bronzed leader briefly thought, *I shall have that beautiful horse in a few minutes after I kill this Templar. Mount him and die, Templar.*

The squire had readied an arrow and rolled away left from his horse during all of Sirocco's theatrics. He then courageously stood and targeted the startled leader, who had believed Roland would mount the horse and run.

Now the leader also tried to roll left to escape death. "Allah be praised," he said, as he believed he had evaded death this day.

Perhaps it was because of the many hours that Roland and Aaron had hunted rabbits, but the enemy's evasive maneuvers were to no avail this day. From fifty feet away, the squire's shot hit the archer's back squarely. It was a near-perfect center-mass hit, a certain hit to the man's heart.

The other warriors looked toward their dead leader. Roland said to them in Arabic, "لها ترديد أن تعيشيا اليوم ثم يقفوا مع يديك عقد هاياته," telling them that if they wanted to live today, they were to stand with their hands held high.

The three surviving enemies stood with hands held high, crying, "رحم، في رحم الله اسم" Mercy. In God's name, mercy!

The young Templar continued in Arabic, "You promise in Allah's name not to raise a hand in combat? If yes, drop *all* your weapons and bring your dead over here. If you break this promise, I will kill all of you. I must also attend to my wounded."

The weapons they were holding dropped immediately. The young man from France let an arrow go speeding toward one soldier. The arrow ran hard and true and struck the man in his upper chest.

"I said *all* your weapons. He was not an honorable man and died. He failed to drop a dagger he had hidden in his belt. I should kill you all as I promised."

Two more small daggers hit the ground from the remaining two prisoners. They picked up the fallen comrade's body and approached Roland.

The young man then took the medical kit from his pack that Doctor Jacob had given him and went to Hugh. The sergeant was in great pain but with some humor and humility asked, "Squire, do you ever obey orders?"

Roland looked up from the wound and said with returned humor, "Well, Sergeant, if they are wise orders, I always obey. It is the unwise orders I tend not to obey." He examined the older man's wound. "This arrow must come out, Brother Hugh, and your wound must be bound. I have had some medical practice, but I am not nearly as good with medical practice as I am with my longbow."

Hugh was an old soldier and had been wounded several times. "Yes, it must come out. Can you do it?"

Roland had watched Jacob perform this surgery many times and had learned from his instruction well. He quickly tied off Hugh's arm with the sergeant's sword belt above the wound. "This will stop the flow of blood so I can work." He then poured a small drink into a cup. "Drink this, Brother; it will take the pain from the wound."

The young squire said with some humor, "My instructor only let me sew up wounded horses. Perhaps some prayers would help. Now turn your head and pray as I take this arrow out and sew you up."

As Brother Hugh drank the cognac, Roland quickly removed the arrow. The old warrior yipped, "God have mercy on my soul. You did not let the cognac do its work, boy."

The squire turned medic cleansed the wound with Jacob's pure distilled cognac. "But it did work, Brother Hugh. You did not fight me when I removed the arrow. The wound is clean."

The lad continued his work and neatly applied twelve stitches to bind the flesh. He quickly finished the job and stood back to admire his handiwork. "Not bad, considering my last patient was a jackass. I mean the patient before you, Sergeant, was a jackass, a mule."

The old warrior looked to the lad as Roland placed linen over the wound and bound it. "With God's grace, all things are possible, boy." The repentant warrior added softly, "Even fixing an old jackass such as me."

Roland just smiled. "Let us see if I did well. When I loosen the belt, pray no blood comes out of the wound. Keep praying, Brother, keep praying."

The lad was pleased as he relaxed the belt and there was no blood. The wound did not seep but was not so tight that the old soldier would not have some mobility in his shoulder.

Roland next placed a mix of a special mold and some spider webs on the wound, telling the brother, "I covered the wound with an herb and some silk so your wound will not fester yet will heal rather quickly." *Jacob would be proud,* thought young Champagne as he made a sling for the wounded arm.

The squire poured a drink and mixed it with a potion that Jacob had made for loss of blood and for inflamed wounds. "Try not to move the arm, Brother Hugh, or the wound will open. Now drink this potion made with fruits and the bark of a special tree."

Hugh replied, "First, you were able to kill those Muslims in a fashion the likes I have never seen in my fifteen years as a soldier. Then you stitched that wound like you served in the Hospitallers. I thank God and you for my life. So they are true, the stories about you, Squire?"

The young man quickly smiled, then spoke. "Sergeant Hugh, frankly, I am never concerned what people think of me. Don't thank me. Thank Brother Mesnil and Sergeant Brittany when you arrive at La Feve for the hundreds of training hours they gave to me."

Looking down on his medical handiwork, the young soldier paid tribute to his mentors. "If we see those lepers we met on the road, thank the shorter of the two. Most important, thank Jesus, as that prayer assuredly helped my trembling hands stay steady. Now rest; I must tend to the prisoners."

Chapter Seventeen

"Jesus said to him, 'The foxes have holes and the birds of the air have nests, but the Son of Man has nowhere to lay His head.'"

Matthew 8:20

Marie and Yvette Baux found the journey from Raymond of Tripoli's stronghold at Tiberius, on the Sea of Galilee, to the 1300-year-old city of Antioch, in the Principality of Antioch, both rewarding and very tiring. This trip was the main reason for Marie's journey from her Baux homeland in southern France to the Outremer.

The long-awaited trip to Antioch had been on Marie's mind since she was a child. She wanted to see where her mother lived and was buried. They were almost there.

Today found them just completing a five-day sea journey from the bustling port of Acre to the mouth of the River Orontes and the seaport Seleucia Pieria. Then the ladies quickly transferred to a smaller river vessel for the last fifteen miles upstream to the once great city of Antioch.

From a secluded corner of the vessel reserved for her and her cousin Yvette, Marie quietly reflected upon the past many months of travel. *Is it possible this nearly endless travel for close to one year is coming to the end of my quest? We have traveled so far—sea travel from Marseilles, along the coast of the kingdoms of Italy, Sicily, and Greece, to Joppa. Nearly kidnapped in Sicily and killed in Greece. Cold, wet, hot, and hungry—all for this quest.*

Marie looked out upon the lands of the Principality of Antioch as the waves gently lapped against the hull of the small river craft making its way up the Orontes River. In a few hours, they would arrive at the city founded by Seleucus Nicator, a former general of Alexander the Great. It was in this very city that the followers of Jesus and Saint Paul had first used the word "Christians."

The approaching lands to the now small town of Antioch were truly beautiful. In the near distances, Lady Baux could see vineyards covering the hills. She saw small oaks giving shade all along the river's edge. She breathed deeply to smell the gentle fragrance of myrtle wafting in the breeze.

The young noblewoman from the Rhone looked east toward the distant mountains and proclaimed aloud, "Praise the Lord. Finally we are here, at the land of my parents. This is why I came here."

Marie smiled and thought, *I must now add Roland to my short list of why I am here. I must have him near to make my life complete.*

Then the stately woman, gently *touching* the small chained cross around her neck, continued her thoughts. *Forgive me, Lord; my lust should not be mentioned in the same thought as you. Certainly, visiting the sites where you walked and your Holy Land were always on my mind.*

She was disturbed from her thoughts by the loud screeching of her cousin. "Marie, this arid air is playing hell with my skin," complained Yvette. "I have long run out of the lavender cream that we brought from home to keep my skin from looking like leather. No wonder these women marry at fourteen. By twenty years of age, they look like old hags." Yvette stopped only to catch her breath, then continued, "This olive-oil mixture Cousin Eschiva gave us is fine for a salad, but not for my skin."

As Yvette examined how rough her skin was, she said, "Perhaps, Marie, it is the bath water. Yes, that may be it. The water is nothing like the spa water we have in France for our baths. Will they have a spa in Antioch and lotions for our skin?"

The older cousin continued without giving Marie time to answer. "Look at those shacks along the river. Most of the people here live in hovels. I will be so glad to get back to Fra—"

Marie was visibly angry with her traveling companion and cut her off mid-sentence. "*Yvette, stop.* Your constant complaining is of no value. Praise the Lord that we have such luxuries that the count has provided. The people along the way have gone out of their way to please us, yet you complain endlessly."

Lady Baux was calming, as she continued, "Yvette, my father would tell me that when he complained, my mother would chastise him. She would recall Jesus's words 'The foxes have holes and the birds of the air have nests, but the Son of Man has nowhere to lay his head.'"

Marie watched a flock of sheep grazing along the banks of the river. "If Jesus did not have these things that you discuss, they are not important."

Yvette looked down upon the deck. "I am truly sorry, Marie. Shame on me for these things I say. You are patient and good to me."

Lady Baux turned her back on her cousin and looked out at the beauty of the land, pointing to the rolling hills and mountains. "Yvette, have you not noticed that this land is much like our land in France? Look, cousin, at the beauty of this river-much like our Rhone. Stop looking inward, and look out there. Feel the beauty."

The young woman continued, "Dear cousin, our journey is nearing completion. I can now tell why my mother and father were drawn here. Look to the valley and to the mountains beyond." She continued, "I understand the attraction. Now I must know the mystery of why my mother left the beautiful land of the Rhone and Provence along with the privilege of our family name to come here."

The petite young woman turned toward her cousin and challenged her. "Dear Yvette, truly, I thank you for coming with me and sharing this journey. The price of losing your father, my beloved uncle and regent, was ample reason for you to return home, yet you did not. For that I am thankful every day."

Marie continued as she touched her cousin's shoulder. "Dear cousin, bear with me a few weeks longer; perhaps a week here. Then we shall take a pleasant sea journey to Joppa and on to Jerusalem for a few weeks. Then we will turn west to finally go back home, Yvette. Home. If all goes right, I will go to a new life that I will share with Roland."

Yvette looked mystified. "You are fixated on this squire, Marie. For what reason other than his looks should you forever speak of him? He has no money, no title, and no land. What can he do for you?"

Marie was not angry. From a conventional worldview, what her cousin said was true. In her world, women married for protection, title, children, and comfort. She smiled. "I just need his love and affection, Yvette. What need of his money, title, and lands do I have? He is a good man, brave to a fault, kind and loving. What more do I need? It is his past that concerns me, Yvette."

The young noblewoman continued, "I know that he shields something in his past. He is no more a common squire than I am a barmaid. Hopefully, when he shares his inner soul with me, I can forgive him. He is special, Yvette, like no other I have ever seen."

She again looked upon the River Orontes and gathered her thoughts, reflecting on the recent events in her trip. She was nearing the end of an uneventful 250-mile journey since landing in the Holy Land. Marie was happy for completion of this segment of the trip. *Thank God. Perhaps it is a message from God that all has gone well?*

Their travel had included a short side trip to Nazareth, the home of Jesus for nearly thirty years. Marie, being a faithful daughter of Christianity, had visited all the places where Jesus had walked and lived. She had insisted on walking from the city to the site of Jesus' first public miracle at the wedding in Cana, about seven miles northeast.

As she had walked the twisting road to Cana, she could not think about weddings without a small thought of her own wedding one day. She had always dreamed of a large court wedding.

She would bubble over at the very idea of a seven-day fest. *No, Marie, make it larger. Make it ten days of celebration, with much feasting, dancing, and, certainly, drinking.*

Often, Marie and her cousin would talk about the bonding time after the wedding known in Provence as the moon of honey, meaning one full month of romance and bonding. Marie's cheeks were getting flushed with impure thoughts, again, as ever, of Roland on the road to Cana.

She was a woman of standing, rich and from a noble house, yet she would marry down to a young man who perhaps was a commoner with no title and wealth. She, in the eyes of her peers, could not marry such a young man. Social norms and circumstances of the time forbade such things. This mattered not to Marie.

She mused, It *would be a small and very private wedding. Maybe just Yvette and Roland's friend Aaron would attend. Surely, due to Roland's lowly standing as a poor squire, it would be in a tiny chapel, and officiated by a country priest.* But she would be with Roland, and that was all that was important.

While Roland was poor, Marie was anything but poor. She did not often think about her wealth, but when she did, she simply said, "I am blessed by circumstances."

The wealth of the estates of Baux in Provence and other southern French counties had come to her upon the passing of her father. Her vast estates and the eighty villages that went with the estates were to have been administered by Marie's uncle until she was age eighteen or married. Now that her uncle had been murdered in Greece, it was up to the king of Arles and Aragon to name a regent to administer the estates, but Marie would prevail, as the Baux family had for hundreds of years.

It was her duty to keep the holdings in the name of Baux and to pass them on to her son or daughter if it should come to that. *Roland will produce many sons, I am sure. With some mentoring, I am sure he will be a good lord of the manor. He is well skilled in war, and surely no man will ever breech our walls.*

Somehow, she must convince the Holy Roman Emperor, Fredrick Barbarossa, King of Arles, and the king of Aragon, who was her feudal lord, to allow the marriage. If she did not do this, either of them could have her marriage annulled. She must face these issues, yet she was certain she would overcome these problems in time.

The young woman was a smart businesswoman. She understood what was required to make things happen—gold. She knew that gold and silver would be required in the negotiations with both king and churchmen. Fortunately, gold and silver were yielded in great quantities by her estates.

Marie was also a strong woman; her very name, Baux, meant "rock cliff" in her native tongue of Provence, named so for the principal dwelling of the family Baux. No man would take her estates or her virginity unless she allowed it. She would fight to the death to protect both, yet willingly, she would give both to Roland for his asking.

Today, she was more concerned for her cousin Yvette's life. Yvette's father had left her a small, modest estate with only a small marriage dowry. Her present dowry would be ample for a marriage to a second or third son of a local lord. Marie wanted to let Yvette know that she would offer a handsome dowry when the right man entered her cousin's life.

After the harsh words to her cousin, Yvette was now weeping alone and in distress. This seemed the right time to discuss the matter with Yvette.

Marie approached her cousin. "I know, cousin that I discuss Roland too often and that is not fair to you. One day, you will find the right suitor, and when you do, know that a dowry will not be your concern." Marie hugged her cousin and whispered in her ear, "Let me say that when you find the right man, I shall make your friendship and loyalty to me right. I will provide you a dowry. I do this out of love, not charity. You are my sister, and no less deserving of a man like Roland."

Yvette hugged her cousin in thanks and said, "Cousin Marie, you are a good person and deserve a much better cousin than I could ever be. Thank you for your generous offer. All I need to do is find that right man." Both girls laughed aloud until they were approached by the ship's master.

"Ladies, we are nearing the dock on the west bank and will be met by an escort from His Excellency, Prince Bohemund. The escort will take you to the fortress, where you and your entourage will lodge. I am to understand that you will complete your business and return to Joppa within a week?"

Marie acknowledged the master, "Thank you, Master, for your courtesy, and yes, please, arrange for us to travel to Joppa." Motioning to her escort, she opened a small chest and withdrew some funds. "Are twenty gold bezants ample for your work, Master, plus an additional forty more once we port at Joppa?"

This was a princely sum, nearly twice the normal amount for such a voyage. "Yes, Lady Baux, this is more than ample. I will await your sailing orders. Here now are the prince's men." The vessel master added, "May I offer some advice concerning the prince?"

Marie nodded. "Of course, Master." The master approached the ladies to speak in a low voice. "The prince stammers in his speech and may have another talk for him. This should not be taken as an insult."

Marie thanked the master for his advice and departed with her entourage down the ramp. She stepped onto the land of her birthplace and the homeland of her parents. She couldn't trust herself to speak. She felt like laughing and crying all at the same time.

The short journey to Bohemund's fortress along the old Roman-built road reinforced Marie's belief that here, her mother and father had found peace. She could see that in its former glory, the city had had many Greek and Roman structures, though now it was a state of ruin. These ruins had a serene look now, however, because all were slightly overgrown with flowering plants while marble and other stones seemed neatly arranged.

Yvette pointed to several ruins along the route. "Look, cousin. What magnificent temples, theatres, aqueducts, and baths these places must have been in their time. To be here as the caravans arrived with silk and spices and have your pick of the many mysteries of the east would be unreal. To see the plays in the theaters must have been exciting."

The driver pointed to a gate and informed them, "This is the very gateway that Peter came through to us, and there is his first church."

Yvette was beaming now. "You are correct, cousin; I do see why your parents came here. This is where our church was started by Saint Peter and Saint Paul."

From the river, the ladies could see the fort-crowned heights of Mount Seleucus, where the present ruling family, the Bohemund's, had placed their palace. The fortress was rather large and had many European and Muslim engineering features embedded into its structure.

During the First Crusade, the place had withstood several Christian sieges, and only from an almost miracle (with the help of a traitor) could the Christians enter its walls to conquer their Muslim occupiers. Since the year 1098, no others had breached the palace walls.

It was the prince's family who had come here in the First Crusades in 1098 to capture the city and the fortress from the Muslim invaders. Prince Bohemund was the third in his line to hold the title Prince to the Principality of Antioch.

From the coach, Marie could see the townsfolk walking about, doing business and marketing their wares. She noticed the abundance of fish, meat, fruits, and vegetables. Entire areas were set aside for spices and herbs.

The people looked healthy. Children played. All the people smiled and bowed in respect toward the passing coach draped with the banner of the House of Baux. The banner was a beautiful golden-embroidered sixteen-point star set upon a field of red.

One older lady approached the coach with a beautiful bouquet of flowers and extended them to Marie. The Lady Baux, seeing the old woman try to approach, exclaimed loudly, "Please stop. Stop now."

The coach stopped, and the older lady bowed. "The rumors are true; a Baux has returned home. Praise Jesus, you are Marie. I was your nanny. I remember you as a toddler. You have grown to be the image of your dear mother."

The older lady then clutched the red banner tightly. "I remember, like many others still here, this noble cloth with the Star of Bethlehem and symbol of your people. It hung with pride from your family home in Daphne, not far from here, south of the city."

Marie wanted to hear more. "Dear lady, may I visit you after my meeting with the prince?"

The lady pointed to a small but well-maintained cottage. "Yes, my lady Marie, I would be honored."

A short time later, the entourage was met in the great hall by Prince Bohemund and several knights. The entire entourage bowed toward the prince in respect. As they had been informed might happen, the prince did not speak.

"Good day, Lady Baux. I am William, His Excellency's sheriff of Antioch. We here in Antioch offer this prayer for all who enter our doors. 'Peace be your coming in, and joy and blessing be to those who stay here.'"

Marie bowed slightly and spoke. "We thank you for your kind words and welcome, my lord sheriff. It is truly wonderful to be here."

Lord William bowed slightly. "I welcome you on the behalf of my liege, Prince Bohemund. We have received a note from His Excellency and dear friend Raymond of Tripoli on your behalf, and we understand the nature of your visit."

Bohemund spoke up, speaking slowly and haltingly. "I knew your fa, fath, father very wwwwell, Lady Marie. He was a, a noble n-n-n-night and b-b-b-brave war, warri, warrior. He was in my ser-vice and was b-b-b-beside me in the 1172 camp, campaign in Arm, Armenia. Your mother wa, was a wonderful and very noble wom-man. I see that you fffa, favvvor her in your b-b-b-b-beauty. You are a da, daughter of Antioch. Welcome home."

Again, Marie bowed deeply. "It is truly wonderful to be here, Your Excellency. I thank you for your remembrance of my parents, as well as your warm welcome. May I introduce my cousin, Lady Yvette of Baux?"

Both the prince and sheriff bowed with pride. The prince announced, "Welcome, Lady Y-Y-Y-vette. I once met your father when he, he came for Marie. A ffffine man."

Yvette curtsied. "Thank you, Your Excellency, for your kind memories of my father. He was murdered in Greece just some months ago."

The prince crossed himself. "May he rest in p-p-p-peace, sure, surely martyred for C-C-C-Christ."

Marie touched Yvette's hand. "My cousin is a great comfort to me. We appreciate your welcome. Today, our family and people have brought you gifts from our lands in Provence as a small token of our affection for Antioch."

The young woman signaled her escort to bring in several chests, which were placed in front of the prince. "My father spoke often of your kindness and the care you took in helping me reach my relatives in Provence after my mother's murder and father's grave wounds. We thank you for that kindness."

Lady Baux opened several chests containing herbs, crafted silver jewelry, and fine clothing. "Please accept these gifts-from our people to your people."

Several men then carried a large box with several locks into the chambers. "This small token is not a repayment, but rather our form of respect and affection for Antioch," explained Marie. Twenty thousand gold bezants were then revealed.

The prince's expression said it all, but he tried to explain his joy. "These are th-th-th-thre, th-threat, th-threatening t-t-t-times, Lady, Lady Baux. Saladin is c-c-close at, at hand. Your g-g-gift to our pe, people will allow us to obtain mmmany mmmer, mmercenaries to guard our home, homeland."

The sheriff continued the prince's thanks. "We all thank you for your generous gifts. Lady Baux, we understand that you wish to see your ancestral homelands? As you know, your father has willed the land to the Knights Templar." Lord William continued, "Fortunately for all, they have an excellent steward who acts on their behalf. He maintains the estate in the highest condition and takes exceptional care of the workers. He takes special pride in keeping your mother's gravesite a place of beauty. After you rest and refresh yourself, we will escort you to the manor house tomorrow morn."

Marie was overjoyed, "I also met a woman of Antioch as we approached the fortress, who knew my parents. She lives in a small cottage near St Peter's Gate. May I have your permission to speak with her?"

William smiled. "That would most likely be my mother, Helena. Yes, she often talked about when she was your nanny. You were a special baby. She too was wounded the day the raiders came from Aleppo and attacked your home. Yes, she will tell you all, and I will personally escort you to your homelands tomorrow."

Later that evening, the prince and his knights hosted a most generous banquet in honor of Lady Baux and her cousin. The food favored the Armenian-Greek style, with much fresh fish, lamb, and chicken. Excellent wines were in abundance and of the highest quality.

After the four-hour meal, Lord William took the ladies out upon the ramparts and pointed out various places as the sun was setting. "In ancient times, Antioch was called the Queen of the East, because of the beauty of its surroundings, the importance of its commerce, and its strategic location on intersecting Silk Caravan routes between the east, west, north, and south."

The sheriff walked with the ladies to the southern wall and pointed. "There to the south are the lands of the Baux family. Your family may have deeper roots that you think in this region." When Marie and Yvette looked puzzled, William continued.

"Many believe your family came from a princely line from the Kingdom of Armenia, not many miles to the north. Many more believe that the House of Baux was formed from descendants of the House of Balthazar. Yes, the very Magi Balthazar of Matthew's Christmas story about Jesus' birth. The red banner you carry is centered on the golden sixteen-point Star of Bethlehem."

Yvette spoke up. "My father would often tell us the Christmas story and say that Balthazar was our forefather and the first 'vassal of Jesus.' That Christmas story is how we received our family motto. I took this story as a fairy tale. Perhaps it is true?"

Marie was equally mystified. "Sheriff, do you know why my father and mother came here?"

"Perhaps," said William. "In 1168, your parents arrived here on pilgrimage. Your father could see firsthand that the Muslims were at the door of Armenia and Antioch. He had observed the many hundreds of churches and shrines destroyed by Islam. He wished to stop them from destroying Christianity. So he and your mother stayed."

William walked now to the northern ramparts and pointed. "Armenia's border is just there." Then he continued, "In 1172, your father with the help of the Templars and others such as my prince, were very close to taking the Armenian throne from Mleh. He was a former Christian who embraced Islam in order to gain military help from the infidels."

The sheriff turned to Marie. "The plan was to have your father reestablish the House of Balthazar and rule Armenia. The plan to reestablish a devout Christian house, your house, in Armenia nearly worked."

Lady Baux pressed, "What failed, my lord William?"

"Your father was an excellent leader. He had Mleh penned in the capital of Sis, and nearly done. Then Mleh received reinforcements from Syria, causing your father to retreat back to Antioch. Mleh's kingdom prevailed for a few more years," stated William.

"Your father's vision of seeing a Christian king sit upon the throne did happen two years later, but in the end, Mleh had his revenge. He had assassins attack your home. They tried to kill all within. Had it not been for a Templar, all would have been killed. Still, the assassins badly wounded your father, nearly killed you, and murdered your mother and many others."

The sheriff continued, "I too was nearly orphaned in that raid. My mother was present and badly wounded. Now, go rest, and we shall see you in the morn."

Early the next morning, the sun shone brightly as the entourage left the fortress for the five-mile journey. The riders and several coaches made a quick stop to pick up William's mother, Helena.

Along the short one-hour trip to the Baux manor house, Helena made small talk with both of the Baux cousins. "Oh yes, Marie was a good baby. Then again, your mother, Anne, was the most caring woman in this horrid world I have ever seen. All those around her loved her. She was as kind to the lowest slave as to the highest-born lord, lady, gentlewoman, or gentleman."

Helena continued, "Your mother ran the household with perfection. She also directed the management of the entire manor's lands and fishing fleet. Yes, she did it all. Lord Baux was seldom at home. He was either preparing for war or campaigning. When he was here, he, too, was wonderful to our people."

Helena looked out over the lands and announced, "I have not been here since that day they nearly killed us all. Were it not for

Templar Knight Walter, of Mesnil, and his friend Martin, of Brittany, all would be dead on that hill. I still wear the scars from the sword wounds of Satan himself, the evil one named Sinan. Many here call Sinan the Old Man of the Mountain."

Marie stopped her. "Were not these the Hassassins, what the Franks call assassins? These are the men that Mleh employed?"

"Yes, Lady Baux. They kill both Christian and Muslim alike for a price. We are nearing the estate. See the vineyards, so perfectly tended," noted Lady Helena. Then she continued, "I understand Lord Gilbert gifted the estate to the Knights Templar?"

Marie agreed, "Yes, my father joined the Templars after the death of my mother and as a Templar gave the Order many of his possessions and estates, save the holdings in Provence."

Helena asked, "I was the one who chose your dear mother's gravesite, high in the vineyards. After we meet the Templar steward, we shall walk to the garden. It is a pleasant walk."

The coach halted. The entire Templar staff was present for their arrival in front of the manor house. "Good day, Lady Baux, welcome home to the Commanderie of Saint Anne, named so in honor of your mother. I am Robert LaBonte, Templar and steward. Please come in the manor house to refresh yourself."

Marie was very pleased. "The manor house is just the way I imagined it with the Provencal design. Yvette, is it not like the Grand Mas of Baux?"

Robert escorted the entourage through the property. "Lady Baux, I must admit that I am rather newly assigned to Saint Anne's. I was a steward on a small Templar property near Chatillion when I was mysteriously ordered to take charge of this wondrous estate."

LaBonte pointed to the many places where Marie's parents had walked and lived as he spoke. "At first I was concerned that the assignment was done in revenge for my mistreatment of a certain squire. Now I have come to believe it was a reward."

LaBonte pointed out the cottages where the older workers and some aged or crippled Templar monks were living. "I believe the person who assigned me here also noted my work. I have recently heard that the then-squire is now an advisor to Grand Master Ridefort in Jerusalem."

Marie was delighted. "My mother would be pleased to see the care you are providing, Robert. The manor, grounds, stock, and fields are in excellent condition."

Steward Robert was pleased. "We provide much of the foodstuff for all the northern Templar garrisons. The squire requires me to pay particular attention to La Feve; so weekly, I send them two wagons of fresh fruits and vegetables."

As she walked, Lady Baux more understood why her mother had chosen this place. With a deep-wooded valley of sparkling cool waterfalls, as well as oak, fig, olive, and bay trees, it was stunning and picturesque. "Well done, Master Robert!"

Marie's look turned serious as she asked, "Robert, you noted your coming here was the idea of a squire? By chance, would his name be Roland of Champagne?"

The steward was amazed. "Yes, Lady Baux! It *is* Roland of Champagne. I always knew the lad would amount to something; he had a certain air. He was the protégé of the great Walter of Mesnil. Now he advises the grand master. Do you know the lad?"

Both ladies began to laugh, but it was Marie who spoke first. "See, Yvette, I knew he was no common squire. He knew that this estate was willed to the Templars and had the good Steward Robert assigned here for good reasons. Roland is your benefactor, Robert."

Robert thought as he gazed upon one of the beautiful servant girls. *Roland, you truly did me a favor as this place is paradise. The Romans called the place Daphne. I understand why the sex-driven Apollo pursued the nymph Daphne if he was on this estate.*

Finally, Marie felt that her emotional journey was culminating. She requested of the entourage, "May Lady Helena and I walk toward my mother's resting place alone, please?"

The walk from the cool valley floor to the heights above the manor house was perhaps 1,000 yards. The fragrance of the myrtle and bay trees made the walk truly pleasant.

"This was Anne's favorite place to be alone," said Helena. "Your mother would come here because she could see many miles in all directions—to the sea, to the mountains, to Antioch and beyond. She said she felt closer to God here. Before the garden was here, we had a small way station so your mother could sit and rest here."

Helena stopped and pointed to a grove. "There, Marie. Robert keeps the site as a garden. I see a candle glowing."

In the distance, Marie could see the garden and the candle. Although the garden was surrounded by lush bay trees, she could clearly see the cross-mounted tomb in the center.

The sun fell upon the white tomb, causing a glow that made the place come alive. Marie's eyes swelled with tears as she said aloud, "Mother, I am here."

Upon the tomb was engraved, Countess Anne of Baux. Slightly below was Anne's favorite scripture, "*The foxes have holes and the birds of the air have nests, but the Son of Man has nowhere to lay His head.*"

Marie felt a warm whisper of air go over her body. The hairs on her arms stood on end, but it was a wonderful, loving feeling. She could feel her mother's presence in this place, not in the tomb, because she believed her mother was in heaven with her Lord. Rather, she felt that this was a special place of love for her mother.

After some time, the entourage approached and bowed in respect. The tearful Marie spoke in soft tones to the gathering. "Thank you for sharing this time with me. I thank my dear cousin Yvette for undertaking this long trek. I thank Helena for sharing her insight and her many moments with my mother. Robert, you have created a special place of peace and rest for my mother, and I so appreciate it. Thanks to all of you here for sharing this time with me. I will soon journey to France, but my heart will always be here with you."

Lady Baux asked Helena, "My mother was lonely, was she not? And yet, I sense that this place was a place of overwhelming love, not death."

Helena looked toward Marie as she replied, "Your mother was a young woman, just twenty years of age, when she was separated from her family and her beloved Provence. She felt betrayed by Gilbert, in that she had believed that after the pilgrimage, she would go home. She did her duty and accompanied her husband to their new home."

The woman pointed to a bench beyond the garden. "Let us rest upon this seat as did your mother."

Once they were seated, she continued, "At first she was angry with Lord Gilbert for breaking his promise of returning to France. Once here, she made this place and the lands into all you see today. But it was not enough. She wanted something she could not have. Your mother wanted love, children, and affection."

"Lord Gilbert was never home but for a few days each month— if that. He was in Tripoli, Jerusalem, everywhere but here."

Helena looked to Marie. "But one was here. I could tell he loved your mother from afar. His love, too, was forbidden. As with your mother, he too had taken vows. But he was here to protect your mother, share with her the simple things. Both were honorable and did not intentionally set upon the path of unfounded love. However, it happened."

Marie was dumbfounded. "They came here to this place, did they not?

Helena knew the answer because she had been Anne's confidant. "Yes, this is where they would meet in secret. It was inevitable; both were young. The knight was dashing, but he was kind and gentle. He began to complete her in ways that Gilbert had failed."

Marie looked toward her mother's tomb unhappily. "I come to this place only to find that my mother was unfaithful to my father?"

The older lady touched Marie's hand. "Your mother was never unfaithful to your father. She loved him but a short time, but she was *never* unfaithful."

Marie was confused. "Helena, you talk in riddles. You just said that my mother was never unfaithful to my father. How is that?"

"Gilbert is not your father." Helena tightened her grip on Marie's hand. "Another is, the man who truly loved your mother—the one who was there for her even in death. The one who still journeys here almost monthly to see this place. The one who gave you life and saved you, yet kept their love secret to protect you."

Marie felt dazed. "Walter, Walter of Mesnil? Why has he not said the truth to me, now that my father Gilbert has passed?"

Helena knew the answer. "Yes, Walter is your father. He wanted to ensure you were acknowledged as a Baux. Your life would be cruel otherwise. He insisted on this place being given to the Templar Order to protect the secret beyond the grave."

The older woman knew that Marie was very conflicted. "Lord Gilbert was a good man. He may have suspected, but he never said a word. He continued to love your mother and you in his way."

Helena remembered the day that Marie left Daphne well. "Once she was dead, Gilbert had his brother come for you, and he then joined the Templars. He insisted on being assigned to Mesnil's lance. Perhaps this was the penance that Walter had to live with? I can't say, as we all answer to a Higher One. Walter was never sure if Gilbert knew about the affair."

"I have two fathers, Helena," Marie said. "Both loved me. God arranged that both were close to my Roland. My father Gilbert died in the arms of Roland. I know that Gilbert loved my mother and me. His last words on earth were my mother's and my own name. I bear him love and affection," said the dutiful daughter.

Marie looked toward the tomb and the candle for the last time. "Yet I see that a candle still burns for the love of my mother, by another, my father Walter. We must go, Helena."

In the heavy woods behind the garden, perhaps one hundred yards away from the bench, was a hooded man clothed in commoner garb. He was stationed behind a tree, sharing this moment from afar. He spoke in a hushed tone as a single eye filled with tears, "My dear Marie."

The old soldier was clutching his heart as he thought, *My dearest Anne, she is so much like you, warm and loving to all, and a picture of your beauty. You would be proud as I am this day to see her complete her journey. The candle burns forever in my heart for you. One day soon, I will be with you, my dearest.*

The old warrior's wounds from that terrible day in 1172 were painful on this day. A long scar from his shoulder to his hand seemed inflamed, yet it was his very soul that was broken beyond repair.

Walter could just barely see Helena and Marie as they left the garden. His one eye was nearly blinded from a steady flow of tears, yet he could see the sunshine through the rain, for today, Walter of Mesnil knew that Helena had told Marie of his undying love for her mother. He knew he had a daughter's love for the first time.

As Marie walked from the gravesite to the gathering of the workers of the estate at the garden's edge, she again thanked Robert. "You have maintained my mother's grave with honor and love, Robert. I am very partial to the candle. Thank you so much."

The steward commented, "Yes, the mysterious candle. Frankly, Lady Baux, we don't know who does it, but each month about this time, it appears. Today's candle was lit just before we arrived."

Marie could feel that someone was looking at her. Suddenly, she turned and looked to the tree line just in time to see a figure lean down, kiss the tomb, and quickly depart from the garden.

The person retreated to a horse several hundred feet away. Marie knew. *It is my father who keeps watch and honors my mother with the candle. He was watching today, and he knows that I love him.*

Chapter Eighteen

"The thief comes only to steal and kill and destroy. I have come that they may have life, and have it to the full."

John 10:9–10

A s planned, Jacob met Roland at the well on the road to Nablus before the meeting with Lord Toron, Isabella's husband.

"Roland, after you perform the Templars' work, your life may not be worth a halfpenny. I can't help you within the castle walls, but if you get back here, I will arrange to have three or four trusted men escort you back to Jerusalem."

The old man paused before continuing. "Toron's life also may not be worth anything. Tell him that you will also have three good men that could escort him once he reaches Jacob's Well. These men will identify themselves only to you, the messenger. I must disappear since the young man now is arriving."

Roland strained his ears. "I can't hear riders approaching. Oh yes, that is why you are the spy and I am the messenger."

Jacob smiled and quickly melted into the gathering of pilgrims visiting the well. One minute he was there, and the next minute he was gone, as if by magic.

Four horsemen approached the well seconds later.

The squire shook his head. *How does that old fox do that?*

The lead rider, a young man of Roland's age, approached in a rather impertinent manner. "So, Templar, why must we meet in such a clandestine manner rather than at the fortress? Where is this message you say is so important? Making me appear at Jacob's Well is a cover to what means I have no knowledge," demanded Humphrey of Toron.

"My lord Humphrey, I am very familiar with the life within a castle. They have many eyes, to see all, and even more ears to hear all.

Thus, I had the sergeant deliver my note to you so we might meet in private," stated Roland.

He motioned, saying, "Come this way, my lord. A wise man once informed me that if you hide something in plain sight, it will not be found. Perhaps that very wise man is eying us as we speak. I am Roland of Champagne. I was sent by Grand Master Gerald Ridefort, with a message from Prince Reynald. This shed will give us some privacy. Please enter, sir."

The squire continued as they entered the building, "I hid the message here in the loft. Ah, here it is. You may open it."

The young lord of Toron read the document and looked up. "Why does Reynald want my wife, Isabella, to take the throne?" he asked.

Champagne was surprised. "I was present in the room with Reynald, Sibylla, Ridefort, and the entire lot of them. That was *not* what was decided. It appears that treason may be in the winds. May I read the document?"

Roland shook his head in disbelief as he read the note "I risk my very ass to deliver a traitor's message. Will this kingdom never unite to save itself? Well, sir, this should make your masters here very happy. Why you or Count Raymond would trust that man for one second, I have no way of knowing."

The young squire explained to the lord of Toron what had happened since the decision to crown Sibylla. "The Lord Joscelin has secured the coastal cities to the north under his control. The patriarch Heraclius has taken control of the Church in the kingdom and sent word to the priests and bishops that if anyone other than Sibylla is crowned, it is unacceptable and it *will* result in the excommunication of any person who follows your wife. The constable Amalric Lusignan has used his troops to secure the city of Jerusalem along with the Templar Knights."

Roland looked at Humphrey and continued, "I believe your stepfather may be planning a way that he can't lose. He has his troops in Jerusalem to play victor for whatever house wins. The princess Sibylla and Guy's people hold the seaports, control the city of Jerusalem, and control the clergy of the kingdom. And Raymond and his legions control the center and Tripoli, so he can't win without Saladin's support."

The squire-turned-herald continued, "I was instructed to present a second message requesting the presence of Raymond and the high court in attending the coronation of the queen on Saturday next."

Champagne offered, "My lord Toron, let us start from the beginning. In order for your wife to take the throne, she must divorce you. Would you submit to a divorce and watch another man from Europe mount the throne but perhaps also your wife? Oh yes, let me explain. They will bring in a man close to the throne of England or France to leverage the contact with the royalty of Europe. Well, that man could very well be me."

Humphrey was confused. "You, a squire, set upon the throne of Jerusalem? That is impossible."

Roland shook his head. "This is complicated, my friend. Pay no attention to this worn Templar garb. I am from the House of Champagne; my brother is Count Henry. My mother is Princess Maria Carpet of France. My grandmother is Queen Eleanor of Aquitaine. Therefore, my uncles include King Philip of France, King Alfonso of Aragon, oh yes, and my favorite uncle, Count Richard of Normandy, soon to be the king of England."

Young Champagne was but two years younger than Humphrey, so it was now a conversation between two young men on a much more level playing field. "I talk plainly to you, sir. I am in love with another, yet to save Jesus' homeland from the infidel, I would take your wife no matter how ugly she is."

Now Humphrey became angry and laid his hand on his sword. "Silence your insults, sir, or I will cut you from belly to throat. My wife is fourteen, beautiful, and has a body of perfection."

Roland shook his head. "God, worse still. So I must produce a son with a fourteen-year-old-girl and be happy with the act? Perhaps I may be required to produce many sons with a beautiful woman. This only gets better, my lord Toron.

"Let us look down the road to the near future," said Champagne. "So this is how this may work. First, civil war could occur between Tripoli and his members on the high court against many of the country's princes, barons, and Templars, and the sister of the king."

Roland looked into Humphrey's eyes. "Waiting for this act to play out on the stage is Saladin. He will have no problem taking the weakened kingdom and principalities. You, most likely, will be dead, working for Tripoli, or die in combat against overwhelming odds."

Roland walked to the door and looked out to ensure that no one was listening before he continued. "Humphrey, you don't want to divorce your wife or step aside and watch me produce sons with her. Does she want a divorce? Or to bed someone else? It could be even worse—she could end up with my unmarried brother, Henry. At least she would not have children, for I don't believe he knows how," he chuckled.

Toron was looking upon Roland more as a confidant now than an adversary. "What must we do, Champagne? What must we do? Isabella does not want to be queen. She knows that the Templars are in league with her half-sister, as are the Church and many of the barons and princes."

"This will not be easy, my lord Humphrey. You must assure yourself that your wife will be loyal to you. If the answer to that is yes, you must go to Jerusalem and, in front of all the court, claim Sibylla as your sovereign. Can you find a safe haven for Isabella until her sister can guarantee her safety?"

"Yes, I can do that. I have my bodyguards, who are loyal to me. I will use a pretense of hunting tomorrow, and we will go to a safe haven. Then I will go to Jerusalem."

Roland was quick with his answer. "Good! I will also have several knights accompany you as an escort. Meet me here at dawn."

Toron trusted Roland. "We will meet you at dawn here. Thank you, Roland, for your service."

"Don't thank me. I just want out of this place with a certain Marie of Baux, and pray for all of you that all ends well. Like Apostle John said, 'The thief comes only to steal and kill and destroy. I have come that they may have life, and have it to the full,'" added the squire.

Toron smiled. "I don't judge you to be a thief. I know this Lady Baux and her cousin Yvette. Both are beautiful women. I understand that they are in Antioch and will return soon to Joppa."

Humphrey looked out a small window toward the castle a few miles away. "Count Raymond and Baron Ibelin are within the castle. Wait several hours until we are clear of the Ibelin lands before you present the invitation," said the young lord of Toron.

Young Champagne's simple life was quickly disappearing before his very eyes. "I will wait until the end of the day tomorrow, as that is when they expect you to be back from your hunting trip. Let us pray that you and Isabella are not too late to stop the civil war."

"I leave now to prepare. I also pray that by Isabella coming out for her sister, we can prevent civil war," noted Humphrey.

Minutes after Toron had left the building, Roland heard a knock at the shed door. " ίναι σας συνεδρίαση κατά τη διάρκεια?" a voice asked if the meeting was over. Roland smiled and responded, "Σας δεν χτυπάει καμπάνα του λεπρός σα ," "You did not ring your leper's bell."

Jacob, once again in his leper attire, laughed as he entered. "So, young Toron has departed. Did you convince him to not take part in this drama?"

Roland smiled. "Perhaps. Somehow, I must get word to Ridefort that Toron rejects the crown and is coming in under safe conduct to swear fealty. He also needs to know that Reynald may be playing both sides, as he wrote a note encouraging Toron to support his wife's claim for the crown."

The squire's expression turned rather stern. "Once Lord Toron is safely on his way, I have the duty to inform the high court that they are invited to the coronation. This is truly one time I pray they don't kill the messenger."

The old doctor agreed. "I see you still have some humor within you. I can help. I will have a message delivered to the grand master in perhaps two, no more than three, hours."

The squire laughed. "Sixty miles in two or three hours? Impossible! Have you learned to fly, dear doctor?"

Jacob walked to the door and said, "No, I have not learned to fly—yet. Come here, see my three friends that do."

Both men walked to a small wagon, where Jacob raised a canvas tarp. Three small pigeons were secured there in cages. "I have not learned to fly, but my three friends have much experience in the skill. We shall use Pegasus; he is very fast and knows the route to Jerusalem best."

The old man encoded a note and placed it in a small capsule on the bird's leg. "Off with you, boy." The bird made one turn and got his bearings, and straight to the Holy City he flew.

The doctor-turned-spy continued, "Brother Roger and I will go to Princess Isabella's safe house near Bethlehem and obtain some additional men to guard her."

Champagne was puzzled. "I did not mention the safe house near Bethlehem because I did not know its location. How did you know the location?"

"Boy, that is why I am the spy and you are the messenger. Go back south along the Jerusalem Road, perhaps two miles. You will find an inn with a red door. Announce yourself as the messenger. In reply, they will say, 'Hurry, messenger.' The people within will feed you and the sergeant, and board your horses. The men–at-arms tomorrow will also use the same password. Now go."

"Why not identify me as 'the warrior,' maybe the 'tall blonde warrior'? Even 'the Templar' would make do. No, you would rather have me known as 'the messenger'? Why does the grand master take me as a counselor and you think of me as the messenger?" challenged the squire.

The old man just smiled. "I will explain one day, Roland. Now go, foolish boy."

Chapter Nineteen

"Suddenly a light from heaven flashed around him. He fell to the ground and heard a voice say to him, 'Saul, Saul, why do you persecute me?' 'Who are you, Lord?' Saul asked. 'I am Jesus, whom you are persecuting,' he replied. 'Now get up and go into the city, and you will be told what you must do.'"

Acts 9:3—9

Roland's host prepared a bath and provided new clothing befitting a royal herald delivering such an important message that would bring a kingdom to its knees. This was the first time in nearly two years that Roland had dressed in attire other than the poorly made Templar garb.

He bathed in a large tub of warm, scented water for the first time since leaving Troyes two years before. He dried himself slowly, noting that his legs were perhaps more muscular then a year ago. Roland thought that perhaps it was all the walking he'd done of late, none of it pleasurable.

His host had laid a Damascus-glass mirror next to the large wooden tub. The young man picked it up and looked into the mirror (also forbidden by Templar rules) for the first time in nearly two years.

He laid the mirror upright and walked backward to see an image of his entire body. What Roland saw was a tall, naked, tanned man who looked much older than he expected. His hair was blonder than he remembered, because of the sun bleaching it. His face now had a Templar's beard, along with a rather tired look.

Then the young man looked down upon his hands and arms to see desert-worn skin where just months before, supple skin had covered his bones.

He was truly disappointed in what he saw. He was no longer the boy who had left Troyes. He had grown into manhood and had not even known it. *My God, Roland! Is this the price you must pay for your past sins? Perhaps Marie will take one look at me and flee in disgust.*

His thoughts continued as he gazed into the mirror. He trimmed his beard in preparation of shaving his face clean. *Why should aging concern me? In a few hours, I could be dead. Anyone at Raymond's court could kill me in rage after I pass along my message. I surely will see the axe if any find out that I assisted in Humphrey's and Isabella's escape.*

The few-mile ride to Baron Ibelin's castle in the late afternoon seemed painfully slow. Sirocco seemed to slowly pace up the hill toward the stronghold. "Well, boy, at least you are not getting old and beat-up like I am," complained Roland.

No sooner had the squire said those words that he was approached by twenty or so mounted knights galloping and looking hurried. "Well, boy, here we go to the axe man."

Surprisingly, the mob of men slipped by him, heading toward Jerusalem on another mission. "Ah, Sirocco, the count has come to the realization that young Humphrey and Isabella perhaps did not go hunting. Beyond that grove of fig trees lies the castle. Here we go, Sirocco."

Count Raymond of Tripoli was a stern man today. He and several others were pacing in the great hall when Roland was admitted. Tripoli's voice barked, "We are busy here. What matter do you bring to this court, Templar herald?"

"Roland of Champagne, Your Excellency. I bring you word from Princess Sibylla and the court of Jerusalem."

Tripoli barked, "I am the regent of this kingdom, and thus *I* am the court of Jerusalem."

Roland bowed. "I am but the messenger, sir. With all due respect, the message I carry is but a waste of your valued time and of the most valued time of the members of the high court. I beg your leave."

A tall man of between forty-five and fifty years of age approached the squire. "Is your father Count Henry? If so, my family knew him well from days gone by."

Young Champagne bowed. "Good day, my lord. Yes, I am Henry's third son, Roland. My father has passed on to his heavenly reward, my lord. My brother Henry the Younger now rules Champagne. Today, I am in the service of the Templars and Princess Sibylla, but soon after this, I should once again be in France."

"I am Baron Balian Ibelin of Nablus. This is my domain and home." He looked toward Count Raymond with a concerned look then returned to Roland with a broad smile. "Your father was a good man and defended the Cross. You are welcome here and have my protection, Champagne. This is my brother, Baron Baldwin of Ramla, and this young man is his son, Thomas."

Now Raymond entered the conversation. "My apologies, Lord Roland. My wife's cousins speak highly of you, and it appears they owe you their lives. But I understand that you are now indentured to the Templars and owe them fealty?"

The messenger bowed. "Your Excellency, I owe certain Templars my sword arm and my deepest respect and admiration, but to none here in this kingdom do I owe fealty, including the Templars. Once I deliver this message, I will seek Lady Baux and recover to France."

Baron Balian replied, "Then we need not interrupt your journey. Deliver your message, herald."

Roland took the message from within his tunic. "Greetings. So says the council and the princess Sibylla to the high court. The high court is cordially invited to attend the coronation of Her Royal Princess Sibylla, Daughter of Amalric, House of Anjou, in the presence of Christ in the Church of the Holy Sepulcher, Saturday hence, at the sounding of the bells at None." Roland came forward and placed the document in the hands of Raymond.

Raymond screamed, *Treason!* They all broke their promise to Baldwin on his very deathbed. They swore to allow the pope and kings of England, France, and the Holy Roman Empire to decide who will marry the legitimate princess of the kingdom. This document will stand as her death warrant at her trial."

Tripoli smirked and focused on Balian, "What say you, Balian?"

Balian and his brother, Baldwin, stood shoulder to shoulder. Balian said, "I carried the young King Baldwin on my shoulders and into the church on his coronation because even then he was ill. When he died, I carried his small coffin to the grave. My family swore a holy oath on the king's deathbed to do his will. My stepdaughter Isabella is the rightful heir to the throne. No, the Ibelin family will stand with you, Count Raymond."

"Where is the princess Isabella? She and her husband need to be here. Humphrey must agree to divorce Isabella. She in turn must marry another, more powerful, husband from Europe."

Raymond looked toward the young messenger. "Perhaps our herald from the House of Champagne will be chosen for marriage to Isabella by his uncles Philip and Richard?"

Roland smiled. "A decision, as you point out, Excellency, made by others. However, I am sure that my brother Count Henry will leap at the opportunity. He would make a better king than I. He has been preparing for the role for many years now. I myself have been preparing for a much lower station in life, apparently as a messenger."

Everyone in the hall laughed out loud. Baron Balian pointed to the door. "Tell your Templar master that we will not attend this farce, as we are too busy sharpening our swords. We have much work to do preparing for war, herald. You are excused, Lord Roland. Two of my men will escort you to Jerusalem."

Roland bowed and withdrew, mumbling to himself, "I am alive—still; now on to Jerusalem to report to the grand master, then to Joppa to find Marie and Yvette. By now, Aaron has received my note telling him to come to Jerusalem. We will all be in France in sixty days. A marriage in the Cathedral of Troyes by spring, and we'll be living in sunny Provence next summer. Next, I will meet the escort on Damascus Road, near the Well of Jacob."

The short ride to the well was filled mostly with thoughts and fantasies of Marie. Roland failed to note the four riders coming from the east who rode Arabian stallions, horses hardly ridden by Franks. Sirocco could sense the stallions' movements and other challenges as they approached the well. He whinnied in response, and his ears twitched.

Roland's mind was not even in the Outremer, but in Provence with Marie. Consequently, he missed Sirocco's cues. Worse, once he picked up Jacob's escorts, he decided he would dismiss Balian's men. It would be a two-day journey to Jerusalem, and then this bad dream would be over.

The riders on the Arabian horses turned and rode the short distance to the shed, perhaps eighty yards from the well. Roland and his two escorts approached. Roland shouted, "I am the messenger."

Someone then shrieked, "Blasphemer, there is only one messenger, and Muhammad is his name."

Before Roland could draw his sword, several arrows struck his two escorts, and they both tumbled to the ground dead. Roland was struck from behind as if he was hit by lighting, and he too tumbled to the ground on the road to Damascus.

His vision was blurry as two of the men quickly dragged him into the shed. He was tossed onto the dirt floor of the shed to join the bodies of four other dead men, all with their throats cut from ear to ear. They were to have been his escorts.

Roland could barely see the men in the darkened shed with only one lighted candle burning. He instinctively rubbed his head, surprised to feel a large bump where his attacker had hit him hard with the pommel of a sword. He also felt a trickle of blood flowing down his back. He could make out the ghostly forms of seven men gathered around him.

One man commanded in Frankish, "Kill him *now*. It has taken me nearly two years to come to this day; now kill him."

That voice was familiar to Roland, yet in his dazed state, he was not sure that any of this drama was real. Perhaps he was dreaming? *Yes, that's it; I am dreaming.*

Two men with drawn daggers approached the boy to do the man's bidding. Two other men grabbed the weakened squire and turned his head so his throat was fully exposed in the pale light.

Roland tried to resist, but it was no good. His body just would not answer the commands from his swelling head. He would soon join the other four men with cut throats.

Then another voice, softer in tone, yet also commanding, spoke. "Stop! Is this the man you wished dead? Is this Roland?"

The man who had ordered the execution nearly screamed, "What are you doing? Saladin ordered his execution. I have been trying to kill him for nearly two years. You dare stop them? Then I will do it. I care not if he sees the man who will send him on to hell. Give me that dagger."

Roland summoned all the remaining strength in his body to break the hold of the two men. His body arched just enough to look his approaching killer directly in the eyes.

In that darkened room, he gazed upon a man he had trusted, a man who had taught him life skills, and a man he never would have believed wanted him dead.

Roland refocused his eyes. *Perhaps the injury is causing me to see poorly?* No, it *was* his friend fast approaching. The man with the familiar voice was the very person who would personally end the squire's life.

The young man from Champagne yelled, "You coward, you paid hired murderers to kill me. Let me stand like a man, and you kill me like a man."

Again, the soft-spoken man ordered,"No one will kill this man until he sees Salah-al-din-Yusuf-ibn-Ayyub. I, ibn-Athir, represent the sultan, and you, Frank, will do my bidding. Now bind him and place a piece of cloth over his eyes and mouth. Place him in the wagon. We must get across the River Jordan soon, before his friends note his absence. Do it *now. Now.*"

Roland could not fully see his savior's face, for the man was behind him, yet he knew this man too. *Where do I know this man's voice from? Why did he not let that coward kill me?*

Bound and concealed, Roland was placed in the bed of a wagon and whisked off east on the Damascus Road.

In some hours, Roland heard the water splash under the wagon as they crossed the Jordan River. They must be at Jacob's Crossing. Then he drifted off to sleep, only to hear Arabic being spoken a short time later.

The prisoner was very weak from his concussion. He drifted in and out of a deep sleep. He was not sure how long he slept, but somehow, he had been transferred to a rather nice coach along the road. In the new coach, he awoke to see several older men placing bandages on his head. Then, he drifted off into sleep.

Sometimes he awoke to find a tasty juice being spooned into his mouth by a young woman with a thin veil over her face. He tried to focus his eyes to better see his attendant, only to see two women, then a single woman again, until he drifted off to sleep.

Then, as if by a miracle, he awoke in a fine bed with an older man holding his hand. The man spoke to him in broken Frankish. "Ah, I believe you are fully back with us. The assassin hit you rather hard and caused a nasty cut on your head. I will have two of the guards assist you in walking. The doctor says that we must get you up and moving."

Roland scanned the room. He could hear Arabic voices. "I know you, but where did we meet?"

The man smiled. "Perhaps I have a face that does not make an impression. Perhaps it was the hard hit on your head. We must make your mind work. It is a good practice, said the doctor. Think back some months in Jerusalem.

Now the squire remembered. "Yes, the alleyway in Jerusalem, the nearly captured spy. You gave me your name and you said if I needed a friend, ask for Ali-ibn-Athir. Now I remember-you are Ali-ibn-Athir."

The man bowed. "Ali-ibn-Athir at your service, young Champagne. Little did I know that I would owe my life to a man that himself is a wanted man by my sultan. It would be right and just that I give you back your life as you gave me mine that day in Jerusalem."

Ali grimaced. "Sadly, you now know who our main contact is, and I can't let you go. I must take you to the man you call Saladin, and he will decide your fate. I will do all in my power to save you. Now you must take nourishment, then walk and perhaps a bath. I will come back in some time to see how you are progressing."

Alone in the room, Roland immediately thought of escaping. He slowly made his way to a window and gazed out onto a busy courtyard. He could see Muslim knights and turbaned men, women, and children all moving about. *My God, I am in the middle of Damascus in Saladin's palace!*

Then he hobbled back to bed because the few feet he had gone had made him wobbly. For now, he understood that his fate was sealed.

The door opened, and a most beautiful lady entered. She was petite, with hazel eyes and light brown hair somewhat covered by an ornate head piece. Yes, she was the one who had spoon-fed him juice, water, and crushed fruit.

"Good day, Lord Champagne. I am Sophia, slave of Ali-ibn-Athir. You must lie down and rest. You must not walk. You may only stand when someone assists you."

Roland did feel very weak. "I remember you from my dream. You gave me juice when I was barely alive. Thank you for taking such good care of me. I believe I am in the sultan's palace?"

The young women confirmed Roland's belief. "Yes, you are a guest of the great sultan of Damascus and Cairo. Lord Ali is one of the sultan's closest friends since childhood. All know of your courage when you saved Lord Ali in Jerusalem. Lord Ali is a good man."

Roland could hear a multitude of doors opening in the hallway outside his door. He could hear people running about, and commands being given. Then suddenly, his door opened to reveal four very large men in full armor approaching his bed.

Sophia ran into a corner of the room, where she prostrated herself upon the floor, covering her eyes.

"It is over Lord Roland. May Allah have mercy on you."

Too weak to do anything else Roland closed his eyes to await his fate.

"Roland, are you awake?" inquired Ali. Roland opened his eyes to see Ali. Standing next to him was a smallish man flanked by two giant guards.

The smaller man said in rather good Frankish, "Lay still, Lord Roland. God is indeed merciful, as he has granted your life. I wanted to ensure that my people were taking care of you. My apologies for not introducing myself; I am Salah-al-din-Yusuf-ibn-Ayyub. Your people call me Saladin, among other unkind names."

Champagne immediately tried to get out of the bed, but one of the large men put his hand up. "No, move *only* when Salah-al-din-Yusuf-ibn-Ayyub tells you to move!" demanded Mustafa al-din Gökböri, Saladin's most trusted and experienced subordinate.

Saladin corrected his subordinate. "Mustafa, our guest does not know our protocol. He was trying to be respectful and remove himself from the bed."

The small man continued, "Please stay still, Lord Roland. I wanted to thank you for saving my friend's life. He is a wonderful friend, scribe, and historian. Alas, he is not much good at spying."

Ali, with humor, added, "My sultan, you are too kind. I make a terrible spy."

Mustafa was not amused and spoke in Arabic, "إنه هو العدو، وقد هنا حيث. إنا لن بين راحمين المرحم من العدية بحياة العدو أحد هنا أوده بحياة اذا هذا. إنا لن والدهه هذا من هتلكائع. هل. فدية من الطب. امبر نحن فدية من تجعل ال على الحياة اورفو الأثري؟" Roland understood him to have said, "He is the enemy, his father fought us, and this one has killed many of our warriors. So he did save Ali's life. That does not make him a hero. Perhaps we can ransom him. His family is wealthy?"

Roland requested to speak by saying, "صاحب السمو، وقد انا تنشأ تكون جزء من هذا القرار؟ أو هل نجلس انه يعانني إهاناات مصطفى في اللورد في

تمصلا؟" Your Highness, may I arise and be a part of this decision? Or do I sit here and suffer Lord Mustafa's insults in silence?

Saladin was amazed. "If you feel comfortable, you may arise. You know our language?"

The young man, still wobbly, arose and bowed to Saladin. "Highness, I speak some of your language, not well, but I try."

The lad now turned his bandaged head toward Lord Mustafa. "Now I am standing. Kill me like a man if you must, for I will not be ransomed and would die first."

The small man spoke. "Enough, all here. Lord Roland, my apology for Mustafa's rude remarks. He speaks each day more rudely like the Frank Raynaud. He needs to beg for Allah's forgiveness."

Saladin motioned to Ali. "I have asked my dear friend Ali to take you to his home in Duma to the north as our guest. I understand that you have knowledge of my spy's identity?"

The squire reacted swiftly by sincerely announcing, "Your Highness, Lord Ali has saved my life and has been very kind to me. For this I thank him. I see why he is your counselor."

Roland's expression now turned rather sour. "Yes, I know the identity of the man who is your spy. He has attempted to kill me many times. To get to me, he has perhaps killed hundreds of innocent people. When I am able, I will kill him. Please note, Your Excellency, I did not say *if* I am able."

Saladin understood. "The life of a traitor and spy is not an easy one, Roland. However, I have an important use for this man. For this reason, I can't release you now, even in return for my longtime friend Ali's life. Perhaps in some months we may release you. I need your word of honor that you will not attempt to escape."

Roland's somber expression filled his face because he knew the next words he uttered may be his death warrant. "It is my duty to escape. It would be easy to lie and tell you that I would not try. I will not break my word of honor to you."

The sultan smiled. "Roland, you do know that your priests tell all Christians that it is no sin at all to break your word of honor to a Muslim?"

Champagne stood as straight and proud as his feeble body would allow. "Your Highness, when I give my word to friend or foe, I keep my oath. I have someone higher to answer to than a priest."

Saladin again smiled. "So you were blinded on the road to Damascus like the Christian Apostle Paul, and now you 'see.' It is said in your Bible that the great prophet Jesus, blessings on his name, told Paul that in Damascus he would find answers and wisdom. Perhaps, like Paul, you will find answers here to your journey, Lord Roland of Champagne."

The sultan of Damascus once again smiled as he turned to his friends. "Ali and Mustafa, perhaps we have found the honest Christian, like my friend King Baldwin, that we are looking for? His name means 'famous' in Arabic and in Frankish. It matches him well."

The sultan turned to Roland and said, "Yes, I knew you would tell me about your duty to escape, so we chose Duma. Many miles in the raw desert and without a horse bring certain death to a person walking. Ali shall watch you closely when you are his guest. Here, let me get some water for you."

The sultan of hundreds of thousands of people offered Roland chilled water. "I have the ice brought from the lands of the Tartars."

Roland was thirsty and had not tasted cool water in many months. "Thank you, it is very refreshing."

The wise sultan continued, "It is our custom that when you are offered water or food, you are under the protection of the person who offered the hospitality."

Many of Saladin's generals, knights, and emirs were in the entourage because they wanted to see this warrior of many stories. He turned to the gathering and announced, "All here and in this kingdom note my hand. I, Salah-al-din-Yusuf-ibn-Ayyub, offered this man, El-Cid-Femes-ibn-Champagne, the water of life. He enjoys *my* hospitality and protection. Remember this decree on the pain of death. Ali, ensure that all my lands are informed."

Saladin turned back to Roland. " El-Cid-Femes, I shall have my personal doctor look at you today, and he will ensure you are fit for travel. I am sure we shall meet again, El-Cid-Femes. Peace be on you, and the mercy and blessings of Allah, praise his Name."

Roland bowed toward the small man as he replied, "Thank you for your kindness, sir. May God give you blessings, and peace be to you, Your Highness."

Chapter Twenty

"Daughters of kings are your lovely wives; a princess arrayed in Ophir's gold, comes to stand at your right hand. Listen, my daughter, and understand; pay me careful heed."

Psalm 45: 9–10

The timid and rather mousy clerk approached Patriarch Heraclius. "It is done, my lord Patriarch. The divorce decree has been read in the churches on the past three Sundays. The divorce between Princess Sibylla and Baron Lusignan is final. You may crown the princess."

The patriarch knew that all that was between him and the axe was a thin gold chain with a large cross with a ruby in the center, but his office would not save him if he got on the losing end of this entire venture.

If he failed to crown Sibylla, her supporter would kill him and find another bishop to perform the task. If he did crown Sibylla and she then lost support, Count Raymond would have his head when they crowned Isabella.

The worried patriarch wanted information before he went to the Church of the Holy Sepulcher to conduct the coronation. "What word have we received from Nablus? Have Princess Isabella and her husband come forth to accept the coronation of her sister? Don't just stand there, man, say something!"

Gerald, the grand master of the Temple, entered the room with a small document in his hands. "A trusted agent gave me this message just minutes ago, Patriarch Heraclius. Humphrey and Isabella agreed that Sibylla should rule. Humphrey should be here tomorrow to confer with Sibylla."

Ridefort, now beaming, was rather proud of his handiwork. "It is nearly done, Heraclius. Let us gather the royal regalia and prepare for the coronation. I have my key to the royal treasury box. The grand master of the Hospitallers, Roger of the Moulins, should be here in moments with his key. All we need now is your key, Heraclius, to open the box and access the regalia."

Roger soon entered the room to witness Gerald turning the key in the massive box. Ridefort could see the large tumblers open the second lock. The patriarch had already opened the first lock.

Ridefort looked to his colleague, dressed in the black of the Hospitallers order. "You have the honor, Roger, of opening the third and final lock. Perhaps history will remember this moment when you made Sibylla the queen of Jerusalem."

Roger pulled out the slender key from his tunic. "You two have forgotten your oath to Baldwin. His wish was that only the kings of England, France, and the Holy Roman Empire, with counsel from His Holiness the Pope, would elect the king of Jerusalem. I have not forgotten my oath. I will have nothing to do with this."

Ridefort was quick to respond, "While we wait without a king, you want the traitor Raymond the regent, to play king for a year or longer?"

Roger remained silent, but Gerald did not. "Perhaps, Brother Roger, we should wait until Tripoli turns the kingdom over to Saladin and the infidels?"

Ridefort, gesturing to a map of the kingdom, pointed toward the River Jordan and the Hospitallers' stronghold at Belvoir. "Your men in Belvoir guarding the routes into Galilee give you the same intelligence as my men at La Feve do. Raymond is allowing Saladin unfettered access to his lands. This is the man you want to trust with the Holy Land?"

Roger turned and quickly walked to the open window over the courtyard. There, he tossed the key into the crowd. "My hands are clean of this matter." He quickly walked to the door and left.

Both Ridefort and Heraclius ran to the window, only to see a huge gathering of townspeople awaiting Princess Sibylla's entrance into the church. No key would be found in this mob.

"That idiot," cried the patriarch. "Now we must cancel the coronation until we get this box open. The people will take this sign as a bad omen from God."

Ridefort was far from pleased. "I will make Moulins pay for this treachery." For several minutes, every curse was raised by Gerald for Moulins' deceit.

Finally, Ridefort walked to the box. "We must think this through." The now calm Templar grand master continued, "We shall never find that key in this crowd. If we force the issue, we may have a riot in the streets between the two factions."

In the corner was his second-in-command, Mailly, who spoke. "I have over 200 knights ready and positioned. If need be, we can clear the streets. This is a sad day, as we may kill our own people and supporters. This is not good, Heraclius. What is your order, Grand Master?"

As the leaders of Jerusalem were in a heated discussion, a small redheaded young man in the courtyard had observed Roger approach the window and toss a small object into the crowd. Many in the crowd had thought that the noble had tossed coins to them, so they had run to the site.

As luck would have it Squire Aaron was approaching the palace at that moment. Keeping a sharp eye and always interested in such things as money being thrown from a window at festival times, the young man in Templar garb approached the site where the object landed. He noted four or five people looking for the item tossed, bobbing along the ground like barnyard chickens in search of grain.

The boy took out a silver coin and was ready to offer a reward for the object but then thought better of it. *If I offer a reward, the holder of the object may think the item is of greater value. No, let me think like the old days in Paris and see if my hand is still quicker than the eye.* "It is good that one of you found the small treasure," he announced, "but be cautioned. Many thieves are also in the crowd, so guard it carefully," he said to the crowd.

The young man noted that one man clutched his two hands closer together. *There you are, my friend,* he thought. *Hold tight, now go to the side of the building to better examine your treasure.*

It was if the man was receiving commands from the redhead. He did surely walk to the side of the building to have a closer look at what he had picked up. It was then that the man felt a long dagger at his back.

The robber warned, "Don't turn if you value your life, friend. Now open your hand. Ah, a key. Not much to lose your life over. Now I will do a magic trick."

The man felt an ever-so-soft touch upon his hand. The old beaten key was gone, and in its place was a newly minted silver coin. For the man, it was worth ten days of wages. He no longer felt the point of a dagger in his back. He quickly turned, only to see people behind him picking up small coins and blocking his way. The robber, or perhaps magician, was gone. What kind of robber was this that exchanged a silver coin for an old key?

Aaron pondered, *So why would someone toss a key from a window? Let's find the door or box that this key fits.*

For an accomplished thief such as the crafty redhead, gaining entrance to the patriarch's palace was an easy task; however, once within the palace, he was quickly found out. Several guards were in hot pursuit of the lad as he ran toward the room from which the key had been tossed.

The lad thought as he ran, *What room was it?* As he turned the corner, two guards were barring a door, and several other robed clergy and Templars were outside. The thief mumbled, "Found it." He turned his run into a walk as he approached the gathering by the door. "I have something of interest that belongs to the men inside this room. I am sure that they will be angry if you do not let me in."

The older guard said, "Give what you have, boy, and I will give it within. Or perhaps I will just take it?"

"Both unwise choices for you, friend. Now, just announce me," remarked the young man.

The younger guard smiled. "You best just give up whatever you have; old Philip here is pretty handy with that sword, bo—"

Before the guard could get "boy" out of his mouth, each men had a long dagger pinching deep into his neck, drawing an ever so slight drop or two of blood.

"Men, I tried being nice; that failed. Now, Philip, open the bloody door, or you will be catching your head as it hits your hands. One move and both of you are dead. Now, Philip, open the damn door."

The door opened and revealed several man: Mailly, Ridefort, and the patriarch among them. All looked toward the door as the young man looked toward the unopened box and smiled. "Good day, Grand Master. Greetings from my commander, Brother Walter of Mesnil." The squire looked at the box and continued. "I have a gift that I believe you may be looking for." The young man then held up a weathered key between his thumb and forefinger.

Mailly smiled. "Aaron of Paris, is it not you bearing tidings from La Feve, and yes, an important gift? Come here, Squire, and let's see if this gift is the one we seek."

Aaron came close, bowed, and presented the key to the marshal of the Temple. Mailly clutched the key and opened the box to all present. Within was the high court's mace, as well as the royal orb, crowns, and scepter.

Ridefort, in a rare mood of generosity, announced, "I think that our squire Aaron should be the royal regalia-bearer today. He's certainly earned it. Well done, Squire!"

Gerald turned to Mailly. "Quickly, inform the princess that we begin the ceremony within the hour. Find the regalia-bearer more suitable attire."

The word was quickly spread among Jerusalem that a queen was to be crowned. The church quickly filled with many of the kingdom's honored dignitaries. Notably absent were the Hospitallers, as well as Count Raymond's and Baron Ibelin's factions.

The Templars provided an honor guard, remembering well when Count Raymond's father had been assassinated as he approached the church for his coronation as king of Jerusalem in 1152.

All was ready as Princess Sibylla made her way into the church and walked slowly down the aisle dressed in a beautiful golden silk gown.

At twenty-six years of age and mother of two daughters, the princess looked more an awaiting maiden than queen-in-waiting, yet she understood the importance of the moment. She had prepared for it when her brother had been declared a leper at ten years of age and doomed to an early death.

Sibylla admired the long flowing gown. *This is truly a labor of love of many women. These simple souls spent hundreds of hours to bring this gown to life—so much painstaking energy and patience, all for me.*

The golden gown was fringed in crimson. Both colors represented the House of Anjou, the same house of the sitting king of England, Henry. It was also from where her father, the king's cousin, descended. The princess remembered these things. *I will bring honor to the House of Anjou today and every day.*

The young princess briefly closed her eyes as she made the trip to the altar. *The next time I wear this gown will be upon my death, as my burial dress.* She tenderly touched the embroidered seal of the Kingdom of Jerusalem, the Cross of Christ, upon her gown as she made her way down the aisle.

The queen-in-waiting looked stern as she approached the altar. This was the very summit of Calvary, where Jesus was hung. Below her feet, the blood of Jesus had dripped onto the stone of Golgotha.

As she looked upon the altar, directly over the traditional location of Jesus' cross, she remembered how the Muslims had destroyed this place, the most holy place in Christendom, three times. She mumbled aloud the words "never again" as she knelt in front of the altar.

She remembered that she had been married in this place, and she considered herself still married. As she prayed, she asked her Lord, "If you will it, I will be buried within the very caves below this church, where you were buried and rose from the dead. I pray that one day I too will lie next to your holy tomb, alongside my family and son. Amen."

The entire church was filled. All stood, as was the tradition. In a remote corner of the church, a cloaked blond man stood and watched the events play out. He too was serious, but he knew his time was about to come.

Just to his left was an older man with a beard. He was observing the events unfold as well. He made careful note of who was present or not present. He knew who the cloaked man was to his right, and he deduced why he was present.

The old bearded man smiled to himself and pondered, *Aha, she would not dare to do that, or perhaps she would?* After all, his task as a spy was to analyze.

The coronation ceremony included a full Catholic high mass, with the patriarch, seven bishops, and a score of priests in attendance.

The many young priests began the service with the ritual cleansing and purification. Each held his thurible containing the fragrant burning incense and began a ritual cleansing called censing. They did this by casting the thuribles using various swings, such as around, back and forth, or in a cross. The number of times the thurible was cast depended upon rules of the church.

First, the priests scented themselves, and then they scented other cleric participants. They completed their task with the approving nod from the pope's representative to the Holy Land, Patriarch Heraclius.

The patriarch stepped forward. He scented the princess and the royal regalia by raising the thurible and making an outward motion of his arm with it. Incense flowed toward Sibylla, then wafted over her.

The princess had a peaceful look upon her face as she breathed the sweet incense. The patriarch slowly walked around the princess with further motions, thereby cleansing and purifying her with the sweet aroma.

Soon, the entire Church of the Holy Sepulcher was filled with sweet-smelling incense. The brilliance of hundreds of burning candles made the otherwise somber church sparkle with radiance.

The air was full of music performed by several choirs of chanting monks. The new style of polyphonic music filled the church. Leading the choirs was none other than Atelier, the choirmaster of the new Cathedral of Notre Dame in Paris, who was on pilgrimage.

Aaron, the royal regalia-bearer, came forth and placed the box containing the instruments of office upon the altar. In turn, the bishops placed the orb, the small round gold piece with a cross protruding above, into the princess's hand, the archbishop of Antioch saying, "This symbolizes God's dominion over the Kingdom of Jerusalem, and your dominion and right to protect the lands."

Then the bishop of Jaffa approached with the royal scepter. "This scepter is a symbol of the Shepherd's staff. It will support you and fend off your enemies."

Each gave a prayer and blessing to the new queen. Then she was approached by the patriarch, who placed the crown upon her head and pronounced, "In the name of Jesus Christ and his saints, and by the will of your people, I crown thee, Sibylla, queen of the Kingdom of Jerusalem, in the name of the Father, Son, and Holy Ghost." The crowning of the queen had taken but a few minutes, but the few minutes would cause monumental results.

Queen Sibylla sat upon the throne as the patriarch said prayers requesting that heaven above send a good man to be the king alongside the new queen. "I hold this crown for the man who will sit beside our queen and wisely rule the earthly Kingdom of Heaven."

Heraclius then placed the crown on a purple pillow, which Aaron held. The queen arose and spoke aloud to all within the church. "Your prayers will be answered, Patriarch. Come, Guy Lusignan, and approach the throne."

From the crowd, the tall blond man with the cloak approached the throne. Guy knelt in front of the new queen. The queen took the second crown in hand and said, "I make choice of thee as king, and as my lord, and as lord of the land of Jerusalem, for those whom God hath joined together, let no man put asunder."

All within the church were astounded. Sibylla's own words came hauntingly back to the patriarch: "You must promise me that you will allow me to pick my consort and *swear* none here will oppose my choice."

An older man, and sometimes spy Jacob, in the rear of the church mused that the Torah scripture rang true: "*Daughters of kings are your lovely wives; a princess arrayed in Ophir's gold, comes to stand at your right hand. Listen, my daughter, and understand; pay me careful heed.*"

Ridefort, too, smiled, as he had also been outfoxed, as had Reynald, as well as other barons and churchmen. They all simply stood there as Sibylla crowned Lusignan the king of Jerusalem.

The grand master of the Temple was heard to murmur at that moment, "This crown is a fair return for the inheritance of Botrun. Now let the good count of Tripoli think of a way from this piece of magic."

It took some minutes for the shock to wear off the assembled gathering. Sheepishly, the patriarch approached the new king. "Sire, do you desire the rite of anointment and for me to acknowledge your position within the Church?"

Guy smiled. "Yes, Patriarch, your king would not want it any other way." Guy was at the high point in his life and did not know it.

After the ceremony, the coronation party withdrew from the church and a magnificent feast was hosted by the Templars in the grand hall. Normally, a squire such as Aaron would not be allowed to attend such a feast; however, as the bearer of the royal regalia, he was an honored guest.

Also attending the feast and adding her tidings to the new king and queen were the newly arrived Lady Marie of Baux and her cousin Yvette, who had returned from Antioch.

Aaron noted them in the long line of well-wishers to the king and queen. "My lady Baux, perhaps you may remember me, Aaron. I am Roland's friend. I expected Roland to be here."

Marie had a look of deep concern. "Of course I remember you, as does my cousin, Yvette."

Yvette was silently admiring the newly coined Keeper of the Royal Regalia, who was clothed in a rather revealing royal purple outfit. *The boy cleans up rather well. I wonder if his new appointment comes with a nice yearly salary,* she wondered.

Marie was extremely concerned. "I received word from Doctor Jacob that I was to meet Roland in Jerusalem. We have been here for three days with no word from Roland. What can be wrong, Aaron?"

The squire from Paris was equally concerned. "Certainly, Roland would have made his presence known by now if were here. The land may be on the verge of a civil war, and Saladin is amassing an army in Damascus. If we don't leave here soon, we all may pay a price. I am not sure what to do."

Aaron had heard a rumor as he circulated around Templar headquarters that Roland had last been seen in Nablus, delivering a message on the queen's behalf. "I understand that Count Raymond was the last person to speak to Roland. Maybe he is the count's prisoner?"

Marie was frantic. "Then we should leave for Tiberius quickly. Aaron, I have need of an escort. Is it possible that you may take us to Tiberius as you return to La Feve?"

Aaron smiled. "I knew this rather cushy job as the regalia keeper would end. The good in all this news is that perhaps in a few months, we will be in France just as the winter will set in. Let me talk to Brother Mailly and search out Jacob."

Aaron knew that Jacob would not be far from such an event as the coronation. He walked toward the Dome of the Rock, talking to himself, as he often did. "Where will that old fox be?"

"Behind you, lad. Stop talking to yourself." It was the doctor, dressed in courtly clothing.

Aaron smiled. "Well, that quest did not take long. It is good to see you, mentor. Now, if you can tell me where Roland is, we can get out of this place and back to France."

The sad look on Jacob's face said it all. "Five days ago, Roland was to meet an escort after he delivered a message to Count Tripoli at

Nablus. I waited on the road about five miles south for them to appear. No one appeared, so I went back to the meeting point. I discovered many of Balian's men-at-arms removing bodies from a shed. It was my escort and men whom Balian had provided, all dead, throats cut or black arrows in their bodies. Surely the signature of the Hashashins."

Aaron nearly dropped to his knees in fear. "Was Roland one of the dead? Oh God, not Roland, please."

The old man clutched Aaron. "Stand steady, boy, stand steady. No, Roland's body was not one of them. I used my contacts to discover that this was the work of the Hashashins led by a Frank."

Jacob looked toward the Dome of the Rock. "This is the Frank I have been tracking for six months—always close but never found. It appears that they injured Roland when they took him prisoner. For whatever reason, they took him to Damascus."

"My God, why Roland? Can we find him and release him? Let us go, Jacob. Why do we wait?"

Jacob smiled and said ruefully, "Ridefort was not about to jeopardize Roland, yet the fool sent him on a risky mission. Now we must cope with the problem." He continued, "Aaron, you can't just walk into Saladin's palace. Even I can't do that. However, even Saladin can't keep a secret, such as having a noted warrior like Roland, for long. People talk about such things. I can get close and find out where he is and his circumstances. It may take several weeks, maybe even months."

"I have Marie and Yvette in the hall. They are very concerned and demanding answers. What can I do, Jacob?" asked Aaron.

"Tell them to get back to Tiberius. I have discovered that the count has a secret treaty with Saladin. I don't know the details; however, Saladin will not attack the count's stronghold if it comes to war. They will be safe there until the spring. Also, Damascus is close to Tiberius and to La Feve, so we all can remain in contact."

Aaron could see Jacob's wisdom. "What do I tell Brother Walter and the sergeant?"

Jacob looked deeply into Aaron's eyes. "Tell them that I will find Roland. Tell them that Saladin is coming soon, perhaps in force in the spring, when the wells are full. This time, Saladin will not be denied."

Chapter Twenty-one

"And you were on the edge of a pit of the Fire, and He saved you from it. Thus does Allah make clear to you His verses that you may be guided."
The Quran 3:103

As Roland approached Lord Ali's castle to the north of Duma, he agreed with Saladin that the place was isolated. No village was within seven or eight miles of the fortress. The terrain was flat and brutal. Unassisted escape would be nearly impossible.

A tall blond Frank making his way over 100 miles of enemy land to the Jordan unnoticed certainly would be nearly impossible, thought Roland.

From a distance, Roland could see that Lord Ali's castle was unlike his home in Troyes. The al-qasr, as the Arab people called such structures, had lines of graceful construction, strong, to be certain, with a stately wall and a single strong entrance.

The flowing lines of the Al-qasr-ibn-Athir made use of rounded archways, airy windows, and several gardens. In the afternoon, the sun made the light colors look golden.

As Roland entered the castle, he noted a rather large tower in the very center of the palace. He also noted several veiled women trying to steal a peek at him from a building to the left of the tower. As hard as they tried, they were doing a rather poor job of concealing themselves.

When Roland smiled at them, he could hear much giggling. Roland had heard that this area was called a harem and only women lived there.

Ali stopped and dismounted. He approached and patted Sirocco. "I must tell you Roland that your horse followed our wagon from Galilee and across the Jordan from a safe distance. He nearly killed two men that attempted to rope him. He only allowed us to secure him to the coach after he noted us carrying you within, yet you mount the animal with ease."

Roland smiled as he patted the noble animal. "Sirocco and I have a special relationship, Lord Ali. Only I can care for him and ride him, no other. He has saved my life many times, and I would do the same for him."

Ali understood. "Yes, horses are special to my people. Your horse is very desirable, and only because the sultan graced you has the animal been safe with you. He must be stabled under guard so that you may not use him to escape."

The scholar Lord Ali looked about. "Now, let us walk together." As they walked, Ali pointed out all the parts of the castle to Roland. "Only two places I ask you not to go: the central tower and the harem. You have free access to all other places within my home. Here is where you shall stay."

A rather large guard opened a door to reveal a hallway with a suite of well-appointed rooms leading to a cloistered garden. Ali pointed the way. "Yes, this should do. Make yourself comfortable. A servant will be along to prepare a bath and offer refreshment and food."

Ali pointed to the guards in the hallway and at his door. "I must insist that you always be accompanied by a guard when out of your room. One will be present all day and night. Rest today, and I shall see you in the morning for my falcon exercise. Shalom onto you, El-Cid-Feimes."

The newly appointed El-Cid-Feimes was amazed at the suite. In one room, he found a small pool surrounded by small and large pillows. Several windows in the room looked out on the garden.

A second room served as his sleeping quarters, with a large bed draped in fine silken bedding. A closet held many fine suits of both Arabic and, amazingly, Frankish-style clothing fitted for him.

A third room had tables with flowers and fruits of all kind in baskets. Roland sat in the large chair at the head of the table and smiled when he looked at the other six chairs. *One day, Marie and I will live in Provence and I will be at the head of that table with our children nestled upon similar chairs.*

A slight rap upon the door begged admittance. "دق دييسيلا جئت؟," a voice called.

Roland said in Arabic, "Please enter." A large guard opened the door, and the petite Sophia entered.

The young woman was trailed by six men bearing large buckets of warm water. "Lord Ali has directed me to attend to your needs. Unless you prefer a guard attend you?"

Roland looked at the large guard and immediately responded, "You will do fine, my lady Sophia. You may dismiss the guard if you please."

Sophia smiled, "As you like, El Cid. I will have your bath prepared in a few minutes. Would you like to eat within or out in the garden?"

Roland was amazed because the last time anyone had poured him a bath was several years before. "Thank you, Sophia. I am hungry, and perhaps the garden would be nice."

Within some minutes, Sophia had prepared the bath. She was standing beside the pool of steaming water with a long towel the likes of which Roland had never seen before. Scented vapors arose from the water. "I will have your clothing cleaned," she told him. "As you bathe, I will lay out some comfortable clothing for you, El Cid."

She smiled and turned away as Roland stripped off his clothing and entered the pool. "Oh my God, is this wonderful!" he said. He could feel the hot water relax his sore muscles to the point that he nearly fell into a deep sleep in the pool.

Sophia came in and spoke to the nearly sleeping lad. "El Cid, the doctor says it is important that we rub this herb potion onto your body. I am skilled in such manners."

Roland was in a near coma. Not a muscle moved. His heart rate was slowing, and he was relaxed as never before. Mumbling, he exclaimed, "Perhaps, Sophia, I can have the herbs applied later?"

"As you wish, El Cid. If you would rather have another do this, perhaps I could get the guard who comes from Anatolia to perform this task? Many tell me that he too is very skilled. I will have Toor, the guard, come in later, as I must attend to Ali's family in a short time."

Roland was suddenly awake, standing naked and reaching for the towel. "Toor. Does that not mean 'bull' in Arabic?"

Sophia blushed because she had not been prepared for Roland's sudden exit from the pool, and his nakedness. "Yes, El Cid. I think he is the next guard on duty, larger than the one at the door. But I am told that his hands will press any mischief from your body."

The young man wrapped himself in the towel and simply asked, "Sophia, where must I be for you to rub the herbs on my body?"

"This way, El Cid. We have such a table set up in the garden. Please lay down, and I will place the towel over you."

Now Roland's senses of hearing, smell, and touch took over. As he laid his head upon the soft lambskin, he could hear all manner of birds that Ali had brought to his home in the garden. He could hear turtle doves cooing; he heard the sound of orioles, even a small owl. In the far distance, he could hear pigeons flying overhead.

The various scents coming from the flowers in the garden, along with the fragrance in the jar of herbal potion, was a bouquet like the lavender of Provence. The scents brought all the pleasures of life back to the young lord.

Sophia's firm touch as she applied the herbals was perfect. She rubbed salves into his muscular body, taking the pain away.

Sophia could see the many black and blue marks, and stitches on Roland's body. She understood why he had earned the warrior name, El-Cid-Feimes, at such a young age; he had paid a heavy price for the wages of war.

Roland drifted off, dreaming of Marie and Provence. He could see children running in the fields. All too fast, he was awake as Sophia gazed at him with the sun to her back.

"I am sorry that I fell asleep, Sophia. Somehow, I rolled over and never recalled myself doing it."

Sophia eyes were gentle upon him. "This is unworthy of an apology. You are still weak from your injury. Please, dress in this clothing while I ensure that your table has been set."

The young woman did not want to inform him that she had seen his nakedness. She had felt warm when she massaged him. She so wanted to tell him that her hands were still trembling from applying the herbal lotions upon his body. Rather, she simply smiled.

Roland's repast of lamb, chicken, and fish was above reproach. He did miss the wine, but this was a Muslim table. The many fruit juices were more than ample to fill the gap of the missing wine.

From his table, he watched the sun set over the desert. As the sun set, he listened to the call for prayers from the tower in the center of the courtyard. He was truly relaxed.

He had no pain in his body or heart. This was a first in many years, that neither ached. It was then that he noticed that the herbal potion had been applied to his entire body. *The things we miss when we are asleep.*

He slept soundly until the break of day, a full two hours later than normal from when he had to awaken as a Templar squire.

In the distance, he could hear a familiar whinnying from his steed, Sirocco. "Coming, boy, I am coming." He found a set of Arabic clothing, along with a Frankish tunic and trousers. *I will try these Arabic clothes. All tell me they are cooler and more flexible.*

After dressing, the young man from Champagne opened the door to find a man larger than he standing guard. "Toor, I suspect?"

The man stood with his kilij saber in his hand sword. "I am Toor, El Cid. What is your pleasure?"

"I need to care for my animal. Rather early, but he normally is fed even earlier."

From the tower came the Muslims' first call to prayer, the Azan. The huge man looked at Roland. "I must pray, El Cid."

Roland agreed, "It is good that we both pray. You to Mecca and I to Jerusalem, but we will both pray to the same God."

With that, Roland went into his suite, knelt, and prayed. "Thank you, Lord, for keeping me another day. Praise your name, and please keep Marie and my friends in your care. Amen."

Sirocco, with the help of Toor, was soon washed, brushed, and fed. They were just finishing as Lord Ali approached. "Ah, you are up early and are looking very Arabic—save for the pale skin, blue eyes, and blond hair. Your Sirocco seems in need of a hardy ride, yes? Come with me, and let us start the day."

Roland passed the tower and asked himself, *Why is this rather strange tower so important?* From the outside, it was nothing to marvel at. It was about thirty feet high, perhaps thirty feet wide, with a staircase and with windows. Four guards were at the door, and he could see others along the staircase. The top two floors had no windows. One man, on top of the tower, was walking to the four points of the winds.

Ali noticed Roland's interest in the tower and smiled. "Aha, young one. We all want what we cannot have."

The entourage of several guards, Ali's falconry team, along with Roland, moved rapidly along the desert floor. They traveled perhaps five miles to a plateau from which they could see for miles in any direction.

Along the way, Roland asked Lord Ali if he could study Arabic and maintain his skills at arms with bow and sword. Ali was rather pleased. "You are interested in our culture, El Cid, and this is good. I will have several teachers call upon you."

Ali continued, "Now, for the warrior training, let me think. I have no one ample on my staff. My friend Mustafa al-din Gökböri is the consummate warrior, though. He comes here to work in my shop. I have a metal shop that is the best for handcrafting swords. He is a good challenge for you in the ring."

Roland dismounted and spoke. "My lord Ali, is this the same Mustafa that wants to either kill me or ransom me? I am not sure that he will just practice jostling with lance or the sword in the ring."

"Aha, El-Cid-Feımes, you are humorous," bellowed Ali. "Remember that you are under the protection of me and the sultan. Once the sultan declared you in his care, anyone—including Mustafa—who dares violate that order will surely have a long and painful death."

Ali beckoned Roland closer. " El-Cid-Feımes, my friend Mustafa is a soldier, and he appreciated your candor in facing death. He admires you, El Cid. He told me he wished you soldiered for him. Now, let us see how my birds are today."

A handler brought a covered falcon to Lord Ali, who petted the bird, then removed the leather cover from the animal. "Here is my Angel of Death. Come to me, my Azrai'il. Is he not a handsome creature, El Cid?"

Roland could see the beauty of the bird of prey. When the hood over the bird's head was removed, he could see that the eyes were ever searching. "See, El Cid, at the plateau's edge, perhaps 300 yards," Ali said. "My man will release a pigeon. Let us see if Azrai'il can search it out."

Ali just made a slight movement of his arm, and the falcon was off. The pigeon made several dives and moves, but to no avail. The Angel of Death came quickly and suddenly upon the pigeon. Feathers were everywhere. Then, as the falcon's talons reined in the small bird, it was over.

The falcon brought his prey to Ali, who rewarded him with a piece of fish, the bird's favorite food.

Roland had done falconry in Troyes but found it boring. He'd rather hunt birds with a bow and arrow. After two more pigeons, the entourage journeyed back to Lord Ali's estate.

Young Champagne found his bow and three new sheaves of arrows with several targets set up in the courtyard. It had been several weeks since he had drawn a bow-in the fight by the Jordan River. He closely examined the arrows, "These are very good quality arrows. The heads are quality steel, and the shafts are made with pure oak. They appear to be English."

Ali agreed. "They are indeed from England. Our friends the Venetians provide our needs from Europe, and in turn, we provide silk, spices, and slaves."

The young man rosined the string and pulled on the draw. It took him several pulls until he could get the maximum draw. "Thank you, Lord Ali. I need the practice and may not hit a target."

He started with a simple drill—twenty-five yards from the target to hit the centers of a variety of round warrior shields. He hit ten of ten targets. "Rather impressive, rather impressive indeed," marveled Ali.

"Please move them back to seventy-five yards, near the wall," requested Roland. "Lord Ali, are the falcons the only ones allowed to hunt pigeons?"

Ali laughed. "Here in the courtyard, any pigeon is fair game; but only here in the courtyard, not near the tower."

Once the targets were in place, Roland set eleven arrows in place in the soil to his front. He drew back the full length of his English bow and let loose all eleven arrows in rapid succession.

All but one hit the shields, and mostly, the strikes were center mass. The last arrow hit a pigeon that was circling the courtyard unnoticed by anyone else until Roland aimed high in the sky to bag his prey.

All in the courtyard were amazed with the young man's skill. Ali added, "Our sultan should have named you Azrai'il."

Roland smiled. "Not that good, Lord Ali. I am still weak. Turn the shields over. See how I barely penetrated the shield? A few weeks ago, I could get eight to ten inches into a warrior's shield. I need to build my strength. Perhaps when you go hunting in the morning, I could exercise?"

"Of course, an excellent idea," said Ali. "What do you suggest?"

Roland replied, "I could run the canyon below and climb the ledge each day. That work, plus a few hours a day on horse and the training rink should do. That will certainly build my body. In between training, I can have your instructors come and mentor me."

Ali smiled. "Yes, just thinking about it makes me tired. Then again, that is why you are a warrior and I am the court scribe."

The men were walked toward the tower when Ali commented, "We must part, as I have duties within. Next week, I shall be gone to the Sultan's court to conduct my monthly court business. Mustafa will be here to entertain you."

So it was that Roland started his training regimen the very next day. The first few days nearly killed him. The running and ledge climbing were truly hard.

Late in the afternoons, Champagne worked on his archery skills. He did his normal bow drill practice. Then, he set the targets in a random pattern and ran twenty to twenty-five yards and fired into the most distant target. He hit most targets on his first attempt. "I must try shooting from horseback. Perhaps next week, I shall try from horseback with an Arabic bow?"

Each day, under guard, he would run three or four miles in the hot canyon. He would finish his run under the plateau, where Ali was conducting his climbing practice.

Ali's guards would drop a rope from the top, and Roland would tie the rope around his belt. The guards would hold the rope as a safety precaution, and then Roland would painstakingly ascend the rock facing of the plateau.

In just six days, Roland was getting along nicely in his newest challenge. On the first day, it had taken him over one hour to ascend the thirty feet to the top. His hands and feet were getting conditioned to the sandstone wall face. Every muscle ached and every joint hurt. The only saving grace was Sophia's routine of a nightly warm pool and magical rubdown.

But this climbing was more than exercise or the challenge of cliff climbing. Roland wanted to enter that tower, and he knew the door was not the only way in. Rather, Roland intended to go up the tower's walls. He had done this type of climbing in two sieges with his uncle Richard.

The young prisoner noted that the tower's outer stone shell offered an opportunity for him to climb. Each stone had an inch or two of indention above and below it—just enough ample material for a trained hand and foot to stage the climb that he had planned.

All his training was not just to exercise his body and mind. He was planning his escape. He needed all the warriors' skills, plus to speak better Arabic to make his escape a success.

On Ali's last day before going off to Damascus for a week or two, Roland knew that it was nearly January. If by February, he had not been released, he would make his escape.

So, each day, Roland trudged forward on a path of hard training. He studied the language, culture, and art of the Islamic people with his mentor to improve his chances of fitting in. With the study, Roland realized that in all aspects of science, mathematics, art, and medicine, the Arabic people had the edge over Europe. It was sad that the religious divide kept the two peoples so far apart.

Ali had received word from the sultan concerning Roland's status as a prisoner. " El-Cid-Feimes, my master the sultan feels that perhaps at June's end, you may leave unabated. That is five months from now. He will not demand a ransom since you saved my life. It is the best I can do."

Roland smiled. "The alternative was death, so this option, while disappointing, gives me a goal, my Lord Ali."

The die was cast; he would not wait five months. Roland had a roadmap and a timetable to freedom. He would escape next month in the dark of the moon.

Jacob had instructed him and Aaron, "To be a successful spy, you must act in a usual manner in the most unusual circumstances. The key is not to act concerned, because concern will alert your foe to your intentions."

It was critical that Roland's attitude and demeanor stay the same. His new mantra was "Act the same way each day and stay the course, Roland," so he acted no differently the following day. He was up early, to the stable, morning prayers, and a breakfast of grain and fruit. He joined Ali and rode to the point where he would run to the ascension point.

As Roland was slowly climbing the sheer face of the escarpment in the desert's morning heat, he knew that he must completely master this rock-climbing technique if he was to gain vertical access to the forbidden tower.

As he was trying to negotiate his large body up the vertical escarpment, he murmured mirthfully, "Where are you, Aaron, when

I really need you?" Aaron could climb cliffs like this just like a mountain goat.

"I must move faster," he said as he approached the midway point, about twenty feet up the wall. Roland's large frame and several hundred pounds of muscles and sinew needed time, and time was the enemy in this heat. The heat reflected off the wall and would drain him of his energy after just thirty minutes.

"Move, Roland, move," he murmured out loud. His hands were bleeding from the sharp rocks that felt like the needles of a porcupine. He could feel the burning from the desert salt as it filled his wounds.

This was his seventh climb, and granted, he was getting better, but he was still slow! He remembered the first few times that he tried to scale the wall, he had fallen as many as ten times. The first time he had fallen, he had been only five feet up and the safety line had been manned by only one small Arab, whom Roland had nearly pulled over the cliff's edge when he had fallen. Now, two large Turkish bodyguards manned the safety lines on the cliff above.

As he climbed, he needed some self-motivation. He knew the climb would be worth it. *Something of great value is within that tower! What great secret exists that six or more guards watch over it? The pigeon near the tower are off-limits, yet just feet away I can shoot them in the courtyard? Why is that? Keep going. Keep moving, and don't look down.*

Hand over hand, Roland made his way up the limestone face. When climbing the tower, he would not enjoy the safety of the rope that hung down from the cliff that two of his captors manned as a precaution. He would get no help when he would climb the tower on the darkest of nights, when the moon would not so much as glimmer, so he tried to ignore the safety and reassurance that the rope brought.

He was closing on the rim when he heard a scream and the clash of metal on metal. It was swords striking swords and shields. Roland felt the rope go limp when he had about three feet to go to the top. *Is this a test or a cruel joke?*

Seconds later, the rope was tossed over the edge to hurtle toward the ground thirty feet below. The noise from swords and screaming in Arabic got louder as Roland's hand reached the rim.

As he carefully brought his head even with the cliff, he saw a terrible life-and-death ballet being played out before his very eyes. Roland thought but one Frankish word, *Assassins.*

Three of the warriors sent by Rashid ad-din Sinan, the Old Man of the Mountains—those same men called the Hashashins, were attacking Lord Ali's bodyguards. Lord Ali's men were the finest warriors in Saladin's army, yet two of the five lay dead on the ground.

One of the bodyguards, who had been holding the safety rope, was fighting an assassin only a few feet from Roland. The assassin warrior was pressing the bodyguard hard. Roland could see a sword wound on the bodyguard's arm and knew the guard was in trouble.

With one swift move, Roland lunged over the edge of the rim and seized the ankle of an extremely surprised assassin. The warrior looked like he had been latched onto by a sea serpent. Roland's great weight, matched by his strength, pulled the assassin over the ledge in one smooth movement. The man never even screamed as he dropped thirty feet to his death.

Meanwhile, Roland leaped over the ledge and picked up his new enemy's sword, then closed in on the second assassin, who had just killed the third bodyguard. Immediately, the warrior turned to meet Roland. As skilled as Roland was, he was evenly matched with this highly skilled man dressed in black. Move for move, the two men parried, lunged, and countered each other's blows with precision.

Roland got lucky first and hit the man's shoulder, issuing a near-fatal wound. It seemed that this warrior felt no pain, though, for he not only ignored the deep wound but managed to plunk a well-aimed blow to Roland's right leg.

The pain shot up Roland's body as blood flooded into his boot. Roland too fought off the pain and came on to the man with an over-head blow that sent the hooded man back three feet. It was now a fight to the death between two wounded animals.

Then the assassin made his fatal mistake. He went for the wounded Lord Ali and was blocked by the lord's best bodyguard. Both men fought well, but the assassin was too skilled, and, in some seconds, the bodyguard was down.

This gave Roland an opportunity to recover and to come to the protection of Lord Ali. As the killer turned to finish his work on Lord Ali, Roland was waiting.

The squire parried and blocked his opponent's sword to perfection. For a brief second, his enemy left a small space unprotected as he extended his sword to strike Roland. Hundreds of hours of training came down to this moment in time. Roland stuck the killer in the chest. He then followed it up with a blow that severed the warrior's head.

As he finished the warrior, Roland realized that the last assassin had dispatched the remaining two bodyguards and had cornered Lord Ali near the rim of the canyon wall. While Lord Ali was a scholar, he had only a rudimentary knowledge of swordsmanship and would not last long against the trained killer.

Roland felt exhausted now and knew he had little fight left in him. Perhaps it was his willpower, or maybe his warrior training, but something inside him took over. With what little strength the lad had left, he ran the five or six feet and tackled the assassin, just as the assassin was about to cleave Lord Ali. The momentum carried both men into the canyon's abyss.

For a brief second, both men looked into each other's eyes as if they were searching for the other's soul—and then both bodies hit the ground. Roland could hear the air rush from the dying man's body with the murmur of "Allah wills it."

God favored the boy from Champagne that day. The assassin's body had cushioned Roland's fall somewhat; however, the badly injured Roland was spinning out of consciousness and slipping into death.

Chapter Twenty-two

"When arguing with fools, don't answer their foolish
arguments, or you will become as foolish as they are.
When arguing with fools, be sure to answer their foolish
arguments, or they will become wise in their own
estimation."

Proverbs 26:4–5

Guy Lusignan was rather pleased with himself this day. All the
rebellious barons, save one, Baldwin of Ramla, had offered
homage to the new king and queen.

It was heard that Baldwin Ibelin of Ramla had exiled himself to
Antioch. Baldwin had placed his oldest son, Thomas, in the care of
Balian of Nablus to save his holdings from being seized by Guy.

Even Count Raymond of Tripoli had come to Jerusalem this very
day to swear homage to the new royals. King Guy and Queen Sibylla
looked out to see Raymond enter the throne room. His small
entourage lacked any friends, peers, or family.

Sibylla spoke first as Raymond approached the thrones. "It is
good to see you enter Jerusalem, Count Raymond of Tripoli. We welcome you. We pray that all is forgotten and you accept my husband
as your king?"

Raymond made a slight bow of courtesy—certainly no more
than the minimum required to even call it a bow—toward the king.

"Yes, Your Highness, we are here to pay our homage and ask
that the past, for the good of the kingdom, be forgotten."

Guy spoke. "Dear Count Raymond, we do forgive you for your
trespasses. Now that that is completed, let us move on. We wish to
discuss another issue as you stand before us. When we ascended the
throne, lo and behold, we found the treasury empty. What say you as
the kingdom's regent?"

The count was rather shocked by Guy's direct insolence. "You,
sir, are you making charges that I took funds unlawfully? I stand here

trying to make amends, and you say this to me? I never used one penny on myself or my fiefdom. All the funds I used were directed towards the security for the kingdom, yet you think of me as a thief in the night?"

Guy pressed, "I did not say you took the funds. I ask you to assist us in seeking the light of day. Perhaps another took the funds when you were not attending to Jerusalem."

Raymond's posture stiffened. "Now you not only imply that I took funds but that I did not attend to the business of state, as well? This is too far a transgression. I beg your leave." With that, Raymond turned and left the room. He rejoined his bodyguard and Baron Balian to immediately return to Tiberius.

The riders had barely gotten past the city's walls when Ridefort, there for this farce, pressed Guy and Sibylla to rise up against Raymond. "The man is a traitor. Besides what you see, my men continue to report that Saladin sends larger bodies of troops within the kingdom, entering and exiting from Raymond's land. Raymond knows this and allows it to happen."

Guy was holding a document in his hand. "True, but we have Reynald, who also continues to break the treaty with his raiding of caravans in the Transjordan. Here I have a document from the infidel Saladin that tells me that I allow this."

Gerald replied, "I have confirmed that my messenger, Roland, was captured by Saladin near Nablus. We have not received a ransom demand yet, but surely it will come."

Now pacing, Ridefort continued. "Once the count of Champagne and his mother hear this news, there will be hell to pay. I have Mailly to thank for this. The boy is a favorite of his uncle Count Richard. Now I must contend with half of Europe's monarchs."

Sibylla rose from her seat. "Honored husband and Grand Master Gerald, we must heal the kingdom, not split it. I, too, have issues with Raymond. Remember that the man has 400 to 500 knights and men-at-arms under his control. The Christian population of Tripoli and Galilee is perhaps another 10,000 people. Raymond must come back into the fold."

The king smiled. "My dear wife, you are the wisest of the lot here. I would add that we must use all our resources to find young Champagne. Our cousin Richard will be very angry, very angry indeed."

Sibylla remarked, "Much like Proverbs, we are damned if we do nothing, and equally damned if we do something."

She then offered, "My brother, Baldwin's, strategy of holding the fortress as logistics bases, building a mobile force, shadowing the infidels, and striking when they least expect it has worked well."

The queen touched her Seal of the Kingdom broach upon her shift. "He would bring the people in to the fortress and make Saladin pay a heavy price to take a city in terms of wearing down his army and time. We can't wait for Saladin to strike. We must prepare our cities and country now."

Lusignan cautioned his wife, "Baldwin's actions have *mostly* worked, my love. Let the men of the kingdom gather and decide on a strategy. More important issues face you. How are our daughters doing in their new home?"

The queen looked at her husband and then excused herself. As she left the throne room in disgust, she thought, *Just perhaps I should have laid the crown on another's head? The young Champagne, perhaps. He surely would have mobilized the kingdom and gathered help from Europe. I will go and prepare Joppa and Ascalon for war.*

As Raymond rode under the Jerusalem city gate north toward home, he said to Baron Balian, "The man will never change; he is an idiot. I was prepared to swear homage, and he calls me a thief. I will have nothing to do with this kingdom. I make my fief of Galilee and my county of Tripoli safe. Whatever efforts that may take, Balian."

Balian was literally in the middle. The Ibelins' lands abutted both Raymond's land to the north and the king's lands to the south. He must live in peace with both parties. "My lord Count Raymond, you have been a friend to my family for a lifetime. Try to understand that I will not choose sides."

The baron had personally seen what the price of political intrigue had done to his family. "You see what my brother Baldwin's hatred of Lusignan has caused. His own son, Thomas, now hates his father for not paying homage to the king and queen. Now, Baldwin has exiled himself to Antioch and left Ramla and Thomas to me to tend."

The older baron remembered when his brother Baldwin, after his wife had died, had had a brief affair with Sibylla, perhaps eight years ago, when she was 16 and just returned from Europe. He believed this was the real reason his brother could not bow to Guy. Baldwin was still in love with Sibylla.

The older man continued, "Raymond, we have seen victories when we, as a kingdom, acted as one, such as the miraculous victory at Montgisard. We have also seen defeats such as Jacob's Crossing, when we split our wisdom and failed to act as one. Both you and I paid for that mistake with many years in prison."

Ibelin again spoke as Raymond pondered. "Now that Humphrey and Isabella have paid homage to the king and queen, we must avoid civil war. I remained a loyal subject of Jerusalem and paid Sibylla and Guy homage."

Balian stopped his horse to emphasize his next statement. Tripoli also stopped to hear him. "Count Raymond, I have no love for Lusignan, or Sibylla. I do this only because I can't let Saladin burn our churches, kill and enslave our people, and drive us out. No, we must not allow him to *crush* Christianity in the Outremer."_

The road intersection to the north and Nablus, and to the northeast and Tiberius was in the distance. As the riders approached the split, Balian asked his old friend Raymond, "I respectfully ask you not to make the Ibelin family raise a hand against the kingdom. In return, nor will I raise a hand against you and yours. Peace be to you. Now I prepare for Easter and Christ's rising."

Raymond nodded. "I respect you, Balian; you are an honest man. I will not call upon you to raise a hand against Jerusalem. With that said, I ride to Tiberius."

For Balian, the road to victory was reconciliation with all the Christian elements within the kingdom. He turned to his nephew Thomas, who had accompanied him. "Thomas, as your regent, I want you to prepare the district of Ramla for Saladin's invasion. Muster all boys over fourteen and all men under fifty; start training and outfitting them with arms."

The baron pointed to the Ramla Road. "Go now. I will prepare Nablus for war. After Easter, the entire high court must go to Raymond and convince him to prepare Galilee. May the Lord help us, since no one else can or will."

As Raymond and his men rode along the Jordan River, he felt alone. For him, the die was cast, because he chose isolation. For

Raymond, his only ally would be Saladin. Jerusalem and his Christian neighbors be damned.

In the early spring of 1187, the clouds of war were gathering and the storm fast approached. Events were soon to be out of control and beyond stopping—on both sides of the Jordan River.

Chapter Twenty-three

"It is but Satan who instills [into you] fear of his allies: so fear them not, but fear Me, if you are [truly] believers!"

The Quran, 3:175

Just a two-day march east from Tiberius, and five days from Jerusalem, was Damascus. It too was a beehive of activity. The last of the 2,000 mounted men from Cairo had just arrived from their twenty-day march and were paraded by the royal palace for the sultan's review.

From the window above, Salah-al-din-Yusuf-ibn-Ayyub and many of his war council stood observing the cream of the Islamic army, the Mamlukes. "They are truly magnificent, Hajib Husam; they will match up against the Franks well. Well done indeed."

Husam was undeniably proud. "Twenty years in the making, my sultan. European slave girls and women bred with the finest warriors we have to create them. Taken from their mothers at ten years of age then trained for hundreds of hours in all warrior skills and Islam. Yes, man on man, they will beat the Franks in single combat."

Salah-al-din-Yusuf-ibn-Ayyub was presiding over a council of war with the sole purpose of planning the demise of the Christians. "They will be the centerpiece of our army. Now we take council. Are you ready, Ali?"

Taking notes in this highly secret room was the wounded Ali. His leg had been badly cut in the Assassin attack of a week before, and it required Ali to use a walking stick. "I am slower these days, my sultan, but alive and well. The Hashashins pierced my leg, not my writing hand. Praise to Allah the merciful."

All laughed at Ali's comment. "Yes, Ali, we are all thankful. We shall talk after the meeting about this attack and El-Cid-Feimes' condition. If all the Franks were like this man, we would not be having this gathering," Salah-al-Din said.

The sultan spoke to the secret gathering. "You all know why we are here. We must act soon, my friends, before the new king and queen of Jerusalem can obtain assistance from the Franks beyond and their pope. You are here today because you are the empire's wisest warriors. You will tell me what I need to hear, not what I want to hear. Can we attack the infidels soon?"

Mustafa al-din Gökböri spoke. "My sultan, we have nearly 15,000 knights and infantry ready. With additional levy soldiers, we can have perhaps 5,000 more soldiers in thirty days. This is more than ample to do the job."

Mustafa pointed to the large map on the table. "With this army, I say we should attack north towards Acre. When Acre falls, or we have it in siege, we will continue down the coast with our vessels from Egypt in support. We will then attack each port city in turn. After Joppa falls and we have nothing to our backs, we can easily go east to Jerusalem."

Salah-al-din offered, "My friend, this is what the Christians did to conquer the lands near ninety years ago. While it did work, it took them nearly two years and more than 50,000 warriors to achieve their goals."

Salah-al-din pointed toward Europe on his map. "We don't have two years, or 50,000 men. Their pope will raise the call, and tens of thousands of skilled warriors will be at our door in a year. We must act more quickly."

Baha ad-din ibn Shaddad was next in line to speak. "Lord, I say go straight to Jerusalem. Within days, we will overrun them, and that alone will be our leverage with Rome. Then we can turn our attention to the port cities but we will control the Holy City."

The sultan was quick to point out, "True, Baha, we shall conquer Jerusalem sooner; however, the word will go out to all the Christians in Europe and they will gather quickly. The large Frank army will use the port cities to come back inside the land and invade us again."

Salah-al-din offered his additional insight. "All here have offered approaches, and while good, all have been tried in the past. I thank you for your ideas and your loyalty; thanks be to Allah.

"Each year, the Christians build new and better castles. Each year, they improve the lands and they increase the crops and cattle.

Each year, more of them come from Europe and stay. The cities are getting larger each year."

The leader pointed to the map and then pointed to each large city or major fortress within the kingdom. "See the line of fortresses they have built?"

The sultan continued, observing, "We must draw them away from their cities and castles. We must make them come to us in the desert. We must be the ones to pick our place of battle. So how do we do this?"

The son of the sultan, one of Salah-al-din's seventeen sons, Al-Afdal ibn Salah ad-din, spoke. "Lord Sultan, Jerusalem is wracked with discourse. Count Tripoli has a hatred of the new king and queen. Let us test his loyalty, as well as the Christians' wisdom and resolve."

Salah-al-din was interested. "Yes, continue Prince al-Afdal. Tell us more."

Al-Afdal continued, "Let me take a large force across Galilee, one that the infidels can't ignore. Perhaps we could raid the lands north or south of Tripoli's lands; possibly even as far west as Acre. If the opportunity presents, I will attack a Templar or Hospitallers fortress or outpost, perhaps La Feve."

The sultan's son pointed to La Feve, below Nazareth, on a map. "The Christians will then have two choices. They can mobilize the cities and lock themselves within them, or they can come out for us. I believe they will send a mobile force, as they always have, against us. When they do, we pick the battlefield and strike with our best knights."

Salah-al-din nodded his head in approval. "Once we defeat the main force, we would then have options to either attack Jerusalem, as Baha points out, or to go for the port cities, as Mustafa suggests."

The leader looked to his son. "You, Prince al-Afdal, and General Husam will take our best warriors, the Egyptian Mamlukes, and make your presence known in Galilee."

The Sultan pointed to La Feve on the map. "When you see an opportunity against the infidel monks, seize it. Kill them all. It is the monks who present a threat, not the others. The monks fight for their Jesus, and that makes them very dangerous. The others fight for gold. Don't attack any of Tripoli's people or lands. Look to late April or early May, when the wells are filled, to accomplish this raid."

Salah-al-din looked pleased. "We shall see the outcome of this raid upon Jerusalem's courage and wisdom. We must remain flexible. I don't want to commit the army to any one plan, not yet. But I want to get closer to Jerusalem without tipping our hand to the infidels."

One of the sultan's most capable and loyal generals was his nephew. "Prince Taqi-al-din, you will prepare the remaining army and arrive near the Jordan River in late June, here at Cafarsset, and southwest of Tiberius. May Allah the merciful look down on us in favor."

Salah-al-din seized the opportunity and pointed to his friend's leg. "Ali, my dearest friend, you have still another wound that you took at my expense. How is El-Cid-Feimes doing? I pray that the doctors I sent saved the boy's life?"

"With Allah's mercy, my leg is healing well. I am not so sure that the young man will survive." The royal historian continued, "No one has ever killed three Hashashins in single combat and lived. No one can fall thirty feet on rock and live. Yet with Allah the merciful, all things are possible. He lives day by day. He lives minute to minute."

Ali continued as he blotted a tear from his eye. "Were it not for Allah the merciful guiding the hand of the doctors, he would already be dead. The doctor called Jacob, the Jew from Joppa, placed a small hole in the boy's head to drain fluids. It was amazing to watch."

The sultan moved closer to his friend. "Ali, we owe this young man much, and we will repay it someday. Is it true that the three who attempted to kill you were the same Hashashins that our spy engaged to kill the boy at the well?"

Ali agreed, "Yes, Sultan, they were the same. We found El-Cid's sword and dagger, which had been seized at the well by our spy, on the person of one of the killed Hashashins. To me, it appeared that their plan was to kill us all and then plant Feimes' weapons on, or perhaps in, my dead body. In this manner, all would think that El-Cid murdered me."

The sultan understood. "Yes, it would look like the young man did it. Certainly, had they not killed him, I surely would have for such a crime."

The sultan looked toward Mustafa and, using his hand, gestured him to come. "Mustafa, the Frankish spy is out of control. He wants to kill this boy at all costs, and anyone who stands in his way, or near him. He is no longer objective, and certainly, he cannot be trusted by us. I want that man destroyed. See that it happens."

Ali was writing the death warrant as his friend and master spoke. He then passed the document to Mustafa. "So it is written, so will it happen, Master."

Chapter Twenty-four

"The Lord sustains him on his sickbed; in his illness you restore him to full health."
Psalm 41:3

Deep within a coma, Roland's mind, battered but still working, labored to keep the lad alive. It appeared to Roland as if the ghostly forms to his front were shrouded by a flowing fog, nothing like he had seen before.

The forms would appear to his front and then disappear, just like ghosts. He was terrified of ghosts. He tried to talk to the ghosts to help allay his fear, but neither he nor the forms made a sound.

Then his mind would be blank. In what seemed like seconds, the fog reappeared. Then the forms reappeared. They were trying to contact him, but why, when he was so fearful of them? He hated this, but this cycle of the ghosts and fog occurred endlessly.

"Doctor, has he made any progress?" asked Ali. "He has been sleeping for two weeks."

"Lord Ali, it is amazing that he lives at all, truly amazing, yet I see things, small things, that indicate he is living within. His lips move when we give him fluids. When I touch him on certain muscle locations, he moves ever so slightly. He has both a strong sprit and body. Slowly, his leg wound is healing."

The doctor pointed to various locations on Roland's body. "See here, Lord Ali; he broke three, perhaps four, ribs. His leg here is broken. The small hole to drain the fluid in his brain is healing. That procedure was at the hands of Allah, the Merciful. All good signs; but soon, he must awake to take real nourishment. The small quantities of water and juice are not ample to fend off impurities that attack his systems."

The doctor placed his listening tubes on Roland's lungs. "Hear the sound of his lungs when I place my listening pipe on his chest."

Ali listened and said, "It sounds like a rattle."

The doctor agreed, "Yes, he is showing signs of lung problems, perhaps pneumonia. Because of that rattle, we must get him to walk soon. The bottom line is that he needs to walk and eat soon."

Sophia came into the room. She carried some juice and a small tube to get the fluid to Roland's stomach. "It is time for him to get fluids, Doctor. When I talk to him, I feel that he can hear me. Doctor, is that foolish?"

The doctor was quick to answer, "We must reach within him to break him free from his bonds of darkness. It is as important as is his herbal treatment and the compounds. When I say something, he does twitch or move slightly. He seems to react to a female voice more than a male voice. Try contacting him again, Sophia."

Ali offered, "Sophia, call him Roland. That name is more familiar to him. We know that a certain Marie, while they are not betrothed, is very special to him. Perhaps he believes you are this Marie. Challenge him to live. Perhaps that may break this curse?"

The doctor listened to Roland's heart, then his lungs again. "His heart is strong, but those sounds in his lungs are not good. If he does awaken, ensure that I am contacted immediately. While we want him up, it must be controlled. He has suffered two wounds to his head in just weeks. We won't know the damage until he awakens. He could be blind or have no use of his limbs."

Ali smiled. "Sophia, you have done wonderful work with Roland. I want you to know that previously he asked me to free you and give you a dowry. He wanted you to have a good man. He has concern for you."

Sophia slowly and lovingly placed the fluid reed in Roland's mouth, down to his throat. She gently raised the bag of herbal tea so it slowly emitted a few drops at a time, as the doctor had wanted her to try some tea instead of the juice.

The young woman looked at Lord Ali and said, "I feel foolish. What do I say to him?"

"You are a learned woman. I know you read Greek and Arabic. Recite the Quran to him. This is good for his soul if Allah the merciful calls him to heaven."

Ali signaled to two older women. "Assist Sophia; arrange to sleep in the next room. He is very special. Treat him as my son."

Sophia went back to feeding Roland. The feeding process took twenty minutes. When it was complete, she slowly removed the small reed and said, "Lord Roland, awaken. Please awake. Lord Ali is right. We must not think that we can do this without Allah's compassion."

The young woman started to recite the Quran from memory. "In the name of Allah, the Most Compassionate, the Most Merciful. All praise is due to Allah, Lord of the Worlds, The Most Compassionate, the Most Merciful. Sovereign of the Day of Judgment. You alone we worship, and to You alone we turn for help. Guide us to the straight-way; the way of those whom You have favored, Not of those who have incurred Your wrath, Nor of those who have gone astray."

Into the night, Sophia recited the Quran, stopping only to feed Roland. She fell asleep sometime just before the first call to prayer.

From her sleep, Sophia could hear a slight sound coming from Roland in a soft tone as the imam sang the call to prayer. He mumbled, "I can't see. The fog. The fog."

Sophia awoke and went to Roland. "My lord Roland, can you hear me? It is I, Sophia. Can you hear me?"

She held his hand. "Praise Allah the most Compassionate. He wants to live. Live, Roland. You *must* live. Come back to us."

Roland's parched lips spoke softly. "Marie, the fog is there." Then as if by a miracle, he slowly raised his hand perhaps two inches, and he used his finger to point. "Who is that behind the fog? What is there?"

The two older ladies came in as Sophia called their names. "Dura, go get the doctor. Tell him that El-Cid-Feimes has talked and used his hand. Casa, get some cool water. Let us see if he can take some water without the reed. Allah be praised."

The room was soon filled with doctors and others, such as Baha and Mustafa, who came to see Roland and thank him for saving Ali's life again. Roland remained asleep during this.

Ali wanted others to come by also. Ali spoke to the assembled in the outer room, "All, come by just for a few seconds and say a few words to Roland. Call him by his Frankish name. It must be Allah's mercy that will move him from the darkness to the light of day. The doctors can do no more. It is for Allah's mercy and us to call him out of the darkness. Please come; thank him for what he has done."

For one hour, they came to Roland. Some whispered words of encouragement, and others prayed. General Mustafa stopped by again, commanding Roland to awaken. He got much movement from the young man when he said, "Arise, Lord Roland, the enemy is at the gate," his hand slightly moved, but Roland remained unconscious.

It was Sophia who again got Roland to move his hands as if he were searching for something. "Have him move his right hand," the doctor told Sophia.

"My lord Roland, hear me," she told him. "Use your right hand and touch my hand. Please hold me." The gravely wounded Roland slightly moved his right hand, and Sophia touched it. "Hold my hand, Roland," Sophia repeated.

To the entire room's amazement, he answered with more strength. "Marie, it is you. The fog is cold, but your hand is warm." Then he blinked a few times and slept.

The doctors were happy with this progress. Doctor Aadam summarized it by saying, "He is moving his hands and fingers. He spoke and commanded other parts of his body to move. He can sense heat and cold. All are good signs. Now we leave, and continue tomorrow."

The same efforts were made by Sophia each day, the same therapy several times each day. The young woman seldom left his bedside. She would bathe him, rub lotions on his body, talk to him, and pray for him.

In between therapy, she constantly talked to him about her childhood and poetry, and of course, she recited the Quran. The doctors were pleased because Roland made steady progress as his body rebuilt itself.

Then, on the twenty-first day since he had fallen into near death, a miracle happened as Sophia was reciting the Quran to him: "Surely those who believe and do good, their Lord will guide them by their faith; there shall flow from beneath them rivers in gardens of bliss."

The young man opened his eyes and asked, "Sophia, how long have I been sleeping? The last thing I remember is falling."

Sophia screamed excitedly, "Allah be praised! You are back among us, El-Cid-Feimes, back among us. For twenty-one days, you have been sleeping among the dead. Don't move, please. Dura, come, come quickly. He has come back from the dead. Get the doctor."

The word went like wildfire through the palace. A miracle had just occurred. Once Roland had been checked by the doctor, he was up and about with the assistance of both Baha and Ali.

He walked a few steps and stopped, and then he walked a few more. A hot bowl of soup was delivered, which he devoured. "More, please?"

The doctor cautioned, "That is all you may have for now. I must see your reaction to eating the food. I must see your urine and excrement. If all is well, you may have a second bowl in some hours. Perhaps in two or three days, you may have some lamb and rice. All praise to Allah the merciful. He wants you to live. He must have plans for you, El-Cid-Feimes."

They were all gathered in Roland's suite: Ali, Baha, Mustafa, Sophia, the doctors, and Roland's attendants. Roland could speak a little in soft tones. "I thank God for keeping me. With his mercy and your help, I am alive. I have much to do to get well. I know with your help, I can do it. Thank you all, with a special thanks to Sophia."

He rubbed his ribs. "I did want so to live, and I could hear voices calling me. I remember this thick fog with forms of people on the other side, and yet I could not see them clearly. The fog kept changing, too. But it was God's will, and you, that made it possible for me to live.

"I understand that I will no longer be a watched 'guest' and that I am now free to leave at will because of saving Ali's life. Let me add here that I would save my lord Ali's life many times over and will always consider him a valued friend. I owe you my life now, but I do plan to leave. Since it is nearly March now, by June, I must be ready to travel."

Long weeks of rehabilitation were before him now. Each day, he would work hard. The young man from Champagne knew he was driven, and he used that motivating force. Each day brought him closer to his goal of reuniting with Marie and his friends.

When Doctor Aadam informed Roland about his bandaged head and "the wondrous work" accomplished by his old friend from Joppa, Doctor Jacob, Roland felt the smile grow across his face. He knew that his friends knew his whereabouts and condition. This further relieved young Champagne.

With Roland rapidly on the mend, Ali knew the young man would be in traveling condition by June. What if he could convince Roland to be a member of Saladin's court? What if the young man converted to Islam? Ali had one more mission for Sophia before she was granted her freedom and rewarded for her hard work.

The wise man could see that Roland was very fond of Sophia. He noticed the affection, those certain looks between both young people. *Roland is a man, after all. Perhaps if it was not for this unseen Marie, Sophia would be wedded to El-Cid-Femmes.*

The scribe had written many chronicles concerning men who made certain that women were above all in their lives, including country or religion. *Many Christians have been converted to Islam for less. Just maybe Sophia holds the key to Roland's heart between her breasts.*

Chapter Twenty-five

"I have commanded those I prepared for battle;
I have summoned my warriors to carry out my wrath—
those who rejoice in my triumph."
Isaiah 13:3

The king of Jerusalem was pleased to see Baron Balian in front of his throne. He was not pleased to hear the subject of the baron's plea. "Let me understand, Balian of Ibelin. You come before us today to plead because of the count of Tripoli's peculiar ways. We owe *nothing* to Raymond. We *know* that he is a conspirator and should be tried for high treason. Tell me one reason this entire kingdom should not rise up against him?"

Balian was a member of one of the most prominent baronial families in the Outremer. He had married Maria Comnena, grand-niece to the Byzantine Emperor Manual, and the mother of Princess Isabella. Balian's sage, sound advice and family contacts were desperately needed.

The baron pointed to the map of Galilee. "Sire, Raymond controls the mostly likely invasion route for Saladin—Galilee. His stronghold at Tiberius and the Hospitallers' fortress nearby at Belvoir make it impossible for Saladin to advance into Galilee without concerns for his back. He must take at least one of these fortresses and siege the second before he can advance safely."

Even Guy Lusignan knew that this much held true. "I agree, Baron Ibelin. Then we should mount an attack against Raymond as soon as possible, take over his lands, and fortify the frontier. This message to Saladin may deter him or at least make his way difficult."

Ibelin went on to explain, "Yes, we may attack Tiberius. But Raymond's ally Saladin certainly will come to his aid, as he, too, will see our plan. We can't win against their combined forces without great assistance from Europe. What will Europe say when we attack one of our own? The count's family still controls Toulouse and the south of France. Perhaps a better way may be afforded to us?"

Sibylla was also in attendance and spoke. "What better way, my lord baron?"

The wise Balian replied, "We form a united embassy consisting of all the high court members, the patriarch or his designated representative, the Templars and Hospitallers. We then approach Raymond as one voice. If he reconciles with this court, all the better, since no blood is shed. If he rejects us, our plea to the pope and kings of Europe will be just. We shall offer them an opportunity to share Raymond's lands. They will come, if our claim is just."

Guy looked to Sibylla, who was in agreement. "We thank you, wise Balian. We will take your recommendation and organize such an embassy. I place you as the leader and ask you to perform this service for the kingdom."

"I shall be honored, sire, to lead such a mission. I will gather the embassy and leave from Jerusalem on April 29. I do have to visit my new holdings at Ramla along the way. We shall rally at La Feve and journey to Tiberius."

Guy turned to the Templars' Grand Master Ridefort and the Hospitallers' Grand Master Moulins. "What say the monks of the kingdom?"

Roger was the first to reply. "I agree with the plan. Baron Ibelin's plan is wise and provides an excellent pathway."

Gerald Ridefort added, "Perhaps the grand master is correct. If this fails, it is a pathway to the block. Agree."

"Patriarch Heraclius, we shall use your good office to contact Count Raymond. Will you go?"

The patriarch meekly answered, "I must prepare for the feast of Saints Phillip and James. The archbishop of Tyre, Josias will attend."

On this same day in Tiberius, Count Raymond received Prince Al-Afdal. "Your Excellency, Count Raymond, I bring you greetings from my beloved father and lord sultan, Salah-al-din. Sadly our, shall we say operatives here in Galilee, inform us that a Christian army is forming. As in our treaty, we would like to investigate this information."

The count answered, "I know that you have several small units spying in Galilee. You must know these operatives are incorrect. No matter; I have nothing to hide or fear. You may bring your people into my lands, but I need to warn my inhabitants to gather their animals and stay within their towns and villages. You may not enter those areas, or bother my people. Also, as stated in our treaty, you have only twelve hours to inspect, and at night only, sunset to sunrise. Agreed?"

Prince Al-Afdal bowed. "You may warn your people now, as in two days' time, I will lead the force. This will ensure it does not get out of hand."

Raymond of Tripoli asked, "How large will this force be, Prince Al-Afdal?"

The young prince's answer was brief. "A few thousand men perhaps." He bowed and left the fortress. He was in the lands of his father in three hours.

The gathering of twenty Arab knights and the royal banner of the House of Saladin did not escape the notice of several people. An old man watering his pony near the well south of town, on the road to Damascus, was one such interested person.

Within minutes, a pigeon launched by an old man from the outskirts of Tiberius on the road to Damascus was making its way toward La Feve. The fifteen-mile trip took the bird less than one hour.

Now the old man would make a house call on a former patient in Duma in five or six days. Along the way, he would gather information.

Marie noted the exiting entourage from high above the ramparts. *What are Arab warriors doing within this castle? No one lets the enemy visit their stronghold.*

The young woman quickly disappeared to the stables. She knew this was where the action was and where the men gossiped over the day's events as they brushed their animals or were dispatched to Tripoli's holdings.

One squire who had eyed Marie before finding out she was Lady Baux was one such rumor monger. She could hear the squire, but she could not hear the second person well.

"So, Squire Edward, are you riding north to warn the villages? I am going towards Hattin and Nazareth. That nice tavern in town is where you will find me. I won't be on the road when those bastards come by. Thomas heard the count say several thousand of them. No, I will be laid up in the inn with a nice slave girl named Fortune."

The small bird landed on the high tower of La Feve. Within minutes, one of the brothers assigned the duty of keeper of the pigeons had the coded message in the hands of the garrison commander, Walter of Mesnil.

The old warrior sent for his second-in-command. "Martin," he told the sergeant, "Get Aaron and have him prepare to ride south towards Nablus. I have a message for him to get to the grand master and Baron Balian. They are somewhere on the road. Tell Aaron to wear that fancy garb he was furnished with in Jerusalem. Also, must he take that mule? Give him a horse."

Martin smiled. "The mule helps him blend in, so to speak, Commander. Yes, the beast is slower, but the thing will go for hours without water or feed. It will be just right for this mission, sir."

Walter just shook his head. "If its best, then fine. I want you to get Brother Philip and send him to our two outposts. Tell him that something major is about to happen."

The wise soldier looked at his map and pointed to Jacob's Crossing. "Our friend the doctor noted several thousand knights in ready just east of the Jordan three days ago. Today he saw Saladin's son leave Tiberius. I believe that Saladin just placed more wager on the table than these five-to-ten-man reconnaissance units."

Mesnil commanded, "Cancel the patrols and double the guard here. Martin, find some pilgrim clothing and go alone to Nazareth. Go to that inn you frequent when I journey to Antioch. Yes, Martin, I know about that. Put that ear to the wall and find out what is happening."

Martin looked up from the map. "It can't be that loudmouth chaplain that told you about Fortune. I just go there in the interest of civil discourse and community relations. I am on my way, Commander."

Count Raymond was up early, because this was the evening when Prince Al-Afdal was to take his large element into Galilee. "Your Excellency, a messenger from Nablus just arrived with a note for you," a servant announced.

Raymond quickly read the note. "The king is sending a delegation to me requesting my reconsideration of homage and support to Jerusalem. Those fools; they will be riding into Galilee the same time that Prince Al-Afdal performs his reconnaissance. I must warn the delegation."

Twenty miles south of La Feve, the embassy and forty knights, save Baron Ibelin, who had a one-day delay, had found lodging in a small monastery. This was where Tripoli's messenger found them at nightfall.

It was Grand Master Roger who read the note. "Count Tripoli has allowed a large force of the enemy to look within his land for an army. Raymond advises us to stay within for twenty-four hours."

Grand Master Gerald could not resist saying, "Tripoli is a traitor of the worst sort. The Templars will not be bullied, and we *will* seek this force. Marshal Mailly, at first light, go to La Feve and inform Mesnil that I want every Templar available as we ride out to find this force of infidels."

About this same time, Aaron and Paris were on the darkened road on the way to Nablus. Aaron complained to Paris, "Girl, I know that monastery is near here, but I can't find it in the darkness. It matters not, as but a few more miles and we shall find Beisan. We will find lodging there and feed for you; and continue on tomorrow to find the grand master."

The sunrise on May 1, 1187, found all the players mounted and acting the parts of a game of chess. One was a king's son; a bishop was there; and another was a queen's son, along with some knights and many pawns. All were in a deadly game of chess. For many, it would be their last move in the game of life.

Aaron had found Beisan and lodging. He was up early in the day. He brushed, fed, and watered Paris. He refilled his goatskin water container, had some fruit and bread, and was off.

As he headed south, behind him perhaps one mile, he could hear a rumble. He observed what appeared to be a dust storm. He urged Paris along south. "Bad weather, girl, just bad weather."

It was worse than bad weather. It was the Islamic army led by Prince al-Afdal and the vanguard of 500 mounted knights. They, like Aaron, had started their day's journey.

A mile behind the vanguard was Prince Taqi al-din with more than 6,000 mounted knights. This was indeed more men than Tripoli had been informed about and to whom he had granted permission to pass. It was one of the largest cavalry ventures in Outremer history.

The force stormed across the Jordan, then flowed northwest toward Acre. Their track would take them near the village of Beisan, then some few miles south of La Feve. They would validate the condition of the water wells at Cresson Springs, and then go back to Syria. Aaron was correct: A bad storm *was* approaching.

The royal delegation completed its trek to La Feve about one hour after prime. Gerald Ridefort found Marshal Mailly gathering ninety Templars and several hundred turcopole infantry soldiers and archers. The secular knights who formed the bishop's bodyguard amounted to an additional forty men.

Mailly said, "Good day, Grand Master. Our turcopole scouts inform us that the infidels are making their way towards the springs at Cresson. They come in two groups, with a smaller vanguard and larger main body. Arab scouts chased our men away before they could get a good count."

Ridefort watered his horse. "We understand that the force may be about 2,000. What is that rabble against 140 Christian knights and supporting infantry, Marshal? Let us move out."

The grand master directed Mesnil, "Brother Walter, I want you and Brother Martin to be my bodyguard today. Martin will carry the beauséant."

Walter protested, "Grand Master, I should be with my lance today. Let me get Brother Edward to ride with you."

Gerald was not having it. "I gave an order, Brother. Now lead on to the springs."

Just two miles from the springs, the Christian force passed a small village. Several of the village leaders came out to see the force. "My lord, what is this?" they asked.

Ridefort advised the leaders, "Follow us with wagons to collect the booty. Bring shovels to bury any Christian dead." He turned to Mesnil, "Well, Walter, we shall make history in but a few hours."

Mesnil crossed himself. "Yes, we shall make history. God save our souls."

Along the road to the south, Aaron and Paris made steady progress. In the distance, Aaron could see perhaps fifteen men riding under the flag of Baron Ibelin. "Well, some good news, Paris. We can save a twenty-five-mile ride since there is the Baron Ibelin. Where are the others?"

Tripoli was already awake and rather worried. "Captain Laodicius, have the troops ready to travel to La Feve in thirty minutes. I must be assured that Prince Afdal has vacated my lands."

Marie, Yvette, and their cousin Countess Eschiva were also concerned. Yvette wanted to leave immediately, "Marie, shall we pack and leave for Acre now, before it is too late?" Yvette asked.

The Countess Eschiva shook her head. "Sadly, we are trapped. Raymond informs me that it is unsafe to leave the fortress for several days."

Marie was distressed. "It has been four months since Roland was captured. No ransom note. I did receive a short note from a friend informing me that he was badly injured and is recovering; and now this? I will ask Count Raymond to arrange a meeting with Saladin and plead for Roland's life."

Countess Eschiva, a mother of four sons, worried. All four of her sons served the count as knights, so they were in harm's way. "Marie, we may be past the point of peaceful discussion. To think, just miles from here, Jesus preached peace."

It was about one hour after Tierce prayers when the Templar force approached east of the springs at Cresson. As they ascended a small rise, one of the scouts reported to Gerald. "Grand Master, they have at least two elements. The one at the springs numbers in the hundreds. The second, about one mile to the south, is immense in size. It has many squadrons, many."

James Mailly looked at Ridefort. "We need to leave and retire to La Feve. Otherwise, they could seize the place and we shall have no stronghold between Acre and Tiberius. If only the hundreds at the spring were present, perhaps we could do damage. Our supporting infantry is two miles behind. This is a forlorn hope."

Grand Master Roger Moulins agreed with Mailly's appraisal of the situation. "We need to leave before they see us. If they combine, it will be hopeless. Without us screening the ground force, they will slaughter the archers and infantry."

Gerald Ridefort was contemptuous of their advice. He taunted his marshal. "You love your blond head too well, Mailly, to want to lose it?" he asked.

Mailly defiantly declared, "I shall die in battle like a brave man. It is you that will flee like a traitor. I will lead, Ridefort, and you will follow me to my death."

Mailly gathered the chaplain and the men around. They all crossed themselves then formed a long line with only a foot between horses. Mailly took to the center and shouted, "Be glorious, Brothers. Templars, charge!"

Ridefort gathered Mesnil and the flag-carrying Sergeant Martin. "You two are with me. Brittany, you shall keep that flag up. Be glorious. Charge!"

Prince al-Afdal was ready to remount when he heard a thundering sound. He looked to the east to see a long line of horsemen, dressed in white mantles, with lances lowered, approaching his position. "Remount quickly, and form. Get my cousin's force here quickly."

Within thirty seconds, the long line of brave Templar men hit the Arab force. Horses tumbled, men screamed, limbs were hacked off. Bloodletting on both sides was unrelenting.

Walter could see the heavy damage done to the enemy. The heavy Templar horses plowed into the smaller Arab steeds. The Islamic force lost perhaps 200 men in this initial attack. If this were the only force, perhaps the Christians would have prevailed, but it was not to be.

Mesnil looked over his right shoulder and saw horsemen approaching in the distance. "God save us," was his simple prayer. Walter then flipped his helmet up to reveal his face to the grand master. His plea: "Let me die with my men?"

Ridefort's bravado had fled. "Stay close to me, Mesnil."

Then, all hell broke out as Prince Taqi al-din's force of several thousand slammed into the Templars' and other knights' flanks, and soon surrounded the beleaguered monks.

Walter could see his men being cut to pieces and, one at a time, dying. Men he had trained and men he had served with were dying before his eyes. Two were childhood friends who had climbed apple trees in Champagne with him and were now bleeding to death. Each Templar had killed two, three, or more of the enemy before themselves dropping from their saddle because of wounds.

Roger Moulins and his small detachment of Hospitallers bravely fought until the last man.

It was Mailly's stand against horrific odds that made friend and foe admire his bravery.

Lying in piles to his front were ten dead Islamic knights. Four others were badly wounded. Mailly had been hit two or three times, and blood oozed from his chain mail.

Then five enemies rushed the brave marshal and brought him to his knees, where they beheaded him. Walter screamed as he tried to get to Brother Mailly, "No, not James!"

Walter, too, had covered himself in glory as he had taken down five warriors before he heard Ridefort yell, "Retreat!"

But it was too late for the force. Each Templar was surrounded and cut down. Each man was dead or dying. They all died bravely, all 140 knights. Even Ridefort was wounded, in his leg and arm.

Martin used the Templar flag to bind his own badly mauled leg. Blood streamed from Walter's head and shoulder. As the three men cleared the hill, they could see in the distance the last of 400 men infantrymen die in a square, slaughtered to the man.

Prince al-Afdal looked over the carnage. Dead or dying men screamed in pain and begged for water. Horses with missing legs were whining in pain all over the battlefield. The few wounded Christians were praying for mercy, but then came the brutality.

Al-Afdal's orders were simple. "Ensure that all wounded are put to the sword and beheaded. I want their heads on pikes so all will see as we leave this place the price they will pay if they resist us. Cut the scalps off the monks; their blond hair will make a fine gift for the caliph in Baghdad. I will deliver them personally. Now move. I want to bathe in the Jordan tonight and wash the Christians' foul blood from my body."

"Lord Prince, we have about 200 of Tripoli's villagers who came to find booty on the battlefield. Many are children and women."

Al-Afdal smiled. "They found their booty. They will be offered paradise as Muslims. Make them prisoners. Sell the men and older women in the slave market in Damascus. The young girls and women will marry our knights who demonstrated bravery today."

On a distant hill, a small detachment of riders surveyed the battlefield. Count Raymond dismounted. He observed the Arabs killing the wounded, then beheading and scalping them. "My God, what I have done, Captain Laodicius? What have I done? I have opened Pandora's Box. We must get word to Jerusalem. Now I must pay homage to Guy and make amends, or I will be forever cursed to hell."

Balian, his escort, and Aaron arrived at La Feve just before None prayers to see the gate opened and two wounded turcopoles near the gate. They saw several tents in front of the fortress as if people had slept in them. No Templars were in sight, and the mighty fortress was abandoned.

Aaron asked the wounded turcopoles, "What happened? Where is everyone?"

An old soldier of many years pointed to the desert, toward Cresson Springs, and said two words, sobbing, "They are all dead-the bishop, the grand masters, all the monks. My wife, three daughters, two sons, all my brothers and family were taken as slaves."

Baron Balian asked Aaron, "Who are dead?"

Aaron, now with tears in his eyes, replied, "The entire garrison and the embassy are dead, my lord baron. Brother Mesnil would never leave the fortress unprotected. This can only mean that war has begun. God save us all. I did not die with my friends, so I will die here alone for my penance."

Aaron walked toward the gate and began to push the door closed as Balian rode south to Jerusalem. Then he saw Balian rush to meet three riders slowly coming along the road from Cresson Springs.

Aaron wiped the tears from his eyes when he saw Walter, Martin, and the grand master slumped over their horses. All had bloody mantles. No others were trailing behind. War had come to Aaron's door, but his mentors were alive.

Chapter Twenty-six

"Then I saw a new heaven and a new earth, for the first heaven and the first earth had passed away, and the sea was no more. And I saw the holy city, new Jerusalem, coming down out of heaven from God, prepared as a bride adorned for her husband."

Revelation 21:1–2

Each day, signs of healing were evident in Roland's body. His side no longer hurt, and his head wounds had healed. He still needed crutches to get around because of his leg, but that too was getting better.

He could do some things, such as work with the bow. He could also do other, simpler, things that did not require much movement. Each day, he also set aside two hours of study that included reading the Quran and other Arabic literature. He also worked with the doctor several hours a day to discover more about the human body.

One day in early May, something different occurred with his recovery routine. Several riders rode into the grounds. They went directly to the tower and to Ali's apartments.

Roland then observed that many of the soldiers seemed to be celebrating. He heard many utterances of "Allah be praised" from the soldiers. As he approached the tower, Ali cautioned him, "Remember El-Cid-Feimes, you may not enter the tower. It would be better for you to go to your apartment."

Once inside his rooms, Champagne asked Sophia, who was preparing his room, "What is happening, Sophia? The soldiers all seem to be celebrating."

The slave girl was evasive. "I can't tell you, master. Lord Ali has cautioned all that serve you or come in contact with you that we must not tell you—under pain of punishment. Please do not ask."

Roland limped over to the window and thought. *Something big has happened. It appears that Saladin's men have won a battle, but I am not sure. You must get stronger, Roland, so you can leave this place.*

His back muscles and some other muscles were hurting. He had perhaps overdone his training program. Sophia noticed him rubbing his arms and legs. "Lord Roland, Doctor Aadam said to give you this potion if you have pain. Here, drink this."

After Roland drank the potion, she lit several sticks of incense, newly arrived from India. The fragrance quickly filled the room.

Sophia picked up a container of salve and pointed to the table. "Here, Lord Roland, let me rub some salve onto your body."

Roland limped over to the table. He noticed a heightened ability in his smelling. It seemed that the incense soothed his head. He could see Sophia extinguishing the candles until only one lone candle was lit.

His pains left his wracked body as the slave girl rubbed his back. "Lord Roland, I want to thank you. Master Ali has informed me that he will free me and provide me a dowry because of your request."

"You are a good woman, Sophia. I don't think I would be alive if not for you."

Then the Templar felt more relaxed. "Perhaps I am sleepy from the day's efforts. Forgive me if I fall asleep. "

Sophia continued to massage Roland. "Just relax, Lord Roland. I will take the pain away. In a few weeks, you will leave us. Your Marie is a fortunate woman to have your love. Perhaps you will see her soon? Would you like to see her right now, if you could?"

The young man's body was drifting off. He could barely hear Sophia—only Marie was in his dreams. "Marie...if I could have Marie, you say?"

Sophia slipped off her shift, revealing her perfect body in the flickering candlelight. She blew out the candle and whispered in Roland's ear, "Marie is here, my dear Roland."

The drug Sophia has given the young lord made Roland slip from reality to living in a fantasy world. He could feel Marie's warm body press against his frame. He was as alive as any eighteen-year-old man could feel. It was real to his body that he was with Marie. He could touch her, caress her, and make love to her as to no other.

He began drifting from one state of fantasy off to another one of sleep, only to awaken and be lying next to his Marie. He could touch her, but it seemed to him that he could hardly speak to her; yet she was there with him. It was heaven. Then a deep sleep came over Roland and he drifted into a place he had never been before.

Lord Ali saw the young woman walking toward her room at midnight. She looked up to her master as he stopped. "It is done," she told him. "It is in Allah, the Merciful hands now. The potion worked. He will not remember, but I will remember all the days of my life. I have done your bidding. Now you must keep your promise to protect me and his child."

The morning call to prayer found Roland in his bed alone. He felt refreshed, and his body did not hurt for the first time in days.

Where he had felt naked in his dream, he now had on a linen wrap, the same one he had had on the previous night, before his massage. He thought, *Roland, it seemed so real that Marie was with you! I think we made love. It was but a dream to yet happen. Get on with the day's efforts, boy.*

As he was walking from the stable and his morning routine with Sirocco, the lad could hear sounds from the forge, mighty blows of hammer on steel.

He soon entered the darkened area to see General Mustafa sweating at the forge and landing blow after blow on a piece of steel. " El-Cid-Feimes, so you have traded your crutches for a small cane. This is good. This is how I stay fit, sane, and in touch with Allah the mighty."

Roland smiled. "I think I understand the fit part, but the maintaining sanity and the praying part, I do not understand."

The general responded between strikes to the hot piece of metal. "Literature and books are not my way. I am a soldier, like you. The quiet prayer in the mosque is also not my way."

Mustafa drove the hammer hard. "I see all the things that I hate on the metal, and I strike sharply. In between strikes, I thank Allah and recall the Quran in my mind. Come, you try it. Start with a smaller hammer, because your muscles have been asleep and need to be awakened. Now, let me heat up the metal."

The general pushed the double bellows mightily. "This steel comes from India. It comes a long way for me to punish it. Now strike here and here, only in those two places. We must work the metal slowly."

The young man in his weeks of coma had lost much muscle. He hit the metal, and within a few attempts, he had the glowing steel beginning to show signs of feathering out.

The general was pleased. "That is it. Let me reheat the metal. Now pray to Allah in between. Do you know the last verse in the Holy Quran?"

In between blows, El-Cid-Feimes answered, "Fear the day when you shall be returned to Allah, then each soul shall be paid what it has earned, and they shall not be wronged."

Mustafa was amazed. "Allah be praised, you are correct! See how my system works. Your mind is clear and ready for such exercise."

The wise general continued, "I will be here for some days. Come by each day, and we shall work the metal into a sword. Unlike most Christian swords, which are much heavier, this sword does not have a weak tip and a strong point near the handle. That is our secret of Damascus steel."

Each day, Roland made the forge a part of his training regimen. The general mused one day, "This work will be my gift to you for saving Ali's life. You will need a sword made from Damascus steel because our friends the Hashashins will not ever forgive you for killing three of their best men. No other has ever done such a feat. We shall make my sword as a model." The general removed his rather dull-looking sword and placed it on the table. He could tell that the young man was less than pleased.

"Aha, because this sword is simple, you believe it has no character? You want a sword perhaps like my master, the sultan's? Yes, it is beautiful, bedazzling with many jewels. He does not take that sword beyond the palace grounds."

The general continued, "Why is that? Simple. Every soldier would soon know that the sultan carried such a valuable sword and would target him even more in combat to obtain the sword. This sword has no rubies, but it will have a heart because you will beat one within it."

The young man smiled. "I understand, General, and you are wise."

The older man beat on the edge of the hot sword. "Come and work the edge like I am doing. Beat character into this sword. Put a heart into it. Like your Frankish and Viking people before you did when they too worked the metal. We need a name for it."

As the young man hammered the metal, he could clearly see that its shape was that of a viper. "El-Ephah, I shall call him—the Viper!"

Mustafa roared, "I like it. I just ask you one thing, El-Cid. I pray to Allah the all-knowing that the Viper never goes against Asad, the Lion, my sword. Promise me this?"

Roland understood. "I will never raise this sword against you in combat, General. Now let us finish the work and place the pattern on the blade and hilt."

The general shared the secret of how the Damascus blade was shaped, flexible and never broke in combat. "It is the final treatment that makes a great or poor sword. It is this certain compound, and how we place it on the edge of the sword only."

Roland painstakingly applied the compound of clay and metallic substances along the edge of the sword. Then the blade was heated for more than one hour. As it was aglow, the lad quickly placed it in the cooling oils to anneal the sword's blade. "It is done, Mustafa."

The general admired the sword as he placed a simple hilt of grooved oakwood onto the blade. Then he ran his hand down the blade to find the all-important center of balance. "The balance is slightly off. Aha, we need to have the soul placed in the sword to create a better balance."

The old man twisted the oak cap to reveal that the hilt had a cavity. He opened a bag and poured out many jewels, including sapphires, rubies, diamonds, and emeralds, onto the table. He then placed them one by one within the handle cavity and sealed it. "Now the sword is balanced perfectly."

The young Templar wore a look of total amazement as he said, "That is a king's ransom!" The general explained, "El-Cid, did you not understand that what lies within your heart is more important than what is on the outside? You are a very handsome young man. Yet, in time you will be weathered. You are the best warrior I have ever seen. Yet, in time you will not have the strength to lift a dagger. More important is that within you beats a brilliant sprit that instills kindness and righteousness. It is what we have on the inside that is much more important than the outside.

"You see the sultan's ruby sword and you think he is rich. Our sultan gives all his money away to the poor. He has nothing. But his heart and soul will glow in paradise. These jewels are his gift to you. He took them off his sword. Now your sword is poor on the outside, yet rich on the inside."

Champagne was amazed. "It is a fine gift without the jewels. I thank you for your patience with me these past days. Tomorrow, I will try riding and getting back to my other regimens. I will try the Viper sword in the ring soon to test her. I will thank the sultan one day soon for his gift."

The general yelled at the guard at the door, "Stand in the hall, soldier. You can't see anyone approaching near the door. It is your duty to walk the hall. Idiot."

The old warrior turned to Roland. "I am always the general, El-Cid, much like you are. He is but a poor guard. He was to guard the hall, not here. I leave tomorrow, El-Cid, for the capital. It is May, and soon the people will do the first harvest, then we—. My apologies, I ramble on."

Roland noted that the general had stopped in mid-sentence. *'Then we'? What did he mean? After the harvest, something will happen.*

The young man worked harder as May turned to June. His combat skills had returned, and even his slight limp had disappeared. He was once again the Roland of past. Not even the highly skilled Mamlukes could match him in the training ring. Viper's punishing blows and distinctive sound on the shields and again the swords of the Arab knights could be heard around the entire palace grounds.

As always, it was his archery skills that amazed the most. Now, he had mastered the shorter compound bow of the sultan's Parthian archers. At a full gallop on Sirocco, he could hit every target in the field.

He approached Ali in late June. "Lord Ali, each time I have asked where Sophia is, the other ladies just giggle. Where is she? Is she in fine health?"

"Yes, Sophia. I have made her part of my harem. She is within and is of excellent heath. She is a fine-looking woman, and I have made her my second wife. Islam allows us to have four wives; may he grant me strength."

Roland was surprised. "Yes, Sophia is a fine woman. Lord Ali, she will make you an excellent wife and, hopefully soon, a wonderful mother to your children."

Lord Ali bowed and remarked that his first wife could not bear children. "We pray to Allah that a boy will come to our family soon."

The young Templar was surprised. Marriage and now talk of children. "Soon, I myself with hope of marriage in the winds. When can I depart, Lord Ali? The sultan said that I could leave in June. While I have enjoyed your hospitality very much, Lord Ali, I must return to my people."

"The sultan has ruled that you can leave in a few days for the coast. It will be important for you to head towards Joppa and seek a vessel. I can't share any more information than that, El-Cid-Feimes. Please, no more questions. After six months here, what are a few more days?"

Ali continued speaking as they walked. "You have come far. You speak our language as you were born to it. You have discovered our Quran. I have seen some of the wounds you dressed on the knights you have trained with in the ring. They are as good as those dressed by Doctor Aadam. Even old Mustafa says you are good on the forge."

Roland was a different person in many ways than the young man who had been kidnapped by Jacob's Well. "Lord Ali, I have eyes and ears. I can see and hear the rumors of war. I want to gather my friends and Marie then leave here. I don't want to fight Islam. I just want to go home."

Ali's face turned stern. "Roland, understand that if I tell you certain things, you will be unable to leave here today. If you did leave, my friend, the sultan would have my head and yours. Agreed?"

"Agreed," responded Champagne.

The royal scribe face was serious. "I fear that your Templar friends may be dead. Your Marie and her cousin are within the fortress at Tiberius, and they have my master's safe conduct."

He continued, "Let me explain. In early May, a terrible battle was waged at the Springs of Cresson between Prince al-Afdal's men and a Christian force. Nearly all the Templars were killed. Only three escaped; the grand master for certain was one of those."

Ali continued, "Since that battle, King Guy Lusignan, Count Raymond, and other princes and barons have joined forces to form the largest Christian army ever to assemble in land, with over 15,000 knights and soldiers.

"They all wait at Acre to see if my lord sultan will invade the lands again. I fear that both sides are out of control. Both kings have stripped all the cities and land of soldiers. Boys and men from everywhere have been pulled in to meet the army's needs.

"Nearly all of the Islamic and Christian cities are nearly defenseless. Whoever wins this one battle will be lord over all."

Roland was shocked. "I stand here as my friends go to war? I stand here as my Marie is defenseless and waits to be a slave or worse? I must leave, Lord Ali. I have saved you twice, and you owe me your life—twice. Release me now."

Lord Ali was apologetic. "I too join the Islamic army tomorrow to serve my master. You *will* be released tomorrow to serve your master, as well. There is nothing you can do for your people other than to die with them, as perhaps I will do alongside my lord sultan."

Ali walked ever so slowly as he turned in to the small mosque, removing his shoes. "I now go to spend the last few hours in prayer. I suggest the same to you. Shalom, El-Cid-Feimes, until we meet again."

Roland would not take no for an answer. It was unacceptable to him. "Why not today? Why is this day in July so important that you can't repay your debt to me now?"

Ali stopped without looking back. "It is the day set for the invasion of Galilee. It is the day Islam takes back what has been promised. It is the day Islam destroys the Christian army."

Historical Notes

Political Intrigue—Roland and his friends found endless internal drama crippling the Christian Kingdom of Jerusalem in 1186 and 1187.

The story of the death of young Baldwin is based on fact. His mother, Princess Sibylla, did divorce her husband, Guy, seize the throne, only to remarry Guy; this is based on fact. The post-coronation events with Humphrey and Isabella are also based on fact.

The count of Tripoli and his factions could not stem the tide. Saladin and Tripoli were indeed allies until the Battle of Cresson Springs. After that battle, Raymond of Tripoli went to Jerusalem and begged forgiveness, which was granted by the king and queen.

Springs of Cresson—The action at the Springs of Cresson on May 1, 1187, foretold the future of the Christian kingdom. As the book points out, the cream of the Knights Templar, including Temple Marshal James de Mailly and the Hospitallers' Grand Master Roger de Moulins, along with about 140 knights and about 400 infantry, were slaughtered. It was also true that the villagers were gathered up and sold into slavery.

As depicted in the book, it is true that only Grand Master Gerald de Ridefort and two other Templars survived the battle.

Not only did the Arab leader, al-Afdal, son of Saladin, kill all, but he had all the monks beheaded and scalped, and their heads posted on pikes. He sent the bag of mostly blond scalps back to the caliph (Saladin's master) in Baghdad as a prize. When the effeminate caliph saw the scalps, it is said, he passed out from fear.

Prince al-Afdal and his father, Saladin, would pay dearly for this lack of civility in later battles with Richard the Lionheart, who would make Saladin remember the massacre with an in-kind slaughter.

Saladin—The name Saladin means "righteousness of the faith" in Arabic. Saladin was the great ruler of the Islamic people. His dominion spanned from Cairo to Damascus, Yemen, and Arabia. In 1186, while the Christians fought against each other, Saladin concentrated his political and military power in preparation for the attacks of 1187. He busied himself with gathering regional allies as the Christians fought among themselves to the point of civil war when the child-king Baldwin died.

Saladin ensured that the vast Byzantine Empire was crippled and out of play before he launched his attack on the Outremer. He knew that he must cut off the Kingdom of Jerusalem from any local assistance to be successful.

He held Islam's third most holy city, Jerusalem, which was always the centerpiece, the center of his conquest. The storm was gathering, and this time, Islam would not be denied.

Knights Templar & Knights Hospitaller—The Holy Land's major defensive force, the warrior-monks of the Knights Templar, along with their brothers-in-arms, the Knights Hospitaller, and other, smaller, military warrior orders, were not immune from indifference and bitter rivalry.

Having said that, it is fair to say that without the military orders stationed and fighting in the Holy Lands from the years 1109 to 1300, the Outremer would have fallen, perhaps as early as 1150, to the Islamic army.

Had this happened, the Islamic armies certainly would have turned their attention even more to Central Europe, having conquered Iberia. Many scholars believe that most of Europe would have fallen to Islam if the Muslim leadership had had free reign in the Outremer.

This defense came at a large cost. Of the 80,000 Templars who served from 1109 to 1307, more than 20,000 died in combat or from illness.

Life at La Feve—Today, the fortress at La Feve stands in ruins just a few miles south of modern Nazareth. Most of Squire Aaron's life at Fortress La Feve is fairly typical. Poor rations and water made many Templars ill at La Feve. Most Templar men stationed at La Feve died from illness rather than from wounds suffered in battle.

Many documents written by Christian and Muslim authors inform us that the Christians were warned of the attack plan many months prior to the engagement at Cresson Springs. Saladin had launched several campaigns in the region of Galilee earlier in the 1170s, with a major Christian defeat at Jacob's Crossing, where Count Raymond, Baron Ibelin, and Prince Reynald were captured.

Warrior monks at Fortress Belvoir and La Feve were the first to discover several Muslim reconnaissance in force movements. Saladin's men carefully scouted out the region of Galilee for more than a year prior to the famous battle at Cresson Springs.

Grand Master Gerald Ridefort—The book did not travel far from documented reality about Templar Grand Master Gerald de Ridefort's poor leadership, lack of honor, and poor sense of duty. Gerald proved these character faults on many occasions as a direct participant in the political intrigue of the kingdom. Ridefort could always be counted on to work against Raymond of Tripoli and others who were tolerant of the Muslims. He also favored Guy Lusignan and his followers.

Gerald's many military failures included his infamous order to attack at Cresson Springs, as well as his poor counsel to Guy Lusignan. All are examples that he was the wrong man for the position of grand master. Roland will confront Gerald one on one in *The Final Glory*, book three of our adventure, for his betrayal and cowardice behavior at Cresson Springs.

Count Raymond of Tripoli—Count Raymond was culpable for his treachery after Guy Lusignan was crowned as king when he negotiated with Saladin and allowed the many excursions onto his fiefdoms. By many accounts, Count Raymond lived the life of an Islamic lord rather than a Christian lord. Raymond had been an Islamic prisoner for nearly ten years at Aleppo. During that time, he learned Arabic, studied the Quran, and dressed in Arabic clothing. Many feel that he may have been co-opted during this time.

King Guy de Lusignan—The king proved to be an ineffective leader and failed on all counts to be the master of his own destiny. Saladin once said, "A single mistake on the part of a Frank commander could lose the field army, the fortresses, and with them, the whole kingdom." Lusignan proved Saladin correct. The story concerning Guy being run out of France because of his robbery and murder of an English nobleman is very much true. He was always a man "on the edge," as well as a "lady's man". It was also true that he would remember only the last things said in conversation.

Queen Sibylla—The queen is very accurately portrayed in the book. Although she had an opportunity to extract herself from her marriage with Guy, she did not. By all accounts, she loved him to her deathbed. She will prove her love of her husband in book three, *The Final Glory.*"

Princess Isabella—Princess Isabella did marry the then sixteen-year-old Humphrey when she was only twelve or thirteen years old.
In later years, Isabella became a strong-willed woman who buried four husbands and, in fact, did marry a Champagne and rule Jerusalem, as we shall see in the third book of the series, "*The Final Glory.*".

Reynald of Chatillion—Reynald had a hand in the destruction of the Christian Kingdom of Jerusalem. His one–sided, total hatred of all things Muslim made him a poor chief councilor to the king. Reynald's many poor decisions included breaking every truce with Saladin, which caused most of the problems in the Outremer when the inhabitants fought among themselves. He attacked caravans and raided Muslim villages. He even attacked Medina and Mecca.

He did more to unite all Muslims than did Saladin's efforts. Reynald surely brought all sides of Islam together against the Christians.

Walter of Mesnil & Sergeant Martin of Brittany, Commander James Mailly— Mesnil, Brittany and Commander James Mailly were real Templars. Mailly and over 140 Templars were in fact killed as described at Cresson Springs. We don't have any documented proof of exactly how old Walter and Martin were when they died. We do know that Mesnil did kill two Assassin's in combat and went to prison for it. We also know that Richard De Brittany did kill the Archbishop of Canterbury and Catholic Church Saint, Thomas Becket. He was sentenced to serve fourteen years as a Templar.

We believe the way Martin, Walter, James Mailly and the other Templars are presented in this book accurately portray the rank-and-file life and death of the Knights Templar.

It was the well-trained and equipped Templar knight, the best heavy cavalry of its day, and the Templar sergeant, the best light cavalry of its day, that struck fear into the Islamic army. When wisely led, even those Templars who were vastly outnumbered were known to beat the enemy.

The novel's chief characters—Roland, Aaron, and Marie are representative of how people lived life at Templar headquarters, or at Castel La Feve. They are also indicative of how the upper class lived.

Roland of Champagne—Roland has completed the many tests of manhood after nearly two years of his continuing journey. He will come onto the field in *The Final Glory* and play a major role with his gathered knowledge.

In fact, the Champagne family were the financial founders of the Templars in France. It was with the efforts of the Champagne family that the Templars were acknowledged as an official Catholic order. Count Henry and his wife, Princess Maria, had two sons, but alas, no son named Roland. Roland in Arabic means "famous."

Aaron—After grueling training and service, many Templar squires went on to be promoted to sergeants. Some even went on to be knights. Aaron represents the hundreds of squires who served, fighting alongside their assigned knights or sergeants. Templar documents reveal that young men, as young as ages twelve to fourteen, served as squires. And yes, many did indeed ride on mules and paltry horses.

Marie of Baux—The Baux stronghold in Provence is much as we describe in the book. In fact, the Baux family does have a connection with the Outremer. The family crest, the sixteen-point Star of Bethlehem, and their relationship to Balthazar, are a proud tradition of the Baux family today. While Marie is a fictional character, she represents the many women who did go to the Holy Land; and worked and fought alongside their family to defend their Christian beliefs.

More on that in *The Final Glory*!

CPSIA information can be obtained
at www.ICGtesting.com
Printed in the USA
FFOW05n2219230215

9 781457 534492